Wicked Garden
By Lorelei James

One woman's past and present collide in the ultimate temptation.

Eden LaCroix loved Billy Buchanan ten years ago, but he ran out on her the night of prom. Now he's back, and Eden thinks a fling will help her move on from their tangled past. She wasn't counting on Billy's wicked side—or the return of her sometime lover Jon White Feather—to appeal so strongly to her own dark, hidden desires.

College took Billy away from Eden, but it's a mistake he can rectify now that he's in town to make the final decision on the fate of the community center Eden manages. Except reignited sparks keep getting in the way of his objectivity. The flames only leap higher when Eden's rock star lover comes home from the road.

Eden considers herself a one-woman man, but in the arms of Billy and Jon she feels truly beautiful for the first time in her life. But does the healing go far enough to prevent her from letting love slip through her hands a second time?

Warning: ain't nothin' sweet about this garden of naughty sexual delights, including threesomes, creative use of a weight bench and bonding over bondage.

A Question of Trust
By Jess Dee

How do you choose between love and honor?

Madeline Jones is having the time of her life with Gabriel Carter, a man who fulfills every one of her sexual fantasies. She's sure it can't get any better than this...until Gabe introduces her to his best friend.

When Connor Regan enters the mix, sparks fly. Suddenly Maddie wants more than just Gabe, she wants Connor, too. The two men seem happy to oblige.

But threesomes have a way of getting complicated. Hearts can be broken. Although Gabe and Connor play by a strict set of rules designed to minimize the damage, true love does not always adhere to the guidelines.

Sometimes, to fulfill the dream of having the love of a lifetime, even the most comprehensive codes of honor have to be challenged.

Warning: This book contains spicy sex scenes, uninhibited voyeurism, m-f-m passion, anal play, and a new sandwich recipe.

Nice and Naughty
By Jayne Rylon

Can one man satisfy Alexa's appetites? Or will it take two?

After a disastrous lesson in heartache, Alexa Jones confines her adrenaline rushes to intense boardroom negotiations. Her legendary control cracks and she indulges in a high-octane encounter on the hood of her sports car. She never planned to see the enticing stranger again. When she finds herself across the boardroom table from him, there's suddenly more at stake than just her career.

Justin Winston got more than he bargained for on his summer drive, but he should have known nothing is ever that easy. He's met the woman of his dreams yet he doesn't know who she is. Luckily, he can always count on his practical brother for the things that matter, and this time is no exception. But, when a web of corporate espionage entangles them all, it's clear Justin isn't the only one who's fallen for their mysterious siren.

In Justin and Jason, Alexa finds something as unique and rare as the patent they will risk their lives to secure. The freedom to explore—and satisfy—the full range of her desires. From naughty to nice. Can Alexa accept the love of two men?

Warning: This story contains light bondage, anal play and smoking hot brothers for double the fun and double the trouble.

Three's Company

A Samhain Publishing, Ltd. publication.

Samhain Publishing, Ltd.
577 Mulberry Street, Suite 1520
Macon, GA 31201
www.samhainpublishing.com

Three's Company
Print ISBN: 978-1-60504-324-1
Wicked Garden Copyright © 2009 by Lorelei James
A Question of Trust Copyright © 2009 by Jess Dee
Nice and Naughty Copyright © 2009 by Jayne Rylon

Editing by Angela James
Cover by Scott Carpenter

Wicked Garden, ISBN 978-1-60504-249-7
First Samhain Publishing, Ltd. electronic publication: September 2008
A Question of Trust, ISBN 978-1-60504-250-3
First Samhain Publishing, Ltd. electronic publication: September 2008
Nice and Naughty, ISBN 978-1-60504-251-0
First Samhain Publishing, Ltd. electronic publication: September 2008
First Samhain Publishing, Ltd. print publication: August 2009

Contents

Wicked Garden
Lorelei James
~9~

A Question of Trust
Jess Dee
~119~

Nice and Naughty
Jayne Rylon
~211~

Wicked Garden

Lorelei James

Chapter One

Eden LaCroix embodied sin. Wicked, sinful pleasures of the flesh that'd lead a monk straight into temptation.

Billy Buchanan never claimed to be a monk, but how on earth had he ever walked away from her?

Walked? Nice try, man. You ran *away from her.*

He traced her outline on the glass partition separating them—slumberous hazel eyes, full lips, auburn curls—and was surprised his fingers didn't come away scorched.

Eden's spine straightened. Before she turned and caught him gawking, Billy stepped from view.

Way to act like a stalker, Buchanan. Real professional.

Minutes later, her secretary found him calmly leaning against the wall in the reception area. However, calm was the last thing he felt when faced with the pleasures of Eden.

"Ms. LaCroix will see you now."

Billy's knees were knocking as loud as his heart when he finally opened her office door.

"Financially unfeasible my ass," Eden muttered. Not every decision had to be about money.

She didn't glance up from the spreadsheet when the door clicked open. Dammit. She wasn't ready to listen to another "expert" regurgitate the same gloomy diagnosis: the building housing the community center couldn't be salvaged. "Hang on. I'll be right with you."

"No hurry. We've got all the time in the world."

A chill skittered up her spine. She'd heard those exact words before. In that low timbre, with that playful tone. Nah. Couldn't be. Her ears were playing tricks on her.

Weren't they?

Curiosity won out. Eden shoved the papers aside and looked across the desk. But the man's zipper—not his face—was at her eye-level. Before she could discern whether he dressed left or right, her gaze traveled up the charcoal-colored suit pants, past a narrow waist and broad chest covered with a crisp white dress shirt. Wide shoulders. Strong neck. Square jaw. Big grin.

A familiar big grin.

Eden's stomach knotted. "Say it ain't so," she half-whispered. "Billy Buchanan?"

"In the flesh." Billy spread his arms wide before his killer smile melted away. "Eden? You look like you've seen a ghost."

"A ghost from prom past, minus the baby blue tux." She shook her head to get the blood flowing, never taking her eyes off him.

"It's been a few years," Billy said. "You look amazing. Last time I saw you—"

"—my prom dress was down around my ankles at Motel 6. I'm surprised *you* remember since the last time I saw *you*, your scrawny ass was high-tailing it out the door."

Billy allowed a sheepish shrug, which fell short of the endearing mark Eden suspected he'd been aiming for.

"Although this trip down memory lane is fascinating..." she smiled—all teeth, "...I don't have time to reminisce. I have an appointment."

Without waiting for an invitation, Billy plopped into the chair, watching her with an intensity that hadn't dimmed despite the passing of a decade. "Feather Light Consulting, right?"

That stopped her cold. "How did you know?"

"Because I *am* your appointment."

Eden's pulse spiked, but she managed a droll stare. "Still the consummate bullshit artist, I see." The wheels on her office chair squeaked as she rocked back. "I'm supposed to believe *you* work for Feather Light Consulting?"

"Yep. Since yesterday afternoon." He clicked open a battered black briefcase, propping it on his lap. "Robert Light had a heart attack Saturday night." When she gasped, he said, "Bob is recovering, but it'll take time, time Feather Light doesn't have in order to meet their current client obligations. Jim White Feather brought me here from Illinois."

Her gaze narrowed. "Why you?"

"Robert gave me a great recommendation with the engineering firm I work for in Chicago. I owe him." Billy reached into his briefcase, withdrawing a manila envelope. "Luckily I'd just wrapped up a job in Calgary. With freelance status, I'm assisting on this project with Feather Light."

"Guess it is a lucky thing for Robert."

"And for you." Billy smiled, flashing a deep dimple. "Isn't it great, us working together again? Just like old times?"

"Marvelous." The last time they'd punched a communal time clock at a local floral shop, any free moment between deliveries and customers her clothing had been askew and Billy's eager body had plastered hers to the flower cooler as they'd played the FTD version of post office.

Billy merely lifted his brows at her sarcasm.

"Although I'd like to renew specific relationships—" his eyes moved from her eyes to her lips, "—I'm not interested in making friends, Eden. I'm here to do a job."

Eden chalked up the fluttering in her stomach to acid reflux, not anticipation, and certainly not from his predatory once-over.

While he rummaged in his briefcase, Eden studied the changes ten years brought to Billy Buchanan. He was still undeniably sexy, and boy-next-door handsome. His hair had darkened from blond to tawny gold. His once lanky 6'3" frame filled out impressively. She imagined a toned athlete's body under his custom tailored clothing. Yet the quick smile with deep-set dimples and his hypnotizing blue eyes remained unchanged. Blue eyes completely focused on her.

"Jesus, Eden. You take my breath away."

The heat of his gaze evaporated every bit of moisture in her mouth. Not many things threw her, but one compliment from him and she reverted to a seventeen-year-old girl; her heart raced, her face burned, her blood pumped hot.

"Sorry. I know that was out of line. Not a good way to start this."

"So how *do* we start this, Billy? Do I ask you how you've been? Do I ask to see your credentials?" *Or do I ask why you ran out on me?*

Billy's eyes didn't waver as the locks on the briefcase clicked. "Sure. We could also discuss the weather, or whether my old boss Nathan and his wife Tate, have contributed to the population explosion in Spearfish." He angled forward, settling his elbows on the briefcase, studying her carefully. "Or, we could skip all that crap and I could tell you why I left you and your virginity intact ten years ago."

"By all means, let's revisit that stellar moment." She lifted a hand, stopping his immediate objection. "You have one minute to get whatever guilt off your chest."

"See you've still got those rough edges."

"If I recall correctly, you were one of the few people who liked that about me," she retorted sweetly.

"Truth was, I liked everything about you."

"Funny way of showing it."

"Can you blame me? You were jailbait and at twenty-two I was a little old to be deflowering virgins."

"I knew exactly how old we both were. I chose you because I trusted you with something that mattered to me." Snapping at him wouldn't change anything. She picked up a pen and drummed it against the desk blotter. "At any rate, water under the bridge. I will admit you did do me one favor by leaving." Her lips curved into a naughty smile. "Now I take my pleasure where and when *I* like."

"Got a steady boyfriend, do you?"

"Don't need one. There are plenty of motorized ways for a woman to stay satisfied that don't involve a man. So, let's cut to the chase. What do you know about this project?"

He flipped through a binder. When Billy met her gaze again, his was all business. "The city hired Feather Light Consulting to assess whether this building can be updated with minimal cost. Or—"

"—whether the city council should sign off on it so they can use the taxpayer's dollars to build a brand new facility."

"Not a big fan of city government?"

"No, which is ironic since I am a city employee." Eden pointed to the folder. "What else does that report say?"

"The other two companies hired to assess the situation filed conflicting results. The first report suggested bulldozing the property. The second claimed it'd be cheaper to make the required updates."

"Feather Light was called in as the tie-breaker?"

"Yes. Tell me why you're so adamant about keeping the community center in this location."

She paused, trying to stay professional when this was an emotional issue for her on many levels too. "When I was growing up, if I wanted to hang out with other kids, or get advice from adults who didn't see me as a pest, I could hop on my bike and be at the community center in ten minutes. This place still caters to kids like me, single-parent, mixed-race kids with little money."

Billy's eyes softened. "Is this 'save the building at all costs' a personal crusade?"

"No. This center is crucial to the community and the hundreds of kids who walk through the doors every day. The size of the building and the state-of-the-art exercise equipment won't matter because few of the kids will be able to get out to the new building on their own."

"Meaning what?"

Eden ticked the points off on her fingertips. "No bus service. Heavy traffic on the highway makes it impossible for kids to ride their bikes with any measure of safety. Too far to walk and few of them drive."

"But the proposed site is within the city limits, even if it is on the other end of town," Billy pointed out. "The city is slated to provide transportation, connection to the bike path and other city services."

She shook her head. "Look at the preliminary report again. If the council passes the ordinance, they could take up to ten years to implement final stages of the required zoning. Ten years. The city is already considering doubling the yearly membership fee *before* committing to a multimillion-dollar building. We have a mix of income levels here, most families struggle to pay the fees now."

"The fees are a non-issue if the building is deemed unsafe."

"True. Maybe the building needs a little TLC, but there are dozens of professional contractors volunteering to make it safe."

"Why?"

"Because so many people see it like I do. This is a community center. We fulfill many needs. We have two counselors and a dozen senior citizen volunteers come in to help out with homework or just hang around to feel useful. I predict the number of kids in juvenile detention will increase dramatically, with no other outlet for their physical and emotional frustrations. Of course, the council members believe I'm exaggerating the potential problems."

"Are you?"

"No. But I am frustrated." Their eyes locked. "I'll do damn near anything to keep the center right where it is."

Billy smiled. "Prove it. Take me on a tour, Eden. I want to see the center through your eyes."

Eden's gaze raked over his clothing. "This isn't a clean, sterile office environment. People sweat here and get dirty. You aren't afraid you'll soil your snappy suit?"

Billy stood and braced his hands on her desk. "I have no problem getting down and dirty. Do you?"

"None whatsoever."

"Good. Then let's do it."

Chapter Two

Two hours later, Eden peeled the damp silk shirt away from her overheated skin. She'd ended Billy's tour in the basement boiler room. Pipes hissed and clattered, then quieted down to the occasional rattle and wheeze.

Billy inspected every square foot of the building. He'd asked question after question, until his low, sexy voice echoed in her ears and throbbed through her bloodstream. His cool efficiency rekindled memories she'd tried to bury years ago.

Eden might've been innocent in understanding the needs and desires that fuelled an adult physical relationship, but she and Billy had clicked on an emotional level. They'd dealt with deeper issues than where to spend Saturday night. His: the lingering effects of his father's death and his need to finish college. Hers: dealing with her drunken mother, and trying to finish high school while working nearly full-time.

In truth, it'd hurt Eden far worse when he'd run out of her life without explanation, than when he'd raced out of the motel room and refused to take her virginity. She'd counted on Billy's stability, his support, his friendship.

Eden's gaze wandered to him as he dutifully made notes. His blond hair was tousled, his funky lime-green tie askew. The smart and sexy aspects of his persona hadn't changed. But he'd honed his youthful intensity to a precise edge. She wondered if he still kissed with the same fire. Did he make love with an engineer's attention to detail and single-minded absorption in the process?

What she wouldn't give for another chance to have those energies directed at her.

Before Eden considered the implications, almost as if he'd read her mind, she became his sole focus.

"Eden?" he murmured next to her ear, sending a delicious tingle down her spine. "You spaced out for a second. Where'd you go?"

A naked **trip** down memory lane. "Nowhere special. Why?"

He drew a fingertip down her sweat-dampened arm. "Really? Seemed special to me. Your eyes turned liquid and soft. You licked your lips." His rapid exhalations teased the nape of her neck. "What were you tasting in your daydreams?"

You. Your lips, your mouth, your skin. She stepped back and faced him, balling her hands into fists.

His gaze dropped to her breasts and the nipples poking against her translucent blouse.

Heat suffused her face. "It *is* hot in here."

"I'll say." Billy zeroed in on the bead of sweat dripping from her temple, wiping it away with a measured sweep of his thumb.

The simple touch heightened her responsiveness and again she retreated. "Have you seen enough?"

"No." Billy started toward her, an animal stalking prey.

Eden backed up until her shoulders met a low-hanging section of ductwork. "What else?"

"I have two questions." His Italian loafers bumped her sensible black pumps. They stood knee-to-knee, hip-to-hip and chest-to-chest, face-to-face, practically breathing the same air.

Could he hear the rapid beat of her heart? Sense the fervor thickening her blood? "Ask away."

"Does this old heating system keep the entire building adequately warm?"

"Yes."

"Are you seeing anyone?"

"Not really."

"Good." His notebook crashed to the floor. He slanted his mouth over hers and kissed her.

At the warm insistence of his lips, the smooth glide of his tongue, Eden gave up both the internal and external fight. She might've leapt over the professional line, but she wanted him. The hard press of his zipper against her belly showed her how badly he wanted her too.

For several glorious minutes, she reacquainted herself with Billy's exhilarating taste; his masculine flavor flowed into her mouth and her memories. His harsh breathing, her throaty moans of pleasure and the rasp of clothing were the only sounds in the humid space.

The ravenous kiss slowed. Billy murmured against her damp skin, trailing kisses down her neck to the swell of her breasts.

His fingertips swept her hair from her face, drifting down her jawline to stroke the pulse beating in her throat. He traced her collarbones to the V of her shirt, testing the weight of her breasts in his large hands; his thumbs strayed to the silk-covered nipples.

Once again heat exploded between them. Billy crushed her against the ductwork so completely she felt every twitch of his cock on her belly, every hard muscle of his body.

The clatter of pipes startled them into breaking the kiss.

Billy backed off, but his passion-darkened eyes never left hers. They stared at one another. He tenderly brushed a curl from her forehead, letting his palm linger near her temple. "Don't look for an apology. I've been wanting to do that for three hours."

"I don't want an apology. But we weren't exactly discreet. Anyone might've walked in." She sent a nervous glance over her shoulder. "I've worked to build a decent reputation—"

"I know." He cupped her chin, urging her to look at him. "I'd never do anything to jeopardize your reputation. Doesn't change the fact I want you. Damn, do I want you, Eden. In every way imaginable."

Her insides seemed to liquefy, sending a hot trickle of excitement between her legs. "Me too. But I don't want anyone to think I slept with you in order to assure Feather Light won't recommend closing the center to the city council."

Billy froze. Then he spun on his dress shoe and crossed the concrete floor halfway before pacing back. "No offense, but nothing you could do with that luscious mouth or your incredible body would affect the outcome of this survey."

"But?"

"But when we're alone can we put the business aside?"

Here was her chance to close that chapter of her life. Might be reckless, but she deserved Billy Buchanan's undivided sexual attention, if only temporarily. "How long will you be in town?"

"A week." He watched her smooth her hair, straighten her skirt and adjust her blouse. "You busy after work tonight?"

"Yes."

"How about tomorrow night?"

"No," she admitted.

He gave her a wolfish smile. "You are now."

♋

Later that afternoon Billy stretched out on the tan buffalo skin sofa in Jim White Feather's office.

He scanned the bold color scheme of Jim's extensive collection of Native American art, artifacts and photographs. The room whispered power, but exuded warmth.

A row of pictures lined a rustic pine bookshelf. Jim and his wife Cindy had taken the "go forth and multiply" suggestion quite literally.

Jim set the phone down. "What are you grinnin' at?"

"The White Feather bunch." Billy faced him, surprised by the gray streaks in Jim's long black braid. "Is eight really enough to fill your house with love?"

"*Shee.* Eight is plenty, especially with one in high school and one in diapers. Our life is never dull. Which brings me to the question of the day: how did your meeting go with the always entertaining Eden LaCroix?"

"You might've warned me she's adamantly opposed to building a new community center."

"Gave you a rough time, did she?"

An image of Eden's mouth, ripe from his forceful kisses flitted through Billy's mind. "Ah, no more than I deserved."

"Our Eden certainly is a firecracker."

"*Our* Eden?" he repeated.

"Eden is *tanka*, practically my little sister. She and Cindy and Jon have palled around for years."

"Then why didn't you handle this project?"

"For that very reason. Look, I wasn't thrilled when Bob took this assignment. In fact, I told him I wanted nothin' to do with it because I agree with Eden's position the community center needs to remain in its present location. That's why I brought you in on Bob's suggestion, for an unbiased assessment."

Billy realized this was his chance to tell Jim he wasn't exactly impartial where Eden was concerned. But the damning words stuck in his throat. "Don't you think *your* opinion might affect the outcome of my recommendation?"

"I hope so." Jim shifted his enormous frame back over the desk. "Bob has absolute confidence in your ability to make the best financial decision for the client."

"You don't?"

"Like you said, I'm biased. The bottom line is different in this case. Eden is the best thing that's happened to the community center since Grace Fitzgerald left. So far the city hasn't offered her the executive position if the center relocates. She'll probably hafta leave town to find a similar payin' position. I don't want that on my conscience."

"So you're putting it on mine."

"That's why I agreed to hire you on a temporary basis. You've got nothin' at stake."

Wrong. Billy stood, pacing to the windows where pine-covered hills stretched in a sea of greenish-black.

His life had been in chaos since he'd finished his last job, one spent damn near in solitary confinement in Canada. Sure, he'd made more money in one year than in the last five, but his restlessness remained after the checks sat unspent in his bank account.

After the stint in Calgary, he realized cash had to stop being the sole factor in his decision-making. He'd wrestled with the idea of tendering his resignation to the Chicago firm, amidst visions of a slower paced life, when he'd received the frantic call about Bob's heart attack. Billy was using his vacation not only to help an old friend, but to make some tough decisions regarding his future.

And his future looked endlessly bleak. On the outside it might seem he had it all—a high-rise condo, a high paying job in a prestigious company, but on the inside, he realized none of that surface stuff mattered.

At thirty-two he was damn tired of being alone. Looking again at the happy pictures in Jim's office, Billy recognized not only did his sleek black, white and chrome office in Chicago seem drab in comparison, his life was pretty colorless too.

"You okay?" Jim asked.

"Fine. I'll keep you updated. Speaking of updates...how is Bob?"

"Better. Mostly he's scared. Betty says he might finally consider partial retirement." Jim's black eyebrows pulled together. "I don't even want to think about that."

"He's what? Sixty-seven? Didn't you consider the possibility he might not want to work forever?"

"Things've been so hectic we haven't had time to consider another partner. And now Bob's heart attack put us even further behind."

"What else can I do? I'm here, you're paying me."

Jim gestured to the stack of folders on the corner of the desk. "Take your pick. Pretty simple projects, especially for a big city hotshot like you," he grinned, "but I'd appreciate you takin' a look."

"I'll get to it right away."

"Oh, and I'm givin' you a heads up my brother Jon'll be around the condo sometime in the next couple of days. He's between tour dates."

Tour dates? Billy frowned before he remembered Jim's brother played in an up-and-coming rock band, which mixed traditional Lakota Sioux Indian folk music with ear-splitting electric guitar and drums.

"Maybe you oughta take him along next time you talk to Eden."

"Why? Think Jon can work some musical Indian magic on her?"

"He's been tryin'. Hell, he's succeeded. Eden goes out with him whenever he's in town." Jim sighed. "I keep hopin' my little bro' will wise up, marry her and settle down, because she is perfect for him. But they're both just satisfied with hookin' up."

Hooking up. A surge of jealousy rolled through him. "With the hordes of gorgeous female fans throwing themselves at Jon on a nightly basis? I don't see the Indian rock star settling down, even with a woman as enticing as Eden."

"Enticing?" Jim repeated.

The secretary buzzing Jim's intercom allowed Billy an easy out. He snagged the folders and left before he said something else he'd regret.

Chapter Three

Eden greeted her charges by name during the influx of after-school kids. The hallways teemed as they raced to the gym, a hotbed of basketball games, tumbling and jump rope classes. Her grin was as wide as theirs. This was her favorite part of the day.

She ditched her heels and played a quick round of Double Dutch, then headed to the kitchen to help serve snacks. After checking on the latest arts and craft project, she verified the volunteer list for the homework help room. Tempting to blow off her remaining paperwork and immerse herself in the enthusiasm bouncing off the walls, but part of her job was to teach responsibility and shirking hers wouldn't set a good example.

In her office, Eden immediately spied the young Sioux boy sprawled in the chair across from her desk. She risked an indulgent smile. "Thomas!"

"What do you want done today? 'Cause they're lettin' me play forward later."

"Didn't see you in the cafeteria. Did you get a snack?"

He angled his Denver Nuggets baseball cap toward the carpet. His unlaced high-top tennis shoes swung beneath the chair. "Not hungry."

Thomas had more pride than the average twelve-year old. But pride didn't fill hungry, growing bellies. She unwrapped the Rice Krispie treat and set it on the edge of her desk.

"Too bad. My eyes were bigger than my stomach."

"S'pose I could eat it." He ate with a delicacy that belied his age and gender. "What'm I doin' today?"

Eden pointed to the cardboard boxes on the floor. "Those are the monthly newsletters from the last four years. I want them filed chronologically."

Panic flared in his brown eyes. "Chrono-what?"

"Chronologically. In order of date, January 1999, February 1999, and so on."

"Do I hafta *read* them?"

"Not all the way through, just enough to put them in the correct order." Thomas had let it slip he lagged behind his classmates in school. Despite his grumbling, she'd decided to challenge his mind, hoping he'd recognize mental aptitude was as important as physical skills.

"Can we at least listen to some music? Like KILI?"

KILI FM was a Native American radio station that played an odd assortment from Powwow music to rap. "Sounds good."

"Cool." He flopped on the floor behind the chair, dumping the box contents into a messy pile.

Eden turned the boom box on low and sorted through her own stacks. The rhythmic chanting and steady beat of the tom-tom drums made soothing background noise. The music reminded her Jon White Feather, a.k.a. Johnny Feather, a drummer/singer with the Lakota musical group, Sapa, was due to roll back into town soon.

Jon personified rock star: long black hair, tribal tattoos, all buffalo-leather clothes and warrior attitude. He was a smokin' hot, sweet-talkin' Indian who could charm the panties off any woman—and probably had, but Eden didn't care. They had a great time together.

With her, Jon could just be Jon, her old college buddy, not Johnny, heartthrob to the Indian nation. With him, she could be Eden, the wicked temptress, not Eden the buttoned-up community center director. Sex was off-the-charts phenomenal between them because neither one pretended it was anything more than two old friends acting on mutual lust.

Would sex with Billy be that explosive?

Not helping you concentrate, Eden.

Twenty minutes later she hit the total button on the calculator and frowned.

"How is it possible you look beautiful even wearing a

scowl?"

Billy's gravelly voice brought color to her cheeks. She glanced up—his crotch was eye-level again—and saw he wore thigh-hugging faded jeans rather than suit pants.

A boyish snort sounded from behind the chair. Thomas leapt to his feet. "Man, that was so lame."

"Thomas. Be nice."

Billy thrust his hand out. "Billy Buchanan."

Grudgingly Thomas accepted the proffered hand. "Thomas Fast Wolf. Billy, huh? Another guy by the name of Billy, *Billy Mills*, came here last year and talked to us. Ever heard of him?" Thomas recited Billy Mills's feats of Olympic glory, while Eden stood by with her mouth hanging open. The kid did pay attention.

"I'm not much of a track and field fan, but I do like the occasional basketball game." Billy regarded Thomas's hat. "The Nuggets aren't as good as the Bulls."

Thomas snorted. "The Bulls are a has-been team."

"Better than a *wanna-be* team."

"Enough." Eden directed her attention to Thomas. "If you're finished sorting, scoot. I don't want you to miss a minute of your game. I'll see you same time next week."

"Aren't you comin' down to watch me?"

His tone was shy of pleading. Thomas, no stranger to disappointment, rarely asked anything of her. "Absolutely."

He treated Eden to a broad smile, but gave Billy a skeptical once-over. "So Mr. Bulls fan, you oughta come down and see how real basketball is played. Some of the guys in junior high are bigger than you. Bet you'd get your butt kicked."

"Thomas!"

But Billy merely shrugged. "Good thing I wore my butt-kickin' shoes. I'll be there after I have a word with Ms. LaCroix." After the door closed, he said, "Interesting kid. What's he doing in the office when he'd rather be wreaking havoc in the gym? Working off some sort of punishment?"

"No. A trade." She fixed her gaze on the calculator keys. "Thomas helps me out once a week, no big deal."

Silence stretched, long and snaky as the calculator tape.

"You're paying his club fees and letting him work it off in

here?"

Why bother denying it? "Yes. That way he doesn't feel he's a charity case. It keeps him out of trouble."

"How many fees are you paying out of your own pocket?"

"It doesn't matter. Thomas is basically a good kid. But that'd change in a heartbeat if he didn't have anywhere to go after school. His family situation isn't the best. Sometimes he sneaks in here at night to avoid a beating. I've tried to tell him how dangerous that is but he doesn't listen and I shudder to think what'd happen to him if the center closed."

Eden squeezed her eyelids shut, remembering Thomas's resentful look turning hopeful when she'd offered him the trade. Having Thomas around was a constant reminder of how far she'd come. One person could make a difference in the lives of kids who had so little. "This place is everything to him."

Gentle fingers touched her cheek. Her eyes opened to see Billy standing within kissing distance. "Seems this place is everything to you too," he murmured, stroking the vulnerable skin by her ear.

She stepped away from his tempting touch. "Not here."

Billy's eyes clouded to murky gray. "If I had my way I'd close the blinds, lock the door, throw you across the desk and fuck you until neither of us could walk out."

The fire in his gaze rushed over her in blast of heat.

"If I'd had my way yesterday, I would've hiked up your skirt, spread your legs wide, bent you over that duct in the basement and pounded into you until you came, screaming my name."

Eden clenched her legs together to stave off the tremors.

"Surprised?"

"Not by the visual. But I was surprised you weren't here earlier today."

"I was. The janitor let me in at six o'clock. I hung around until nine, videotaped some footage."

She frowned. "You should've told me yesterday you planned on checking out the building at the crack of dawn."

"Why does that matter?"

"Because I'd have made a point to be here to answer any of your questions."

"Or to try to steer me away from areas you don't want me to see?" he countered.

"Not true. I didn't deny you access to any area yesterday, and you damn well know it." Eden folded her arms over her chest. "I just don't like the idea of you sneaking around unsupervised."

"Need I remind you, you aren't my client and I don't answer to you?"

"As administrator of this facility, I expect you to give me advance notice on when you plan to be on site."

"Keeping tabs on me?"

"No. Like every other person who walks through those doors, when you're here, you're my responsibility. And if something should happen—"

"—like if a chunk of that water-damaged plaster ceiling on the third floor fell on me? Or if I tripped over the four-inch foundation crack in the basement and split my head open?"

"See?" Eden jabbed a finger in his sternum. "That's exactly what I mean. We haven't discussed a damn thing about any of your initial findings. I'm sure the other companies reports made you aware of the safety concerns—"

Billy pressed her palm flat to his chest. "I haven't read the other reports."

She blinked. "What?"

"I haven't looked at them. They're still in Bob's office."

"Why?"

"Because they don't matter. Those reports are their opinions, not mine. I didn't want my judgment skewed beforehand." Billy brought her wrist to his mouth, kissing the soft skin until her breath hitched. "I'm sorry. I blew it, all right? I should've informed you first. So, in the future, I'll give you a heads up before I start poking around."

"Good."

"When and where can I see you tonight?"

Eden disentangled herself and grabbed a piece of paper. "Here's my address. Come by after seven."

"I can't wait."

Chapter Four

As Billy sped through Eden's neighborhood, he scarcely noticed the architectural details—the Victorian painted ladies, the quaint brick bungalows or the structural designs inspired by Frank Lloyd Wright.

He parked in front of the detached garage, nearly vaulting the evergreen hedge separating the sidewalk from the driveway. After passing through the arbor twined with yellow roses, he paused at the steps. A white envelope was tacked to the front door, fluttering in the evening breeze.

Disappointment clenched his gut as he strode across the spacious porch and snatched the envelope. The note read:

Since you're so adept at sneaking around my building, you have five minutes to find me. If you succeed, you get to be in charge tonight. If you fail, be prepared to surrender to my every whim. Ring the doorbell and the timer starts.

A thrill shot through him that buttoned-up, professional Eden hadn't neglected her playful side. He set his watch, swung open the door, poked the doorbell and stepped across the threshold.

Billy's gaze darted up the staircase but he started his search in the living room. She wasn't hiding behind the velvet drapes or in the coat closet. In the dining room, the space under the antique trestle table remained empty. The mahogany china cabinet was too small to crawl inside, even for a sprite like Eden.

He dashed through the doorway to a kitchen painted in

tones of lavender and purple. When he paused in front of a bright red half-bath tucked underneath the staircase, he realized Eden hadn't shed her funky bohemian side.

Damn. Two and a half minutes had passed.

Billy took the stairs at a dead run.

Upstairs he faced seven doors—all closed. The first one revealed a small linen closet. The second and third, empty bedrooms. The fourth room displayed a four-poster canopy bed and was sumptuously decorated in lace, velvet and silk.

Behind the fifth door he found a large pink and black bathroom, complete with a claw foot tub. Door number six led to an attic. Billy flicked on the light switch and barreled up the wooden stairs. Boxes covered the wide-planked floor. No Eden. He raced down the stairs.

He turned the crystal doorknob, pushed open the heavy oak door to the last room, and found Eden sprawled on a weight bench. A Stairmaster stood in one corner, a TV/DVD combo in the other. A purple yoga mat was spread on the carpet.

Somehow he ripped his gaze away from her to check the time.

Four minutes, forty-five seconds. He'd made it. His triumphant smile increased when he got his first complete look at the sexy outfit Eden was *almost* wearing. Red bustier. Red garters hooked to shimmery black stockings. Black fuck-me stilettos.

Instantly, his dick stirred to life.

Her cherry-colored mouth curved into a secretive feminine smile. "I was beginning to wonder if you'd gotten lost."

"Just losing my mind when I think of you." He stalked toward her. "You were lounging here the whole time?"

"Mmm." One finger stroked her plumped cleavage. "You cut it close." She tossed the timer to the floor. "Ten seconds left, by my calculations."

"Fifteen seconds by mine," he corrected. "But I am the winner. I can do whatever I want, right?"

"Within reason."

"I'd never do anything to hurt you when I've thought about nothing but touching you all day." Billy crouched in front of her, his hands glided up the outside of her stocking-clad legs, over lace-covered narrow hips and rib cage. His thumbs brushed the generous swell of her breasts, purposely avoiding her nipples, lingering across the graceful sweep of her collarbone. He palmed her shoulders, lightly trailing his fingers down her arms to clasp her small hands.

He tugged her to her feet, angling his head to draw in the fragrant scent of her hair. "Kiss me."

Her lips parted and she latched onto his tie, hauling his mouth to hers. Not a sweet, welcoming kiss; Eden inhaled him with a tongue thrusting, clash of lips and teeth.

A heartfelt groan had him gathering her silken hair in his fists.

Eden broke her mouth free, nibbling over his jawbone up to whisper, "The bed's in the other room."

"We don't need a bed. I want to look at you. Stand right here." Billy expected her to protest, but she placed her feet on the carpet where he'd indicated. "Beautiful. Close your eyes."

Her long lashes drifted shut.

Billy circled her, dusting his fingertips over her petal soft skin. Standing behind her, he let his breath waft across her damp nape until she shivered. "Did you wear this outfit to tease me?"

"Yes."

"Hold still while I take it off." He sank to his knees, running his palms up the back of her muscled calves, across that expanse of fabulous thigh. The gap between garter and stocking held his fascination and he bent to taste it.

Eden gasped. Her gasp morphed into a full-blown moan when his tongue licked a wet path up to the sweet curve of her hip. He explored that exquisitely sensitive skin, using feathery strokes on the outside of her legs.

"Unhook the garters," he said gruffly.

She fumbled with the stockings until they were free of the clasps.

The sight of Eden bending over, smooth ass pushed out, the line of her spine flat, made him adjust his erection. He'd take her that way, cock grinding into her sweet, hot pussy as his fingers dug into those curvy hips.

"Turn around and sit on the bench."

"Can I open my eyes?"

"Yes." Billy fell to his knees. "Let's get those sexy shoes off."

She lifted her leg, placing the toe of her black pump on his shoulder. Cupping her ankle, he removed her shoe and slid off the stocking, licking, nibbling and kissing each portion of newly bared skin. He repeated the agonizingly slow process on the other leg. Once finished, he scrutinized her, noting her ragged breathing as he placed his hands on her knees.

He tugged at the bustier. "Take it off."

"The zipper is in the back, so if you're expecting a sexy striptease—"

Billy blocked up her dissent with his mouth. He fed on her sweetness, groaning at the press of her lace-covered breasts to his chest. He hungered for this hot-blooded woman moaning in his arms and wouldn't be satisfied until he memorized the distinctive taste of her as she climaxed against his tongue.

Reaching behind her, he yanked on the zipper. The bodice fell and he tossed it aside. He blazed a trail of wet, hot kisses to the tops of her breasts.

"These are perfect. I want to take hours learning how you like to be touched here. But for now..." He sucked as much of that soft flesh into his mouth as he possibly could. Feasting on her breasts until the pink tips bloomed a darker rose.

She cried out, arching her back, straining against him.

His cock swelled from her throaty growls. He leapt to his feet and eased her back onto the inclined bench seat.

Billy unknotted the tie and threw it behind him. He made short work of his dress shirt, shoes and socks. He only unbuttoned the top button of his slacks. Again he slipped his hands up her body, savoring every sexy inch. "What's really going through that sharp mind, gorgeous?"

Her eyes turned liquid, a soft hue that bespoke of raw passion. "I've thought of this since I was seventeen."

"Tell me what you want."

"I want you to put your mouth on me."

Smiling, he bent and kissed her knee.

"Smart-ass," she hissed.

"You weren't very explicit."

She propped herself up on her elbows, eyes gleaming. "I

want your mouth sucking between my legs until I come."

He stared at her and grinned. "That's the hottest thing I've ever heard."

"And I want it right now."

He hooked his fingers inside her red lace panties, dragging them down her long legs and carelessly tossed them over his shoulder. "You asked for it. Remember that when you're begging me to let you come."

Chapter Five

"I can take it," Eden said boldly, even when the sparkle in his eye sent shivers to her core.

Billy gently nudged her and she lowered her back flat, staring at the ivory ceiling. Perched on the end of the weight bench, he placed his hands on her knees. "Wider. Show me what I've won. Show me what's mine tonight."

A wave of desire washed over her. She stretched her legs, letting her heels rest on the metal rungs of the bench. Her eyes closed when his hot flesh moved into the space she'd created between her thighs.

His finger slid through the wetness of her pussy, stopping to trace the triangle of curls. "So pretty. So pink." One hand stroked her thigh. His mouth came into play, kissing her hipbones, the sensitive line of skin below her navel. A warm tongue skated across each rib as he made a thorough journey up her body.

His thumb flicked across that pouting bundle of nerves at her center, gliding down to rest in her slick opening. He repeated the path up and down her wet slit, gradually increasing the rhythm so it was a constant stroking.

Eden began to thrash. Even the fake leather bench seat was too much stimulus on her skin. She wanted his mouth everywhere—on her lips, on her breasts, on her aching sex. Finally that wayward mouth reached her nipples, using the tiniest amount of tongue on tips. "Please, Billy."

As he latched onto her nipple with his teeth, he slid two fingers deep inside her pussy.

The sensation of his hungry mouth suckling her breast, his

long fingers pumping in and out, his thumb rubbing her clit, sent her careening into space. She pressed up to meet his demanding fingers, clutching his strong shoulders, shudders racking her from scalp to toes as he milked even the tiniest spasm.

After her sex quit pulsing, Eden opened her eyes, mortified by being so quick on the trigger.

But Billy's intense gaze indicated he hadn't minded her speedy trip to climax. His hand slid from between her thighs, smoothed a wet line up her belly, which he followed with this tongue. "Beautiful," he growled against her flushed skin.

Eden dove her hands into his thick hair. Her impatient palms tracked the iron contours of his broad shoulders, down his powerfully muscled back. She tugged at the wool fabric of his suit pants. "I want you," she murmured against his mouth.

"No." Billy pressed into a push-up position, using the bar above her head as leverage. "I want to look in your eyes when I make you come this time." With that declaration, he stepped back, circled her ankles and planted her feet on his shoulders.

She struggled to sit up. "What are you doing?"

"Putting my mouth on you." His tongue swirled a path up the inside of her thigh. "Stay like that," he warned, "watch me taste you."

"B-but, it's too soon, I-I can't possibly—"

"You can," he said, licking a wide swath over the center of her, "you will." His thumbs spread her folds apart, dragging his mouth up and down the dripping furrow. In a breathless second, he jammed his hot, wiggling tongue inside her pussy as high as it would reach.

"Oh. My. God." The muscles below her belly button rippled as his mouth worked magic. Soft hair brushed the inside of her thighs making them tremble anew.

"Jesus, you taste like some dark exotic fruit," he groaned, lapping at the moisture pouring from her sex. Billy's head lifted, his mouth glistened with her juices. "Keep your eyes on mine." Again his nimble tongue connected with her clit, drawing a series of figure eights.

Blood rushed to the swollen membranes as that elusive point pulsed. The steel bar dug into her lower back as her legs tensed, her nipples beaded, a zing of white-hot heat shot straight to her core.

When the vibrations started, Billy trained his eyes on her face, and his callused fingers tweaked her nipple.

Eden moaned as orgasm number two flooded her. She watched Billy's heavy-lidded eyes as the climax he'd wrought emblazoned a mark on her.

The delicious throbbing slowed. Stopped. He scattered kisses along the tops of her thighs. Replete, she flopped back on the hard bench with a gusty sigh.

Billy's mouth meandered up her torso, tasting the dips and valleys of her sated flesh until he reached her lips. His gentle breath swept her mouth open and his tongue plunged inside, sharing his heat and her musky tang. He lifted her from the bench and settled her on the yoga mat.

Eden stretched, coiling around him with the languor of a sun-warmed snake. After endless, glorious minutes of Billy's loving caresses and reverent touches, he pulled away. She opened her eyes lazily. "What?"

"You are amazing."

"But I haven't done anything besides let you have your wicked way with me."

Smiling, he twined a damp curl around his finger. "Would you believe me if I said that *was* my biggest fantasy?"

"No." To prove her point, she slid a bare thigh up his leg until it connected with the hard ridge of his erection. "I'd say my biggest fantasy involves ripping those pants to shreds." She reached for the zipper, but he blocked her move. A warning flashed in the back of her mind.

"Before you scorch my hair with that dirty look, I'm not going anywhere." Billy pinned her arms above her head. "Leave them there."

"Why?"

"Because you haven't called mercy yet." His wicked mouth wended between her aching breasts. He lapped at the generous curves until she writhed beneath him. He coated his middle finger with her juices, slipping it down to rest on the rosy bloom of her anus.

She froze, half in fear, half in excitement, automatically contracting that muscle.

"Has any man ever fucked you here?"

"No."

He looked her square in the eye, his questing finger stayed in place. "Since I blew taking your virginity ten years ago, will you let me take this one? Let me be the first man to put my cock in your ass?"

Eden's mouth went as dry as the Badlands. She'd been curious about that particular act, but hadn't trusted other lovers to initiate her into the dark pleasure of anal sex. But Billy had figured out her secret desire and offered to make it come true.

She nodded.

Billy growled, clamped his lips to hers, snaring her attention in a drawn out, tongue numbing kiss. Her body arched closer to his, lost in passion flaring between them.

When he finally, slowly breached that untried area, the sensation was so acute she gasped in his mouth.

He steadily pumped his finger, and slid his thumb into her slit, wiggling it inside her. "Tighten your pussy muscles. Now."

Right when Eden squeezed, Billy pressed his thumb and his middle finger together, so she felt him stroking both walls.

"Oh. My. God."

"Wild, huh?"

"Yeah. Is that sort of what it'd feel like to have..."

His eyes glittered. "Tell me. To have what?"

"To be filled in both places at one time."

"Would you like to try that? Have a cock in your cunt and another one in your ass? At the same time?"

"Uh. Yeah."

"Real? Or a facsimile?"

"Both."

Billy kissed her, not a hard punishing kiss, but softly. Sweetly. He whispered, "Where is your vibrator?"

She went utterly still. "W-w-what?"

"Your vibrator." His hand slipped over her sweat-slickened belly to the thatch of curls and stroked her clit. "Don't play coy. You told me you don't need a man to take your own pleasure. Tell me where it is."

It was hard to create a plausible lie when he used such sublime diversions. "Umm...What are you going to do with it?"

"I won't use it for double penetration right now."

Her brain stuck on *right now.* "Oh." Eden swallowed hard. "What do you have planned?"

Billy's low chuckle rumbled against her breast. "Guess you'll have to trust me to find out." He lifted his head a fraction. "Do you trust me, Eden?"

"I-I—"

His pink tongue lapped shiny wet circles around her equally pink nipple. His cool breath drifted across the moistened tip and she gasped when his demanding fingers began plucking her other nipple. "Where is it?"

"Bottom drawer in the bureau in my room," she blurted.

He grinned, raced out and was back in the room with the buzzing purple rubber vibrator before she felt the sting of embarrassment. "Billy, it's not what you think—"

"No? I think you're sexy." The vibrating tip teased her puckered nipples. "I think you should relax and enjoy this." He drew circles around her breasts, zigzagging the buzzing wand down the length of her torso. "I sure as hell am."

Billy nipped love bites along her hips. He slipped the pointed end over her clit and held it there. "Like that?" he murmured, watching every pleasurable twitch of her body.

Eden's breath caught. "Too intense. Move it down."

The rubber shaft slipped through the wetness between her thighs, creating pulsating warmth. He traced the mouth of her sex, dipping down to press the tip into the strip of skin separating her two openings. She tensed, half-afraid, half hoping he'd just dive right in to the naughty temptation.

But he moved the vibrator up to the wet furrow of her pussy and pushed it in.

Her mouth opened in a cry of delight, which he seized with a bruising kiss. He rocked the buzzing shaft in and out. With his hard cock grinding into her hip and his lips controlling hers, she wanted to wallow in the feeling of utter wantonness.

Instead, she exploded, gasping as shards of pleasure erupted. Heart racing, sweat dripping, pelvis pumping, she thrashed against the sticky mat as the most intense orgasm of her life nearly knocked her unconscious.

At one point Eden was vaguely aware of Billy removing the vibrator and whispering soothing words, gifting her with tender kisses, prolonged caresses. He enfolded her in his arms, and whisked her off to her bed. Cool cotton sheets brushed her skin, then his firm body nestled against hers beneath the comforter.

She closed her eyes. "Let me catch my breath, then it'll be your turn."

"No hurry." His warm breath ruffled the hair on the back of her head. "We've got all the time in the world."

Content, she snuggled into Billy's embrace.

And fell fast asleep.

Chapter Six

Eden woke up naked and alone, darkness shadowing her room. She called out a tentative, "Billy?"

No answer. Not that she blamed him for taking off.

She flipped the covers and shivered. Donning her chenille robe, she tiptoed into the hallway. The Tiffany-style lamp threw a pattern of rainbow colors against the wall. She double-checked the doors downstairs, but Billy had locked them before leaving. Still, she felt every bit a selfish idiot. What'd possessed her to fall asleep?

When she'd crawled back into her bed and turned on the nightlight, she noticed the sheet of paper perched on the adjoining pillow. She grinned. Cocky man. He'd used her vibrator as a paperweight. The note read:

> *Eden,*
> *I didn't have the heart to wake you. Late lunch tomorrow? You pick the place.*
> *Billy*
> *PS-Tomorrow it's your turn*

She clasped the letter to her breast. He wasn't upset? How had she forgotten his innate sweetness? Right. She'd been so bowled over by his sexpertise; she'd forgotten Billy Buchanan was comprised of more qualities than talented fingers and a skillful mouth. Smiling, she switched off the light and returned to sleep.

♋

"Mr. Buchanan is here," Shelby announced through the intercom early the next afternoon.

Eden's pulse spiked. She peered at the clock. Late lunch meant little interruption for the surprise she'd planned. She fluffed up her hair and smoothed the crease from her black linen mini-skirt. "Send him in."

The door swung open, but Billy's handsome face was hidden behind a camcorder. He kept the camera trained on her as he folded his solid frame into the chair opposite her desk. "Today we're in the office of Eden LaCroix, administrator for the Spearfish Community Center. Ms. LaCroix, I'd like to record your opinions on the future of this facility."

"What is this?"

Billy depressed a button and rested the compact machine on his knee. "I told you I tape footage for every project."

"Why?"

"Easier to find problems in case I missed something pertinent the first time around."

"Does that happen often? You miss something important?"

He frowned and fiddled with the angle of the LCD screen. "Sometimes when I least expect it."

"And if I refuse?"

His eyes met hers in challenge. "I'll use my toy on someone else."

Hoo-boy. Her body heated, remembering his proficiency with *toys* last night. "Fine. Let's get started. Don't forget we have a lunch date and I'm starved."

♋

As Billy trained his camera on Eden, he felt like he'd been split in two. The professional half calmly asked questions and appeared in perfect control. The testosterone-laden half gloated at the shine in Eden's eyes, the high color in her cheeks, the way the lens caught every beautiful nuance of her face.

Had his attention to her sexual pleasure last night put the

41

extra glow in her today? Nah. He couldn't take credit. Eden was smart, striking, determined and it showed in person as well as on tape.

He listened as Eden rattled off the comprehensive history of the community center. She presented him a detailed list on how the city could improve and promote the community center in its present location. Some of her suggestions were unfeasible, but the majority of the ideas were reasonable.

Billy kept his questions to a minimum and let Eden's passion for the project speak for itself. "That should be enough for now," he said, powering down the unit and shoving it in the carrying case.

Eden rounded the desk, cocking a slim hip on the corner. Her short skirt rose up, showcasing an extra inch of marvelous thigh. Automatically his attention traveled higher. She rolled her shoulders back, the buttons on the sleeveless cinnamon-colored blouse stretched, exposing a creamy line of breast encased in a lacy peach bra.

Billy's hungry gaze met her impish glimmer.

"Seen enough?" she murmured throatily.

"Not nearly." He stood and pressed closer, letting her knee brush the bulge beneath his fly. "I wish I'd had this camera last night."

"Sorry I conked out."

Billy slid a quick glance to the closed metal blinds separating her office from the reception area. "I want to kiss you," he said, leaning close enough to taste her sweet breath. "I need to feel your mouth on mine so I know last night wasn't another elaborate fantasy I'd conjured up when I'm alone in my bed thinking about you."

"You've been thinking about me?"

"For years." Before he could erase those scant inches and fasten his mouth to hers, Eden ducked under his arm.

"If you've waited that long then another few hours won't matter. You're not kissing me in here." She snagged an oversized purse. "But if you're really good, I might give you a kiss in the car on the way to lunch." Her amused eyes zeroed in on the swelling beneath his zipper. "Probably won't happen though, because we both know how much you enjoy being bad."

Billy's response, "I'll be good, I promise," fell on deaf ears as she sailed out the door.

She'd chosen an upscale Italian restaurant in a renovated turn-of-the-century warehouse showcasing exposed maroon bricks, metal beamed ceilings, original wide-planked wooden flooring with deeply weathered grooves. The structure appealed to him on a professional level. Add in old-fashioned gas lamps updated with electricity, crisp ivory linen tablecloths, pots of fresh herbs and private high-backed booths and it was charmingly romantic.

The college-aged male waiter recited the lunch specials, warning them the kitchen was about to close. After ordering, Billy noticed Eden's fingers nervously plucking the tablecloth.

"What's wrong?"

"Nothing. It's just weird, us having lunch together."

"Because we're in public?" Anyone strolling by had to look damn hard to see them, as they'd chosen a secluded booth away from the kitchen and the front door.

"No. Because when we were younger neither of us had enough money to eat someplace this nice. And we'd rather have been..."

Billy twined her fidgety fingers through his. "We'd rather have been making out like crazy, all hot mouths, frenzied hands and unfulfilled aches."

Color rose on her cheekbones. "Like last night?"

"Regrets?"

"None. Except for me falling asleep. I'm really sorry."

"Don't be. I told you. Last night was for you." He grinned. "I'm not worried. I'll get mine."

Eden grinned back, a bit smugly, in his opinion. "Sooner than you might think." She deflected his next question by pointing to his briefcase. "Is this a business lunch?"

"No. But it'd appear that way to anyone who might see us eating together."

"Good thinking." She settled into the cushioned leather backrest. "So, with all the stuff going on at the center, you haven't told me about your fabulous life in Chicago."

Fabulous. What a laugh. "What do you want to know?"

"The usual. Do you go to Bulls games? Do you walk along

the waterfront?" She brushed a lock of hair from her forehead. "Do you and your friends heckle the hapless Cubs? Or do you prefer fine dining when you're out on the town?"

"Sometimes I do those things. I've also been known to wolf down a Chicago style pizza and a hot dog or two. But mostly, I work, so my social life is pretty pathetic. Plus, I've been in Canada for the last eighteen months working on an intensive restoration."

"Eighteen months? Isn't that a long time to be away from home?"

Funny, he'd never considered his condo home; he was so rarely there. He spent more time in his battered office chair than on his brand new living room couch. "I'm used to it. The majority of my projects are done in other cities."

"Bet you've been some pretty cool places?"

"I guess. What about you?"

"Me? I've never ventured from here. Spearfish has always felt like home." Frowning, she stirred her tea. "But now with the future of the community center up in the air, it's a little scary wondering where I'll end up."

An awkward silence lingered until the waiter interrupted with their salads. Billy was determined to get the conversation back on personal ground. "I love the Black Hills. Now if I can only convince my baby sister Maggie to stick around here."

Eden's fork stopped midway to her mouth. "You have a sister who lives here?"

"Maggie lives in Rapid City. She signed on as a civilian computer programmer at Ellsworth Air Force Base a few months back. I hadn't been able to visit her until the job in Calgary ended."

"You planned on coming back to South Dakota *before* Jim called you?"

Here was the moment of truth. Billy fixed his gaze to hers so there'd be no misunderstanding. "Yes. Bob's heart attack just speeded up the process. I'd intended to spend time in Spearfish long before that."

"Did you know... Never mind. Don't answer."

"Yes. I knew you still lived here."

She rooted around in her salad. "Why didn't I know you

had a sister?"

"Actually, I have two sisters. Lacy is married with two kids and works as a publicist in New York City." He focused on the muted fresco covering the far wall. "I didn't tell you about my family because my senior college year wasn't an easy time for me. My mother went off the deep end after my dad's death. Luckily, Lacy had escaped to NYU. I'd ended up here on a full scholarship and lived with my grandma, but poor Maggie was stuck with our mom."

He remembered the guilt, the hysterical, late-night phone calls from his frightened sister. His sister who was the same age as Eden. Talk about a wakeup call. The night when Eden doffed her dress in the motel room and stood in front of him completely naked? As much as Billy wanted her, his brain got stuck on whether his little sister was losing her virginity to a lecherous college boy in a sleazy motel after her senior prom.

That idea literally deflated his plans and he was too embarrassed to tell Eden the truth. Instead, he'd yanked his pants up over his limp cock and vanished into the night.

The next week college finals had started. After the last stunt his mother pulled, he'd had no choice but to leave right after exams, skipping his college graduation ceremony. As soon as he'd settled Maggie in New York with Lacy, he'd joined the Chicago firm.

A warm, soft hand covered his. "I'm sorry. Guess I was so self-absorbed back then I didn't see you suffered with your own family problems."

"Not self-absorbed, Eden. Self-conscious, maybe. Self-reliant, definitely. But you are the least self-centered person I've ever known."

The meals arrived and they ate in companionable silence. Eden sucked a fat piece of shrimp from her fork, releasing the tines a millimeter at a time, swallowing with gusto and then licked her lips.

An image flashed of her wrapping those shiny red lips around his cock. Sucking frantically and her beautiful throat muscles working as she swallowed. The urge surfaced to sweep everything from the table, spread her wide and fuck her fast and furiously on top of it.

The air thickened and the booth seemed to close in.

When the waiter appeared to clear plates and detailed the dessert menu, Eden fished around in her purse, pulled out a twenty and handed it to him. "Nothing else. We won't have to bug you and we can get on with our business."

Before Billy considered Eden's motives, she'd squeezed next to him in his side of the booth, her right thigh pressed to his left. Her body heat seared him and her heady, dark scent made his already shallow breathing more difficult.

"Put your briefcase on the table and open it, so it looks like we're working."

A tiny kernel of anxiety unfurled in his gut, but he placed his briefcase on the middle of the table and popped the locks. "Are we working?" he asked inanely, removing file folders.

"Not you." Eden's cool mouth suctioned to the hot skin below his ear. He shuddered at the simple touch. Her left hand arced down the center of his body from the knot in his tie to the buckle on his pants. "However, I have catch-up work to do. It is my turn, remember?"

The full impact of her words sunk in when she unbuckled his belt. "Eden—"

"Billy," she whispered back in a mocking tone, making quick work of his zipper. "I'm going to stroke your cock right here under the table until you explode in my hand. And you're going to let me."

Turned on beyond measure, he said not a word.

"Sit back and open your legs wider." Eden's exhalations tickled his neck. "Pretend you're studying a market analysis." Her fingers slipped into the gap in his boxers. When the warmth of her hand circled his aching cock, Billy groaned.

She stroked from root to tip, letting the plump head rub against the hard ridge of her palm. Drops of pre-come dribbled down, making the glide of her hand easier, increasing the sensations until his buttocks tightened and the vein running up his cock began to pulse.

If anyone passed their table, all they'd see was two heads bent close, engrossed in the sheaf of papers on the table between them.

Eden repeated the words he'd said last night. "Tell me what you want."

"I want to fuck you. Hard. Fast. Right now." His hand

moved under the table and he tried to stop her activity on his dick. "Let's go."

"No. You let go." She nipped his earlobe, knocking his hand away with her knee. "My turn to call the shots." She stopped the slide of her hands to feather butterfly touches from his balls to the weeping tip. "You're so damn sexy, Billy. I want to feel you come. I won't stop until you do."

As he nuzzled Eden's soft hair, his tension slipped away. No doubt if he would've slid his hand under her skirt, he'd have expected her compliance. Hell, he was a modern man, equal time and all that. He admitted it felt good to let Eden be in charge. And if the euphoric look on her face was any indication, she was getting off on the naughty exhibition as much as he was.

"I wish it was my mouth on you." She squeezed from the bottom of his shaft up, her fingers a tight ring as she rubbed her thumb over the slick tip. "My lips, teeth and tongue. I'd get your cock really wet. See if I could deep throat you. Then when you were teetering on the edge, I'd suck you dry and swallow every drop."

"Enough. God, I can only take so much." Damn. He was close. Too close, but he had no intention of trying to hold back.

"Do you like me talking dirty? You'll like it even better when I do this." She increased her strokes.

The muscles in his groin tightened, his balls drew taut. Helplessly he gathered the linen tablecloth in his fist. He focused on a rainbow glimmer of crystal reflecting on the table as his rigid sex pulsed toward completion. A white-hot flame shot out of the end of his cock, his head fell back and he groaned long and low as his seed flooded her hand.

A tender kiss brushed his lips, followed by a soft cloth on his crotch wiping away the remnants of his explosion.

Billy slowly cracked his eyelids, half-afraid he'd been dreaming again and he'd wake to nondescript walls of another hotel room with his dick clutched in his own hand.

But his eyes met Eden's and clashed in a heated frenzy of desire. She lifted her hand and wickedly licked the tips of her fingers.

A possessive need ignited his blood.

Billy tucked himself in and zipped up. Briefcase closed, he

hauled Eden from the booth, out the door and into his car.

His hands clutched the steering wheel. He didn't utter a peep after his Neanderthal tactic of practically dragging her by the hair from the restaurant. He didn't dare touch her; once he started he wouldn't stop. When he finally screeched to a halt outside the condo, he faced her.

"Look. I didn't mean to make you mad."

"I'm not mad."

"Why were you in such a hurry to get away?"

Billy's hands shook when he reached for her. Somehow he kept his touch gentle as he traced her baby-soft cheek with his knuckles. "Feather Light owns this condo. I'm staying here. It was the closest place with a bed."

Her hazel eyes widened. "But I have to go back to work—"

"No. You have to get out of the car, Eden, or else I'm taking you right here on the front seat. Your choice."

Chapter Seven

Eden couldn't move. She stared at the rigid set of Billy's jaw. Need and the underlying darker impression of hunger made his body still, too still, like an agitated jungle cat about to pounce.

Her eyes slid to the condo entrance. Six redwood stairs led to a covered portico. The door was set back far enough into the structure she couldn't discern the color. Besides the scraggly lilac hedge separating the driveway from the sidewalk, they were out in the open. No trees, shade or shadows from nearby buildings. Surely Billy hadn't meant he'd take her right here on the leather seat of his rental car? In broad daylight?

"Well," he demanded. "What's it going to be?"

Holy cow. Guess he *had* meant it.

Before Eden lost her nerve, she grabbed her purse, flung open the door and stumbled out of the car.

Billy was on her before she reached the top step.

He kissed her with an openmouthed mating of tongues, hard, wet, divine. He pushed her toward the entrance, his body plastered to hers. As he fumbled with the house key, he kissed her. As he struggled to unlock the door, he kissed her. As he opened the door and half-carried, half-dragged her inside, he kept his voracious mouth on hers.

Eden fell headfirst into desire, letting her own long denied needs break free.

"God, I want you," he groaned, slamming the door shut behind them only to flatten her body against the hard surface.

Her purse plunked on the rug. He began a fresh assault on her mouth, little nips and kisses, watching her eyes glaze over while he hurriedly unbuttoned her blouse. The satiny material slid an erotic path down her arms and dropped on the tile.

Then his hands were everywhere.

Sensations bombarded her. His sharp teeth on the swell of her breasts. His shaking hands fumbling with the clasp of her bra. His warm mouth dragging kisses across her moist skin. The ridges of the wooden door digging into her bared back. Her eyes fluttered shut when his lips closed over the peak of her left nipple.

Eager fingers tugged at the side zipper until her skirt met the floor in a soft *whoosh.* Nylons were peeled down her legs, stopped by the barrier of her high-heels. She kicked off her shoes, shed her hosiery. Eden was barefoot and completely naked, except for a damp pair of peach bikini panties.

Ripped out of her sensual daze, she opened her eyes and realized Billy was still fully clothed. She pushed him back a step, her fingers tracing the delineated lines of his chest. One hand unknotted his tie, while the other worked on the buttons of his ivory dress shirt.

Billy toed off his loafers, unfastening his shirt cuffs as she continued to undress him.

"Stand still," she hissed, struggling with his belt buckle. He swayed, trying to remove his socks one-handed. His pants hit the floor, leaving him in boxer briefs and an unbuttoned shirt, looking every inch a male underwear model. She smoothed trembling hands over the golden blond hair dotting his broad chest.

His thumb traced the outline of her lips. "I can't get enough of this mouth."

"Billy—"

"Ssh." His blue eyes were wild, his cheekbones suffused with color. A resigned sigh drifted over her temple as he molded his hard body to her soft curves. "I don't think I can get enough of you, either."

Eden moaned.

Billy swallowed the sound in a greedy kiss. Fingers inched up the inside of her thigh, pushing aside the lace barrier of her panties and plunged into her slick channel, and back out, spreading moisture to the heart of her begging for his attention.

She arched, pushing her pelvis closer, blindly jerking his

boxers down his hips to reach for the erection teasing her belly.

He trailed his lips over her jaw. "You are so wet. Do you have any idea what that does to me?"

"Show me."

"Let's go. Condoms are in the bedroom."

"No. Now. Right here, right now." She wrenched away from him and groped on the floor for her purse, coming up with a square package from the inside pocket. She ripped it open with her teeth and shimmied out of her panties.

When Eden looked up, his underwear was history and he stood before her magnificently naked, strangely vulnerable. She couldn't offer him reassurance that taking this next step wouldn't result in broken promises or broken hearts, nothing but mindless sex. They both knew better.

He helped her roll the condom down the straining length of his cock. Panting against the hollow of her throat, he lifted her higher, pressing her to the door. "Wrap your legs around me."

Eden's arms circled his neck. She dug her heels into the back of his muscular thighs and dropped her hips to feel the tip of his cock demanding entrance to her body.

Billy paused and gazed into her eyes. He lowered his mouth and kissed her at the same time he pushed inside her to the hilt.

His gentle passion nearly undid her.

"Eden." He uttered her name as a reverent sigh. His large hands gripped her butt, tilting her pelvis for the deepest penetration.

What a rush, finally feeling Billy Buchanan inside her body, skin-to-skin, soul-to-soul, man-to-woman. Sweat beaded on her skin. Her mind shut down to everything but pure pleasure.

Billy's controlled thrusts changed to short, hard strokes, which made it impossible to sustain the frantic kiss.

Eden ground into him, her fingers buried in his soft hair, her teeth scraping the rigid cords in his neck. She loved the taste of him on her tongue. The brush of his solid chest against hers. His crisp pubic hair abrading her clit and his firm muscles beneath her hands. The sexy sounds their bodies made at each thrust and retreat.

His forehead dripped sweat on her shoulder and his hips

flexed beneath her clenched thighs. Billy shuddered and slowed down, pulling out until just the tip of his cock met the greedy mouth of her sex, then glided back in inch by inch.

"No. Harder." Her heels spurred his butt to remind him to keep up the frenzied pace, cursing his restraint.

Warm lips followed her collarbone. "God. This feels so fucking perfect I can't hold off much longer."

She tilted Billy's face up to meet her eyes. "Don't hold off. I'm there right with you."

Billy's hips began pounding again. Hard. Relentless.

"Yes." Eden's midsection tightened. Her ass slapped into the door with a satisfying sting, and Billy's upper body pressing into hers was the only thing holding her up.

A moment later, she began to come apart. A shiver started in her scalp, zinging through her system like a wayward electrical current.

Billy licked and bit at her neck, his satisfied male chuckle echoed across her skin as tremors rocked her body.

His humor disappeared on a groan.

Feeling drunk from the intensity, her head thunked back. Stars exploded behind her lids.

"Hang on." His hands left her tangled hair and smacked flat beside her head against the door. Four powerful thrusts coaxed another climax from her and she cried out, her vaginal contractions prolonging his release as Billy slammed into her high and hard, growling her name.

Even in the near silence, their harsh breaths, their blood synched as one.

Sweat plastered them to each other and Eden to the door. Several bliss filled seconds passed before she finally whispered, "It was worth the wait."

Chapter Eight

Sweat dripped into Billy's eyes. His toes were cramped and his arms felt like bands of Jell-O.

Beautiful. He'd taken her against the front door. He'd waited ten years and banging Eden fast and furious in the foyer was the best he could offer her?

It was a wonder he ever got laid.

A contented sigh drifted against his neck, followed by a string of openmouthed sucking kisses. Evidently Eden hadn't minded.

Billy leaned back, taking their weight in his legs as he attempted to pull out.

But her thighs gripped him tight. "Stay." She nuzzled his cheek, burying soft lips in the cup of his shoulder. "Just for another minute until my brain can function."

A sense of rightness washed over him. He'd never felt so completely...complete. "You okay? You're not mad that I—"

"—fucked me stupid?" Her lips curved into a smile against his neck. "Are you kidding? I imagined it'd be good between us, but not like that."

"It was pretty spectacular."

She shivered delicately and seemed to burrow even deeper into his skin. "You think it was a one shot deal? Years of wondering 'what-if' made it impossible *not* to combust when we finally came together?"

He nudged her back against the door, not surprised she'd kept her beautiful eyes closed, hiding her feelings from him. "There's only one way to find out."

"How?"

"We have to do it again." He peppered kisses down her jaw. "And again, and again, and again, until we're sure it wasn't a fluke."

Her laugh soothed his soul.

Billy smoothed an auburn tendril from her flushed cheek. "Eden."

"Mmm?"

"Baby, look at me."

She glanced at him from beneath lowered lashes.

"I have to tell you something."

"No." She tried to squirm away, an impossible maneuver since they were still physically connected. "Whatever happened in the past doesn't matter. And if this has to do with the community center, I don't want to hear it right now, okay?"

He stared at her, the words stuck in his throat. How could he tell her it wasn't their past that caused his sleepless nights, but thoughts of their future?

"I need to get dressed and go back to work."

Billy cautioned himself to keep it light as she was already on the verge of retreat. "You sure you can't stay and play hooky?"

She gave him a sexy grin. "The word you're looking for is *nookie*. And no. I have to go."

"Smart ass." He nipped her chin and she yelped.

"The kids are probably running around driving Shelby crazy with their questions about where I am."

"Are you there every day after school?"

"Without fail." Eden's fingers trailed a path across his shoulders and her mouth tasted the skin she'd touched.

Another whip of desire cracked through him. "Then you deserve a break. Stay. Please."

"Tempting...but no." She whacked his butt and he withdrew from the warm place that strangely felt like home.

When her feet touched the tile, she shivered and bent to grab her clothes, muttering, "Looks like a damn yard sale in here."

Billy plucked up his clothing on the way to dispose of the condom. In the bathroom, he peered at his reflection, turning his profile left and right. Yep. Same guy on the outside, but the emotions jumping inside told a different tale. The last few days he'd been revitalized.

Scrubbing his hands over his face, he slumped back against the wall. *Face the facts, man.* His return to Spearfish hadn't been about helping out an old friend or an excuse to checkup on his sister. He'd come back for her. Now that he realized the magnitude of the mistake he'd made years ago, how could he walk away? Now that he was certain she'd always been *the* one for him?

Worse yet, if he loved her, how could he close the center?

A soft rapping on the door ripped him from his reverie. "Billy? Look, I hate to screw and run, but I've got to get back."

He grinned at her phrasing, hoping it indicated there'd be no awkward silences between them on the drive back to the center.

♋

Eden primly crossed her bare legs. She hadn't bothered putting her nylons back on. As she surveyed the landscape out the window of the rental car, she sensed Billy's confusion. He'd tried to delve into what'd happened and she'd blatantly ignored him. And she'd practically jumped from his car when he pulled up at the community center.

Shelby didn't pester her about the overly long lunch but Eden's relief was short-lived. She'd nearly ducked into the safety of her office when a soft voice startled her.

"Aha! I knew I'd catch you goofing off someday."

Eden faced her friend, Tate LeBeau. "As you can see, I'm back at the grindstone."

Tate's blue eyes turned shrewd. "What's up with those rosy cheeks and sparkling eyes?" Her gaze traveled up Eden's exposed shins and narrowed on a spot below her ear.

Dammit. Had Billy given her a hickey? Ten years ago he'd delighted in marking her his, everywhere, but he'd outgrown that impulse, hadn't he? Eden resisted the urge to rub her neck.

Unfortunately, Billy chose that moment to saunter around

the corner. His contented smirk disappeared and he stopped dead in his tracks. Eden suspected their guilt was obvious.

"Oh my God. Billy Buchanan? Is that really you?"

"In the flesh."

Tate rushed forward, blond hair flying as she enveloped him in a hug. "It's good to see you, even though I haven't forgiven you for leaving Nathan in the lurch all those years ago." She whapped him lightly on the arm. "Poor man was forced to finish the fire station project all by himself."

Billy had the grace to blush. "I wish I'd had another choice." His troubled gaze connected with Eden's before he gave Tate a boyish grin. "You look exactly the same."

She patted her pregnant belly. "Not exactly."

"Dare I ask how many kids make up the LeBeau household these days?"

"This one is number five." With pride she rattled off, "Sophie is seven, Ben is five, the twins, Michael and Sasha are three."

He whistled. "Been a busy decade. How is Nathan?"

Tate beamed the pure sunshine of a woman wildly in love. "Wonderful. Business is great. He has four fulltime employees, which means he has time to coach the kids' various sports teams and knock me up on a regular basis."

When Eden attempted to sneak into her office to let them catch up, Tate firmly grabbed her elbow. "Excuse us. Eden and I have some...ah, issues to discuss." She propelled Eden into the office, slammed the door and clicked the metal blinds shut.

No escape. Pregnancy hormones seemed to have given Tate super-human strength and eagle-eyed detection skills. "Spill it, girl. How long have you been sleeping with Billy?"

Eden didn't bother to lie; Tate knew her too well. "Since about an hour ago." She skirted the desk but was too wired to sit. "Don't start." During Eden's teenage years, Tate had become her mentor at the community center. Eleven years later, Tate was still a mentor, but also a close friend, so Tate was aware of Eden's devastation when Billy had abruptly left her life.

"You expecting a lecture? From me? You know better. No bull. What is going on?"

"If I tell you I don't know, will you believe me?"

"Yes." Tate's eyes softened. "Talk to me."

The words tumbled out in a rush. "This is all so surreal. Get this: Billy's working for Feather Light, deciding the future of the community center, which means my future is in his hands." She inhaled a deep yoga breath to keep the hysteria at bay. "But from the minute Billy walked in the door, it hasn't been about business, or my future, but our past."

"I imagine that drives you crazy."

"Not only haven't I seen any of his notes regarding the center, I have to deal with my stupid hormones wanting to get naked with him. All. The. Damn. Time. When he smiles at me, every professional thought sails right out of my head." A shiver moved through her. "Maybe I'm more like my mother than I want to admit."

Memories of men parading out of her mother's room in the early morning hours flashed in Eden's mind. Whenever her mother stared into space, mooning over some new guy she'd met at work, inevitably her mom lost her job.

"Eden LaCroix, you are nothing like your mother," Tate muttered. "Although sometimes I wish you were."

Her astonished gaze snapped back to Tate. "What?"

"You're so caught up in making sure your reputation in this community is beyond reproach, you've forgotten there's more to life than work. No one will begrudge you a relationship."

"With the man who's come here to shut down the community center?" Eden said incredulously. "How could I ever explain my way out of that?"

"Billy already told you he's closing you down?"

"No. Whenever he gets within three feet of me, we both forget the real reason he's here." But he'd mentioned concrete concerns in the car. Had he been serious? Or angling for an excuse to relive their delicious lunch? Sad thing was, it wouldn't take much to convince her she should spend all of her meals with him, stripped bare and screaming for another course.

"Regardless of the business end of things, he still cares for you," Tate said.

"You can't know that. You've seen him for what? Two minutes?"

"So?"

"So, neither of us is the same person we were ten years ago." Eden glanced at her framed college diploma, then at the high school one hanging beside it. "We can't go back."

"But you don't want to go forward either. For years you've used your experience with Billy as an excuse not to get involved with any man." Tate held up her hand, stopping Eden's protest. "And no, banging Jon White Feather like a drum whenever the mood strikes you does *not* count, because both you and Jon use your pasts as an excuse not to move on—either together or separately."

Stupid insightful pregnancy hormones.

"Now that Billy has returned, apparently willing to make amends to you or to change your opinion of him, you're unwilling to do either."

Eden barely held on to her temper. "What do you expect me to do? Blindly give him my heart and my trust again?"

"Sweetie. Why won't you admit he's *always* had your heart?"

Dammit. She refused to respond.

"Lord, you are stubborn as a mule. Seems no matter what Billy does or doesn't do, he can't win."

"You're defending him?"

"No, I'm pointing out the facts. If Billy doesn't close the community center, you won't believe he didn't do it to get in your good graces. If Billy does recommend closing it, you have a legitimate reason not to pursue a relationship with him."

"What relationship? He lives in Chicago. I live in Spearfish. This 'relationship' is nothing but another loose end he's tying up while he's here."

Tate studied her face until Eden squirmed under the intensity. "Think about what you really want and don't be such a chickenshit about going after it." Then Tate was gone.

Eden slumped in her office chair. She was no closer to knowing what her future held than she was three days ago.

She did know one thing for certain—ten years of life experience only added to Billy's appeal. Yet, she suspected when it was all said and done he'd walk away. Unscathed. Just like he had before.

Despite Tate's observation Billy carried a torch for her, she didn't believe he wanted more than a mutual slaking of lust. Her feelings for him were her problem. But she'd be damned if she'd spend time brooding about it. Life went on.

Eden flipped on her computer and lost herself in work while she still had a job.

♋

A lush male voice sang, "Knock, knock, knockin' on heaven's door..."

Eden looked up and smiled at the longhaired, leather-clad Indian casually leaning against the doorjamb.

Simply put, Jon White Feather was a beautiful man. His angular face, courtesy of his Swedish mother, was as striking as his pale blue eyes. His broad forehead sloped into high, wide cheekbones. A regal nose gave way to lush lips and a pointed chin. Copper-colored skin bespoke his Lakota heritage. Tall, muscularly lean, his meaty biceps and the insides of his forearms were decorated with tribal tattoos. His black hair flowed past his shoulders, giving him the look of a bad boy rocker mixed with an Indian warrior. He was built, he was hot and his intense gaze still made her belly quiver after years of friendship. "*Hoka-hey, kola.*"

"Jon. I was wondering when you'd get into town."

He quirked a dark eyebrow at her. "You haven't seen me in six months and that's my welcome? How about some sugar from my best girl, eh?" He spread his arms wide.

She skirted the desk and launched herself at him. Jon spun her in a circle amidst her laughter.

"Didja miss me, my wicked little garden sprite?"

"No."

He whispered, "Liar."

"Fine. I missed you. Put me down."

"Only if you promise to go out with me tomorrow night."

"Where?" The last time she'd forgotten to ask specifics she'd ended up in a strip club in Wyoming with Jon and six of his bruiser roadies, watching them jump into a bar fight with a group of hot cowboys. After the blood and the insults dried up, the dozen or so guys had shot whiskey in the tour bus until dawn.

"How about dancin', someplace off the beaten track?"

When he rolled into town, Jon preferred to lay low somewhere he wouldn't be recognized. "Like the Silver Star?" The honky-tonk was one of the few places in town that didn't cater to college students.

"I'll probably be the only Indian in the place amidst cowboy hats and shitkickers, and you know what happened last time, but it's a deal."

She returned to her chair while Jon flopped across from her desk. "So what're you doing at the community center? Working out that buff bod of yours?"

Jon gifted her with a smoldering look. "I'm here just for you, dollface."

"Wrong. Try again."

"Man. I can't pull nothin' over on you." He grinned pure mischief. "I told Jim I'd pick up Micah from basketball practice since Cindy is dealing with sick kids. But I really did volunteer so I could pop in and see what you were up to."

Eden gestured at the piles. "The usual."

"You work too hard, which is why I'm taking you out for a night of fun. How long's it been since you cut loose?"

"Months. I've had a lot on my mind."

"I heard. Jim says the center might be in trouble. What's up with that?"

"The same old bullshit. It's been coming for a year so I'm not surprised."

He frowned. "Is your job in jeopardy?"

"Yeah." She looked away to avoid his pity.

Papers rustled as Jon leaned across her desk and clasped her hand in his. "Hey. If the city is stupid enough to let you go, their loss, eh?"

Underneath Jon's sexy persona of rocker Johnny Feather lurked a really sweet, thoughtful guy. "I guess."

"You could always go on the road with me."

"What would my job be?"

"My personal love slave."

Eden snorted. "You've already got that position filled. They're called groupies."

Jon brought her hand to his mouth and kissed her knuckles. "None of them hold a candle to you."

"Flatterer. But I will take it under consideration if this place goes belly up." She threaded her fingers through his. "How long are you here?"

He sighed. "Only two days. This break isn't near long enough."

"And you say I work too hard?"

"Yeah, well, I'd like to hang out to catch up with Jim and his tribe, but unfortunately, most of my time will be spent in Eagle Butte."

"Another last minute gig?"

"No. My bass guitarist is getting married." He dropped his gaze to their joined hands. "I oughta be thrilled for him, right? His woman is awesome. He's never been happier."

"But?"

"That's the thing. But nothin'. Him getting hitched won't adversely affect the band, so it's not a professional issue. I can't figure out why I'm...pissed. Frustrated."

"Jealous?" Eden offered.

"Maybe." Jon's thumb stroked the inside of her wrist. "He's the first one of the band members to pair off. Which is cool. When he's with her, it's like they're the only two people in the world, even if there's a dozen people on the bus. I'm surrounded by people almost twenty-four/seven so why do I always feel so damn lonely?"

Eden was familiar with that feeling, but as this was one of the few times Jon had opened up in recent years, she didn't interrupt.

"Do you ever look around at your life and feel like you're missing out on what's really important, even when you aren't sure what that important something might be?"

"Yeah. We all have days like that."

"Some of us more than others. I just wish..."

"What?" When his startling blue eyes connected with hers, her stomach cartwheeled.

"I forget how beautiful you are."

Her face heated and she yanked her hand back. "Jon. Stop."

"I'm serious, Eden. You're beautiful. Smart. Successful. Funny as hell. Sweet as pie when you ain't bein' a pain in the ass." His grin was there and gone. "You've dealt with the same Indian/white racist shit I have. The sex between us is great. My family adores you. *I* adore you."

"I assume this sweet talk has a point, *kola*?"

"Sometimes I don't just want to be your friend, Eden. I want more." His eyes went from playful to haunted. "You are the perfect woman for me. So why can't I settle down with you and let you fill the lonely spots in my life?"

"A—because you aren't ready to abandon your wicked rocker ways and pledge your life to one woman. B—because you snore. C—because you don't love me."

"I should. You'd be good for me."

"Would you be good for me, Jon?" Eden asked softly.

"No." Jon sighed again. "It wouldn't be fair because I don't know if I can ever..." He briefly shut his eyes. "You deserve so much more than the pittance I can offer you, *winyan*."

Eden's heart clenched at the raw pain in his melodic voice. "Are you ever going to forgive yourself? It wasn't your fault Juliette died."

"Yeah, it was."

They'd had this conversation dozens of times and it always ended the same way: with Jon changing the subject.

"You're one of the few people in my life who doesn't automatically say, 'Yes, Johnny' to whatever crazy thing I suggest. Not only do you know the real me—Jon the half-breed Indian with a checkered past—but you don't want anything from me."

"Except hot sex," she teased, hoping to lighten his mood.

"But even that is different, truer, than with the groupies hanging around, waiting to fuck me in the tour bus strictly for the bragging rights that they nailed Johnny Feather."

"The price of being semi-famous."

"Price," he scoffed. "My agent, the promoters, the tour director, the radio stations, the assorted tribes, the fans; they all see me as a commodity. Dollar signs. A brand. It gets old."

Eden didn't say anything.

Jon grimaced. "Listen to me. I have everything I ever dreamed of as a poor kid on the rez and I'm complaining? You probably think I'm a self-indulgent prick, eh?"

"No, I think you need a friend."

"Thanks. You are a damn good friend, Eden, and I missed you." He kissed her knuckles again before releasing her hand. "But we're still friends with bennies, right? Because I'm about a quart low on sweet lovin'."

What kind of woman even considers a round of no-strings-sex with one guy mere hours after screwing another one?

The answer was a stab in her gut, *the kind of woman who raised you. You're just like your mother.*

"Eden?"

She smiled tightly. "The truth is, I'm sort of seeing someone."

"Anyone I know?"

"No."

"Is it serious?"

Eden shrugged.

"Doesn't matter. I still wanna hang out with you while I'm here." Jon gave her a shrewd look. "Tell you what. Bring him along tomorrow night. I'll check him out to see if he's good enough for my best girl."

And wouldn't that be an awkward situation? *Billy, meet Johnny. Johnny and I play naked Indian poke-her whenever he rolls into town. Johnny, meet Billy. Billy is here to fuck up my life on a professional level, but that doesn't matter because I let him fuck me any other way he pleases.*

"What's goin' on in that pretty head of yours?" Jon murmured.

"Nothing. Just wondering if I should pick you up at Jim and Cindy's tomorrow night?"

"Nah. Bebe and Stephie are both sick so I'm not staying with them. I'm crashing at Jim's old condo."

Eden frowned. Something about that seemed familiar.

"I'll meet you. Silver Star at seven?"

"Deal."

"You dressing up full-on bad boy rock star?" Eden asked slyly.

"Nope. I'm sticking with the poor Indian look. So don't be surprised if you don't recognize me."

"Right, dollface," Eden repeated his oft-used term of endearment. "You could wear sackcloth and ashes and you'd still be the hottest guy in the room and you damn well know it."

"Now who's the flatterer?"

Micah and Thomas burst in, dribbling a basketball, creating chaos and Eden was grateful for the diversion.

Chapter Nine

Billy's workday was a lost cause.

His focus centered around reliving Eden's husky moans of delight as he slid in and out of her slick feminine heat, the satisfying weight of her lissome body wrapped around his, the remembrance of her sweet and hot kisses. Occasionally he'd catch a whiff of her scent on his skin and he'd go as hard as his protractor.

Before he'd left Bob's office, he'd grudgingly grabbed the files concerning the community center. The logical thing would be to hole up and decide on a course of action for the city council.

Sometimes logic was highly overrated.

Almost on autopilot, Billy drove to the community center. He justified the burning need to see her because they had business to discuss, preferably in a room without a bed.

He winced. That hadn't seemed to matter a few hours ago when he'd taken her hard and fast against the front door.

No regrets, but there hadn't been any finesse either.

Her Jeep was parked in its usual spot and he wasn't surprised she was working late. Briefcase in hand, he passed by the gym, stopping to observe a raucous basketball game. The men appeared to be his age, but that didn't stop the cheap shots or the adolescent taunts. After a nasty elbow jab, in the next play, the jabber found himself facedown on the court courtesy of the jabbee.

Billy squinted at the kid leaning against the back wall. Was that Thomas? He waved.

But Thomas didn't wave back. A stricken look crossed the

kid's face and he disappeared beneath the wooden bleachers.

Dammit. According to Eden, Thomas wasn't supposed to be here this time of night. Had he snuck in again? It made Billy absolutely sick to think the kid had to figure out a way to avoid getting a beating on a regular basis. He suspected Eden's bond with Thomas was partially because she'd been in that same "duck and run" family situation. Billy's childhood hadn't been ideal, but physical violence hadn't been an issue. So did he keep Thomas's secret so the kid would be safe tonight? Or did Billy tell Eden he'd spied her young friend hiding out again?

The empty corridors were quiet, save for the far-off mechanical whine of a vacuum cleaner and the shuffle of his hard soled dress shoes on the marble floor. Light shone through the half-closed blinds in Eden's office.

He knocked and heard a brusque, "Come in."

Billy hesitated on the threshold. "Am I interrupting?"

"Would it matter?"

"No."

"Why are you here?"

"I need to talk to you."

A deliberate pause. "Is this a matter concerning the center?"

Concerning the center. No surprise she wouldn't discuss their mind-scrambling sex that'd ruined him for any other woman. "Actually, yes, I do have some questions." He slid into the chair opposite her desk and opened his briefcase, shuffling through the papers until he found the one he needed. "My research shows nothing's been done with the electrical system since the city took over this building twenty-five years ago?"

"We've hired an electrician to put in additional outlets or fix some minor glitch, but as far as major rework? Not in the five years I've been in charge. Why?"

"Seems the city only did minimal changes back then," he said, scanning his notes.

"Didn't it pass inspection?"

"Yes, but neither the city nor the contractor kept a detailed list of what'd been updated. My understanding is that this building was a temporary solution, so they only made the most rudimentary updates."

"Which means...?" Eden looked at him expectantly.

"A whole different set of unforeseen problems with wiring codes."

"I don't understand. How can you assume the wiring is faulty if you can't see it?"

Billy snapped the briefcase shut, using it as a lap desk. "That's the crux of the problem. The only way we can determine whether the wiring is coated with asbestos is to rip out all the walls. And if we rip out all the walls..."

"The city might as well rip out everything and start from scratch." Her glance darted to the fire alarm across the room. "Is there a danger of an electrical fire?"

"Certainly it's a possibility."

Eden mulled it over. "What the hell else can go wrong?"

The bitterness in her tone didn't surprise him. If his livelihood were at stake he imagined he'd be testy, too. "The family who owns the land has no interest in buying the building. It's a tricky situation when the landowner and the building owner aren't the same party, but I've seen this type of situation before—where one party puts land in a trust and another party builds on it in the guise of civic improvement."

"Have you spoken with the landowners?"

"No. It seemed irrelevant. Why?"

Eden's shrug was nonchalant, yet her fingers folded a neon post-it-note as if she was practicing origami. "Rumor has it if the city's findings are against improving the center, and they level the building, the landowners will use the lot and the empty one directly behind us to construct a fitness center that'd be in direct competition with the city's new digs."

Billy smiled, even if it felt a bit grim. "No love lost, huh?"

"No. I'm surprised the land trust agreement hasn't been challenged in court. Not only have the council members been bickering among themselves about this situation for years, the family owning the land has been stuck dealing with the bureaucracy."

"Have the landowners asked you to get involved if they do build the new facility?"

"Probably they won't, since I am a city employee. They'll assume I have a job." She sighed. "I hate politics. My main concern, my only concern, has been how this will affect the kids."

Devoted to others needs before her own—that was Eden to the core. He paused to gather his thoughts in the pretext of double-checking his notes. When he glanced up, she was rubbing her temple. "You okay?"

"Makes my head hurt thinking about this stuff."

"I'm not trying to give you a headache, Eden. I'm just trying to do my job."

A second passed. Then two. If this were a normal relationship, Billy supposed he'd cross the room, gather her in his arms and offer reassurances. So why was his dumb ass still glued to this cheap chair? Why were his hands still gripping his hard leather briefcase instead of her soft curves? He scooted forward, determined to prove this "thing" happening between them could be permanent and he was finally man enough to stand up for what he wanted: her.

But it wasn't her voice that stopped him cold; it was her utter look of defeat. "So what do we do now?"

"Have you eaten?"

"I'm not hungry. I had a late lunch."

Their gazes locked. "I know. I was there, remember?"

Eden opened her mouth then snapped it shut.

"Can we talk about our lunch date today?"

"No." She wheeled back and stood, snatching her keys from her desk. "Did I answer all of your questions? Because I—"

Billy was next to her before she could retreat. "Don't do this, Eden. Don't pretend nothing changed between us and we're just opposing sides in a business disagreement."

"What do you want me to do? Ignore it?"

"Yes." Billy tilted her chin up. "Put it aside. Just for tonight. Be with me. Let me come home with you."

Her eyes darkened with reproach as he leaned close enough to kiss her. "Not here—"

"Then invite me over. Please." He swept a tangled strand of hair from the corner of her mouth. "I want to be with you."

Eden twirled her car keys on her index finger. "Who the hell am I kidding? I want to be with you too. Let me lock up."

"While you're locking up, I think we should look for

Thomas. I thought I saw him in the gym."

"That little sneak. He knows he's not supposed to be here this late. I'll check his usual hiding spots and meet you at my house."

"Do you need help?"

"No. Actually it'd be better if you left. He might stay hidden if he sees you."

"Be careful."

Chapter Ten

Eden didn't find Thomas, but she'd managed to get filthy while looking. She jumped in the shower and didn't bother getting dressed afterward. No sense pretending they wouldn't be naked together within minutes anyway.

Carnal images of red-hot pleasure ran through her head, heating her blood so the cool water practically sizzled on her naked skin. She imagined the prickle of Billy's beard rubbing between her thighs. His rough fingertips trailing over every dip and swell of her body. His clever mouth doing all sorts of clever things.

Stop. If her thoughts traveled that route, she'd melt into a puddle right there on the bath mat. She tightened the belt on her robe and ventured downstairs. Billy was gazing out the living room window.

"Nice neighborhood."

"Thanks."

"This is a great house. How long have you lived here?"

Eden pressed her face into the middle of his back, wrapping her arms low on his hips. She inhaled. Mmm. The scent drifting from him ought to be classified as dangerous because it certainly made her reckless. "Did you really come over so we could talk about real estate?"

"No."

"The romp this afternoon wasn't enough?"

"If I say *no* will you think I'm a sex fiend?"

She laughed. "No. I'll chalk it up to ten years of wondering how it'd be between us becoming reality. We'd be stupid not to explore every down and dirty sexy fantasy we denied ourselves now that we have the chance."

His back snapped straight. "That's what it boils down to? This is just about sex?"

"For tonight it is." She grabbed his shoulders from behind, pulling him down so her teeth could nip his earlobe. "I want you."

Billy faced her. "Eden—"

"Let me have you." She smoothed her hands up the crisp navy cotton of his shirt. "It's a damn shame I haven't taken my time undressing you."

"We have all the time in the world. Let's take it upstairs."

"No. Here." She closed the blinds. By the time Eden's fingers reached the last pearly button near his groin, she saw Billy was having difficulty breathing. She slowly parted the halves of the shirt, gliding her soft hands over the breadth of his chest. So solid. So rough and silky at the same time.

Her lips followed the path her fingers started. She slipped the shirt off his shoulders, down his muscular biceps and forearms until it fluttered to the floor. "You don't spend all your time behind a desk." She seeped her senses in his scent, laundry soap, a hint of aftershave and the dark manly musk of his skin. Her tongue flicked the flat coppery disk of his nipple.

Billy groaned.

So she did it again. And again. Sucking both sides. Worrying the nubs with her teeth.

His groan was louder. Primal.

She skimmed her fingertips from his Adam's apple to his navel, loving how his belly muscles undulated beneath her touch.

"Eden. Baby."

"Ssh. No talking." Eden kissed his stomach. She dipped her tongue into his belly button and drew big, wet circles progressively lower. She licked the faint line of blond hair pointing to her target.

"This looks promising." She unbuttoned his pants to reveal the ultimate precision engineering tool.

Oh yeah. Eden knew just how to fine-tune this bad boy. She didn't tease. She sucked his cock into the wet heat of her mouth until the plump tip poked the back of her throat.

"Jesus." He latched onto her head and threaded his hands through her hair.

"Mmm," was all she managed, lost in the slick sensation of velvety male hardness sliding across her lips, looking up, seeing the raw need in his eyes. She let the end of her tongue zigzag lazily from his scrotum to his glans, licking at the tip of his cock.

"That's so good. Woman, you're killing me."

Then she slipped her hand between his thighs to massage his balls, pressing her thumb into the strip of skin right behind the taut sac. She loved everything about this intimacy. The musky male way he smelled. His clean, salty taste. The feel of the hardest part of him stretching her lips and brushing the roof of her mouth. His tiny shudders when she lapped the sweet spot below his cockhead and at the sweet fluid coating the slit.

"You want to come fast or slow?"

"Ah. Fast. Christ. Please."

Eden circled her hand around the base of his shaft and jacked him while her mouth counter-stroked, lips and fingers meeting in the middle. Her head bobbing, her mouth watering, her teeth-scraping, all rhythmic sucking, heat and wetness. Worshiping that marvelous male flesh.

Billy's hips pumped. His thumbs spread across her hollowed cheeks as she took him deeper yet. The wet, sucking sounds of her mouth on his sex and his answering moans of ecstasy made her thighs sticky and her blood race.

"Eden. Stop or I'm gonna shoot."

"Shoot in my mouth, Billy."

A low growl rumbled from his chest. "Then you'll swallow every goddamn drop." His hands returned to her head and he gripped hanks of hair in his fists, adding an erotic pinch of pain as he fucked her mouth.

His body tensed. "Here it comes." His cock lifted slightly, the length tightened and twitched as pulse after pulse of hot come flowed over her tongue and dripped down the back of her throat.

She kept swallowing, stroking, wringing every ounce of pleasure from him until he begged, "Stop. Jesus. I can't take any more, baby," and his spent cock slipped from her mouth.

Billy hadn't opened his eyes. His hands were clenched into fists by his naked flanks. A beautiful red flush colored his cheeks and his breathing was decidedly ragged.

Good.

Quietly, Eden stood and padded to the kitchen. Her hand shook so badly that she spilled water down her neck. The cold glass felt heavenly against her hot lips. Liquid cooled her mouth but washed away the taste of him.

She heard his footfalls stop on the linoleum behind her.

Billy pulled her against his chest. "That was fucking amazing," he muttered gruffly.

"For me too. Are you hungry?"

"Only hungry for you, Eden." His lips brushed her ear. "I want you."

"But—"

"Stop talking. Let me have you."

Amidst drugging kisses, his thumbs feathered touches on her stomach near her belly button and the muscles rippled in response.

"Hang on." Then he lifted her onto the counter. "Take off the robe. Now."

"Right here? In the kitchen?"

"You just had me in the living room." The heat in his eyes contrasted with the gentle hands he placed on her collarbones. "So yes. Right here, right now." His mouth sought hers and he oh-so-slowly lowered the robe, allowing the silky material to slither over her bared back.

As he cranked up the kiss, his hands drifted across the slopes of her breasts, slipping over her torso and briefly landing on her midriff. Billy grabbed her butt, tugging her half-on, half-off the counter.

Eden jerked back. "I'm falling."

"I won't let you." Sweaty palms glided over the breadth of her legs to her knees. He watched her eyes as he splayed her thighs apart. Wide. "Put your hands behind you and dig your heels into the cabinet door."

"But—"

"Do it," he growled, shutting her up with another carnal kiss that curled her toes, her hair and her internal organs.

When he ripped his mouth free, the desire in his eyes almost toppled her off the counter.

Billy warned, "Brace yourself," and dropped to his knees on the rug in front of her.

Every bit of blood drained from Eden's upper body, plummeting to the lower regions currently *not* in need of additional blood flow.

He clamped his fingers securely around her quaking knees and rubbed his mouth there. "Jesus, you smell good." His labored breathing echoed hers as he wended his way toward his target via the inside of her thigh. The slow, steady rasp of his razor-stubbled jaw made her squirm. After one quick swipe at the throbbing center of her heat, he nibbled a path to the other knee.

A frustrated sigh escaped her.

Billy repeated the teasing tactic on her legs, getting closer with each wet pass of his tongue, until Eden groaned at the erotic combination of his soft hair and hot mouth brushing her hypersensitive skin.

Finally Billy's tongue darted out for a thorough taste of her pussy, probing, licking and then retreating before he blew one soft breath over her molten core.

"You are so wet. So hot. So unbelievably delicious." He continued torturing her with smallest flicks of the tip of his tongue. "Mmm. Same pretty pink color here as your mouth. It was hot as hell seeing my cock disappearing between your sweet lips." He detoured and licked the crease of her thigh.

Eden's leg spasmed involuntarily and he chuckled, the low rumble shot a spike of heat from her groin to her nipples. But Billy avoided the area where Eden craved his elusive tongue.

Her breath sawed out of her lungs. Sweat dampened her neck, her back, between her legs. She wanted to plunge her hands in his silky hair and force his wandering head closer.

"Such soft skin right here," he whispered, nipping at the curve of her inner thigh, while his thumbs drew feathery circles behind her knees. He tortured her with openmouthed kisses down the front of her shin to her ankle.

Not up.

Damn him.

Billy licked the shallow dent near her heel; his fingertips stroked the back of her calf. Lightly. Like raindrops. He nibbled the top of her twitching foot, then set his hot mouth right above her anklebone and sucked.

"Oh. My. God." Eden's eyes rolled back in her head. Whoa. Since when was her ankle an erogenous zone with a hyperlink to her burning pussy?

"Like that, do you?"

He did it again and her sex contracted.

A small scream burst from Eden's throat. "Billy, I thought you said no more talking. And there you are, *jabbering* for God's sake—"

"Fine. I'm done." His tongue blazed up her moist channel. Making her wetter and wetter. Stopping to suckle her swollen pussy lips. Swirling that naughty tongue in circles. Fast. Slow. Teasing. Blatant.

Billy pressed his thumbs above her pubic bone, peeled back the hood hiding that little bud, and fastened his mouth to her clit. He used his lips, his teeth—God—his *tongue*— persistently until she thought she'd burst.

And she did, climaxing in a flash, gasping his name as he sucked and sucked. The pounding, pulsing waves flared from her sex, sending shudders of pleasure throughout her whole body.

Sated, dazed, spent, Eden forgot about bracing herself and let her head fall back in utter abandon. The resounding whack against the cupboard and sharp pain barely registered.

When the tremors stopped, she gazed down at him.

His blue eyes were ablaze, his mouth glistening with her juices. "Remember the other night? When I told you what I wanted from you?"

His explicit words rang in her ears, promises of exactly what he planned to do to her. "Uh. Yeah."

"I'm gonna take you that way tonight. Now."

Pulling her from the counter, Billy rocked his erection into her pelvis and captured her mouth with a wet, soul-sucking kiss. He detached his lips from hers. "Go upstairs. Get your vibrator. And a towel. I have to get something and then I'll be right up."

Chapter Eleven

After taking the condoms from his pocket, Billy left his clothes where he'd shed them and headed upstairs.

A small light on the nightstand suffused the room with soft amber light. Eden had rolled down the bedspread and was sprawled in the center of the mattress.

He stopped and stared. "You steal my breath."

But her eyes were glued on the bottle of oil in his hand.

Billy set the stuff next to the vibrator and perched on the edge of the bed. "Hey." He smoothed his hand from the curve of her shoulder to her wrist. "You okay?"

"Ah. Yeah. What's the oil for?"

Keeping his gaze on hers, he traced her index finger in a sensual line from the nail to the knuckle and across the webbing, eliciting her deep shiver. "You know what it's for." He leaned forward and kissed her, a slow tango of sliding lips and dueling tongues.

The kiss changed from sweet to hot to molten. Gentle caresses turned into uncontrolled touches. Billy ended up on top of Eden, with his hand buried between her soft, moist thighs. God. She was wet again. He wanted her so badly it was painful.

"I can't wait. On your hands and knees."

Eden didn't look at him as she rolled over.

Billy slipped on a condom, grabbed the vibrator and placed it next to her right hand on the bed. He caged her body below his and put his lips on her ear. "Do you know how incredible you look? With your ass in the air waiting for me? It's sexy as hell. I'll go slowly. Nothing to be scared of." When he nuzzled her nape, she trembled. "Nothing to be ashamed of either, Eden."

"I know. I want this. I want this with you." She turned her head and nipped his jaw. "Do it. Take the last of my virginity, Billy."

Somehow he kept from ramming his cock into her right then. He set his hand in the middle of her back and pushed her upper body flat on the bed. "Be easier for you to use the vibrator in this position. Now spread your knees wider. Tilt your hips up. Oh, yeah. Perfect."

The little pucker and her pussy were completely visible, a wet, pink oasis amidst the tawny skin of her rounded ass and slender thighs. His cock went hard as a ruler.

He reached for the bottle of vegetable oil and tipped it, dribbling the liquid down her ass crack.

"Oh. That's warm."

"I heated it." He cupped oil in his hand, using some on his cock and the rest to coat his fingers. He probed the tiny hole with one finger, added more oil, inserted another finger and poured the remainder a little at a time as his fingers fucked in and out of her untried ass.

Eden shuddered.

"You okay?"

"Yes. Just do it."

For a second he couldn't focus beyond his animalistic lust, his need, the male possession thumping in his chest. But somehow he held off impaling her to the hilt in one lightning fast stroke. "Just a little more." He scissored his fingers inside her narrow opening to stretch her, bowled over by the tight, slick heat. When Eden pumped her hips back with a whimper, he knew she was ready.

Billy slowly circled the plump head of his cock around the slippery entrance, knowing the stimulation of pressure on the nerve-endings would drive her crazy. Then he popped just the cockhead in and stopped.

"Oh God."

"No, baby, don't clench. Does it hurt?"

"Yeah, but keep going."

I'll show you how I can keep going. Harder. Faster. Make

you burn. Prove to you who this ass and everything attached to it belongs to; always has, always will.

Reason shoved the male glutton aside. *No. Hold off, hold off, hold off, don't be a brute, don't be selfish. Be the tender man she deserves.*

"Billy?"

"I can't reach your clit. Do you want to slide the vibrator in your pussy before I'm in fully?"

"No. God. Please. Just finish what you started."

"Then say it. Say the words, Eden."

"Fill my ass."

"I love it when you talk dirty." He eased all the way into that tight, hot channel and groaned. Damn. He wasn't going to last long even if he wasn't moving much. Even if he wanted to pull her ass cheeks apart and ream her. Watch that small hole stretching to accommodate his dick. Feel that close-fitting heat sucking him in, the tight muscles milking him dry, making him mindless with lust.

"Why did you stop?"

"Because it feels so damn good I want to savor it. You're like silk inside, Eden. Warm, tight, hot silk around my cock."

The buzz of the vibrator brought him out of his pleasure stupor. When she rested the phallus against the length of her pussy and Billy felt the vibration in his balls, his hips snapped back and he plunged to the hilt again.

The noise from her sweet mouth was indistinguishable as pleasure or pain so he kept the next few strokes measured. Rivulets of sweat snaked down his temple. His molars damn near cracked from clenching his jaw. His fingers gripped Eden's curvy hips in an effort not to fuck her virgin ass like a wild man.

He tried to concentrate on the sweet perfume of her arousal not the supreme tightness of her anal passage. The sight and sound of her arm moving between her legs as she pleasured herself and not her ass muscles clenching and unclenching around his cock. The brightness of her auburn hair flowing across the pristine white sheet and not how erotic his cock looked disappearing between those softly rounded bronze cheeks.

But it didn't help. His awareness was solely in his dick and the *tight hot tight hot tight hot faster faster faster* mantra urging him to plow into her ass. He gave in. One hard, deep thrust from cockhead to root.

"Just like that. Do it like that again. Fuck my ass harder, I'm so close—"

Eden didn't finish the sentence before Billy jackhammered into her tight portal over and over.

When Eden began to come, gasping, thrusting her hips back, her anal muscles contracting, the vibrator buzzing near his balls, Billy lost it. He fucked her without pause, lost in that *yes yes yes* blur of unconsciousness, where nothing mattered but expelling every ounce of hot seed into those clenching walls.

What a fucking rush. Like being in a Formula One car, bungee jumping into a gorge and on the steepest drop of a roller coaster—all at the same time.

After he reclaimed his brain cells from pleasure overload, Billy kissed his way up Eden's spine. "That was amazing."

"I...damn. I don't even know what to say."

"You okay?" he murmured.

"Yeah. Tired. You wore me out today, Billy."

"Mmm." He tasted the sweat on her neck and softly blew in her ear to distract her while he pulled his semi-soft cock out of her ass.

Eden hissed.

He scattered more soft kisses across her shoulder. "Be right back."

A few minutes later, he brought a warm washcloth. He cleaned her up amidst flirty kisses, thorough caresses and whispering sweet words against her sweet-smelling skin. Billy couldn't get enough of touching her, running his hands and mouth over every inch of her sleek curves. He hauled her upper body across his, continuing to drag his fingertips up and down her spine.

Eden propped her chin on his chest and gave him a pensive look. "I have to ask you something kinda weird."

He twirled a section of her hair around his finger. "What?"

"Would you like to go to the Silver Star tomorrow night?"

"Is it a restaurant?"

"No. It's a bar. There's music and dancing."

"I thought you preferred to keep our relationship off the radar."

"That's why it'd be perfect. It's off the beaten path."

Billy wasn't sure he liked the direction this conversation was headed.

"A good friend is only in town for a couple of nights and I promised I'd hang out with him."

"Him?"

"Yeah."

"Are you involved with him?"

"Yes and no. This'll probably sound awkward, being that we're in the afterglow of butt sex and all—" she flashed him a quick grin, "—but you should know that Jon and I have a casual sexual relationship."

Fuck. He asked, "How casual, Eden?" knowing that his tone wasn't casual at all.

"Very. We're good friends, but we're also lovers when the mood strikes us."

A surge of jealousy rocked him so hard that he was surprised his body wasn't convulsing.

"Say something," she demanded.

"I don't know what you want me to say. I've never been in a situation like this."

"Like what?"

"Like my lover asking me to hang out with her other lover."

"Jon and I are friends first." Eden idly stroked the area around his nipple. "Don't you have female friends you've slept with who are still your buddies? Who can fill that need for intimate physical contact once in a while, without strings?"

"No. Truth is, I don't have a ton of friends of either gender. Been too damn busy or I've been on location."

"Well, I think you'll like Jon. He's a great guy."

Billy kissed her nose. "I hope so, since he's my roommate."

"What?"

"I'm assuming you're talking about Jon White Feather, aka Johnny Feather, rock sensation?"

A stunned look crossed her face. "You know him?"

"No. Feather Light owns the condo I'm staying in and Jim White Feather warned me his little brother Jon would be crashing there. I saw his luggage today, but he wasn't around so I haven't met him yet." He trailed his fingers across her collarbone. "And Jim had mentioned you and Jon hooking up whenever he rolled into town."

"Jim just threw that out there in casual conversation?"

"No. I think he didn't want me to be surprised if I saw you wearing Jon's bathrobe or something at the condo." He paused. "Jim doesn't have a clue we knew each other before or that we..."

Eden sighed. "I know Spearfish is a small town and we know some of the same people, but this is just bizarre."

"Tell me about it," he muttered. What were the odds he'd be rooming with the only other person Eden had slept with in the last three years?

"So is that a no for tomorrow night?"

"It sounds like fun."

"Good." She yawned and snuggled into him. "Are you staying over?"

"Do you want me to?"

"I'd like that."

Holding Eden all night? Definitely heaven. His arms tightened around her. "Me too."

Chapter Twelve

The next evening Eden and Jon exited the dance floor and returned to the table where Billy waited. The night was going far better than Eden anticipated. Billy and Jon showed up together, acting like best buds. Apparently they'd spent the morning playing basketball and shooting the shit.

The cocktail waitress swung by and pressed her boobs in Jon's face. "Need anything, darlin'?"

"Sure I'll take another Coke. What about you guys?"

Billy and Eden shook their heads. After Miss Look At My Tits sashayed away, Eden asked Jon, "You ever get sick of all the female attention?"

Before he could answer, two rhinestone cowgirls approached and demanded a dance. After Jon politely declined, they focused their attention on Billy. When he also declined, they focused their venomous looks on Eden and stomped off.

The single women in this place were hostile. At first she chalked up their attitudes to the fact she, Billy and Jon weren't regulars at the Silver Star. Then she decided the women were jealous because she was in the company of two great-looking young guys. But she also suspected the sneers and whispers were because she was an Indian woman with two gorgeous guys, one of whom was white.

Putting aside her paranoia, she refocused on the conversation.

"Too bad you're only here temporarily," Jon said. "I know Feather Light needed another full-time engineer before Bob's heart attack."

She listened while Billy launched into a detailed

explanation of the other projects he'd been handling.

"The bottom line remains they are swamped. I'm doing what I can while I'm here."

"*Has* Jim said anything to you about staying on permanently?"

Billy shrugged but wouldn't meet Eden's inquisitive gaze. "He's hinted, but I think he's waiting to see how my report on this initial assignment turns out."

Eden swigged her beer and feigned interest in the neon bucking bull above the bar.

A warm hand pressed into the small of her back. Equally warm lips brushed her ear. "Dance with me." Billy tugged her onto the dance floor, holding her against his body with a firm possessiveness that heated her blood.

They swayed together, lost in the rhythm of the music, secure in the synchronicity of their bodies. By the end of the third song, Eden needed a break from the intense feelings Billy aroused with just a simple touch.

She escaped to the bathroom and locked herself in a stall, attempting to regain control of her emotions. Was there a chance Billy would stick around? If so, where did that leave them? Would he be interested in pursuing a relationship?

The outer door slammed against the garbage can. An angry female voice whined, "He turned me down again. And that ugly Indian bitch wasn't with him this time."

Eden peeked out the crack in the stall door. The two pesky rhinestone cowgirls from earlier were primping in front of the mirror.

"Give it up, Jackie. So what if he's gorgeous? You can ask him until you're as red in the face as he is and he ain't gonna say yes. Them Indians always stick together."

Her stomach lurched. They were talking about her.

"But it don't make sense the white guy with them said no."

"Why are you surprised? She's probably doin' both of them."

"What the fuck do they see in her? She ain't pretty. Her clothes look like Salvation Army rejects. She's probably always drunk, and dumb as tipi post."

"So she's another fuckin' slutty Indian squaw. Why do you

care?"

Eden felt sick and lowered herself to the toilet seat.

"Because they're the best lookin' guys in here tonight."

"They're not the *only* guys. You don't wanna be with a white dude who sticks his dick in red meat anyway."

The bimbos exited in a burst of braying laughter.

Eden cooled her heels until her temper waned, but nothing erased the embarrassment. A couple of cutting remarks and her hard-won confidence disappeared, allowing the pitiable little Indian girl who still lurked inside her to resurface. She slunk from the bathroom, keeping her eyes on the concrete floor until she reached the table.

Jon sat by himself. When he saw her, his smile died and he stood abruptly. "Eden? What's wrong?"

"Where's Billy?"

"Had to take a phone call from his boss in Chicago." Jon cupped her face. "What happened?"

"Same shit, different day." She tried to wriggle out of his hold. "Look. I can't stand to be here. I'm leaving."

"The hell you are. What happened to make you turn tail and run?"

"Nothing." She cringed when the women passed by their table and Jon caught her reaction.

He swore softly. "What did they say to you?"

"It doesn't matter."

"You know you'll feel better if you talk to me." He swept her hair over her shoulder. "You know I'll understand."

"I know. But not here. Please. Let me go."

"Fine." Jon's gaze was laser sharp. "Come to the condo. We'll talk there."

"No. I just want to go home."

"Not a chance. I'll get Billy—"

Eden was near tears. But she'd be damned if she'd give those women the satisfaction. "Just drop it."

"Drop what?" Billy's hands squeezed her shoulders.

"She won't tell me what happened, so let's get out of this redneck dive and head back to the condo." Jon's thumbs stroked her hot cheeks. "You want Billy to drive your car?"

"I'm fine. I need some air. I'll follow you."

Billy's voice tickled her ear. "You sure?"

Eden nodded.

They released her and somehow she made it to her car without bawling.

Chapter Thirteen

Eden felt ridiculous, seated between the men on the small sofa in the condo, Jon holding one hand, Billy the other, as she told them what'd transpired in the bathroom.

In retrospect, she'd heard worse things, racial slurs barked directly in her face, so she didn't know why she'd gotten so upset and worked up over it this time.

Billy demanded, "Does this bullshit happen often?"

"Yes," she and Jon answered simultaneously.

Thick silence descended.

"Is that why it's easier for you two...to be together?"

Eden looked at Billy oddly. "Indians always stick together?"

"That's not what I meant."

"Love doesn't discriminate about varying skin colors, but everyone else does. Jim's wife Cindy is white. They've been married for almost twenty years and they still get dirty looks and snide comments."

"Same thing with Tate and Nathan LeBeau. She says it's not just white people who are prejudiced. Some Indians claim that's how the whites are conquering their race. By intermarrying and reproducing half-breeds."

"Not like we can do anything about it, either," Jon said. "We're either a social experiment or socially shunned."

"No one needs shit like that. Jesus. People are fucking idiots," Billy muttered.

"It's just another thing to deal with. We poor half-breeds hafta stick together, eh? Especially since our families can be the worst offenders."

"Is that true for you?" Billy asked Eden.

She inhaled and released a long breath. "Yeah. I don't know if you remember me telling you, but my mother got knocked up when she was drunk. She had no idea who my father was and resented me when I came out of the chute looking like an Indian. Or part Indian. Or whatever the hell I am."

"Hey." Jon grabbed her chin in his hand, turning her face to his. "What you are is beautiful." He pressed a soft kiss to her lips.

Billy cleared his throat and Eden's head whipped back to him. But no censure darkened his eyes, just heat. He touched her face exactly as Jon had. "And sexy." His mouth brushed hers and he expanded the kiss from Jon's simple peck.

Two quick tugs on her hair had her facing Jon again. "And smart." Jon licked the seam of her lips until she opened fully and he dove in for a slow tangling of tongues.

Jon's kisses were more practiced than the raw hunger Billy's mouth unleashed. Their tastes were different too—Jon's was exotic, like cinnamon and sage. Billy's was darker and sweeter, like red wine laced with honey. Both were delicious. Both were intoxicating. Both went to her head as fast as a shot of whiskey.

Jon released her mouth and Billy was back for more. "And you're sweet, Eden. You are so damn..." The rest of his response was lost as he inhaled her in a kiss so blistering hot she wondered if her lips would bear scorch marks.

Her senses were overwhelmed. She didn't want to analyze what was happening. She just wanted to exist in the moment. Eden closed her eyes, dropping her head back on the couch cushion when four male hands began caressing her. Her throat. Her breasts. Her thighs. Her body shuddered from their erotic attention.

"Eden? Baby, do you want this?"

"Want what?" she managed.

Billy's breath tickled her ear. "Want both of us."

"At the same time," Jon said, his lips drifting down her neck.

Heat sparked inside her and she moaned.

"Is that a yes?"

She nodded.

"Say the words," Billy insisted. "Tell us what you want so there won't be any misunderstandings."

Could she do this? Have two men at once? Two men not just kissing and petting her, but licking and sucking and expecting the same in return. Two sets of rough male hands touching her everywhere. Two mouths to kiss and bite and suck on her skin, on her sex. Two cocks demanding entrance to her body.

Was she a carbon copy of her mother if she admitted she wanted that sexy scenario as much as her next breath?

No. Billy and Jon weren't some random guys looking for kicks from an easy lay, they were special to her. They'd treat this—and her—as a sexual experience to be celebrated not as just another kinky threesome. They both knew how to make her body weep with want and vibrate with pleasure. She'd be damned if her mother's ghost would ruin something else for her.

"Baby?"

"Yes. I want both of you to fuck me. At the same time. One night of anything goes down and dirty wicked sex."

"Good answer," Billy murmured. "But make no mistake about who's in charge. You will do whatever we say."

Eden cracked her eyes open. "Have you guys been planning this all day?"

"No. But neither of us is about to let a golden opportunity pass us by, right Billy?"

"Damn straight."

Jon stood and held a hand out. "Come on. Bedroom. Now."

She gripped Billy's hand and allowed Jon to lead them into a room at the end of the hallway.

A bout of nerves surfaced when she saw the bed.

"Relax," Jon said. "Trust us to make you feel as beautiful as you are to us, Eden." His head dipped and he captured her lips. He began to unbutton her blouse. As soon as it hit the carpet, another set of eager hands unhooked her bra and the scrap of lace disappeared.

Then Billy's hot, hard male skin pressed up against her back. He swept her hair aside, nibbling from her left shoulder to her nape.

Her skin became a mass of goose bumps and she trembled.

Eden gasped when Jon tweaked her nipple. He slid his lips free from hers and replaced his fingers with his hungry mouth.

"Oh. God."

"Do you know how fucking hot it is to watch him sucking on your tits?"

"Help him. I want to feel both your mouths on my breasts at the same time."

Billy growled at her request and moved in front of her. He watched her face as his abrasive tongue lapped the pebbled tip. The same motion in the same spot. Over and over.

Jon mirrored Billy's actions. Tiny flicks of a tongue. Suckling the point with pursed lips. Blowing a soft stream of air across the wetness. Drawing as much of her breast into the wet heat as possible, sucking long and deep and hard.

She'd never experienced anything so visually and physically arousing. Jon's dark head on one side, Billy's blond head on the other. The sensations of each hungry mouth focused solely on her nipple, the same, yet different.

The dual sharp nip of teeth made her cry out. A hot burst of moisture soaked her panties.

"Get her goddamn pants off," Billy said.

Zip. The denim pooled around her ankles. She kicked the jeans away. Keeping his smoldering eyes on hers, Billy knelt and oh-so-slowly dragged the lace underwear down her legs.

A wave of heat nearly buckled her knees.

"On the bed."

Eden scooted into the middle and propped herself on her elbows to see both men undress without a striptease. Not that she complained. She didn't want to wait for all that gorgeous, male flesh that was hers for the taking.

"Toss me a pillow," Billy said. He tapped Eden's ass and she lifted her hips. "Spread those legs wide. I want to see every inch of that pussy."

Jon swept the pad of his thumb across her lower lip. "You ready to have my cock in your mouth?"

She nodded.

"Jon, do you have something we can bind her hands with?"

89

Holy crap. "But—"

Then Billy was right in her face. "But nothing. You agreed to being with both of us, which means you are ours to do with as we please. And it'd please me greatly to see you tied up and at my mercy."

Three bandanas appeared. Two were looped around her wrists; the third was used to tie her bound hands to the iron slats in the headboard.

It was hot as hell, seeing the lustful sexual greed on Jon and Billy's faces. The inside of her thighs were drenched. Her skin was so hot she feared she'd inadvertently set the cotton sheets on fire.

Jon straddled her chest on his knees. He braced one hand on the headboard and used the other to grip his cock as he circled the mushroomed head over her lips. "Lick it."

Her tongue darted out to swipe the bead leaking from the slit. Another pearly drop appeared and she licked it too.

"That's good. Now open up, dollface."

Eden's lips parted and Jon fed his cock into her mouth, past her teeth, over her tongue until the tip poked the back of her throat. When her lips tightened around his considerable girth and she swallowed, Jon groaned.

"Gonna fuck this sassy mouth." He pulled out and pushed back in, each stroke more insistent. "Suck harder. Like that."

When Billy dragged his tongue from her hole to her clit, she arched up, moaning around Jon's rigid cock.

"Jesus. You're so fucking wet I feel like I'm bathing in you." Billy burrowed his tongue into her slick channel, licking the juices from the inside out. She bumped her hips higher, desperate for contact on her clit, but he allowed her no control. He held her hips down and fucked her pussy with his tongue.

The pace of Jon's rigid cock slamming into her mouth increased. He shoved one last time, staying balls deep as his cock twitched and jerked on her tongue.

Thick, warm ejaculate coated her throat and she swallowed repeatedly even as his hips continued to pump into her face.

Jon stilled and glanced down; his blue eyes glittered triumphantly. With his cock still buried in her mouth, he tenderly stroked her cheek with his knuckles. "Eden. You're beautiful. Honest to God beautiful from the inside out. Don't ever forget that. Don't ever let anyone make you feel less than you are." He pushed off the headboard and slipped from between her lips.

But Eden didn't have time to bask in Jon's compliments. Billy zigzagged the flickering end of his tongue up her labia and demanded, "Fly apart for me."

Then he suctioned his mouth to her clit and tongued her relentlessly, imprisoning her hips as she bucked and thrashed. The rush of blood to the sensitive nub wasn't a slow, sweet throbbing, but a tidal wave of epic proportions. One second she was floating toward heaven, the next she was sobbing Billy's name in the maelstrom of pure sensation.

After she'd descended back to earth from the sexual high, Billy untied her hands. She couldn't help but notice his cock was still hard as a club. How'd that happen? Jon had gotten off. She'd gotten off. But Billy hadn't.

Billy's heavy-lidded gaze locked to hers as he gently rubbed the red marks on her wrists. "My turn. On your knees on the floor. Now."

She scooted off the bed, parking herself between Billy's outstretched legs. It didn't matter she'd just finished blowing Jon; she ached to wring the same explosion from Billy. To experience that rush of erotic power when he gripped her head, thrust deep and detonated his male essence in her mouth. To see his sated expression and feel smug she'd taken him there.

Eden bent forward and licked the thick vein pulsing up the center of Billy's cock and suckled his purple cockhead.

"That feels good but that's not what I have in mind."

"Then what?"

Billy picked up her hand and circled it around the base of his stiff cock. "I want your mouth on my nipples while you jack me off, Eden."

That was blunt. But sexy as all get out.

With deliberate sensuality, Billy's fingertips created a path of fire from the upper swell of her breast to the tip of her nipple. "Then I'm going to come on your tits. There's something very appealing about marking you with my seed."

Everything in her that'd been pliant and sated went hot, tight, wet and wanting.

"Watching that'll make me hard again," Jon said.

"Come on, baby. Give Jon a real show. He's a showman. He'll appreciate it. But not as much as I will." Billy knotted his hand in her hair and tugged her to his right nipple.

Eden pursed her swollen lips over the flat disk and began to suck softly. After several attempts of trying to work his cock, she realized the angle was wrong. She stood, propped two fluffy pillows beneath her knees and yanked Billy's slender hips down so he was barely balanced on his elbows on the edge of the bed.

"Mmm. That's better. Need a little lube, though." Rather than use the tube of K-Y on the bed, she reached between her legs, getting her hand wet from her juices. Then she wrapped her fingers around Billy's cock again and pumped from root to tip.

Behind her, Jon groaned. "Fuck. That's hot as hell, Eden."

Billy's response was an unintelligible male grunt.

Smiling, she nipped at the flat disks and began to vigorously stroke that beautifully hard prick. No slow build up. No tease and retreat. She jacked him faster and faster. Biting and licking and sucking his nipples. Appreciating his groans. Loving the taste of his sweat and need. Relishing the feel of his hips pumping up to meet her strokes.

"Jesus. Fuck." Billy knocked her hand away from his cock and clamped his palm on her shoulder, holding her in place. He pumped frantically as long streams of come jetted out the end of his cock and splashed on her breasts. His eyes were wild blue flames and he growled as spurt after spurt dotted her chest. Pure animal satisfaction was etched on Billy's face as he stared at the milky liquid dripping off her nipples.

Her pussy was sopping wet again. As her sex clenched and throbbed, she squeezed her thighs together and gasped when a tiny orgasm rocked her. She looked up and saw Billy's eyes were still on fire, still devouring her.

"Jesus you're beautiful. Absolutely steal-my-fucking-breath beautiful, Eden."

Her heart damn near turned over in her chest.

He released her shoulder and his hand moved down to cup the underswell of her left breast. His thumb brushed a thick rivulet of come from the tip of her nipple and he brought it to her lips.

Eden opened her mouth and sucked his thumb inside, swirling her tongue, savoring his taste.

"Again." Billy dragged his finger through the sticky wetness cooling on her breast and held the offering to her.

Eyes on his, she licked away every drop.

They made it through two more rounds of erotic finger painting before Jon said brusquely, "Enough. It's my turn and after that little display I'm hard enough I could fuck her clear through the wall." Jon helped Eden to her feet and wiped away the remnants of Billy's spent passion.

She shivered at the cool washcloth skating over her heated skin, wondering when Jon had left the room. No surprise neither she nor Billy noticed.

"Eden." Jon's melodic voice tickled her ear and she trembled.

"What?"

He didn't answer immediately, he lazily traced every vertebrae down her spine, causing the buzzing sensation in her skin to hum back to life. She'd never experienced arousal this prolonged. Never believed she could ache for more.

"I want you." Jon's teeth sank into the slope of her shoulder and she cried out from the pleasurable nip of pain. His next words and his hot breath burned her like a brand. "But I want to tie you up first."

"Why?"

"Not only do I get off thinking about fucking you as deep and as long as I want, but it's a way for you to give yourself over to us, before we take you completely." He clasped her hands together behind her back, twisting the bandanas around her wrists again. Then he gently spun her around. "Close your eyes."

Eden feared she might topple over from too much stimulation on her sex organs and not enough blood reaching her brain.

Soft, moist lips drifted down her jawline, starting on the left side below her earlobe, ending at the right. Those sweetly arousing lips traveled up her hairline from her temple across her forehead and down the left side. Then Jon rained kisses on her eyelids. Her cheekbones. The corners of her mouth before taking her mouth in a wet, sizzling kiss that robbed her lungs of air and her mind of reason.

"On the bed." Jon crawled on first and stretched out on his back. He rolled on a condom and looked at Billy. "Help her. She's going to be facing you as she's riding me."

Anticipation quickened her pulse. Without use of her hands it was difficult to balance, but Billy steadied her, helping her straddle Jon's pelvis.

"Your knees need to be wider."

Eden shot him a panicked look over her shoulder. "But I'll fall forward."

Jon smacked her ass and she yelped. "No, you won't. I'll be holding your hips. Now spread 'em."

Billy braced her shoulders as she lowered on Jon's cock.

"Oh yeah, you're really wet." He guided his shaft inside her to the hilt and stilled all movement. His hands floated up her bound arms. "You okay?"

"Yeah."

"Slow and easy. Let Billy tend to you while I enjoy your beautiful body and prep you to take both of us."

Her eyes were focused on Billy as Jon began to rock his hips. The movement was subtle but accurate. The widest portion of his cockhead continually pressed her G-spot.

"Oh. That's good." She gasped. "Really good."

Billy caught her next gasp in his mouth. His tongue speared past her lips, languidly dueling with hers. His hand stretched from her collarbone and curled around her neck, holding her in place. He flattened his other hand and it drifted down her quivering belly. The long middle finger reached her bikini line and kept going until the tip connected with her clit. He rubbed tiny circles and more wetness flooded her pussy.

Jon fucked her in a steady rocking motion. His hands roved from her calves to her arms to the crack of her ass in a constant caress. "So beautiful. Every part of you."

She was teetering on the edge of complete meltdown. Jon controlled her sex and the movement of her hips; Billy controlled her mouth and her clit.

And her heart.

No time for that emotional detour now.

Concentrate on nothing but physical pleasure and the

pulsing, throbbing, sexual adoration these men are bestowing on you.

Billy put his mouth on her ear. "It's right there, Eden." He increased the pace of his stroking finger. "Scream, baby. Come for me. Come for Jon."

Just like that, her body erupted. She cried out as her clit spasmed and her internal muscles clamped down on Jon's cock like a vise. Surge after surge bombarded her.

When the throbs became little pulses, Billy licked the sweat running down her throat, latched onto the sweet spot on her neck with his mouth and sucked, shooting her into orbit again. "Oh God, oh God, oh God, stop. I can't take any more."

"Ssh. Baby, it's okay. I've got you."

Breath sawed in and out of her mouth. She had to rely on Billy to keep her upright. "Please."

"Eden. Look at me." He tilted her chin up and she blinked her eyes open. "I need you to turn around so Jon and I can take you together, okay?"

"But—"

"This is what you wanted."

You're what I wanted. You're all I ever wanted.

Why couldn't he see that?

And just for a moment, she thought he did realize it when he murmured, "Trust us. Trust me. This is a one time only wicked, wild thing, remember?"

Jon untied her hands and massaged her wrists. He patted her ass and she lifted on her knees, letting his still hard erection slip free from her sheath. Then Eden threw her leg over Jon's hip and faced him.

His grin was pure conquering warrior. "I apologize in advance. This ain't gonna last long, because I'm about to blow."

"You don't have to prove your staying power to me. You've wrung me out."

Plastic crinkled behind her as Billy donned a condom.

Jon gathered her against his chest and kissed her. Keeping her focus on the soft, wet, warm recess of his mouth as Billy coated her puckered hole with cool gel.

Eden shuddered with want when Billy inserted one slippery finger past the ring of muscles. More gel, another finger coating her, stretching her. Fucking her. Marking her.

"So tight. So hot. So *mine.*" Fingers were replaced with the head of his cock. "Gonna be good, but baby, it'll be hard and short."

"Such an adventurous girl, taking us both on. How's it gonna feel to be stuffed with cock?" Jon cranked her head to the side and sucked the sensitive skin above her collarbone, ratcheting her need another level.

A tickling tongue zigzagged up her spine. "Ready?" Billy breathed against the back of her head.

"Past ready. Do it now."

Billy canted her pelvis to his liking. Jon reached between their bodies, poising his cock at the entrance to her pussy.

They plunged into her simultaneously.

"Oh God." She felt every twitch and jerk of their cocks in her ass and her pussy and her womb, even when they weren't moving.

Billy stayed in place while Jon pulled out. Then they switched. Back and forth. Their bodies shook uncontrollably, yet they kept an easy, careful penetration. But that wasn't what Eden wanted. She wanted roughness, no-holds-barred passion. To be used shamelessly. "Stop."

Both men froze. Jon said, "Are we hurting you?"

"No. I want you to let loose. I want you guys to fuck me like you mean it." She tightened her anus and her pussy around their cocks and they both hissed. "I won't break." She turned her head and challenged Billy. "But I dare you to try."

Billy snarled, "You asked for it," and rammed deep.

Jon twisted his fingers in her hair and jerked her head up so he could watch his cock impaling her. Over and over.

They fucked her without pause. Thrusting together. Each taking what they needed. Sandwiched between slick, hard, pounding bodies, surrounded by the scents of sex and the sound of primal male grunts, she started to come apart with a prolonged scream of complete female satisfaction, taking both men over the edge with her.

No one said a word.

Billy pulled out first and left the room. She rolled off Jon, landing flat on her back on the mattress. Several seconds passed as she acclimated her breathing.

Then Jon's serious face was above hers. "You're beautiful. Thank you for sharing yourself with me one last time."

"Oh, I see. Now that you've proven your rock star penchant for threesomes, you're tossing me out?"

"No." He pushed a section of hair behind her ear. "I'm stepping aside."

"What?"

"We're still friends, great friends, but no more friends with bennies. Billy is a great guy and he really cares about you."

"How do you know?"

"Any man who'd willingly share his woman with another man because that's what she wanted, even when it makes him see red, is a man insanely in love."

"But—"

"No buts. Trust in it. Trust in him. Be happy, dollface. You deserve it." He kissed her forehead. Like a friend would. "Now scram. I need my beauty sleep."

Eden hopped off the bed and dressed, noticing Billy's clothes were already gone.

Chapter Fourteen

Billy heard her footsteps coming down the hall and wondered how he should play this. Knowing Eden, ignoring it was his best option.

He faced her. "Hey, beautiful. You okay?"

"Yeah. Worn out. I should go."

No. Stay. He smiled tightly. "I'll walk you out." It surprised him when she reached for his hand as they left the condo and walked to her car.

Cicadas sang in the trees, filling the silence.

Finally she spoke. "Can I ask you something?"

"Sure."

"Are you done with the Feather Light project?"

"Almost."

"What happens now?"

"I'll have a final decision by tomorrow." Feeling helpless, he let go of her and shoved his hands in his jeans. "You know I have to give the city my recommendation first?"

She nodded and glanced away.

But not before he caught her hopeless look. Were her eyes tearing up? Or was that a trick of the moonlight? His stomach muscles knotted. "Come over for dinner tomorrow night."

Her suspicious gaze whipped back to him. "You cook?"

"No. But I do a mean take-out order. It'll give us some time alone before—"

"—you go back to Chicago."

"Does it bother you? The thought of me leaving?"

"It doesn't surprise me." After opening the SUV door, she

stopped. "Good luck with your reports. Call me tomorrow and let me know what time I should come over."

"Eden—"

"Goodnight, Billy." The door clicked shut. She started the engine, the radio blared Stone Temple Pilots and she sped off.

"That went well," he said to her taillights.

Several hours later Billy rubbed the grit from his eyes. Decision made, he signed off on the report, printed two copies and hastily shoved the sheaf of papers on top of the desk in the living room.

He'd drop off the original tomorrow. Maybe put it off until the next day if it'd give him more time with Eden. He crawled in bed, unsure for the first time in his career whether he'd made the best choice.

The white ceiling wasn't particularly interesting, but he stared at it for an eternity before he drifted into an uneasy sleep.

Chapter Fifteen

Billy made one last visual sweep of the setting. Timer set so the food didn't dry out. Candles lit. Music playing. Wine uncorked. He expelled a nervous sigh. How would Eden react to his confession? Especially after he told her he had to leave first thing in the morning? *Hey, I love you, but I gotta go.*

The doorbell dinged.

Eden slunk in wearing a skin-tight black cat suit and a cat-like grin. "Hope I'm not too early."

Billy wrapped his hand around her neck and took her mouth. The taste of her burst on his tongue. "Might be a little early for dessert."

"Mmm." Her dainty fingertips traced a straight line from his throat to his stomach, lingering on the waistband of his jeans. "I was thinking more along the lines of an appetizer." On tiptoes, she brushed a fleeting kiss on his chin. "But I guess I can wait for dessert, if you can." She sauntered to the breakfast bar separating the small kitchen and the living area.

Damn. He drooled at the curve of her ass and followed her like a dog on a leash. He'd need every ounce of patience to survive the night. While he poured the wine, she silently assessed the condo's sparse furnishings.

"What's your apartment like in Chicago?"

"A lot like this." Boring. Bland. Lonely. "Although it does have a better view."

Eden murmured her thanks when he passed her a glass of red wine. "You've made your decision?"

"Yes. But you know I can't tell you—"

"I know." A beat passed, then two. "I am anxious, but

mostly because I'm not sure *what* I want anymore."

"Professionally?"

"And personally."

If he said the wrong thing she'd clam up. He kept his tone offhand. "Well, you already own a charming bungalow with the picket fence. Looking for a husband and the 2.5 kids to go along with it?"

"I have three hundred kids right now who count on me," she said dryly. "It's a pretty hefty responsibility. Besides, I can't imagine with my upbringing that I'd have any parenting skills." She poured merlot in her empty glass. "I've focused all my energies at the center. I don't have time for much else. Didn't you say your social life was pathetic? Mine is worse. My friends are more forgiving than the men who've tried to have a relationship with me."

"Which is why hooking up with Jon works out?"

"Yeah. We've been buddies since college. No chance either of us wants more." She smiled. "Last night was unbelievably hot."

"No regrets?"

"No. But it's not an experience I ever have to repeat. Guess I'm more of a one-woman man."

He'd be that man if he had anything to say about it. "So, if you've been hooking up with Jon whenever the mood strikes you, when was your last actual relationship?"

"Three years ago."

"How long did it last?"

Eden's eyes narrowed. "How long did *your* most recent relationship last, Billy?"

"The longest relationship I've ever had lasted a month."

She truly looked shocked. "So what is wrong with us?"

"Maybe we're not willing to settle for second best when we've had the real thing."

"Real? Lord. We were so young neither of us knew what that meant."

Billy angled across the counter and briefly placed his mouth over hers. "I know you don't want to talk about this. But what we had ten years ago was real."

The timer on the stove dinged. *Saved by the bell.* Billy

dropped the discussion. "Come on. Let's eat."

During dinner Eden was as animated, slyly sarcastic and charming as ever. After they'd devoured the meal, she washed the dishes while he dried. Peace settled over him. What would it be like to come home to her every night? While her hands were occupied, he snugged his body behind hers, holding aside her silky hair so he could trail warm kisses down her neck.

She angled her head letting him take what he wanted.

"Coffee?" he murmured.

"No. I'm too wired the way it is."

"Why?"

"Partially because you've made the decision regarding the center and you're so damn good at hiding it. Partially because I'm anxious to be with you all sweaty and naked in the dark."

He chuckled. "Soon. But I have a surprise for you first, so why don't you make yourself comfortable in the living room?"

She spun around and placed a soapy hand over his heart. "Billy, you didn't have to go to all this trouble."

"I know. I wanted to." He'd meant to say something witty, but the seriousness in those tawny depths changed his mind. "I can't think for wanting you. Just you." His mouth met hers in a sweet, slow, bone-melting kiss. "Go sit down before I forget my own damn name."

She turned on her high heel and left him gawking after her like a tongue-tied boy.

Once Billy regained control, he removed the box from the fridge and dimmed the lights in the living room.

Eden was tucked in the corner of the white leather couch. She looked so small, so wary. So damn perfect his heart nearly stopped.

He handed her the clear plastic box. "This is for you."

A beat passed. "That's exactly like the corsage you gave me for prom."

"I know. Remember you threw it at my head when I took off?"

"Pretty childish, huh?"

"No. It was childish I left without explaining why."

Eden's lower lip trembled before she firmed it. "I can't believe you remembered."

"I can't believe you'd think I'd forget." Billy helped her to her feet and slipped the corsage from the package. The heavy scent of gardenia filled the room. Eden held out her wrist, he slid the stretchy silver band over her small hand.

An eternity passed as she fingered the white roses surrounding the creamy gardenia. She lifted the corsage and inhaled. "Why?"

"To show you I've never forgotten you. Leaving you is the only thing in my life I regret. Can we go back in time, just for tonight and be those two people who were so crazy for each other?"

♋

Eden fought a wave of tears. Dammit. She should tell Billy the truth. She wanted him the way he was *now*—the gentle, thrilling, demanding man he'd become and not the confused young man he'd been.

Before the end of the night she'd tell Billy how she felt about him. Before she found out his decision on the community center. Before she lost her nerve and let him walk out of her life again. "I'm still crazy about you, Billy."

"Show me."

His gentle caresses turned energetic. Mouths, which had teased with slow, deep, wet kisses, became frantic. When Billy pulled his lips away, Eden whimpered and tried to reconnect their hunger.

"No. I want to do this right. We have all the time in the world." He opened his hot mouth on the tender skin beneath her jaw line and sucked.

She allowed him this fantasy and repeated the words she'd said that night at the Motel 6. "Make love to me."

Billy studied her face, his blue eyes filled with longing. Slowly, too slowly, his deft fingers peeled the silky material off her shoulders and down her arms. Breathing unevenly, his hands clenched on her hips, he merely stared at her.

Her skin tightened, spreading the aching, needy feeling throughout her body. "You gonna gawk at me all night?"

"Maybe." He tugged until her one-piece outfit slithered to

the carpet. Clad in black bikini panties and a black demi-bra, she shifted on the knee-high spike-heeled black leather boots and kicked her clothes away.

"Should I call you 'Mistress Eden' in that get-up?" One blunt finger traveled from the hollow of her throat to the dip in her navel, sending waves of heat rippling across her skin. "Or should I ask if you have a cat-o'-nine tails hidden in your purse?"

"Seems you're well-acquainted with pleasure tools. Got some bondage fantasies, Mr. Buchanan?" she murmured silkily.

"Only with you. Next time, leave the boots on, but for now, take them off. I want to feel nothing except your skin on mine."

Eden sensed Billy's control had stretched to a thin line. She sought to shatter it.

She swiveled her hips, bracing her hands on the back of the couch. With her back flattened, her ass curved up in blatant enticement. Exposing the dampness between her thighs was like waving a red flag in front of a bull, but she did it anyway. Glancing over her shoulder, she wet her lips. "A little help removing the boots? I'm having a hard time catching my balance."

"I'm having a hard time catching my breath." Next thing she knew, Billy slung her over his shoulder in a fireman's hold and was striding to the bedroom like his feet were on fire.

She squealed, "Billy!" when he sharply smacked her ass.

"You definitely need to learn submission." He tossed her on the bed and yanked her boots off. Darkness disappeared as he lit the candles lined up on the nightstand.

She melted as easily as candle wax when faced with his romantic side. "Maybe I'm dominant. I like being on top."

"You'll get your chance later. For now," he started to unbutton his dress shirt, "you get to be on the bottom."

Soon as he was naked, Billy swept the bedding to the floor. Eased her panties off, unhooked her bra. In one graceful move he tumbled them both to the mattress, her underneath him.

The coolness of the cotton sheets on her back exaggerated the feverish feeling of his heated skin on hers. She couldn't help the small shudder of anticipation.

"Cold?" he asked, smoothing tangles of hair away from her

face.

She shook her head.

His hand looked enormous drifting down her body, so capable of exacting pleasure as it skimmed over her beaded nipples, past the indent of her navel to disappear between her legs.

Her breath caught.

Billy didn't stop his indolent caresses as he pressed his lips to the delicate skin below her ear. His middle finger slid inside her sheath. He made circles inside her, lazily licking down her throat. "I want you nice and wet. Open and ready for me."

Eden wriggled her hips higher to meet his rhythmic strokes when he added another finger. With a hint of steel in her voice she clamped down on her internal muscles, trying to pull his fingers deeper and said, "I am ready."

"Not yet."

With his continual attention to her clit, an orgasm rocketed through her. She moaned his name as every region of her pelvis contracted in pulsing billows that didn't end until he gently withdrew his hand.

A condom package rustled. Billy spread her thighs wide.

"Eden. Look at me."

She focused on those serious blue eyes as his body covered hers.

The scent of Billy, vanilla candles and sweet flowers surrounded her, making her dizzy. "You're smashing my corsage."

"Forget it." Billy's hips pressed forward and he slipped just the head into her opening. "The only thing I want you thinking about is me." He kissed her. "About us." He kissed her again, longer, sweeter. "How if we'd done this years ago I wouldn't have had the guts to leave you." He thrust inside her completely.

Their joining was as tangled as Eden's emotions, fierce one minute, tender the next. And when neither could hold back any longer, he whispered, "With me, Eden, always with me."

They came together in a molten rush.

As she lay crushed beneath Billy's spent body and the weight of his words, she knew losing her job paled in comparison to losing this man.

Chapter Sixteen

Billy snored like a damn freight train.

At first, Eden was amused by the escalating snuffles. With his arm firmly wrapped around her waist and her body tucked against his, she couldn't move and she couldn't get back to sleep. She lifted his arm and rolled away, hastily jamming the pillow in her empty spot.

Billy didn't notice.

She snagged his shirt off the floor and buttoned up while creeping from the room.

Moonlight beamed through the skylight in the hallway. The ceiling fan above the dining room table whirred softly and the refrigerator quietly hummed. A shiver broke free when her bare feet hit the cold kitchen tile.

It was weird, wandering through the condo alone in the dark, knowing Billy was as much a stranger in this place as she was. A tickle in her throat reminded her she'd worked up quite a thirst. She plucked a wine glass from the dish rack, turned the faucet on low and gulped three cold glasses before the dryness disappeared.

Eden rested her backside on the counter. The digital clock on the microwave read one-fifteen. They'd been in bed roughly four hours.

Every single time he'd touched her had been different tonight, urgent, sweet, raunchy. He'd been amazingly attuned to her needs just by looking into her eyes. She was half-afraid the man knew she'd fallen in love with him again.

Again? Why won't you admit Billy's always had your heart?

She meandered into the sparsely furnished living room, too

keyed up to sleep. No magazines littered the coffee table. The shelves held not one paperback book. She didn't want to skulk away without so much as a thank you for the orgasms. Plus, she did have that whole confessing her love for him thing to get through.

A single window separated the living and dining areas. She skirted the small desk, pulled back the heavy curtain and stared outside, watching the moonbeams throw shadows across the pavement.

As she turned away in the darkness, her thigh bumped the desk, scattering stacks of papers and file folders. Eden muffled a curse, set down her water glass and tried to straighten the piles.

That's when she saw an envelope addressed to the City of Spearfish.

Her stomach dropped to her toes. The contents of that flimsy envelope held her future.

Then she noticed something else: the envelope hadn't been sealed.

Did that mean Billy wasn't certain of his decision?

No. Billy was completely confident where his career was concerned. Still, the open flap stuck out like a sore thumb.

Or a dare.

She reached out and touched the stiff paper, then dropped her hand as if it'd been burned. She really shouldn't. No. She *couldn't*. Peeking would be wrong. Unethical. A breach of trust. If he ever found out...

But the devil on her shoulder reminded her Billy was in the other room making noise which put a chainsaw to shame.

Eden gnawed her lip, racked with indecision.

The jangle of her cell phone broke the eerie silence.

Her gaze encompassed the room as she tried to remember where she'd stashed her purse. She followed the sound to the far corner of the couch. By the time she dug out the phone, it'd stopped ringing.

The blue light glowed as she scrolled through the messages. Ten messages? In the last hour? All from Shelby?

Why would Shelby call her ten times?

She dialed Shelby's cell number. Shelby answered on the

second ring. "Eden? Thank God! Where are you? I've been trying to reach you for over an hour."

"Why?" In the background, Eden heard sirens, the squawk of police radios and people shouting. She felt the first stirrings of real panic. "What's up?"

All sound stopped. For a second Eden was afraid they'd lost the connection. Then, in a normal decibel range, Shelby said, "I'm in a police car now so I can hear you."

"Shelby, what the hell is going on?"

"I'm outside the community center. You'd better get here fast."

After hearing Shelby's next words, Eden plummeted to the carpet. "When? No. I'm okay," she lied. "Of course. I'll be right there."

Dazed, she snapped the phone shut.

"Eden? Baby, what's wrong?"

How long had Billy been standing there? In shock, she just stared at him. Through him. She couldn't seem to make her legs work.

Billy crossed the room. "What is going on?"

"Seems your concerns about the electrical system were dead on. The community center is on fire."

He hauled her to her feet and held her.

Eden dug her nails into the bare skin of his shoulder blades. "Oh God." Another horrifying thought jarred her. "What if Thomas snuck in and spent the night?" Hurriedly she redialed Shelby's number and relayed the information about the young boy. She shut the cell phone with a snap and looked up.

"Come on." Billy ushered her toward the bedroom. "Get dressed and we'll go."

♋

Eden stared mindlessly out the window of her car as Billy drove. She'd called Shelby to relay the information the building might've been occupied.

Seemed to take forever to reach the center. Fire trucks, police cars clogged the side streets after blocking off Main

Street. When Eden saw the flames licking fifty feet into the air, she bailed out of the car and ran.

She stopped and gaped at the broken shell. The windows had blown out. The roof completely collapsed. The brick interior walls were charred black. Smoke billowed and curled into the cool night air. She gripped the barricade and watched the firefighters lugging equipment. Cops trying to get control of the growing crowd. But her gaze kept returning to burning building.

Desolation took root and settled deep, increasing that sick feeling.

"Eden?"

A large hand jostled her shoulder and she looked up into the grim face of Detective Danley.

"I'm so sorry. The fire department got here as soon as they could but it was already too late."

Was he talking about Thomas? She swallowed hard. "Did they find him?"

A frown creased the Detective's brow. "Find who?"

"Thomas Fast Wolf. A twelve-year old boy who sometimes sneaks in and sleeps here. He has family problems..." Tears blurred her vision. Images of sweet Thomas danced in her head until she wanted to throw up.

"Eden!" Shelby trotted up and hugged her.

She was too numb to move. The detective pulled Shelby aside and they conversed in low tones. Eden didn't bother to listen; her heart was so heavy with grief she thought she'd collapse beneath the weight of it.

Shelby returned and shook her. "Listen to me. Thomas isn't in there."

Eden blinked at Shelby. "What?"

"After you called me I called Nathan LeBeau. He's had some dealings with Thomas's parents so he drove over and checked the Fast Wolf house." Shelby grabbed her hands. "Thomas is home. He's been there all night."

Immediately, Eden began to cry.

Shelby hugged her again. "It's just a building. No one was hurt, that's the important thing, right?"

People started to gather around her and offer support. The community outpouring stunned her, but with nothing left but a burned out skeleton, there was no doubt the direction the city would take with the community center.

Finally at about four, the blaze was under control; there was nothing left to burn.

Exhausted, Eden looked around for Billy. Several times in the last few hours she'd wanted him by her side, needing his quiet strength. Wishful thinking because he couldn't have offered it in front of all these people anyway.

As she wound her way through the emergency vehicles, Billy stepped out of the shadows.

Tempting to throw herself into his arms and damn the consequences. Did it really matter if these people knew she needed Billy Buchanan? So what if the mayor and the whole city council saw them? Billy's report wouldn't matter now. Her job was history.

Billy kept his gaze trained on the building. "I overheard the firemen talking. They think it was a gas leak since it spread so fast. Not the electrical system after all."

So cold. So clinical. Eden's hope shriveled and died. He'd already reset the distance between them. His job, his time in Spearfish was done. She wanted to cry but she found she didn't have any tears left.

"You okay?" he asked, finally looking at her.

"Not really." Eden exhaled the breath she'd been holding. "I can't believe it's gone. Makes your job easier, doesn't it?"

"Eden—"

"I suppose you'll be heading back to Chicago sooner than expected?"

Billy's mouth stayed unsmiling, his tone flat. "Actually, I'm leaving tomorrow."

The sweet, romantic night she'd spent in his arms meant nothing? It'd been his way of saying goodbye? "I'm sure you'll be glad to get back. It appears your time here was wasted."

"Wasted? What the hell are you talking about?"

Eden gathered her courage even as her heart shattered. "I saw your recommendation letter to the City Council."

"When?" he demanded.

"Tonight. At the condo. When you were sleeping."

Although she hadn't read the document, by the expression

on his face, she knew what his final recommendation had been.

Billy exploded. "For Christ's sake—"

"Don't you dare yell at her." Shelby bulled her way between them. "Leave her alone, Mr. Buchanan."

"You stay out of this."

"No. I've watched you waltz around the community center, charming her, getting her to trust you. She's lost enough tonight with losing her pride, too."

Billy reared back, speechless like he'd been slapped.

As Shelby herded Eden to her car, Eden discovered she had more tears left after all.

Chapter Seventeen

One week later...

Eden shoved the box in the backseat and slammed the door. "That's the last of it."

"Thanks. I don't know what I would've done without you. You've been the best boss I've ever had." Shelby launched herself into Eden's arms and sobbed.

"Hey. We promised no crying, remember?"

Shelby sniffled. "I'm gonna miss you, though."

"I'll miss you, too."

She shuffled back and straightened Eden's collar. "Promise you'll email me and let me know what's going on?"

"Scouts honor." They wandered through the piles of boxes spread out on Eden's driveway.

A black Ford F150 pickup pulled up to the curb and parked.

"A friend of yours?" she asked Shelby.

Shelby fidgeted beside her Grand Am, strangely hesitant. "No. Yours?"

"No." Who could it be? Then Billy jumped from the cab.

Holy crap. What was he doing here?

Shelby moved in front of her. "You want me to stay?"

Eden murmured, "No. I'll be okay." What a lie. She'd been an absolute mess since Billy left, just like ten years ago. If she thought she'd been hurt then, it was nothing compared to the total annihilation she'd experienced the night of the fire.

Tires squealed as Shelby roared away.

Billy stalked toward her. Did he have to look like he didn't have a care in the world?

"What the hell is this?" He gestured to the boxes. "You going somewhere? I've been trying to call you, going crazy because you never answer."

Maybe he wasn't as blasé as she'd first believed. Deep circles marred his face, along with a scruffy beard. "Hello to you too, Billy."

He stared at her. His eyes roved over every inch of her face. "Sorry. I-I—" He scrubbed his hands over the stubble darkening his chin. "Are these your boxes?"

"Yes."

"Then you are leaving town," he said flatly.

His anger surprised her. Why did he care? A sliver of hope unfurled and she called herself every kind of fool. "I haven't decided what I'm going to do. These boxes were for Shelby. She can't wait around for the new community center to open, so she's taking a job in Cheyenne with her cousin."

A profound look of relief crossed his face. "Thank God." Billy hauled her against his body, locked his mouth to hers and kissed the daylights out of her.

She pushed him away. "Stop. What are you doing here?"

"I'm here for you. For us."

"What? But you left."

"For a lousy week." Billy imprisoned her head between his hands forcing her to meet his eyes. "I didn't have a choice. I had to go back to Chicago and hand in my resignation in person. So, I have a few things to say to you and you'll damn well listen. No interrupting."

"I don't interrupt."

He lifted a brow.

"Okay," Eden said, "so maybe I do."

Billy smiled and some of the tension in his eyes vanished. "First off, you never read my recommendation to the council or you'd have known I'd urged them to keep the community center right where it was."

"You did?"

"Yes. And second, maybe if you weren't so damn determined to think the worst of me, scared that I'm always going to leave you, you'd realize that I love you and I'm not going anywhere this time."

Tears stung her eyes; she was too stunned to interrupt.

"I'd planned on telling you the night of the fire." He brushed the wetness from her face. "Truth is, I've never stopped caring about you. It took being with you again to drive the point home. So maybe I was young and stupid and we've wasted ten years, but we have lots of years left ahead of us. I think we can make it work. I want to try. Robert and Jim asked me if I wanted to buy into Feather Light as a partner."

"What did you say?"

"Yes, immediately, before they changed their minds." Billy pressed his forehead to hers. "When I came back here, I saw you've built a support network of friends who've become your family. I want to set down roots with you. Be part of a community. I want a life with you, Eden."

When she didn't speak or move, Billy moved back so he could peer at her. "Say something."

"You told me not to interrupt."

"Smart ass. Please. Talk. Yell. I don't care. Your silence is killing me."

Eden let her finger trace the worry lines by his eyes. He looked so vulnerable, so unsure of her reaction it made her ache inside. "Oh God, Billy, I'm so in love with you—"

His lips slid over hers in a gentle kiss as tears fell freely from her eyes. "Say it again," he whispered against her mouth. "I feel like I've been waiting my whole life to hear you say it."

"I love you. I've always loved you. I wanted to die when you took off for Chicago, even when I planned to track you down and kick your ass for leaving me again." She wrapped her arms under his shoulders, taking refuge in him, his strength, his warmth. "Everything in my life went to hell in one night, but losing the community center wasn't the worst of it. It was losing you all over again."

"Didn't you know I'd be back? I'd do whatever it took to convince you we belong together." He placed her left hand on his chest. "We've always belonged together."

Billy's heartbeat thundered beneath her palm. She gazed into his eyes, wondering how she'd ever doubted this man's feelings for her.

"Marry me. Right now. The courthouse is open until five."

"Yes, I'll marry you, but not today." She skimmed her hands along the ridge of his pecs. Her future husband had the most remarkable body, but it wasn't nearly as remarkable as his heart.

"Why not?"

"I have a job interview in an hour."

He frowned. "Already? With who?"

"The Patnoe family. They own the land beneath the rubble of the community center. Seems Jim White Feather showed them the tape you made and my passion for keeping the center there. They were so impressed they've vowed to rebuild as soon as possible. They want me to run it. Of course, I'd planned on turning them down."

"Why?"

"Because I was headed to the Windy City."

"You'd have left all this behind for me?"

"Without question. But now it seems I have the best of both worlds."

Billy kissed her again, slowly, sweetly, with love. "Me, too." His mouth wandered down her throat. "I missed you, baby. Let me show you how much. What do you say we go inside?"

"Mmm." She arched her neck, giving him full access to all the good spots. "I say what's your hurry? We've got all the time in the world."

He groaned. "I deserved that."

"I know." Eden whispered, "But think about all of the delicious ways you can make it up to me. I'm thinking it'll take hours."

"Wrong. I'm thinking it'll take years." Billy hoisted her over his shoulder and barreled up the steps, amidst her shrieks of laughter.

"Well, then. We'd best get started right away."

About the Author

To learn more about Lorelei James, please visit www.loreleijames.com. Send an email to lorelei@loreleijames.com or join her Yahoo! group to join in the fun with other readers as well as Lorelei! http://groups.yahoo.com/group/LoreleiJamesgang.

Look for these titles by
Lorelei James

Now Available:

Rough Riders Series
Long Hard Ride
Cowgirl Up and Ride
Tied Up, Tied Down
Rode Hard, Put Up Wet
Rough, Raw and Ready
Branded As Trouble
Shoulda Been a Cowboy

Wild West Boys Series
Mistress Christmas
Miss Firecracker

Dirty Deeds
Beginnings Anthology: Babe in the Woods
Running With the Devil
Wicked Garden
Wild Ride Story: Strong, Silent Type

A Question of
Trust

Jess Dee

Dedication

To D, who finds it impossible to think inside the box.
To Angie, for giving me this incredible opportunity.

Chapter One

"Dump him," Connor Regan told her. "I'll make you happy in ways you never thought possible." He grinned as he said it, but his eyes held a gleam of something serious, something that gave Maddie gooseflesh.

She slapped him lightly on the arm. "You have got to be kidding me. There's more chance of me scaling Everest in a bikini than dumping Gabe." Maddie was having the best sex she'd had in years, possibly even in her whole life. Hell, just thinking about physical therapist, Gabriel Carter's touch made her skin prickle with a lust she'd never experienced before.

She might not be crazy head-over-heels in love with Gabe—yet—but they were having a brilliant time together, and who knew where things might lead? No way could she consider calling an end to things now—especially not for Gabe's best friend.

Connor's appreciative gaze settled briefly on her breasts—breasts that had tightened with wanton desire at the thought of Gabe's touch—before returning to her face. "You have to. It's the only way to save my sanity. Do you have any idea how long I've waited to meet someone like you, the woman of my dreams?"

Maddie smiled, unable to take him seriously. She knew Gabe trusted Connor. He'd told her so. He trusted Connor with his life, so it stood to reason he trusted him with his woman as well. "No. Why not fill me in?"

With his looks and slim, athletic build, she doubted Connor'd waited more than a week at most. No doubt women were flinging themselves at his feet on a daily basis. But cute as he was—with his unshaven whiskers and longish blond hair—

slim and trim didn't work for her. She liked big and ripped. Like Gabe. She had a thing for bulging biceps and huge, hard chests. She had a thing for men who could make her feel dainty, and with Gabe she felt as petite as a doll.

Connor sighed dramatically. "Longer than I can remember. The only women who seem to like me are too thin and too shallow for my...needs. I like voluptuous, with more to the personality than an empty smile and blank eyes." He grinned wolfishly. "Someone more like you." Slowly he drew his gaze down the length of her body and then back up again. "Someone exactly like you."

She liked that Gabe's friend thought she had some depth to her character, but still Maddie shifted from one leg to the other. His gaze was hungry, and while it didn't make her uncomfortable, it made her...something. Something she did not want to explore too deeply. "Someone exactly like your friend's girlfriend, you mean."

Amusement danced in his eyes. "You think I'm a bad person."

"I'm trying to," she confessed, "but it's hard to think badly of you when you can't seem to find one single woman to satisfy your needs. Poor thing. How you must have suffered."

With a dramatic gesture, he placed a closed fist over his heart. "Oh, I have suffered. Enormously." He looked at her with a soulful gaze. "Make it better. Take me in your arms and comfort me. Please?"

She shook her head. "I'm sorry, sweetie. My arms are reserved for Gabe."

The look he flashed her was delightfully evil. "Trust me," he said, "if you held me in your arms, the last thing you'd call me is sweet."

Maddie looked at him suspiciously and harrumphed. "What happened to the charming man I met at dinner last night? To the perfect gentleman who is staying at Gabe's flat for the weekend? Who are you and what did you do with him?" Charming was a perfect word to describe Connor. In the two hours she'd sat beside him at dinner, he'd utterly bewitched her. Drawn her into his world with humor and wit, fascinating conversation and eyes that made her feel like the only other person alive.

"He met a girl." Connor sighed. "At dinner last night. The girl of his dreams. And he fantasized about her right through to the wee hours of the morning."

Maddie couldn't help herself. She gave a snort of laughter. "You've known me what? Less than a day and you're fantasizing about me?"

"Just one look, Maddie. That's all it took." His tone teased, but his eyes told her he spoke nothing but the truth.

"Connor, you hardly know me." Okay, so they'd spent a long time chatting the night before. They'd clicked immediately, laughing and talking about anything and everything. Still, what he said now bordered on preposterous, even if it was all spoken in jest. "How could you possibly think I'm the girl of your dreams?"

He shrugged. "I'm thirty. I've been around long enough to instinctively know who's right."

"That so, huh?" Maddie raised an eyebrow. "Well then, let me let you in on a secret, a little something women know instinctively themselves." She summoned him closer and whispered in his ear. "Simple rule of thumb: The right woman can never be your best friend's lover."

Connor pulled his head back and gave her a smile so wicked it made her heart skip a beat. "I guess that would depend on whose rules you're playing by."

She gaped at him, at a loss for an appropriate response.

A muscle ticked in his cheek. "Close your mouth, Madeline Jones. Otherwise I might be tempted to put something in it you're not at all prepared for."

She snapped her jaws shut, then opened them again tentatively to speak. "And by that I'm assuming you mean a cigarette or something equally unpleasant?"

"Not even close, sweetheart, and you know it."

It was her turn to sigh. "I miss the man I met last night. I would have liked to get to know him better."

"The man would like to get to know the woman he met last night better too." His smile was devilish. "Infinitely better."

She shook her head and laughed. "Even though said woman is sleeping with his best friend?"

"Especially because said woman is sleeping with his best

friend."

Pardon? "You realize, of course when I say sleeping, it's just a euphemism? We don't really sleep much at all." Oh, Lord. Was she honestly saying these things? How could she be bantering like this with him? Surely it wasn't appropriate, being that Connor was her new boyfriend's mate and all?

His eyes danced. "You're kidding me. Really? Dang, and here I was getting my pajamas ready to come and join you for a sleep over."

She chuckled. Their repartee didn't feel inappropriate. It just felt like a little innocuous fun, a little harmless flirting. Of course Connor knew she was sleeping with Gabe. It was hardly a state secret. "Sorry, mate. No pajamas at this party."

"No worries," was his immediate reply. "I'd be happier without."

Connor, she was quickly learning, was incorrigible. "No Connors at the party either," she clarified. Then she shrugged and added conciliatorily, "The bed's too small."

Connor tsked. "The bed? Gabe's restricting your pajama party to the bed? Not a good sign." He shook his head in sympathy. "Once again, dump him. I'll make you happy in ways you've never imagined possible."

"Once again, I'm sorry, but Gabe makes me happy in ways I'd never imagined possible." Oh, okay, she'd imagined them— but only when she was alone, and only when she let her mind drift to the naughtiest, most secret parts of her imagination.

"Come to my room with me," a voice said from behind. "I'll make you even happier." Gabe's hand came to rest possessively on her shoulder. The warmth of his touch scorched her skin, sending tingles racing down her spine.

She twisted her neck around to look at him and couldn't stop the smile that burst onto her face. "I would love to," she told Gabe. "Unfortunately, I can't just yet. I'm trying to explain to Connor that it's not cool to hit on your best mate's girl."

"Even if your best mate says it's okay?" Gabe asked innocently.

It was hard to gawk at him when the play of his fingers on the back of her neck sent warm flurries whistling through her belly. "Pardon me?" she spluttered. "You told Connor to hit on me?"

"I told him to give it his best shot." Gabe's voice filled with an amused I-told-you-so tone. "But he never stood a chance, did he?" Gabe leaned in and kissed the sensitive spot just below her ear, shooting her powers of concentration straight to hell. "Because this is what you really want. From me."

Oh, sweet Lord, yes she wanted that. That and so much more. "Gabe..." His teeth grazed her skin, and she forgot what she'd wanted to say anyway.

He pressed up close behind her, fitting his groin against her ass. "Am I right?"

She barely heard him. With that single move he'd hurtled her thoughts away from Connor, out of the living room and back to Gabe's bedroom last night. The same bedroom where Gabe held her against the wall, dropped to his knees and kissed her slick folds with his hot, wet mouth until she'd almost passed out from the pleasure. Even now, just thinking about it, moisture pooled between her legs and the low hum of desire buzzed in her stomach.

"Right, baby?" Gabe chuckled in her ear.

Concentrate. "I...yes. Of course, yes." She focused on Connor's eyes, eyes that looked straight through her, into her soul. God, did he know what she was thinking? Could he read her lust and her passion?

"Did he ask you to share?" Gabe asked, startling her out of her thoughts. He shifted minutely, making Maddie aware of the way his rigid cock pressed against her bottom, teasing, arousing.

"Share?" she repeated, confused. What on earth was Gabe talking about? Honestly, she could hardly function when he was around. Her head became all foggy, her body so awash with desire she could not even comprehend basic questions. But how did he expect her to concentrate when the promise of pleasure pressed into her like that. "Share what?"

Connor's lips parted and his light blue eyes dilated. A lock of wheaten hair fell over one eye. "Us."

From nowhere, her heart skipped a beat. Since she'd met Connor all of sixteen-odd hours ago she had not given his physical allure a second thought. Sure, she appreciated his boyish charms and sculpted good looks. What woman wouldn't? Her thoughts however, were so full of the massive, dark-haired, dark-eyed Gabe it was virtually impossible to consider another man sexually.

Virtually.

But the way Connor's blue eyes glowed and with the contemplative look on his face, suddenly Maddie couldn't help but picture him naked. More than that, she couldn't help but picture him pressed up against her, chest flush with her breasts, his hips against hers. And she couldn't help but picture Gabe behind her, like he was now, close and hard. The only difference was, in her unexpected thoughts Connor, like Gabe, wore nothing.

She swallowed a whimper. Gabe's loving must be driving her crazy. Already it had sent her to new sexual planes, opened up doors she'd never ventured through before. Now that those doors were open was she having a problem closing them again? Was she seeking out more doors to open and explore?

Had to be, otherwise why was she suddenly imaging herself in the centre of a very sensual, very sexy Maddie sandwich?

She laughed out loud. "Connor! You were actually considering it?"

Connor didn't respond. The teasing and jokes had vanished. He simply looked at her, the contemplation still clear in his eyes.

Behind her Gabe moved and even with two pairs of jeans between them Maddie could feel the heat of his erection. He placed his hands on her hips and pulled her back more firmly against him, leaving her with no doubt about his thoughts on the Maddie sandwich idea. She grew lightheaded.

"I don't know," Connor replied with a wink. "Seems like you're more woman than one man can manage. Especially a man like my friend over here."

Maddie's world shifted slightly left of centre. Oh, sheesh. How could she not have noticed Connor's enigmatic appeal before? One wink and she was almost reduced to a shivering bundle. Or was that the effect of Gabe's erection pushing into her backside? Didn't matter. Maddie was suddenly finding it difficult to draw breath.

"She's more woman than *you* could handle, Regan," Gabe told him good-naturedly. "I, on the other hand, am more than capable of keeping her satisfied. Alone."

God, yes he was. He'd kept her satisfied all through the night and well into the early hours of the morning as well. She shuddered against him as she remembered the bone-melting orgasm he'd given her in the shower.

"Oh, yeah, baby," Gabe muttered in her ear so only she could hear, "do that again."

She shuddered again. This time though, she didn't just relive a memory, she expanded on it. This time, another person stood in the bathroom with them, watching as Gabe bent her over the vanity and took her from behind. This time, her orgasm seemed even more powerful than it had last night because Connor's gaze burned through her as she lost control.

Connor nodded. "Yep, I can see you're keeping her satisfied. For now." The right side of his mouth lifted in a sly grin. "Guess I'll leave the two of you alone for a while, huh?"

"I guess so," came Gabe's reply. "This time."

Connor's small smile turned into a full-on beam which he flashed at Maddie, blindsiding her. She must have had blinders on up until now. The man wasn't just ridiculously attractive, he was sex on legs.

"I have a meeting anyway. See you at dinner." He waved and backed out of the room.

The door was barely closed before Gabe had his hands on her blouse, unbuttoning it.

"Gabe," she gasped. "We're in the living room." Sure, Connor was on his way out, but what if he'd left something behind? What if he had to nip back into the room to collect his mobile phone?

"No worries, baby. Regan's already said he won't be disturbing us." He tugged off her shirt and made short work of her bra. "Unless you want him to," he added in a mischievous tone. His massive hands covered her exposed breasts, the palms feather-light against her nipples.

Tiny bumps covered her skin, beading her nipples into tight, sensitive peaks. Was it his hands or his words that worked their magic over her? Did she want Connor to disturb them? Good grief, was she really even thinking about it?

"The only thing I want right now is you," she whispered, her head already hazy from the rush of sensation from her breasts to her pussy. A month down the line, it still stunned her that Gabe could find her attractive. That a man with a body and face worthy of godliness could have picked her.

While the rest of the world viewed her as plump, gentle Maddie, Gabe seemed to see her as a sex kitten. A woman made for loving, as he'd put it. And in his hands that's exactly how she felt. Sexy as a nymph. Small, thin and hot as hell. In Gabe's hands she was a sex kitten. While long, deep conversations weren't big on his to-do list, long, deep thrusts were—and Maddie was willing to overlook the lack of small talk for the glut of physical satisfaction.

More than willing.

He ran his fingers down her waist and over her hips. Beneath his hands she felt petite and sexy. She wiggled her ass against his cock.

In less than a minute her clothes were removed and she found herself on the couch, straddling a naked Gabe. She practically drooled over his massive chest and his immense shoulders.

"You sure we're alone?" she asked. It was one thing pushing her physical boundaries with Gabe, it was another doing it while his closest friend stayed at his apartment.

"Completely sure." His fingers delved between her legs finding her swollen nub. "Regan's meeting is one he won't want to miss. His future depends on it." He caressed her, igniting a fire she couldn't wait for him to douse. He closed his mouth over her breast, drawing in a nipple, sucking away her breath and Maddie forgot to ask why Connor's meeting was so important.

Christ, sex had never been like this. Ever. She wanted to touch him, needed to, but the way he'd positioned her, she had no access. Instead she gyrated her hips in time to his movements, rubbing her clit on his finger. The more he touched, the wetter she became, until her juices streamed from her, down his hand. His dick was encased in the crease in her ass and she rode him, innocently, with no penetration at all, the cream of her desire easing the way.

"Maddie," he croaked. "Jesus, I want to fuck you so bad. I want to shove my dick in your ass."

Maddie gasped. Before Gabe, no one had ever ventured there. No one had been allowed. Before Gabe. But she'd been with him four weeks now and there was very little about her body that he'd left unexplored—including her ass. She wanted it too, but what if Connor *had* left something behind? What if he walked in and found them locked in a passionate embrace, locked with Gabe's dick in her ass?

The thought brought a fresh gush of moisture between her legs.

"No protection." She grasped at lifelines, trying to prolong the inevitable. Not while Connor was here. But Gabe slipped a finger inside her, and even as she said it, she knew she was fighting a useless battle. Gabe could do whatever he wanted to her—wherever he wanted. She was his willing victim.

"Condom in my back pocket." His hands were full—of her—so she reached over and grabbed his discarded jeans, pulling out the condom and a small packet of lube.

"You always carry this around?"

"Only when you're with me," he muttered and fastened his lips to her other breast.

As her useless fingers struggled with the packaging, he released her breast and slid lower on the couch. At the same time, he wrapped his hands around her hips and lifted her higher, until his mouth was level with her clit. Then he kissed her. She forgot the condom as a million tingles began in her lower lips and radiated outwards. His tongue devoured her as he slid his finger back inside, and Maddie exploded in a heated rush.

Gabe licked until the shudders died away and she was a trembling bundle in his arms, then he dipped her backwards on the couch, knelt before her and raised her feet to his shoulders.

"Condom," he gasped.

She passed it to him with shaky hands, searching for the right words to tell him how desperate and alive and beautiful he made her feel. Lucky for her, Gabe was not a big talker, because at the moment all she could manage was a husky, "Hurry. Please." The orgasm wasn't enough. She felt achy, empty, needed him inside, needed to be filled by him.

Gabe sheathed himself. "Maddie," he said in a voice as rough as sandpaper, and all her instincts clicked to hyper alert. While not a man of many words, Gabe loved to speak about their lovemaking. Loved to tell her exactly what he would do to her and how, and she had learned to anticipate every promise. "I am going to fuck you. I am going to make you come three times, at least, in the next five minutes. And then, when you think you don't have the strength for even one more orgasm, I am going to put my dick in your ass and make you come again. Screaming."

Maddie's trembles multiplied.

"And then, and only then, am I going to come. Deep, deep, deep inside you."

Desire shook through her. No one had ever made her scream, until Gabe. "Do it," she begged as fears of Gabe's friend walking in on them were shoved aside. "Do it now."

He did. In one fluid motion he plunged into her, filling her, delighting her. The breath left her body in a whoosh, then returned slowly, unevenly, as slowly, skillfully, Gabe moved, filling her then withdrawing, only to drive into her again and again.

While Maddie's responses to his ministrations became wild, almost frenzied, Gabe's control was impeccable. His movements were careful, deliberate, filling her in the ways he'd learned turned her on the most, plunging deep inside her then withdrawing gradually, teasing her lips before plunging in again.

It didn't take long. A few torturous strokes and she was close, on the verge—and he knew it. His eyes narrowed to slits, sweat beaded on his forehead. "Come for me, baby," he coaxed. "Come just for me." He inched his way out, drew the tip of his dick around her slick folds then drove into her, again and again, taking her little by little over the edge, until reality blurred, her eyelids drifted shut, pleasured blossomed and she came.

When she opened her eyes again, a small, smug smile played on Gabe's lips. "That's number one."

She couldn't help her own lazy, answering smile.

Gabe was far from finished with her. Removing her feet from his shoulders, he lay down over her, supporting his weight on his elbows. Instinctively she wrapped her legs around his waist, locking him between her thighs.

She wasn't letting Gabe go. Not for anything. At least not until he'd seen through on his promise to make her come screaming.

The change in position changed the angle of his penetration. His thrusts were shallower this time, but no less enflaming. At this angle, he found her G-spot and tormented it, until once again she found herself on the brink of explosion.

Gabe's eyes were hooded, his mouth slightly open as puffs of warm air left his lips, heating hers. "Three more thrusts, and you're going to come," he promised.

She clutched his shoulders, held on for dear life and let him take her over the edge in three deep, erotic strokes.

This time, it took her a little longer to recover. Her heart beat madly, her pulse raced.

"Two," Gabe growled.

"Too good," Maddie agreed in a haze. Her eyelids had become leaden weights, impossible to open.

"Two more to come. At least." He flipped her, so she knelt on the couch with her butt in the air and her breasts resting on the arms.

Her legs trembled, her body on the verge of collapse. Three orgasms in such close proximity had to have an effect on a girl. She wasn't sure her legs could hold her, but Gabe grasped her hips, steadying her, and she quit worrying. Gabe would support her.

He pulled her back, penetrating her at the same time and she whimpered in delight. When he began moving she lost herself to his rhythm, his heat, to his strokes and touch. The world narrowed to the couch, to them. Perspiration trickled between her breasts.

She should be exhausted, sated, but she wasn't. Instead she pushed back greedily against his invading thrusts, her lips gripping his cock, reluctant to release him. She was close, so close, and so hot. Flames of lust burned through her, detonating fireworks throughout her body.

Gabe played his hand over her butt, caressing, tickling, exploring. His fingers were hot. Red hot, burning.

Heat. Hot, hot heat.

Which made the unexpected, cool wetness against the crease of her ass all the more shocking. Shocking and delicious all at the same time.

And then his thumb was there, touching, teasing, tantalizing. She clenched her cheeks together, trapping him, uncertain whether she wished to stop the slow torture or fast forward it. Her inner walls clenched around his cock, squeezing him, and his breathing shallowed.

"Relax, Maddie," Gabe rasped behind her. "Relax and enjoy number three."

How could she not comply?

His thumb teased the sensitive entrance to her ass, pushing against the tight ring of muscle but not through it. Expectation built. Uncertainty turned into an achy desire and then became raw, naked need. Christ, she wanted his thumb in her ass, wanted it bad. She rocked back against him, burying his cock deeper inside her pussy and begging silently for more.

With a sharp intake of breath, he pushed slowly, gently into her.

The instinct to push his thumb out warred with the need to feel him plunge deeper. Sensation rocketed through her, pain mixed with pleasure, intense, feverish pleasure, and she repressed her instinct. She relaxed further, giving his thumb full, free access.

The intensity of it took her breath away. She groaned long and deep as he removed his thumb and replaced it with a different finger. A longer, thinner one. And then he began to move again, fucking her like he had before, but this time, moving his hand in time to his thrusts.

"Ah, Christ, Maddie," Gabe gasped. "Jesus, you look so hot like this. You're killing me, baby. Killing me."

Maddie wanted to respond, wanted to tell him he was the one driving her to a sweet and certain death, but she couldn't talk, could barely draw breath. How could she explain he took her to another plane, a physical plane which knew no boundaries, which knew only desire and lust and need and bliss? How could she tell him when words fluttered through her mind like butterflies, so close yet impossible to catch?

"You like that, don't you?" Gabe's breath was choppy now. "You like the idea of both holes being filled at once." His withdrawal was gradual, then he pushed back in little by little, going deep. Deeper then he'd been before. The movement reverberated all the way up her spine and through her scalp, tingles of delight whispering through her.

Yes. Sweet Lord, yes. She loved the idea. Loved the reality. She felt full, snug and good. So damn good.

"Double penetration...baby." His voice was scratchy, as though talking was too difficult. "It's your thing. It gets you so damn hot. Gets...me so...damn hot."

Hot. Hell yes she was hot. All that existed in her world was his dick and his finger and his voice. And they made her *hot.* A fresh wave of moisture flooded from her and he groaned and thrust deep again.

"You still worried about doing this in the living room?"

She shook her head. She was so into this, so hot for what he did to her she hadn't given it another thought.

He waited a heartbeat, then thrust into her and stopped dead. "What if Connor walks in?"

Holy crap. *Connor.* She'd forgotten him, forgotten everything in the sexual tornado that was Gabe.

He toyed with her butt. "What if Con walks in and sees you like this? With my dick in your pussy and my finger in your ass?"

Maddie stopped breathing.

Gabe dropped the bomb. "What if he wants to share?"

Her nipples tightened painfully and her head spun.

"Double penetration, baby," he whispered. "It's your thing."

It was suddenly impossible not to think about *the Maddie sandwich.* What if Connor truly did want to share? What if, instead of just Gabe fucking her, it was Gabe and Connor? Gabe behind her, like he was now, and Connor beneath her. Gabe fucking her ass and Connor's dick wedged between her slick folds?

Maddie moaned out loud. Her clit began to throb, and her pussy started to drip.

What if—

Gabe twisted, pulled out and drove in, and Maddie dissolved around him. *A Maddie sandwich.* Spasms rode through her like lightning. *A Maddie, Gabe and Connor sandwich.* Thunder roared in her ears. Her orgasm stretched out, encompassed her thoughts, and intensified. Not just Gabe. Connor and Gabe. Gabe and Connor. Gabe and Connor and

Maddie.

Oh, Christ, she was still coming, still in the lingering throes of orgasm.

Gabe, Connor, Maddie. The names whirled through her mind, until finally she collapsed, her knees shaking so hard she could no longer remain on them.

Gabe gave her no recovery time. He withdrew and turned her around so she lay on her back. Then once again he settled between her legs. Seconds before their lips met in a hungry kiss, he whispered again, "Double penetration." The tip of his cock swept against her clit and his tongue slipped into her mouth. He rocked them, sliding his dick back and forth over her tender nub. Once, twice and another tiny orgasm broke over her. Or maybe it was the same one, just not quite over yet.

"Gabe..." She moaned helplessly against his lips.

"Gabe?" he asked, "Or Connor?"

Which one? God, which one? "Gabe," she said out loud, orientating herself. She bucked against him. "Fuck me. Again. Please, Gabe, fuck me." Yes, she was talking to Gabe, but she still thought about his friend, couldn't help it.

He pulled back then and lifted her shaky legs. This time he placed her feet on his chest, leaving her wide open and mere inches away from his impressive erection. He rubbed his dick against her, starting at her clit, and working his way down, over her slit and lower until he touched her ass. Then he dragged it back up again, torturing the swollen, sensitive flesh. Again and again he caressed her like this until the sensation broke and another mini orgasm rippled through her. This time he did not wait for her to recover. While the shivers flowed over her body, he pressed his dick down, with the tip against the tight ring of muscle, and pushed forward.

Maddie expected pain, she expected the now familiar burn as her body adjusted to fit his girth. But to her surprise, in this position there was no pain. There was only sweet, exquisite ecstasy. Gabe pulled back and then moved forward, burying himself in her ass. Slowly, exquisitely, he built a rhythm, filling her completely, then withdrawing totally before filling her again.

After so many orgasms Maddie did not have the strength to swing her hips up to meet him. Instead she gave herself to Gabe fully, relaxing altogether into the delicious, wicked act. She kept her eyes open, watched Gabe watch her. His eyes were dark. Midnight black and glazed with lust.

"You like this, Maddie?" he asked and wet his lips with his tongue.

Maddie wet her own lips, mirroring his actions. "You know I do, Gabe."

"You like it when I...touch you here?" Without losing momentum, he slid his finger over her clit.

"Mmmmmmmm."

"And...here?" He slipped the same finger between her wet, swollen folds.

"Ah! Mmmmm."

"You want Connor to touch you here?" In slid another finger.

She gasped incoherently. *Connor. Charming, funny Connor.*

"And here?" With his dick in her ass, and his fingers in her pussy, fucking her, he stroked her clit with his other hand.

Connor, with his devilish grin and sexy wink. She couldn't talk, just stared at Gabe with wide eyes. Yes, Goddammit, she wanted Connor touching her there—while Gabe fucked her.

"Do you?" Gabe asked again, his eyes dark as sin.

She panted in reply. Could she answer him? Could she tell him the truth? Did she feel secure enough in their steamy, yet young relationship to confide in him?

"Do you, baby? Do you want Connor to touch you while I fuck you?"

How could she not trust him? After all they'd shared, after what she let him do to her, how could she not? Of course she trusted Gabe. Of course she could tell him.

With the last ounce of energy she possessed she opened her mouth and whispered, "Yes, Gabe. I want it. I want...Connor."

Gabe let out a roar of pure male triumph. He lengthened inside her and his movements increased in pace and intensity. His fingers drove her wild, their precise actions drawing to attention millions of nerve endings. His dick filled her, stretched her, pleasured her, his speed rocketed her into another universe and thoughts of Connor filled her head.

This time when she came, it was wild and all consuming.

She screamed as her muscles tightened around Gabe, gripping his dick like an iron fist. Cream poured from her, coating his hand, dripping down to mix with the lube and further coat his cock.

Gabe pressed harder into her, faster, and then he roared again and buckled, and in the middle of her gut-wrenching release he came as hard as she did.

Chapter Two

"Was it good?" Connor's chest heaved as he asked the question.

"Was what good?" Maddie answered innocently.

It was all he could do to hold himself back, to not haul her into his arms and kiss her senseless right there in the middle of the restaurant. She had the look of a well-loved...no wait, a well-fucked woman. The color in her cheeks was heightened in a way no make-up could cover and her lips were full and swollen. Her honey-blond hair, which earlier she'd tied in a neat ponytail, now hung long and free, wispy tendrils floating over her eyes and cheeks. The look on her face was lazy, satiated.

He grinned. "The pajama party."

She leaned close to him and whispered, "I told you, Connor. We don't really wear pajamas." Then she turned to him and smiled. "But yes, it was very good. Thanks for asking."

"No problem." His grin faltered. Shite, maybe he shouldn't have sat down next to her. Maybe he should have gone to the other end of the table and spoken to John and George about their new business venture. A burgeoning erection was hardly appropriate fare at the dinner table. Unless, of course, Maddie was feasting on his cock and not on the pasta prima vera on her plate.

Maddie watch him shift in his seat. "How did your meeting go this afternoon?" She must have picked up on his discomfort and purposefully changed the subject.

"Yeah. It went okay." He liked that she was curious about him.

"Sounded like it was important. Gabe said your future

137

depended on it."

He laughed. "Not quite that important. I'm considering moving back to Sydney. The job will help me decide one way or the other." Usually he wouldn't have organized a meeting for a Saturday, but there was no other way he could have fit it into his week day schedule. Not with the amount of work piling up on his desk.

The problem was, it wasn't his job that he wanted to change. He was happy with his position in Melbourne— although heading up the IT division of a blue chip company was mighty appealing. Something else in his life wasn't working, but he couldn't pinpoint exactly what. It had begun as a vague restlessness, a stirring in his gut, and over time had gotten bigger, more pressing. There was an emptiness in his soul, as though part of it was missing. Perhaps returning to Sydney and starting a new job would settle this agitation.

"So what did you think after your meeting?" Maddie asked.

"I'm not sure. I liked the company. I liked the people. But then I feel the same about my current position."

"Not much help then, huh? Looks like you have a tough decision ahead of you."

"Don't I know it."

"Come back to Sydney," Maddie suggested. "I know Gabe would be happy to have his best mate living in the same city again."

"I wish it were that simple." If his restlessness could be eased by making his pal happy, he'd move back in a shot.

She smiled wryly. "Yeah, if only real life were that easy."

Connor did not want to talk about his life and his decision. He'd thought about it altogether too much already over the last few months. For now, while he could, he preferred to lose himself in the magic that was Maddie.

"Tell me something, Maddie." He lowered his voice so only she could hear him. "You know this afternoon, after I left?"

She looked at him through eyes narrowed by suspicion.

Good. He smothered a grin. She was obviously getting to know the way his mind worked. "Did you think about me while you partied?"

Maddie went very still. Then she sat a little straighter,

patted his hand and shot him an amused look. "Yes, sweetie. You were upper mind in our thoughts the entire time."

He couldn't let the opportunity pass. Connor placed his other hand over Maddie's, trapping her there. The warmth of her skin heated his entire arm. "I don't just need to be in your thoughts, you know."

Maddie gasped and then did her best to hide it.

Across the table Gabe turned to look at her with an indulgent smile. Maddie's return smile was shaky at best. Gabe's gaze came to rest on the spot where Connor and Maddie's hands were joined. He raised an eyebrow and looked back at Maddie. Maddie turned scarlet.

Connor grinned like an idiot.

Maddie dropped her gaze to the table.

Gabe winked at Connor.

Connor nodded at Gabe.

No further communication was necessary.

Shite, he was stiff as a rod. His jeans pulled tight across his straining cock, paining him. He pulled his hand away, freeing hers, desperate for some form of distraction. "So, Maddie, tell me. Do you like lateral thinking puzzles?"

Maddie stared at her hand, perplexed. Then she shook her head and looked up at him. "From pajama parties to lateral thinking puzzles. That's quite a jump."

"Humor me, sweetheart. Thoughts of you in your pajamas have got me hot as hell. I need to think about something else. Anything else."

Her eyes clouded and she looked away as a waiter leaned over her, filling her glass with merlot. By the time the waiter moved on, Maddie's gaze was clear and her voice bright. "It just so happens I'm an expert at lateral thinking."

Connor sure hoped so. Tonight Maddie was going to be asked to think outside the box. Far outside the box. To put all her usual expectations and moral codes on hold and view the world differently. Would she be able to do it? Would she want to?

Gabe seemed to think so.

Connor hoped so. "Two men walk into a bar. They each order a scotch on the rocks. The one downs his drink and goes off to play darts. The other plays a game of darts first, and then sips his drink slowly. Five minutes later, he's dead."

"And I need to explain...?"

"Why the one man is dead and the other still alive."

She nodded musingly. "Did he have a heart attack?"

Connor shook his head. It wasn't working. Watching her mull over the puzzle was not making him any softer. "He was in perfect health."

"Was he murdered?"

Ah ha. She was beginning to think outside the box. Good. He liked that. "He was."

"By a dart?"

"Nope. The dart had nothing to do with it."

"Was he attacked?"

"Nope." He hesitated a fraction of a second before adding, "nothing happened to him that did not happen to his friend." Just like with him and Gabe. But that was a whole other story. A whole other conundrum for Maddie to dwell on at a later stage.

"And yet his friend was fine..." Her voice trailed off as she contemplated the puzzle. Absently, she picked up her water and took a sip. Connor watched as her lips touched the rim of the glass, as she poured the clear liquid into her mouth. He watched as she swallowed delicately, once and then twice.

Christ, he wanted those lips on his dick. Wanted her to swallow any liquid she found there.

Ice tinkled against the glass as she set it down on the table. She raised an eyebrow and lifted the glass again. "The drink. There was poison in the drink."

Beautiful, sexy and intelligent. Gabe, the lucky bastard, had struck gold. "Ah, but both men were given the identical drink. If there was poison in them, why did one man die and not the other?"

She tilted the glass beside his ear and jiggled it. The ice tinkled again.

He was right. There was more to Madeline Jones than blank eyes and an empty smile. The woman was sassy and savvy and sensual, and he liked her. A lot.

"Because, smart ass, it wasn't the scotch that was

poisoned, it was the ice." Her smile was jubilant. "By the time the second man had his drink, the ice had melted and the poison had seeped into the scotch. The first man drank it straight away. There was no time for the poison to reach the drink."

Connor nodded. "Not bad. Not bad at all." She was the first person who'd ever worked out the puzzle. Everyone else gave up too easily or begged for clues. Not Maddie. She stuck at it and worked it out.

Would she stick with the Connor-Gabe conundrum too?

"I told you, I'm an expert." Her tone was haughty, her nose in the air.

He laughed. Maddie wasn't just smart and sexy, she was funny. Never mind the urge to sleep with her, he was enjoying her company just like this. Enjoying it a lot. Did Gabe get this much pleasure from spending time with her?

"Did you know I have a sister?" Maddie asked him.

"No, I didn't." He didn't know much about her at all, other than the bits and pieces Gabe had shared, but now he found himself wanting to discover as much as he could. "Tell me about her."

She gave him a cheeky smile. "She's the same age as me. In fact we were born on the same day, to the same parents. But you know what?"

Maddie had a twin? There were two of her? "No, what?"

"We're not twins."

"Huh?"

"Yep. We're not twins. Go figure."

Connor frowned. "What are you talking about?"

She snickered. "Explain it. We're born on the same day— the same hour even—to the same parents, but we're not twins."

And then it struck him. She wasn't sharing bits of herself with him, she was giving him a lateral thinking puzzle. He grinned at her. No worries. He'd solve this and then find out the real facts about Maddie Jones. He looked forward to it.

"Do you look the same?" he asked.

"Oh, yes. Identical. You can't tell us apart."

Holy crap. He had a sudden picture of himself caught between two Maddies. Two naked Maddies. "Oh, Christ," he muttered to himself. "A Maddie sandwich."

Maddie's fork dropped to her plate with a noisy clatter.

Conversation stopped as everyone turned to see what the commotion was. Gabe shot Connor a questioning look.

Connor shook his head.

Maddie's cheeks flamed. "Sorry. Clumsy me," she said by way of explanation. "Dropped my fork. No biggie." But as soon as the talk around the table resumed, she hissed at Connor. "What did you just say?"

"I was thinking about the possibility of there being two of you. I called you a Maddie sandwich. Why?"

"I...oh...no reason."

She was flustered. Interesting. He was flustered too, but that was because the idea of two Maddies made his jeans feel like a new form of Chinese torture. He decided not to question her further. His dick couldn't take the agony.

"There are three of you," he told her instead.

"In the sandwich?" she asked, her voice squeakier than usual.

"No sweetheart. In your puzzle. You're a triplet."

His answer broke the tension. She smiled. "You're right. Well done."

"I guess I should have told you before you mentioned your sister that I too am an expert lateral thinker."

"There anything else I should know about you that you're keeping secret?"

"Well, I don't have an identical twin sister if that's what you're asking."

She laughed out loud. "And brother?"

"I have one. But we're not identical either. He's five years younger than me. How about you?"

"Two sisters. One older, one younger, and nope. Not identical either."

By the time the dishes had been cleared from the table and all that was left were coffees, Connor had learned that Maddie's parents had recently celebrated their thirty-fifth anniversary. Her sister, Claire, was twenty-nine, and two years Maddie's senior, and Julia was twenty-four. The older sisters ran a small children's bookshop in East Sydney, and Julia would join them as soon as she completed her studies. They planned to turn the one bookstore into a chain of three or four over the next few years, and Maddie was excited by the prospect.

He also learned that Maddie loved cats but was allergic to them, had a compulsive need to buy nail polish (her collection currently sat at ninety-three bottles), and she detested *Desperate Housewives.*

He also learned that whenever she smiled her eyes crinkled up and a tiny dimple teased her left cheek. He noted that laughter made her plump breasts jiggle appealingly and when she frowned only one corner of her mouth tilted downwards.

Alas, by the time dinner was finished, the desire to kiss her had not receded the tiniest bit. He wanted to kiss more than her mouth though. He wanted to strip away her sleeveless, gunmetal grey shirt, rip off her black jeans and sample every inch of her delectable body. What would she taste like? Would her juices taste as good as her lips looked?

Godammit, would he ever be soft again?

Gabe's voice broke through his musings. "We're going across the road for a drink and to play pool." He gestured to the front entrance of the restaurant, where the rest of their dinner companions were headed. "Want to join us?" Gabe stood behind Maddie's seat, his hand caressing her neck. Maddie, Connor noted, stretched like a contented cat beneath his friend's touch. Her eyes closed and a small sigh escaped from her parted lips.

Christ, it didn't take much to imagine her naked and writhing under Gabe's hands. He'd seen how his friend could reduce a woman to a shivering mass of desire, and more than anything he wanted to see Gabe work his wonders on Maddie. Fuck, he wanted to work his own charm on Maddie. He wanted it. Bad.

Without opening her eyes, Maddie said in a low, sexy voice. "Here's something you never knew about me. I'm not much of a pool player."

"You and Connor both," Gabe muttered. "He's lousy with a cue."

Connor raised an eyebrow at Gabe, and Gabe nodded. Good thing Maddie could not see their silent communication or she'd know right off the understanding that passed between them had nothing to do with pool.

143

"Tell you what," Connor suggested. "Why don't you go ahead and play pool. I'll take Maddie back to your place."

Maddie opened one eye and looked at him suspiciously. Again. Clever woman.

He grinned, and not for the first time, gave silent thanks to his friend for insisting he make use of his spare bedroom, insisting he meet Maddie. "I'm going back there anyway," he said with innocence. "I assume you are too?"

"I am." She raised an eyebrow, telling him her suspicion had in no way been allayed. Then she turned to Gabe. "Would it be okay if I didn't join you? Pool really isn't my game. I'd rather just go back to your place and relax." Then she added in a far softer voice. "And get ready for you to get back."

Gabe's pupils dilated. He leaned over and whispered something in Maddie's ear, something Connor could not hear.

She tilted her head closer to Gabe's mouth and smiled.

Gabe whispered something else.

Maddie's eyes bulged and she gasped. Gabe kept whispering. Her gaze darted to Connor as she flushed a dark red.

Connor suppressed a howl of pain as his jeans bit back at his straining penis. Knowing Gabe the way he did, and knowing what Gabe and he had planned, he had a fair idea what his friend had said to Maddie.

The rush of blood to her cheeks did not divert his attention away from the other ways in which her body responded to Gabe's comment. He couldn't help but notice how her nipples poked through her blouse, teasing him, or that goose flesh had broken out over her arms.

Gabe smiled at Connor. Connor smiled back.

"Go with Connor," Gabe told Maddie. "Get warm and cozy in my bed. I'll see you later." In full view of Connor, he turned Maddie's still flushed face to his and kissed her.

Connor watched as Maddie's lips softened and relaxed into the kiss. He watched her mouth open to Gabe's probing. Her pink tongue met his darker one, and damn, he wanted to be the one kissing her, making her sigh like she'd just got a taste of heaven.

Christ, he wanted to be the one showing her heaven.

When Gabe pulled away, Maddie moaned her disapproval. "Later, baby," he promised, then looked up at Connor. His mouth curved into a knowing smile. "She's all yours," he said with a wave and walked away.

"Don't I wish," Connor muttered under his breath.

"Wish what?" Maddie answered. Her voice was all lazy, her pupils tiny pricks of black in her hazel eyes. With her kiss-swollen lips, her beaded nipples and her luscious body, she looked like sex personified.

"That you were all mine," he told her without skipping a beat.

She stood up, drawing her wrap around her shoulders. The glow from a light above her caught the gold glints in a wisp of her hair. She didn't look like sex. She looked like an angel.

"I'm Gabe's," she said. "You know that."

He too got up and touched her shoulder, indicating she should walk ahead of him. "I'll share," he told the back of her head. "You know that."

Her footsteps faltered. "A Maddie sandwich," she mumbled to herself

That's when he grinned. He guessed she hadn't meant for him to hear, but he had. And he was very happy indeed. It appeared she had conjured up a different version of a Maddie sandwich. A version which turned him on no less than his original recipe.

"Is it on the menu?" he asked. "Because I would like to order one. To go."

She almost tripped, but he caught her arm, steadying her, and led her out of the restaurant. Her skin felt like silk beneath his fingers and he did not let her go until she was seated in the rental car and he had no choice.

The minute he switched on the engine Maddie spoke. "Connor—" She floundered, seemingly at a loss for words. "I...it's... Look, it's not..." Her voice dropped off and she shook her head. "How am I supposed to respond when you say something like that?"

He glanced at her and lowered his voice. "Tell me you want a bite too."

The full moon and clear sky provided enough light in the

dark of the night for Connor to see her color deepen. "I... I..."

"Okay, I'll make it easier for you." Christ, that virginal blush played havoc with his hard-on. "Tell me you *don't* want a taste."

She blanched. "*Connor.* Dear God, how did we even get on to this subject?"

When he noticed her nipples poking through her shirt, bathed in the moon's soft rays, it was with a certain measure of satisfaction. This time Gabe was not the one who had induced the response. Connor's desire hit him like a blow to the gut, hard and fierce. "You can't do it, can you? You can't deny you'd like to be the middle of a you, me and Gabe sandwich?"

She stared out of her window, silent for a long time. "I can't do this, Connor," she said at last. "I can't play these games. I'm with Gabe. You know that."

Such strong words. So why did she sound so unconvinced by them? He couldn't help it, he had to touch her. Reaching out, he tucked a tendril of hair behind her ear. Beneath his hand she trembled.

"What if..." Shite, he had to change gear, had to pull his hand away, "...this wasn't a game. What if the two of us, Gabe and I, turned your sandwich into a reality?"

Maddie let out a shuddery breath. Fog steamed up her window.

Connor forced his attention onto the road in front of him. "What if I really did join your pajama party?"

She whimpered out loud.

Focus on driving. Don't crash the car because you're thinking with your dick. "You, me and Gabe, sweetheart. What do you say?"

Maddie opened her mouth, but no words came out, just a strangled groan.

Think outside the box, Maddie, he urged in silence. *Open your mind to any possibilities, not just the obvious ones.*

Connor pulled up outside Gabe's building. He turned to her, took her hand in his, and noticed with satisfaction that she did not draw away. "Here's a new puzzle for you, Maddie. One only you can solve." Her skin was warm and just a little damp. Nerves? "A man sits down to dinner. He meets a woman who makes his world shift slightly off its axis, who makes him hard as a rock and horny as hell. But the woman has a boyfriend—the man's best friend. Tell me, Maddie, what happens next?"

Maddie stared at him, her face wild. Her chest rose and fell in uneven ripples, like her choppy breath.

"Ponder that one, sweetheart," he said and swung open his door.

Maddie sat where she was, looking dumbstruck.

He circled the car and opened her door, waiting chivalrously as she climbed out. They walked up the stairs to Gabe's apartment in silence, but Connor could sense Maddie's tension, could hear her knuckles crackling as she clenched and unclenched her fist.

He let them into the flat.

"I know the answer to that one," Maddie said as Connor put his keys down.

Connor's heart rate slowed.

Maddie ran her tongue over her lower lip. "The...the woman goes to bed." She nodded, as though to emphasize her answer. "With the man's best friend. Just like she did last night and the night before that." She gave him a tight smile. "Goodnight, Connor, and thank you for the lift."

Maddie turned towards Gabe's bedroom.

Before Connor had time to register the crushing disappointment wrought by her departure, she swung back round and their eyes locked. Gone was the contained woman who'd answered with such certainty. In her place stood a vixen with fire in her eyes and lust in her gaze.

His heart slammed into his ribs.

"Fuck you, Connor." Her whisper was harsh. She took three paces forward and poked her finger into his chest. "Fuck you for putting me in this untenable situation." Without giving him a chance to defend himself, she raised her head in defiance, swore again and pressed her lips to his.

It was over too soon. She'd messed with his brain and sent a hurricane hurtling through his stomach and it was over. He hadn't even had a chance to appreciate her actions before she pulled away.

"*No!*" She couldn't leave. Not now, not like this. He grabbed her arm, halting her retreat. He looked into her eyes, acknowledged the hunger and the confusion and the awkwardness he saw there, and then he kissed her.

Connor had experienced his share of first kisses. Some were nice, some were hugely erotic, some needed practice and one had just been bloody awful. Indescribably bad. Kissing Madeline Jones was like nothing he had ever encountered before.

Never, ever had a kiss stopped his heart beating before kicking it into overdrive. His pulse drummed to an erratic, irregular rhythm, pounding so hard it sent blood roaring through his ears, drowning out sounds.

Her lips parted to his seeking tongue, offering him entry into the warm, wet cavern of her mouth. He tasted wine on her breath, and honey, and a bewitching mix of woman and desire. Lord, a man could become inebriated on her taste alone.

Time lost meaning as her tongue twined with his, as she wrapped herself around him, pulled his chest to her breasts, brought her hips to his groin. Space no longer existed, it was just him and her. Together. He felt himself slipping, dropping and falling into Maddie. Whatever she ultimately did or did not agree to, Connor knew it would never be enough. One kiss was all he needed to know that with Maddie he wanted everything.

And then she groaned, twisted and pulled away. She stared at him in horror for perhaps five seconds, pressing her fingers to her puffy lips. Then she looked at her hand as if not comprehending what it was, before wheeling around and racing down the hall.

When there was nothing left but the soft echo of her footsteps ricocheting through his head, Connor found his voice again. "I'm coming after you, Madeline Jones," he promised her absent form. "Sooner than you think."

Chapter Three

Guilt pounded through her chest as she raced down the passage. Oh, sweet heavens, she'd kissed him. Kissed her boyfriend's best friend, and more than that, she'd liked it.

Hell, who was she kidding? She hadn't just liked it, she'd lost herself to the exquisite sensation Connor's mouth brought to life in her.

Shaky knees and breathlessness made her getaway virtually impossible. Each step was a battle against logic. Her head told her escape was essential, her body told her to turn back—*now!* What really rocked her soul though, was the fact that when Connor kissed her, really kissed her, when his lips melded with hers and his tongue took possession of her wits, Maddie felt as if she had finally come home.

Kissing Gabe sent fireworks rocketing into space and darts of lust shooting through her loins. Kissing Connor touched the most private, most intimate of places—her very heart.

Gabe. Shit, she'd have to tell him what she'd done. She couldn't betray him like this—no matter what he'd whispered in her ear earlier. She headed for his room, but when she reached it, doubt stopped her short of opening the door.

How could she tell him? How could she not? What would she say? She'd kissed Connor, and her life had changed? Gabe would laugh at her, right before he kicked her out of his life for good.

Or maybe he wouldn't. Maybe he'd smile triumphantly and reward her for taking his advice?

She couldn't do it. She couldn't tell Gabe the truth. No matter what his reaction might be, she wasn't prepared for it.

The image of her Maddie sandwich was indelibly pasted on her eyelids, the taste of Connor was forever planted in her mouth and shivers from Gabe's lovemaking were eternally racing down her spine. Thank God Gabe had gone to play pool. Right now she couldn't be with anyone but herself and her thoughts and her guilt and her desire. She couldn't face her own uncertainty and desires, she definitely was not ready to show them to Gabe.

Grabbing the handle with a certain measure of desperation, she flung the door open and slammed it shut behind her, sinking back against it for support. With her eyes closed, she rested her head against the solid oak and wished to God she knew what the hell had just happened to her life.

Alone. Thank God. No Connor No Gabe. No one to see her confusion. Just her.

"Maddie."

Gabe's simple acknowledgement nearly sent her into heart failure.

She grabbed her chest. "God. Gabe. Jesus. You scared the hell out of me." He wasn't supposed to be here. He was supposed to be at the pub. Instead he lay sprawled out on the bed, looking for all the world like a demigod. He'd shed his clothes and wore nothing but his underpants. Underpants that highlighted the heavy bulge beneath them. "I thought you were playing pool."

He gave her an indolent smile. "I changed my mind. After your kiss at the restaurant I decided not to play after all. At least not pool."

Her chest heaved. Moisture flooded between her legs. Holy crap. Confused, uncertain, shocked, guilty and horny to boot. One look at Gabe and she turned into a puddle of wanton need.

He slipped off his undies.

She licked her lips.

His eyelids drooped sexily over his eyes. "Did you do it?"

She gawked at him. God, he was asking? He actually wanted to know?

"Did you do it, baby?" Gabe coaxed, and Maddie began to shake. From guilt and from lust and from the simple task of watching Gabe. "Did you kiss Connor?"

"I..." Could she do it? Could she tell him the truth? "I...

Yes. I kissed him."

Gabe grew harder under her perplexed stare. "And?" His voice was a low growl.

"And wh...what?" He wasn't angry? He had honestly expected her to go through with it?

"And are you?"

Her heart hammered. "Am I what?"

"You know what?"

She hung her head. In shame? In embarrassment? "Yes."

"Yes, what?"

Sweet Lord, he was making her say it. Heat crept into her cheeks. "Yes, I'm wet."

He growled. "Wetter than you get when I kiss you?"

She couldn't answer that one directly. Wouldn't. "I'm wet, Gabe. Very wet."

"C'mon here, baby," he demanded. "Let me see."

With legs heavy as lead and with anticipation thrumming through her, she put one foot in front of the other.

"Wait."

This was it. The anger was coming. The resentment. He'd stopped her. Now he would make her leave. She couldn't look at him, couldn't stand to see the rejection in his eyes.

"Take off your clothes."

Startled, she snuck a peak at him. Gabe's eyes were smoky, his lips parted. His hand rested in his lap, his fingers wrapped around his cock. She'd kissed Connor, told Gabe about it—and Gabe was turned on.

Maddie took a breath, the first one to reach her lungs since Gabe had spoken. He liked the idea of her kissing Connor.

"Remove your shirt first."

She obeyed, undoing each button one by one before letting the blouse drop to the floor. Loathe as she was to admit it, she liked the idea of kissing Connor too.

"Now your bra."

She reached behind her back and unhooked the straps. The bra slipped off and her breasts swung free, heavier than usual, more needy.

Gabe watched each move, nodding. His gaze took in her

breasts, her belly and dropped lower.

"More," he said, and she stripped off her jeans.

Where the hell had her inhibitions gone? What had happened to the Maddie who was shy to show her body to men? Who could only picture the too-large breasts and the too-round butt? The soft, fleshy belly and the ample thighs? Where was she and who was this new woman? This woman who found even the cover of her panties too conservative? Who was the Maddie who could kiss her lover's best friend and then return to her lover dripping with desire for another man?

Who was she?

"All of it," Gabe rasped, and Maddie ditched the panties.

He tugged at his cock. "Now, come here and let me see what Regan did to you. Let me see if he has the power to make your pussy weep as much as I do."

Her stomach clenched with desire. Maddie closed the space between them, climbed on the bed and knelt before her lover. The old Maddie was gone. The woman she presented to Gabe was sensual and hot and uninhibited. The woman she presented to him was wet. Dripping. With lust for her lover—and for her lover's best pal.

Gabe reached out and ran his hand between her legs, ran his fingers between her drenched folds. She bucked at the glorious sensation.

"Fuck," he muttered. "You are wet." He slipped his finger inside her and pumped his cock a little faster. "Did Regan do this to you, baby? Did he get you this excited?"

She'd come too far to lie to him now. "Yes. Connor did this to me. His kiss...it made me hot." She lowered her eyes, then lifted them again. "He had an erection, Gabe. He was hard as a rock."

"Did you make him hard?" Gabe's voice sounded scratchy.

"Yes."

"Did he make you wet?"

She whimpered. Lord, thoughts of Connor's mouth, of his hard dick pressed against her belly, were still making her wet. And frustrated. She needed relief, needed something to take the ache and the want and the hunger away. "Very. Very, very wet."

His kiss had made her more than wet. It had made her,

quite unexpectedly, yearn for something permanent, something long lasting. Something more than just sex.

Gabe slipped another finger in, reminding her that, for now, sex would do just fine, thank you very much. Her slick entry offered no resistance and she rocked on his hand, desperate to get him deeper, to feel him move inside her.

"It's not just Connor, Gabe. I'm this wet because of you too, because you turn me on, you make me hot." Oh crap, did he ever make her hot. There might not be visions of wedding dresses and white picket fences with Gabe, but there sure were images of frenzied sex and wild orgasms. "Because I know you are about to fuck me, and I cannot wait. Not one more minute."

Gabe pulled his fingers out and plunged them back inside her. At the same time, he rubbed her clit with his thumb. He kept up the sensual assault as he got to his knees. "Be honest, baby. Be very honest now. Is it me you want to fuck—or Connor?"

Maddie was past even questioning her need to tell him the truth. Gabe's fingers had her so far beyond the point of sanity she was seconds away from coming. She answered without thinking. "Both of you, Gabe. I want you both to fuck me."

Gabe added pressure to his thumb. "Tell me more."

"Together. I want you to fuck me at the same time," she cried.

He pumped his fingers into her a little faster, shaking her senses.

"And separately. One of you inside me while the other watches." She hadn't even known she wanted this until she said it aloud, but now she knew it to be the truth.

Precome spilled onto the tip of his cock and she licked her lips. "Will it make you hot, baby, me watching, while Connor fucks you?"

She nodded on a long groan and eyed his dick.

"You want to suck my cock, baby?"

More liquid spilled out, coating his tip. Boy, did she ever. She loved the taste of him, the musky salt of his come. Loved the feel of him, the satiny smoothness of his skin stretched taught over his thick erection. "*Yes.*"

"While Connor fucks your pussy?"

"*Yesssss.*"

He plunged his fingers in a little deeper and pushed her over the edge. She came with thoughts of Gabe and Connor fucking her at the same time. And of them fucking her separately, one while the other watched, and she cried out as sharp blasts of delight tore through her.

Gabe pumped his dick a little harder, and even as the orgasmic shudders continued, Maddie shuffled backwards, leaned over, and dragged her tongue over the tip of his penis. She could not wait another second to taste him.

Connor stared out of the window, the light from the moon reflecting over the waters of Coogee Beach. He'd given her time to retreat, to gather her wits about her. Given her a chance to assimilate what their kiss had meant. He'd also used the last ten minutes to get his own head sorted out.

He'd intended for the kiss to be a greeting. An introduction to the world of Connor and Gabe. Instead it had been a crash course in losing his heart. The instant he'd tasted her sweet lips, licked her wet tongue, he'd fallen. Hard. Flirting with her over dinner was fun, provocative. Kissing her was life changing.

Connor rolled his eyes.

Whatever the hell that meant. He didn't want to ponder the workings of his heart right now. He wanted to find Gabe's girl.

I'm coming after you, Madeline Jones.

He walked towards Gabe's room.

I'm coming now.

Gabe was there, he knew. Not playing pool like he'd intimated. Anticipation tightened his stomach. Would Maddie invite him in—or slam the door in his face?

He paused outside the room, adjusted his shirt so it covered his aching dick and then opened the door. The sight that greeted him almost brought him to his knees. It would have sent any other man running, but Connor was not any other man.

Gabe knelt naked on the bed, his head thrown back, his mouth open. Crouched before him, on all fours, was Maddie.

Her face was nestled in Gabe's lap, her head bobbed up and down. Her clothes were scattered on the floor and her bare butt stuck up prettily in the air, facing him.

The scent of sex permeated the air.

Connor's tortured lungs searched for oxygen. Christ, hadn't he been able to breathe just a few seconds ago?

Maddie had a perfect backside. Her ass was round and plump. Not skinny or scrawny or muscular, but soft and inviting and feminine. Connor clenched his fists at his side, repressing the need to run his palms over all that womanly flesh. He drew in a shuddery mouthful of air, groaning in frustration when it did not reach his chest.

Gabe lifted his head at the sound and found Connor watching them. Their gazes met and held. Gabe hid nothing. His expression was open, intense, and Connor raised an eyebrow. Gabe smiled the smile of an alpha male. Dominant, triumphant and confident.

Connor returned his grin with equal conviction. Maddie seemed oblivious to his presence.

In a tender move, Gabe scooped up handfuls of Maddie's hair and bunched it on top of her head, giving Connor the tiniest glimpse of her lips wrapped around Gabe's dick. Fuck, he'd commit murder just to have that mouth on his cock.

"Is this what you want, baby?" Gabe asked Maddie. "Just you and me in the room together like this?"

Maddie muttered something unintelligible.

Gabe glanced at Connor. "Or would you prefer it if Connor stood behind you, watching as you sucked my cock?"

Her low moan reverberated straight through to Connor's spine. Maddie shifted then squeezed her legs together and moaned again.

"Thinking of Connor watching us makes you wet, baby." Gabe's eyes glinted. "Doesn't it?"

Maddie gasped. She shifted again and this time drew her legs apart, affording Connor a most enticing view. Hidden between the soft flesh of her thighs was her pussy. It was pink and pretty and puffy—and drenched. As he watched, a trickle of cream slid down her inner thigh.

Connor did not move an inch. Not one single inch. He stood

where he was, rooted to the ground.

Maddie released Gabe's cock with a wet pop. She lifted her head and looked up at Gabe. "Yes. It makes me wet." She licked his shaft, from the very bottom all the way up to the very top.

Gabe's jaw clenched and he swallowed.

She pulled back. "But not as wet as the thought of him watching me fuck you does." Another trickle of moisture down her thigh corroborated her words.

Connor leaned back hard against the wall. The soft thud echoed through his ears.

Gabe nodded and reached for a condom. "Do it, baby," he urged as he sheathed himself. "Fuck me while Connor watches."

Still on all fours, with her butt perched in the air, Maddie twisted her neck to look at Connor.

Holy fuck. She'd known he was there all along. He could see it in her eyes, in the sinuous way she looked at him, in her heavy-lidded gaze. She'd deliberately opened her legs, deliberately shown him what thoughts of him did to her.

Maddie ran her tongue over her lower lip, then drew the same lip into her mouth with her front teeth. Connor felt it in his dick, felt the scrape of her teeth over his tip and he bit his cheek hard.

The impulse to reach out to her was overwhelming. The need to crouch behind her and bury his face between her cheeks almost choked him. He checked his actions, forcing himself to relax against the wall instead. Maddie might be turned on by the idea of her and Gabe doing it while Connor watched, but she had nothing on him. He wanted to watch her fucking his friend almost as much as he wanted to slide his own dick into her slick, wet pussy.

Maddie turned away from Connor. She pushed herself onto her knees and gave Gabe her full attention, leaning forward to kiss him. As their mouths met Gabe drew his hands around Maddie's hips and then down over her butt, drawing her cheeks apart, offering Connor another look. Then Gabe slipped a finger inside her.

Maddie let out a strangled cry and Gabe slipped another finger in. Connor could not tear his gaze away. He watched as his friend drew his hand down then pushed it back up again, clearly saw his fingers disappear into Maddie's body.

Fuck, his jeans suddenly shrunk two sizes. Connor loosened the button and fly. He had no intention of touching himself, but if he continued like this, within the tight stricture of his pants, he'd lose the ability to ever perform again.

Gabe fucked Maddie with his fingers, while Maddie wrapped her arms around his neck and continued kissing him. Her juices streamed from her pussy down over Gabe's hand.

Shite, the woman was responsive. She threw herself into the act with no reserve. It didn't take long before Maddie gasped. Tremors wracked her body and Gabe's hand stilled—trapped, Connor imagined, in the tight clenching of Maddie's vagina. Then her head dropped to Gabe's shoulder and she sat panting, Gabe holding her weight.

He whispered into her ear, loud enough for Connor to hear. "Do it, baby. Now. While I watch Connor watching you as you come on my dick."

She nodded then and swiveled around languidly. Her face was flushed, her lips full and swollen. Her hair was a mess of tangled honey. Connor couldn't drag his gaze away.

He watched as she pushed up high on her knees and straddled Gabe's lap, her back to his chest. He watched as she reached down and grabbed Gabe's cock, positioning it just so. And he watched as gradually she lowered herself down onto him, her hips pushing lower, her pussy welcoming his cock, inch by slow inch until Gabe was buried deep, deep inside her.

"Oh, Christ," Gabe gasped. "Jesus, you are so fucking wet, baby. So slick. So hot."

Connor cursed under his breath. Was this the same woman who had sworn at him for putting her in this—what had she called it—untenable situation? Was this wanton, sexual being the same woman he'd kissed in the living room?

Damn straight it was. He'd known all along she would be like this. His instinct had told him she was ripe and ready for a lot more than just the old classic missionary position. What his gut hadn't told him was that he'd be ready for so much more. That watching her and Gabe would never be enough. That even joining them would not touch sides. His gut had not told him right from the start that with Maddie he would want everything.

Maddie caught his gaze and held it. Her pupils had dilated

in her hazel-green eyes, like tiny black pinpricks of desire. Without wavering, she rocked on Gabe who thrust back up to meet her. Then she did it again and again, and Gabe matched her at every turn.

Gabe placed his hands on her sides, framing her breasts for Connor. Connor nodded appreciatively, watching as they jiggled up and down in time with Maddie's movements. Her breasts were like the rest of her, full and plump and rosy. Her nipples were swollen and distended, and Christ, they looked good enough to eat.

"Look at his eyes, baby," Gabe said to her. "He can't take them off you."

Maddie watched Connor staring at her breasts. She gave him a shrewd smile, grabbed Gabe's hands and used them to cover his view. Gabe shaped his palms to the curve of her breasts and rolled her nipples between his fingers.

Maddie whimpered.

Connor thought about the queen. And his dog. And the pressing need to either accept the job offer or get back to the obscene amount of work piling up on his desk. None of it made a damn's worth of difference to his throbbing penis or his aching head. Fuck, she was Gabe's. He'd found her first. No, Gabe would not resent sharing her, but he wouldn't give her up. Not for Connor. He'd be a freaking lunatic to give up Maddie.

Gabe must have seen something in his expression because he raised an eyebrow.

He placed his mouth close to Maddie's ear. "If you won't share your breasts with Connor, at least give him something else to watch, baby. Something good."

The little witch. She actually had the audacity to smile again—and run her tongue over her upper lip.

"Keep your eyes open, Connor," she whispered. "You don't want to miss this."

Yeah, right. As if Connor had even considered that an option. Someone would have to stitch his eyelids together to prevent him from looking now.

Maddie lifted herself a little higher so that Gabe slipped out of her. She took his cock in one hand and stroked it against her pussy lips, over and over again. Then she dropped her other hand into her lap and rubbed her clit.

"Ahhh!" The sound escaped from Connor's mouth before he even realized he'd made it. Drops of precome leaked from his dick.

Maddie's eyes closed as a look of rapture crossed her face. She called out Gabe's name, arched her body and used his dick to manipulate her clit. Just like that a fresh set of shudders rocked her body.

Fu-uck. Connor thought he might lose it completely without even touching himself.

She kept on, first slapping Gabe's cock against her swollen nub, and then rubbing it there in tiny circles, coming all the while. Gabe grit his teeth. Strain showed on his face. He closed his eyes and grimaced.

When finally Maddie's hands stilled, and her head flopped forward, Gabe let out a fierce oath. He released her breasts and grabbed her hips, slamming her back down on his cock. Without giving her a chance to catch her breath, he began to fuck her, driving himself into her over and over again.

The blood left Connor's body and drained to his groin.

Maddie screamed, once, then twice and came again. It took Connor's oxygen-depleted brain several seconds to comprehend that she was screaming his name and not Gabe's.

Gabe gave one final mighty thrust, then froze. He roared as his body bucked upwards, straining into Maddie's. Connor beat his fist against the wall, desperate for the pain, for anything to dampen his own need for release.

Then Gabe collapsed backward. He pulled Maddie's still shuddering form down with him, exposing her pulsing pussy as it clamped repeatedly around Gabe's cock. He wrapped his arms around her and held her through the last few moments of her violent orgasm, until at last, Maddie lay shivering and panting on Gabe's chest, the pair of them sated and exhausted from their coupling.

Connor gave the wall one last mighty thump, turned around and limped from their room. Thank God he'd undone his jeans earlier, because time was not on his side. The second he was in his own room, he hauled his dick out of his pants and pumped it. Once, twice and he blew. Spurt after spurt of come shot up into his shirt and onto his stomach.

This time he'd provided his own relief.

Next time the onus would be on Maddie.

Chapter Four

Maddie wrapped the towel around her breasts and walked out of the bathroom. The water pressure had been lousy, leading to a very unsatisfying shower.

"Something worrying you?" Gabe lay naked on the bed, in the exact same position she'd left him in. On his back, with his arms spread wide and legs stretched in front of him. There was only one word to describe the look on his face. Replete.

She could have complained about the shower, blamed her unease on the water pressure, but that would be a lie. "It's Connor," she admitted. "The way he left the room. It isn't right." She'd watched him walk away as the last shudders of orgasm rippled through her body.

Maddie had never been more aroused. Watching Connor watching her and Gabe had been the single most erotic experience of her life. Yes, Gabe made her horny as hell, but Connor's presence had increased her arousal a million fold. Had intensified the encounter to a point where even Gabe's tiniest touch felt like a mini orgasm.

Connor had unbuttoned his jeans. She'd expected him to join them. Instead, as soon as Gabe had come, he'd walked away. Left them. In the middle of the most powerful sexual experience ever, Connor's departure had created a gaping hole in her fulfillment.

He'd watched, he'd lusted, he'd enjoyed and he'd slipped away. It wasn't right. The night was...incomplete. She was incomplete. She wanted more. *She wanted Connor.*

Gabe flipped onto his side, rested his head on his hand. "You would have preferred it if he'd stayed?"

Maddie began to lower her head then stopped herself. She'd just fucked Gabe—used his cock to masturbate herself—in front of his best friend. Awkwardness hardly had a place in their relationship anymore. She'd crossed that line less than thirty minutes ago. Instead she looked directly at Gabe and nodded. "I would have preferred it if he'd joined us."

Gabe said nothing, just gazed at her with a strange light in his eyes.

She walked over to the bed, sat on the edge next to him. "Does that make me a terrible person? Wanting him and wanting you at the same time?"

He trailed his free hand up her thigh. "No, baby. It makes you exciting. It makes you a sexy woman, with a healthy appetite for men."

Her pussy tightened. "Not any men. Only you...and Connor." She bit her lip. "You don't resent me for wanting him? For wanting both of you?"

He shifted, showing her his rapidly growing dick. "Does it look like I resent you?"

Her heart lurched and her confidence grew a notch. "You like the idea of him fucking me, don't you? You like it just as much as I do." Moisture gathered between her legs.

Gabe's eyes darkened. "Yeah, baby. I like it. A lot." He pulled himself closer to her and flicked her towel open. "I like what it does to you, and I like what it does to me." His finger found her drenched curls and slipped lower.

She moaned.

"He's watched me fucking you," he said, his gaze never wavering. "Now I want to watch him in action."

Maddie's chest stilled. Her breath caught in her throat.

He played with her clit, using her cream to moisten it. "Go to him, baby," he whispered. "Go and find him and tell him what you want."

Maddie nodded. Lack of air made her dizzy. Or was it his words? His permission to be with Connor? His finger drove her insane, bringing her blood to boiling point. "Only if you're sure you're okay with it." As much as he'd teased, encouraged, she would not do this without Gabe's absolute consent.

"I'm sure." He nodded in affirmation, then slid his finger

inside her. "But there is one thing you must understand. I am not okay with just standing back and watching. When Connor fucks you, I will be right there with you. With both of you. You going to be okay with that?"

Okay? The very thought made her weak. Her breath left her lungs in a whoosh. "More than okay," she whispered. "I...I can't wait." She couldn't. The Maddie sandwich was about to become a reality.

"Stand up," Gabe told her as he withdrew his finger.

She got to her feet as he rolled even closer, so her pussy was inches from his face.

"Go to him, Maddie." He leaned over and nuzzled her hip bone. "Go to him, and when he feels how aroused you are tell him it's because of him, and it's because of me." And then he buried his head between her legs and licked her. He burrowed his tongue between her wet folds and used it to fuck her.

Cream poured out of her, wetting his face, wetting her thighs. She called Gabe's name, called Connor's name, and Gabe pulled away. "Go now, baby, while I can still taste you in my mouth and you can still feel me on your lips."

"Wh...what about you?" she stammered. Good grief, Gabe had never stopped before he'd seen her through to orgasm. Her pussy throbbed, desperate for release.

He sat up and tucked her towel around her breasts. "I'm going to shower. I'll join you soon." With that he walked into the bathroom, closing the door behind him, leaving Maddie alone and aroused.

Connor had walked away and Gabe had walked away and she wanted them both.

There was only one thing to do.

Maddie stood outside Connor's room staring at his closed door. She should be nervous. She should be shaky, but she wasn't. She was needy, she was horny and she was hot as hell. Her pussy pulsed from Gabe's tongue, her breasts tightened at the memory of Connor's face as he eyed them. Her body hummed.

Not giving herself time to regret her actions, she tapped lightly on the door.

Eternity passed before she heard footsteps. The door opened.

Connor stood on the other side. Like her, he wore nothing but a towel. His was wrapped around his waist, leaving his upper torso bare. Water beaded on the whiskers on his chin, and dripped from his hair down his shoulder.

That would explain her crappy shower. She'd shared the water with Connor. Maddie's breath caught in her throat. Next time, perhaps they could share the shower.

The towel fit snug against his waist, showing off his chest and arms. Connor was built like a runner, slim and hard. The same height as Gabe, but smaller, by far. Weight training had fully developed Gabe's muscles, doubling their size at least. When Gabe moved, his muscle bulged. Connor on the other hand was all graceful lines and sleek angles.

He was lean and beautiful and for the first time, Maddie desired someone who did not dwarf her.

"Maddie."

She had to swallow before speaking. Saliva had filled her mouth at the sight of his almost naked body. Images of white picket fences and white dresses filled her head again. "You know earlier, when you asked me the puzzle, about meeting a woman who had a boyfriend?" Her hands were damp and she wiped them on her towel. "I think I might have given you the wrong answer."

He didn't say anything, just stared at her with his penetrating gaze.

"I was too quick to answer. You didn't give me enough information." Was it just her, or did the temperature climb at least twenty degrees?

He raised an eyebrow. "What else do you need to know?"

Lord, even his voice turned her on. Smooth as scotch, and low as a rumble. "You said the man met a woman who made him hard as a rock. My question is..." She hesitated, bit her lip. This wasn't so easy. "Is it just the woman who turns the man on, or is it the man's friend as well?"

Connor gave a snort of laugher. "You want to know if Gabe gives me a hard-on?"

Maddie stood a little straighter. Yes, she wanted to know. Two men and one woman was one thing, but she did not feel capable of dealing with three-way dynamics. "I'm a selfish woman, Connor. I like the idea of you and Gabe together." She liked the idea of Connor alone as well. Too much to give it further consideration in Gabe's home. "But, uh, well, not with each other. Only with me."

The amused glint in his piercing blue eyes vanished. "The only time Gabe gets me hard is when I watch him make love to another woman. A woman I want."

"Could it be any woman?" Was she interchangeable? Were Gabe and Connor specific about wanting her, or could she just have been one of many contenders for the position?

"Right now, Maddie, it could only be you."

Good answer, Maddie thought, but she needed to know more. "Have there been others? Other...Connor and Gabe sandwiches?"

Connor nodded slowly. "A few. Over the years."

She liked his openness, his willingness to share. "Have there been other...threesomes for you? I mean apart from Gabe."

This time he shook his head. "Gabe is the only person I trust enough to do this with. And if you ask him, he'll say the same about me."

That gave Maddie pause for thought. Why hadn't she asked Gabe? Why had she waited until she was alone with her boyfriend's friend before asking all of these questions? The answer eluded her, perhaps because Connor's towel slipped lower on his hips, showing how the line of hair that led down from his navel led to far more interesting bits. She struggled to pull her gaze away, to look him in the eye.

"And after everyone you've shared, Gabe's still your best friend?" Wasn't there ever any jealousy or competition? What if the woman wanted one man more than the other? Or one of the men wanted the woman more than the other? What if one, or both of them, fell in love?

"That depends. Did Gabe send you here, or did you sneak away from him after he fell asleep?"

His question was asked in jest, but still Maddie frowned. "I'd never sneak away from him, Connor. Gabe knows where I am. He sent me to you because he knew I wanted to come."

"Then yes." He smiled. "He's still my best friend."

Oh, Lord. That smile. Surely he must know how deadly it was? "Then I'd like to change my answer."

Connor went very still. "Go ahead, Maddie. A man desires a woman who happens to be his friend's girlfriend. Tell me—what happens next?"

Maddie stepped into Connor's room. Since he stood in the doorway, there wasn't much space to move except very close to Connor. "The woman goes first to her boyfriend's room, where she makes love to her boyfriend while the man watches." The blush returned. Heat filled her cheeks as she acknowledged her own brazenness. "It arouses her beyond anything she's ever experienced before, takes her to new heights of sexual awareness. But it's not enough."

They stood so near they almost touched. Almost, but Connor did not close the tiny gap between them. "It's not?" he asked, and she almost whimpered because his breath stirred her hair and warmed her cheek.

"No," she whispered. "Not by a long shot. At the exact moment the woman thinks the man is going to join them, he stuns her and leaves the room, leaving the woman...empty."

"She wanted the man to join them?" His voice was rough, and his breath drove her slowly mad.

"You know she did."

"So what happens next, Maddie?" He inched closer, close enough that the hair on his chest touched her towel.

The almost touch teased her, driving her nipples into hard peaks. "The woman goes to the man's room." She swallowed. "And she prays to God her boyfriend's best friend wants her as much as he says he does." Because, God help her, she wanted him. Perhaps more than she'd ever wanted her boyfriend.

"He does," Connor rasped. "Believe me, sweetheart, he does."

When his lips touched hers, she melted into him. His mouth seduced her, heated her, sucked her into his world. Again she had the overwhelming sensation that in Connor's arms she was home. He felt right, familiar, as if this was where she was supposed to be.

He was slimmer than Gabe. Wrapping her arms around his shoulders was much easier. She could reach his neck with both hands, wind her fingers through his long, wheaten locks. With

Gabe she had to content herself with holding his shoulders.

Connor drew his mouth away from hers, looked deep into her eyes and then groaned and kissed her again. And again. His kisses were long, intense, delicious. She wrapped herself around him like a kitten, winding her leg between his, twining her hand through his hair while the other stroked down his back. She couldn't get enough of holding him, touching him, kissing him.

With Gabe fireworks erupted when their lips met. With Connor the world slowed down, narrowed. All that existed were the two of them. Together. Kissing, touching, being. Connor.

He moved to close the door, but she stopped him. "Leave it. For Gabe."

Connor smiled. "For Gabe," he agreed and kissed her again.

Gabe would have lifted her, carried her to the bed and told her in no uncertain terms what he intended to do with her. Connor continued to seduce her with his mouth until she was a boneless heap in his arms. Then he pulled away to stare deep into her eyes again.

"Madeline." His voice was a gentle growl. "God, you're beautiful."

She saw the truth in the blue depth of his gaze. He believed it. He made her feel beautiful.

"You're everything a woman should be." He pressed soft, sweet kisses to her forehead and her eyelids. "Smart, funny, sexy." He tilted her face up to his. "Beautiful."

She kissed him before he finished speaking. His lips were fuller than Gabe's, his mouth hotter. While Gabe tasted of sex and musk and man, Connor tasted of, well of homemade apple pie, with cinnamon and ice cream. Okay, and he tasted like sex and like man as well—just not the same man as Gabe.

When Gabe kissed her she could barely wait for him to rip off her clothes. When Connor kissed her she was content to stay there in his arms, oh, for about the rest of her life or so.

With Gabe, the need to fuck him kicked in about three seconds after his lips touched hers. With Connor, desire seeped languidly through her bones, starting in her belly and rippling gradually outwards. His touch was no less lethal than Gabe's, it was just different.

When he unwrapped her towel so she stood naked in his

arms, he did not make wicked promises of what was to come, he simply adored her—with his mouth and with his words. Between drawing her heaving, sensitive nipples between his lips and dragging his tongue over the hardened peaks, he whispered of her beauty and her magnetism and her appeal.

As he feathered his lips across her shivery belly, he adored her in silence, choosing instead to cover every inch of flesh with butterfly kisses that both aroused and awakened. On his knees, he dropped his head lower, ceasing his tantalizing kisses as his mouth found her essence.

For several seconds he did nothing, simply knelt where he was, with his eyes closed, and breathed. He rested his forehead against her mound, and the warm air from his mouth blew lower, stirring the sensations between her legs.

"Connor, please..." Liquid heat gathered, slipped past her lips, trickled onto her thigh.

Connor shuddered. "Madeline. God, you smell like heaven." He inhaled. "So wet, so ready."

Maddie struggled to find words. She'd made a promise to Gabe, had to keep it. "Gabe," she said on a moan and realized immediately that had come out wrong, like she was moaning Gabe's name. The last thing she wanted was for Connor to think she'd confused the two of them.

She couldn't. Neither of them was the type of man you could confuse with another. "Gabe sent me here...wet. He told me to tell you...when you...you see how aroused I am, that both of you have done this to me." His hot breath burned her clit. "You and Gabe...you've both made me wet."

Connor groaned and touched the tip of his tongue to her engorged bud, licking it once. "Did Gabe do this to you, Madeline?" His breath was hot. "Did he lick you here?" The growth of his unshaven beard scraped her hip.

Her eyelids drooped. Lord, she couldn't keep them open. All the pleasure his tongue stirred made thought impossible. Blinking was out of the question. "Y...yes."

He drew his tongue over her again. "So I'm placing my mouth where Gabe's was only moments ago?"

"Y...yes." More liquid leaked from her. Gabe and Connor's mouths, right there, only minutes apart. Gabe's cheeks had been smooth, hairless against her thighs. Connor's whiskers abraded the sensitive flesh there. It was sinful. And decadent. And delicious. So very delicious. Even Connor moaned.

He kept his tongue relaxed, licked at her like she was an ice cream, building the mood, increasing the sensation, slowly bringing her to the brink. Gabe usually tensed his tongue, kept it focused, made her come within seconds. Now seconds passed, minutes, days. She lost track of time, her only conscious thought was the sweet ecstasy that Connor's tongue built in her as he drank his fill.

Her orgasm was inches away, sensation built, grew. Connor licked, sucked. He inhaled, moaned. "Connor, I'm going to…"

He withdrew his tongue. "No, Madeline." His voice was hoarse. "You're not."

Maddie cried out. God, so close. So, so close. "Connor, please," she begged.

He shifted back on his haunches and looked up at her, his blue eyes determined and filled with lust. Drops of her desire glistened on his half-beard. "Not yet, Madeline. Not without me." Then he raised his hand and drew his finger through her slick folds. "Not without Gabe."

She shook her head, desperate for relief. "You don't understand, Connor, please, I need…" She needed to come, needed to quell the maddening frustration.

"You will," he promised and slipped his finger between her lips. "In good time."

She clamped her inner muscles around his finger. God, it felt good there. Good, but not enough, not what she needed. Her clit throbbed, ached for fulfillment, and he would not give it.

"Please, Connor… Gabe… I need Gabe." He'd help her. He'd give her an orgasm. He liked watching her come. Liked making her climax several times before taking his own release.

Connor added another finger, pumping his digits in and out of her as she stood shaking. "Gabe will be here soon," he soothed.

"Not soon enough," she ground out. Christ, he was ruthless.

"Shhh. Relax, Maddie, enjoy." Three fingers now, and to her surprise, Maddie found she did enjoy. A lot. The ache in her clit receded gradually. Not altogether, but enough that she could relish the pleasure his skilled fingers provided.

Gabe would have gone straight for her G-spot, manipulated it until she writhed on his hand. Connor titillated, delighted, pleasured, but did not push. Again, sensation began to build, her pussy started to pulse. Slowly but surely, every nerve ending responded to the hand that caressed, cried out for more. She rode his fingers, pushing down hard on his hand. God, she was close. So close her legs trembled. She cried out.

Connor put his arm around her hips, held her upright and withdrew his hand

"*Connor.*" Her voice was a strangled plea.

"I told you, sweetheart. Not without me."

Fuck, she'd never been this close before, never been this deprived. Connor was dementing her. Driving her slowly insane.

"Not without Gabe." His fingers were between her legs, drawing her cream across her pussy lips and backwards.

"Gabe would let me come," she moaned. She felt physically bereft. Empty. Cheated. Desperate.

"Gabe will let you come," Connor assured her. "When he gets here." He played with the crease of her ass, wetting it with her juices. "We both will."

Sweet Lord, he wasn't going to go there too, was he? He wasn't going for a hat trick. He couldn't. He'd drawn her to the edge with his tongue, left her pussy stranded on the verge of surrender, and now he was tormenting her ass.

Ah, fuck. He was. A billion tingles shot down her legs as he found her bud, tickled, stroked. She couldn't stop herself, she wanted him to have better access. Lifting her leg, she draped it over his shoulder, steadying herself by grasping his other shoulder.

"That's it, sweetheart," he urged. "Open yourself up to me." As his finger, wet from her cream, probed and gained entry, his tongue darted out and tasted her clit again. It took no time before she felt the tension mount again, before a thunderous orgasm threatened to rip through her.

The shivers began deep in her ass and rippled outward into her pussy. Her clit ached and swelled. It was happening, starting, relief was a heartbeat away. Finally.

Connor closed his mouth and removed his finger.

"Nooooo."

"Yes."

"No. Fuck, Connor, no. Let me come," she howled. *"Please."*

He removed her leg from his shoulder, waited until he was sure she was balanced, and stood up. "You will come. I promise." Then he kissed her again.

She was horny, she was frustrated, she was hot, she was dripping and she wanted to come. She did not want to be kissed. She did not want Connor's lips on hers, she wanted them on her clit. She wanted his fingers in her pussy and in her ass and she wanted them there now.

So why did she melt into his arms again? Why did she plaster herself against his chest and hold onto him as though she would never let go? Why, if the only thing she could think about was finding relief, was she suddenly content to kiss him until tomorrow morning at least?

"What have you done to me, Connor?" she asked when they came up for air, when he looked at her with eyes filled with amazement. "You've taken me to the edge three times and I'm happy just to let you kiss me. Forever."

He shook his head. "I have no idea, sweetheart. But whatever it is, you're doing it to me too. Christ, I never want to stop kissing you."

"Then don't." Their lips met again. They clung, they kissed, they caressed.

Maddie ached for him. She wanted him, wanted everything. She'd ached for Gabe, but that was different. That was a physical pull, a hunger to mate, to fuck. With Connor it went deeper. The ache was a longing, a yearning for something more—not just sex.

Closer. She needed to be closer to him, needed for him to feel the same way she did. Needed for him to teeter on the edge, yet long for her kiss. How? What could she do? How could she make him ache for her the way she ached for him?

"More," she murmured into his mouth.

"Hmmm?" He toyed with her tongue.

"More." At least that's what she tried to say. It was impossible to speak clearly when she refused to pull her lips away from his.

She used sign language instead—or she used her hands at any rate, tearing Connor's towel off. His erection sprang free between them, poking into her belly. Finally, she had reason to break the kiss.

"My turn," she gasped and pulled away from him.

She could have started on his chest, like he had, nibbling happily on his nipples. She could have moved down to his stomach, become intimately acquainted with every muscle there. She could have, but she didn't. She chose instead to head straight for the heart of the matter, to bring him to the brink, to make him as achy and as needy as he had made her, and when she was done—and he had found no relief whatsoever—she would kiss him again. And again and again, and maybe not stop until tomorrow morning. Anything so she could show him just how much he had affected her.

Could he see the picket fence, the delightful cottage behind it?

Like Connor had done minutes ago, she dropped to her knees and took his cock in her hand. It was longer than Gabe's and thinner but no less impressive. It was also slightly curved. Maddie's mouth watered. She rested her head on Connor's stomach and inhaled deeply.

Lord, he smelled good. Like Gabe. Man and musk and sex. But there was something more. Something familiar. Home?

His dick lurched in her hand.

Maddie leaned forward and, placing her tongue beneath his balls, licked upward, laving first one testicle then the other, then started on his shaft, encompassing every last inch, from his base to his tip. By the time she withdrew her tongue, pearly beads glistened on the head of Connor's penis.

"Oh, Jesus... Maddie..."

She suspected Connor would have said more if she hadn't repeated her actions. This time she only stopped when she'd swallowed the tasty drops Connor had produced—for her.

Did he still feel it? The magic that crackled between them? The connection. It was there. As sure as she held him in her hand, it was there. She ducked lower, pushed his legs apart and licked the tender spot between his testicles and his ass.

Connor groaned her name.

With Gabe, she could never reach there. His thighs were

too wide, she had to stop at his balls. With Connor she kept on, licking and feeding, teasing with tiny dips of her tongue between his ass cheeks, but never going further.

Connor groaned and twisted.

Two could play at the same game. Just like he had brought her to the edge and stopped, she could torment him. She did. In one full, long sweep, she brought her tongue back up to the tip of his cock and swallowed down the new drops he'd left for her. Then slowly, slowly, she drew him between her lips, taking him inch by glorious inch until her mouth was full.

Apple pie and man. With cream on the side. If his mouth had been intoxicating, his dick tasted like paradise. Maddie lost herself to the fantasy that was Connor. She loved him with her mouth and with her hand, wrapping her fingers around his base, ensuring that all parts of him were taken care of. Using her other hand, she caressed his balls and the sweet area beneath them.

Pleasuring him was no less erotic, no less arousing then his teasing had been for her. Maddie's pussy hummed, yearned. Damn Connor. He might be able to withhold her pleasure, but he couldn't prevent her from touching herself.

She released his balls and lowered her hand until she found her pounding clit. Such was the level of her arousal, it almost hurt to touch it. She winced before sighing around his cock. It wouldn't take long. A little quick, focused circling, apply some pressure, and she'd have her orgasm.

"Don't." Connor's voice was strained. "Shite, Maddie, if you touch yourself, I won't be able to hold back." His dick twitched in her mouth. "Not...fair to...Gabe." He grabbed her head, stilled it, and reluctantly Maddie let her hand drop away. So much for self satisfaction.

He was right though. This was Gabe's pajama party too. Instead she focused on providing him with the sweetest head imaginable.

"Stop!" It wasn't an order but a plea, wrenched from somewhere deep in Connor's body. "Gabe... Not...fair," he panted and tugged on her hair, urging her up.

Maddie released him with a pop and rose to stand face to face. Her jaw tingled, her lips felt swollen.

"You...made your point." Connor's eyes were tiny slits, his

chest heaved. "Very effectively." And he kissed her.

This time when Maddie found home, there were no towels between them. There was nothing but Connor's naked flesh flush against hers, his damp cock pressing into her belly, his chest squashing her breasts. Maddie wondered if it were possible to climb into someone, to become part of him. She wanted him so bad she couldn't get close enough. She didn't just want his body, she wanted all of him—his soul, his affection, his love.

Raising her leg, she hooked her knee around his waist. God, she needed him to touch her pussy, to feed his long, hard dick into it. So much so, she could have wept.

"Where is he?" she cried out in frustration. "Where is Gabe?" She needed to come. She needed Gabe there, now, to take away the agony, the longing.

"I'm right behind you, baby." Even as he spoke, his hand found her back and stroked downwards, stopping at the top of her ass. He pressed his lips to her neck and sucked the skin there, hard enough to inflame and soft enough so he would not leave a mark.

As usual, a thousand fiery sparks exploded beneath his touch.

"Gabe," she wailed. "Oh, thank God, thank you." At last, he was here. Relief was minutes away.

"What's wrong, baby? Is Connor hurting you?" He sounded distracted, and she understood why when he pressed his mighty erection against her ass.

Holy mother of light. Connor was pressed against her front and Gabe her back. There were two hard dicks prodding at her, and she was dissolving in a puddle of man heaven.

"Not hurting me. No." Unless of course presenting her with toe-curling kisses was a new form of sadism. "But he's killing me, slowly."

"He is? How?" Gabe turned her head and kissed her mouth. His tongue took possession of her wits, her control.

Connor ran his hands over her breasts, tortured her nipples.

Maddie moaned as Gabe pulled away. "He won't let me come, Gabe," she complained. "I... I need to...I—"

Gabe's warmth against her back disappeared. There was a cold breeze, and then something nipped her buttock.

She yelped and Gabe soothed her with his tongue.

"I'll help you, Maddie. I'll make you come," he promised. "We both will."

She couldn't talk. He nibbled lower, and his tongue found the cleft of her ass. At the same time, Connor leaned forward and placed his open mouth on her aching nipple. Then he sucked lightly.

"Oh!"

Gabe pulled her cheeks apart, and his tongue delved deeper.

She gasped. He'd never done that before. It felt...it felt exquisite. Like thousands of tiny bubbles exploding around his tongue, light prickles of sensation spearing through her.

Connor scraped his teeth over the tight bud.

Red heat flooded through her. There was no pain, but Gabe's seduction from behind, and Connor's previous teasing had her hypersensitive to touch. Hypersensitive to everything, damn it. Even the tiniest sound was amplified.

Connor trailed tiny kisses up her neck until he reached her ear, then he nibbled her earlobe.

"Please," Maddie begged. "Please, I can't take any more. I need you to make love to me. Please. Connor."

He concentrated on her ear lobe.

"*Gabe*, please. Fuck me."

Gabe's warm tongue left her ass.

"What do you say, Regan? Should we put Maddie out of her misery?"

Misery? This was hardly misery. This was the most intense, profound experience she'd ever had.

"Put *me* out of my misery," Connor groaned. He pulled his mouth away from her ear. "Call it, Gabe."

Maddie yelped as something cool and wet touched her ass.

Gabe growled and ran his hand down her leg, the leg that still stood on the ground. "Hold on to her, just like this, buddy. You take her front, I'll bring up the rear." He caressed her buttocks, dipped his finger between them and Maddie began to tremble uncontrollably. "You ready, baby? You ready to take both of us?"

Ready? Hell, if Connor had been wearing a condom, she'd already have mounted him. "I am, Gabe. I want you, both of you. I want you inside me. *Now!*"

It was really happening. She was about to become the centre of a Maddie sandwich.

Connor kissed her lips. "Don't go anywhere." He pulled back and reached around her, taking something from Gabe.

Maddie waited as both he and Gabe sheathed their cocks. *Their cocks.* Not just Gabe's. Or Connor's. *Theirs.* Both of them. At the same.

Lord, she shook so bad she should have fallen, but desire was a potent drug. It kept her upright while her bones dissolved in her legs. Nothing would stop this moment from happening. Nothing. Her lover stood behind her, ready to take her like he had countless times before. And his best friend stood before her, as aroused and frustrated as she, hungry for the chance to finally become one with her.

She turned around to look at Gabe, check for reassurance. He pulled her head forward, pressing a hot, hard kiss to her lips. "Double penetration, baby," he whispered. "It's your thing."

"You...you still sure you don't mind sharing me?"

He took her hand, wrapped it around his rock hard cock. "You tell me."

Her voice eluded her, so she simply nodded. His body didn't lie. She'd never felt him this hard before.

Gabe's eyes were black, predatory. "You're going to turn around in a minute, baby, and you're going to wrap both your legs around Connor's waist, so he can fuck you while he's standing up." He used her hand to pump his cock. "Christ," he swore. "I can't wait to see his dick disappearing into your hot little pussy." His erection thickened in her palm. "When..." Gabe cleared his throat. "When Connor's inside you, and I'm so fucking horny I can hardly stand, I'm going to slide my dick into your ass." He looked over her shoulder at Connor, then back at her. "Believe me, baby. I don't mind sharing you. I want this. Real bad."

He kissed her again, his mouth setting off a firework display behind her eyelids, then he drew back and turned her to Connor.

His beautiful face was glazed with lust. "You'll get your orgasm, Maddie," Connor promised. "We all three will."

Liquid slid down her thighs and her knees shook so hard it was almost impossible to lift her leg. Almost, but she wanted Connor too damn much to ruin things over a little tremor. "Help me, Gabe," she begged.

He was there, behind her, hoisting her up so she could wrap her legs around Connor's waist and her arms around his neck.

Connor stared at her with desire-darkened blue eyes. "Kiss me, sweetheart. Kiss me and welcome me home."

How could she do otherwise? Her lips found his in a hot, moist kiss. As his tongue slid inside, Gabe's support dwindled and Connor took her full weight. Finally, finally, *finally*, she slid downwards, until her pussy lips touched his cock. She moaned into his mouth as he thrust upwards, and the interminable journey to reach this point came to an end.

Or was it a beginning?

Connor slid into her, fitting inside like a hand in a glove. She did not have to shift to accommodate his size, or shuffle for an easier entrance. With Connor it just worked. She held him tighter, kissed him more intimately and sighed with sheer bliss.

Home. At last.

His heart banged against her breast, his chest heaved against hers. Whatever she experienced, he felt it too. Their coming together was not as simple as a quick fuck. There was more to it. So much more.

"Connor," Gabe rasped behind her. "Fuck, mate, that is so hot. Whatever you're doing, keep doing it. She's on fire."

She was. Flames licked at her pussy, her ass, her breasts.

Connor kept on doing what he was doing. Kissing her like she was the most precious thing in the world, and making love to her like she was the sexiest woman he'd ever met. Blood pumped to her pussy, making her lips swell.

It wasn't enough. She wanted more. Wanted Gabe too. She wrenched her face away from Connor's. "Do it, Gabe," she demanded, pushing down on Connor's cock, and back, offering herself to Gabe as well. "Fuck me."

"You got it, baby. Hold her, Regan. Hold her tight."

177

Connor's arms tightened around her. And then Gabe was there, his groin beneath her butt, the head of his dick probing her ass.

This time there weren't bursts of a million tiny bubbles. This time there was just the utter desperation to get him inside. She bucked and pushed down again, making Connor groan. "Easy," he panted. "Gotta make this last."

"That's it, baby," Gabe urged. "Let me in." He pushed, and the tip of his penis penetrated her tight ring of muscle.

Maddie froze. *Fuck.* The burn. It stung like hell.

"You're okay, sweetheart," Connor whispered. "The pain'll pass. I promise."

Gabe pushed in a little further.

"No!" Christ, she couldn't do this.

He stopped dead.

Shit, that was even worse. "Don't stop. Not now." It might hurt, but she wanted him inside, wanted them both there.

Connor held her tight, then shocked her by withdrawing completely.

Maddie groaned in complaint, bereft.

"You know what to do," Connor told Gabe.

"I'm with you, mate," Gabe answered. He thrust once and filled her ass completely with his cock.

She froze again. Not because it hurt, but because it didn't. Gabe felt unbelievable there. Unbelievable. "Gabe," she whispered. "Sweet heaven...Gabe."

"I'm here, baby. I'm not going anywhere."

She shifted slightly, so Gabe could hold some of her weight, and a spark of pleasure shot through her. "Connor?"

"Maddie?"

"You too. Please. I need you too." How was it possible to feel full and empty at the same time? Connor's withdrawal worried her. She needed him back inside, needed to share herself with him. She needed to find home.

"I don't want to hurt you, sweetheart." Connor kissed her forehead, tenderly.

"You...won't," she muttered. Unless he decided not to see her through on this. Her heart contracted with sudden fear.

"Please. You promised."

Connor moaned.

Gabe pulled her thighs open a little more, giving Connor better access. "Do it, Regan," he panted. "For all of us."

And then Connor was there again, pressing into her.

She clung to him, moved back on Gabe, taking them both in at the same time. Was it possible? Could they fit?

There was no space. But there was. Connor's gentle but determined thrusts stretched her, filled her, slowly, exquisitely, until finally, he too was embedded deep within her. Full. She'd never felt so full. So snug.

Gabe muttered wordlessly.

For long seconds no one moved. They remained motionless, content to just be. She clung to Connor and burrowed her head into his neck. He held her thighs and her ass, while Gabe's hands circled her waist. They both filled her. Completely. She was now officially the centre of a Maddie sandwich. It was mind blowing. Profound.

It was magnificent.

She wriggled her butt.

Both men groaned. Then slowly, slowly Gabe withdrew. Just short of pulling out of her altogether, he pushed back in. At that exact moment, Connor took his cue and gradually withdrew. As Gabe pulled out again, Connor drove his cock back up. Slowly, gently, they fucked her, one thrusting in as the other pulled back.

It was like nothing she'd ever experienced before. She felt full. So very full. And good. There was not an inch of space inside her that was left untouched. Nerve endings she never knew existed danced as they awakened.

Maddie was wedged between Connor and Gabe, two men who took her breath away. Two men who aroused her to levels previously unexplored by humankind. This was the ultimate physical connection. They could not get closer, could not experience further intimacy. They were so entwined with one another, Maddie could no longer tell where she began and they ended, where Connor began, where Gabe ended. They were three, yet within her body, they were one.

Maddie almost wished she were not so aroused. Almost

wished the urgent need to come was not pounding on her insides. She wanted this to go on, to last forever. She wanted to be a part of this unique contact for always. To be three. To be one.

But dear God. Gabe was in her ass, and Connor was in her pussy, and they were plunging in and out of her. Her clit pulsed, so engorged that every time Connor's hair scraped against it, abrading it, she thought she might explode with desire. They had her covered, every angle, and she couldn't last.

Gabe thrust. His cock filled her ass, then withdrew. Connor plunged inside, burying himself in her, then stopped.

"Together?" His voice echoed in her ear.

"Together," Gabe agreed. One second later, both men were inside her, together. Connor in front, Gabe behind.

"Now?" Gabe asked.

Connor nodded. His head bobbed once against her ear.

Both men withdrew, and then together, as though the move had been choreographed, drove back into her.

Maddie screamed. Nothing had prepared her for this. Nothing. She'd thought it couldn't get better, fuller, but it had.

"Feel that?" Connor demanded

"Fuck, yeah," Gabe growled, and they fucked her again. And then again. "I feel it, mate."

She didn't need to ask what they were feeling. She knew. Wedged together, deep inside her body, with only a thin film of skin dividing them, they felt each other.

She couldn't hold back the flood gates. Didn't try. Knowing what they knew sent her toppling over the edge. There were no tiny tremors of satisfaction this time. Her orgasm was all consuming. It swept over her, knocking conscious thought from her mind. She bucked between Connor and Gabe, jostling wildly on their cocks. Waves of mindless bliss rocked her, sent her hurtling through space and time.

"Hold her. Tight," one of the men ordered.

The walls of her pussy and her ass clenched around their dicks, grasping them, holding, squeezing. Spasms of delight—of unrivaled pleasure—demanded, commanded.

Connor roared and pushed deeper, harder than before.

She couldn't take all the pleasure. Couldn't not. She

screamed and sobbed, tears poured from her eyes. She bit Connor's shoulder.

"Baby. Fuck—" Gabe was in so deep his balls touched her pussy lips.

God. They must have touched Connor's testicles too.

Her climax intensified, stretched out, encompassed first Gabe's wild release and then Connor's as well.

And when, at last, the blinding ecstasy of her orgasm subsided, and her legs had no strength to hold Connor's waist any longer, she collapsed, boneless against him.

Gabe was the first one to pull out of her. His withdrawal was equivalent to Chinese torture against the walls of her ass and she whimpered.

"Lean back, baby. I'll catch you."

With the last drop of energy she contained, she obeyed. Gabe caught her as Connor slipped out of her pussy. She cried out as violent tremors wracked her body again.

"I've got you, baby," Gabe told her, his voice a gruff whisper. "We both have."

Chapter Five

Maddie lay on Connor's bed. Her breathing had finally normalized and her body had relaxed almost to the point of slumber. Her limbs were heavy, sedate, as though she were asleep, but she wasn't. Her mind was far too active to allow her the oblivion of sleep.

Behind her, Gabe shifted and snored. His arm tightened reflexively, pulling her back flush against his chest. She cuddled into him, enjoying his warmth.

Connor smiled. "Never fails to amaze me how he can lose consciousness like that. My mind is buzzing. No way I could sleep now."

Maddie smiled back. They lay on their sides facing each other. "Same here. I have a million thoughts racing through my head."

Connor reached over and tenderly ran his thumb over her cheek. "Want to share them?"

She frowned. Could she voice her thoughts, her questions out loud? Sure, they'd just shared an intensely personal experience, but did that give her the right to probe into his life, his psyche? Did that give her the right to expose her own?

"I do," she admitted. "But I don't want to pry and anything I say now would be a question." Either that, or admit to the plethora of unexpected emotion twirling in her belly.

He smiled wryly. "It's a bit late to clam up on me, wouldn't you say?"

Oh, she'd say. "Okay, then, I'm curious," she confessed. "About you and Gabe."

"You want to know about our threesomes."

"Is it that obvious?" Were the rest of her thoughts that obvious?

"You've just had sex with both of us, Maddie, at the same time. I'm guessing it's a first for you. You know it's not for Gabe and me. You want to know more."

She nodded. "Do you mind?"

"That depends on the questions. Ask away. If I'm not comfortable answering I'll let you know."

She nodded. That was fair enough. "Mind if I start with the one that baffles me the most?"

"'Course not."

"See, I don't get how two men, best friends at that, could gain mutual satisfaction from one woman at the same time without wanting to kill each other in the process. Or compete for possession." Weren't men territorial by nature? Didn't they protect what was theirs—fiercely? "Do you and Gabe truly feel comfortable sharing one woman?"

Connor nodded. "We do. I know. It seems weird, but there are times, with the right woman, when sharing isn't just fun. It intensifies the pleasure dramatically." His voice deepened. "You noticed that, didn't you?"

She did. The experience had been so profound because it wasn't just her and Gabe. Connor's presence had increased the pleasure and the emotion exponentially. "Yes. Having both of you inside me at the same time...it was...powerful. In the extreme."

"For us too, sweetheart. But it's not just the sex itself. Watching you masturbate on Gabe's dick? Fuck Maddie, that was about the hottest thing I've ever seen."

The appreciation evident in Connor's face stopped any embarrassment his comment might have provoked. "But, it was Gabe's dick, not yours. Wouldn't you have preferred it if it were you? Uh, your dick?" Would she have preferred it?

His eyes gleamed. "I would have loved it if it was my dick," he said in a voice that sent a billion goose bumps scuttling over her skin. "But if you'd done that with me I wouldn't have been able to see a damn thing. The very act of watching you—Christ, it's making me hard just thinking about it."

"Down, boy," she teased. "I don't have the strength for anything more right now." Her joke was all bravado and brave front. Watching him watching her had not only made her belly lurch, It had made her heart flutter too.

"Know what? I don't think I do either." He grinned. "You wiped me out, Maddie." Then he added as though as an afterthought, "Me and Gabe both."

Somewhere between her legs something flickered. "You're distracting me," she chided. "I haven't finished asking my questions."

"Sorry. I'll behave," he promised.

The light in his eyes made Maddie wish he wouldn't. "How did it start? How did you know you'd enjoy a...ménage?"

"Physiology, my dear. Eighteen-year-old boys will enjoy anything, as long as it means they're going to get laid."

"Eighteen? You were that young?"

He grinned at her. "Oh, we were very mature for our age, I assure you. That, and we just wanted to get laid."

She shook her head in amusement. Connor made her laugh. "Was it your idea? The first time? Or Gabe's?"

"Actually it was the girl I was dating. Gabe and I shared a place after school, and the first time I brought her home, she made no bones about...wanting him as much as she wanted me. She initiated us."

Maddie frowned. "You were okay with that? Hell, if I brought home a date who wanted my best friend, I'd boot him out the front door."

He winked. "I got laid, Maddie. Of course I was okay with it. Look, I won't lie. The first time was awkward—for Gabe and for me. But then isn't any first teenage sexual experience awkward? Fortunately, Sally didn't mind the red faces and the clumsy groping. She hung around for a while, taught us well. After four months, there were no more inept moments."

"She certainly did a good job," Maddie agreed. "Neither of you fumbled at all," she praised him with a teasing smile.

"We aim to please," he smiled back.

Oh, Lord, and their aim had been perfect. She bit back a moan. Perfect. "How many..." Her voice stuck and she had to clear it. Connor was doing funny things to her insides, making her belly twist and her heart pound.

"Maddie?" Connor asked with his wicked smile. "Are you

getting turned on again?"

"No," she answered indignantly as moisture gathered between her legs.

Connor raised a knowing eyebrow.

"Okay, yes," she confessed. "But it doesn't mean anything. Like I said, I'm too tired to act on it."

His eyes turned a midnight blue. "You won't need to move a muscle, sweetheart." Connor shuffled a little closer, ran his hand down her side, and rested it below Gabe's arm, in the dip between her hip and her ribs. "Just lie back and I'll do all the work."

She stared at him, wordless. She could not possibly be considering this. Not after the evening she'd just had. Yet, the weight of Connor's hand, the heat that pulsed from it, straight through her flesh and into her bones, had her tingling all over.

"Lean into Gabe," Connor said, "let him take your weight."

"But...but it's not fair. He's sleeping." Her chest tightened. Gabe was unconscious, and she was aroused. Aroused and considering Connor's suggestion. Hell, she was aroused because of Connor. Gabe did not feature in the equation at all.

"If things get interesting, we'll wake him," Connor promised.

She didn't want to wake Gabe. "I can't handle interesting," she told him. Or was it both of them she couldn't handle? "I can barely spread my thighs I'm so tired." Maybe for Connor she'd make the effort.

"That's okay. I can't handle another erection. Not after what you did to me."

"Then...?" Was that disappointment echoing through her chest?

"My hand still functions, Maddie." To prove his point he slipped it down over her belly.

Her heart tripped. Liquid dripped between her legs. She looked into Connor's eyes.

He gazed back into hers.

Silence filled the air.

Her breath caught. It was all there, in his gaze. Everything she felt. "Connor—"

"Tuck your foot over Gabe's calf," he said, his voice lower, rougher than she'd heard it before.

Yep, probably better not to question what she'd seen in his eyes. She obeyed, leaving herself open to, and anticipating his exploration. When Connor's finger glided over her clit and around her slick folds a jolt went through her body.

Home, she thought.

"Home," he muttered and leaned in and kissed her.

Maddie dissolved.

Their lips clung, their tongues explored, their hearts banged in time, and when he pulled away, Connor's eyes glowed. "Home," he growled.

Maddie's eyes welled with tears. As intense as the night had been so far, this was perhaps the most intimate moment of all. "Home," she agreed, and for long minutes neither of them spoke.

Then Connor inhaled, exhaled, and inhaled again. "Was there something else you wanted to know? About me and Gabe?"

How did he do that? Seduce her, make her fall in love with him, and then pick up the thread of their conversation as if nothing life changing had just occurred? As if his hand was not delving between her legs, or his heart not stealing hers?

She could barely breathe, could barely focus on anything but the exquisite vibrations of his finger caressing her pussy, and his eyes adoring her face.

But damn it, if he could pretend the air did not stir between them, so could she. There were more questions, and she still wanted the answers, so she nodded and asked in a stilted voice, "How...m-many women have there been?"

His gaze searched hers. "Over the last twelve years? More than five. Less than ten."

"Oh, very specific, Regan." She tried for sarcasm, but the way she felt, the sensations Connor evoked in her, her words came out like a whisper.

He grinned and rubbed tiny circles around her clit. "You're number seven, Maddie."

Was it possible to trap his finger? To keep it right where it was for, oh, another week or so? Was it possible to trap Connor, to keep him with her, oh another lifetime or so? "Did you know about me? I mean before you got here?" She held her breath, nervous to hear the answer. Had Gabe prepared Connor, told him he'd found number seven? How did she feel about that?

"Gabe phoned me the day he met you. He knew right off you were...my type. He was right."

"So you came to Sydney expecting this?"

"Christ, no." He moved back to her pussy lips, caressing her lightly, but not pushing inside her. Thank heavens. After the double penetration, she wasn't sure she could endure anything more inside her right now. "I came to Sydney wondering what to do with my life. You were an added bonus." He frowned, touched his lips to hers, drew her breath away. "Gabe and I might enjoy the same woman every now and again. That doesn't mean we take every relationship for granted, or assume every woman will want to be shared. It also doesn't mean I want to sleep with every woman Gabe dates, or vice versa." His eyes took on an odd gleam, and his finger seduced, caressed. "You were different, Madeline. The first time I saw you I knew Gabe was right. I liked you. Very much." He closed his eyes. "Perhaps more than Gabe bargained on."

Maddie's heart leapt into her throat. "I like you too, Connor."

He smiled, kept his eyes closed. "You have to say that. Your next orgasm depends on it." He drew his finger backwards, found the bud between her ass cheeks and stroked it.

She gasped. "No. I don't. I said it because I mean it, not because you have your hand between my legs."

"I like having my hand between your legs," he said softly and opened his eyes to look into hers again.

"I like having your hand there too." She shuddered. "Perhaps more than I'd bargained on."

He kissed her. Small, gentle kisses on her mouth. Using similar small, gentle strokes, he moved his finger from her ass, over her pussy lips and to her clit, then back again. Over and over he did it. Kissed her and stroked her. Never demanding, just giving and giving.

Her orgasm started slowly, building up at the same speed as he moved his finger. It did not explode inside her. It simply, gently overwhelmed her, sending sweet tingles flowing through every nerve cell she possessed. For an eternity it continued, with Connor's warm mouth just the right complement.

She sighed against his lips, melted into the mattress and just felt. And when it was over, and Connor withdrew his finger, it took several moments before she floated back to him. Several moments before she could focus on his face. His beautiful, precious face.

"Thank you," she whispered.

"My pleasure," he whispered back.

Gabe snored behind her, startling her. She'd forgotten he was even there. She'd lost herself in Connor.

"Connor?"

"Hmmm?"

"What happens if one of you falls for the woman you're sharing?"

Connor sighed and collapsed onto his back. He put his arm over his eyes. "Hasn't happened," he said vaguely.

"Never?" she wondered out loud. "You've never fallen in love with a woman Gabe's introduced you to? Or vice versa." What was she asking? Why was she asking?

He was silent for a long time.

"Connor?" She reached over and touched his hand, needing to renew their contact. He jerked away.

Sharp arrows of hurt shot through her. Had Connor just rejected her? After what they'd shared? As profound as the threesome had been, what Connor had just given her was perhaps the most intimate, most personal experience of her life. He'd felt it too. She knew he had.

She burrowed into Gabe, took comfort in his solid form. Or tried to anyway. It didn't help. She did not find the reassurance she sought. Gabe was not the one she needed the reassurance from.

"We have boundaries," Connor said in a strained voice. "Limits. I don't fall for Gabe's women, and he doesn't fall for mine."

His answer emitted a cool chill down her spine. "Ever?" Oh, dear, her question came out more as a plea.

"There are rules, Madeline." He sighed. "If Gabe and I want to remain friends we have to follow them."

"What about the woman involved? What if she doesn't know

the rules—and falls for the man who isn't her boyfriend?" Even as she said it, she knew why she'd asked. She was guilty of that exact offence. She'd fallen for the wrong man. She'd fallen in love with Connor.

Connor's hand clenched into a fist. He tensed visibly. "We still honor the rules."

"Connor—"

"Enough, Maddie. No more questions." He withdrew completely. He rolled over, onto his other side, and then sat up, with his legs over the edge of the bed.

The empty space where he no longer lay was cold, vast. "Connor, I'm sorry. I shouldn't have..." Shouldn't have what? Asked the question, or fallen for her boyfriend's friend?

"I need a drink." He stood up and strode to the door.

"Connor... Please. Don't leave." *Not now. Not ever.*

"Go to sleep, Madeline. Curl up in Gabe's arms and go to sleep. After tonight I'm sure you need the rest."

And with that he walked out the room, closing the door behind him with a resounding click, leaving Maddie gaping in his wake.

♋

Connor kicked the fridge door shut. He slammed the bottle of water on the counter and reached for a glass. Then he banged the cupboard door shut.

Fuck. Fuck, fuck, fuck.

The drink didn't help his agitation. He'd fucked up royally.

He marched into the lounge room and turned on the telly.

Fucking moron, that's what he was.

Incomprehensible scenes flashed on the screen in front of his eyes as he flicked through the channels.

Why hadn't he stopped this? He'd known, as soon as Maddie kissed him, that she wasn't like the others. She was different. Why'd he go through with it? He should have told Gabe right from the start this wouldn't work. That sharing Maddie would fuck with his head.

One kiss. That's all it had taken, and he'd—what was the

word Maddie had used?—fallen for her. Hard. Toppled off a sheer cliff and plummeted down thousands of meters.

As if his life wasn't fucked up enough. He didn't know where he wanted to live, didn't have a clue what job to choose, his future lay before him with not even the slightest hint of direction and now he'd gone and fallen for Gabe's girl.

He'd broken the rules. He'd pushed past the boundaries, and in doing so, he'd betrayed his best friend. He'd fallen in love with Madeline Jones.

Agitated and irritated, Connor threw open the balcony doors. He stood outside watching the moon vanish behind a cloud. Cold wind stirred his hair. Gabe's girl. Not his.

So why, *why* if she was so obviously the wrong woman for him, had the restlessness that had plagued him for months disappeared the instant her lips touched his?

Chapter Six

Dawn could not come fast enough. Maddie had to go, had to get out of Gabe's flat. She couldn't stay there any longer. She felt trapped in his arms, claustrophobic.

Connor had not returned to his bed. He'd left it to Maddie and Gabe.

The moonlight that filtered through the blinds flickered and vanished as she gently shook his shoulder.

Gabe's eyes opened slowly, but the minute he saw her, he smiled. "Hey, baby."

She bit her lip. "Hey, Gabe."

He yawned and stretched, pulling his massive arms high over his head. "Where's Regan?"'

"I...I'm not sure." Damn, he'd left her and it hurt. "He went to get a drink." Over an hour ago.

Gabe looked at her. "You all right? Feeling a little tender? You took quite a...pounding."

Oh, she felt tender all right, but it had nothing to do with the pounding she'd taken. "I'm fine," she reassured him and watched as his face broke into a smile.

"Ready for another round then?" He waggled his eyebrows suggestively.

Maddie burst into tears.

Gabe was up and holding her before she'd drawn her next breath. "Baby, what is it? What's wrong?"

She shook her head helplessly. "I'm sorry," she sobbed. "I...I can't do this. I don't want another round." Only she did, and that was the reason she was crying. She wanted another round—just not with Gabe.

"Jesus, Maddie, did we hurt you?" His voice filled with horror, and affection for him welled in her chest. It didn't stop her crying though. If anything, it made the tears come harder. She didn't want to feel affection for him. She wanted to love him—not Connor. That was the way it was supposed to go. You were supposed to fall in love with your boyfriend, not with his best friend.

She shook her head.

"Did we push you too hard? Make you do things you didn't want to do?"

"No, Gabe. No. It's nothing like that, I swear." She sniffed and wiped her eyes. "It was...amazing. Really, truly amazing."

"Then what's the problem? Tell me, so I can make it right." He held her like a baby, like she might break in his arms if he squeezed too tight.

How could she tell him there was no way he could make it right? Her problem wasn't his to fix. If anything, it would only complicate matters for him.

Tears streamed down her cheeks. "Gabe, you were perfect. Incredible. Thank you. For showing me what it's like."

He rubbed her back. "You know it was my pleasure. Mine and Connor's."

Her heart constricted at his name. "I'm sorry, Gabe, I have to go."

"Go where?"

"Home."

"You're leaving? Now? It's two in the morning." He sounded perplexed.

"I can't be here anymore. I...I can't see you anymore."

Gabe pulled away to stare at her incredulously. "You what?"

"I'm so sorry. You are wonderful. This was wonderful. But it changed things. It changed everything." For a brief second she wished she and Gabe and Connor could have something more permanent than one night of passion, but she dismissed the idea instantly. While the sex had been mind blowing, it was not something she would want to repeat. Maddie was a one-man woman. Yes, double penetration aroused her beyond decency, but two men and one woman on an ongoing basis did not appeal to her.

She was too conventional. She wanted marriage and children and the whole bangshoot. With two men the dynamics would be too complicated, too complex to even consider such a future. With one man the possibilities were endless. With Connor she could picture the whole bangshoot. But Connor was the one man she could not have.

Connor would not break his rules for her, and she could never hurt Gabe by messing with his and Connor's friendship.

"Maddie." Gabe gave an exasperated sigh. "You're talking in riddles. Just tell me what the problem is so we can set it straight. We've just started something, something good. Don't throw it away now. Tell me what's bothering you."

How could she possibly admit the truth without hurting him? She'd fallen for her boyfriend's best friend.

She grimaced and told Gabe as much of the truth as she could. "I'm a conformist, Gabe. I work within the guidelines. Threesomes with two men, no matter how beautiful and how wonderful the men both are, simply do not conform to my standards. I can't do it again, I don't want to." She dragged air into her lungs. "If I continued seeing you, it would be with the knowledge that every time we slept together I'd be desiring Connor too. I'd be betraying you whenever we had sex, and I can't live like that."

Gabe frowned. "You don't need to betray me, Maddie. I want you to want Connor too. I want you to desire him. Didn't I make that clear?"

"Oh, you did. And while we all made love I did not feel disloyal." Well, not until she realized she'd fallen for Connor. "But as I said, I cannot live with, or love, two men. Nor can I be with one and desire another. It won't work. Tonight changed our circumstances. It changed me." Or maybe it clarified things for her. Now she knew what she wanted—one man to be with her for always. Just one. To live with, to love, to start a family with. But that man was not Gabe.

Gabe narrowed his eyes, searched her face. "That's not all, is it?"

Shit. Did he know? Had he sensed she'd developed feelings for Connor? "What do you mean?"

"I don't know. You're keeping something from me, not telling me the full truth." He shook his head. "What is it, Maddie? What are you hiding?"

Again, she couldn't deny him the truth, but she wouldn't hurt him with the extent of it either. "It's me, Gabe. And you. I...I... As much as I wish I were, I am not in love with you."

"Love?" Gabe sounded as taken aback as he looked. "Who said anything about love?"

Maddie floundered. Dang, of course he wasn't in love with her. Who had ever mentioned love in this twosome? It was only when Connor entered the picture that she'd started thinking in terms of the L word.

"Baby, don't misunderstand me. I think you are beautiful. And I love spending time with you. I love sleeping with you." He grinned impishly. "Sex with you is freakishly good. Good enough that I want to carry on sleeping with you for a very long time. But I'm not in love with you either. Not yet anyway. We need time to see if what we have could develop into something more permanent."

Relief washed through her, strong, but not strong enough to alleviate her guilt. "It won't. That's what I'm trying to explain." She sniffed and dried her tears with the back of her hand. "I started dating you because you turned me on something silly, and I couldn't get enough of your body."

He smiled at her. "Yeah? Well that makes two of us."

She sniffed again and smiled back. "When you're that fiercely attracted to someone, you want to know if it has potential to go any further."

"We've only just started exploring that potential."

She shook her head. "No, Gabe. I can't do it anymore. What we just shared? You, me and Connor? That was too big for me. Too huge to do when I'm not in love with someone." Only she was in love. Just not with Gabe.

Gabe looked at her, frowned sadly. "You want to be in love."

She nodded. "I do, Gabe."

He nodded back. "Just not with me."

"You're not in love with me either."

"Yeah, but I still want to sleep with you," he said with a cheeky smile.

She returned his smile with a half-hearted one of her own. "I'm sorry, Gabe. I can't do this anymore."

"Yeah, baby. I'm sorry too." He held her in his arms.

She pressed a kiss to his lips. This time there were no fireworks.

"G'bye, Gabe. Thanks for showing me the time of my life."

"You're welcome, baby," he said as he pulled away for the last time. "You are very welcome."

Maddie dressed quickly. She hesitated as she made her way to the front door. Connor stood alone on the balcony. Even from this distance she could see the tension in his back, in the way the muscles pulled taught around his shoulders.

He'd felt it too. She knew he had.

"I fell for you, Connor," she whispered, knowing he could not hear her. "I didn't mean to, but I did." Iron fists squeezed at her heart. "I found home in your arms." Her voice caught in her throat. She couldn't talk. Instead she brought her hands to her lips and blew him a kiss. One last kiss goodbye.

Then she slipped out of Gabe's flat and closed the door behind her.

Chapter Seven

"I'm going back to Melbourne," Connor told Gabe at breakfast. His eyes were gritty from lack of sleep and he blinked several times trying to clear them.

Gabe poured a cup of coffee and sat down opposite him at the kitchen table. "I thought you liked the company and the job offer they made. Thought you were going to accept it."

Connor inhaled, surreptitiously sniffing the air, searching for Maddie's lingering scent. The only thing he got was a whiff of Gabe's spicy aftershave. "Yeah. I considered it, but Melbourne's my home. Pointless leaving when I've made a decent life for myself there."

Wrong. It was pointless staying in Sydney when Maddie lived here. There was no chance he'd be able to live in the same city and keep his hands off her. And there was no possibility he would share her again. Nope. If Connor ever got his hands on Madeline Jones, it would be with the understanding that he would be the only man ever to touch her intimately again.

Zero chance of that happening since Maddie was Gabe's girl.

"Mate," Gabe said, "you told me something was missing. Told me you needed a change. How much of a change are you going to get remaining in your old, stagnant life?"

He shrugged with a nonchalance he did not feel. "So what should I do? Come here and share your life with you? Share your girlfriend?" Connor shook his head. "I'm too old for this shite, Gabe. I can't do it anymore. I want to find a woman of my own, possibly settle down. I can do that just as easily in Melbourne as I can here." Except for the tiny fact that the woman he'd pick to be his own was in Sydney—and totally off limits.

"That's what your midlife crisis has been about? A woman? It's got nothing to do with your job or the city you live in?"

Connor bristled. "I'm thirty, pal. This is hardly a midlife crisis."

Gabe grinned at him. "You want to find a wife and make babies, don't ya?"

He squared his shoulders, ready for a fight. So what if he did? Then he loosened up and relaxed. Gabe was just taking the piss. It was nothing he wouldn't do if the situation were reversed. "Yeah, so what of it?"

"So nothing of it. That's cool, mate. I'm happy for you."

"Yeah?" Connor looked at Gabe, surprised. He'd expected a shiteload of teasing and mockery. He hadn't got it. "Well, hold back your tears of joy. I don't even have a woman." *You have her.*

Gabe frowned. "That makes two of us."

What the fuck? "You have a prime lady upstairs, Carter. You have perfection." *Easy, Connor. Don't say another word or he'll figure out exactly what you think about his lady upstairs.*

Gabe sighed. "Perfection walked out on me in the middle of the night."

"Pardon?" Connor sat up straight.

"She dumped me. On my ass. Said something about not being in love, and about last night being too intense and she left."

"You're kidding?" Christ, Maddie had ended things with Gabe. Right after their conversation.

"Wish I was."

"She's not in love with you?" Dear God, she didn't love his friend.

"Nope?"

What about Gabe? How did he feel? "You in love with her?" Connor held his breath.

"Nope. But I like her. A lot. And she's a goddess in bed."

Holy crap. Maddie and Gabe were over. Connor let the news sink in. "I'm sorry, mate," he said at last. "You lost a good one there." He was sorry, in a fucked up kind of a way. He wanted

Maddie and Gabe to be happy—even if he couldn't be. Yet he couldn't deny that a selfish part of him sagged in relief.

"Yep, I'm sorry too." Gabe shrugged. "Shit happens."

Man, did it ever.

"Carter?"

"Yeah?"

"You ever been in love with one of our women?" Aw, shite. He was heading into no man's land. He should just shut the hell up.

Gabe regarded him with brooding eyes. "Nah, mate. I'm a possessive guy. I couldn't share a woman I loved with you. I'd be forced to kill you afterwards."

Connor chuckled but called his friend on his answer. "You're lying."

Gabe sighed. "Okay. I liked Tina. More than I should have." He held his hands up in surrender. "But she was yours first. And rules are rules."

Tina. Connor had dug her. A lot. But he'd never been in love with her. In retrospect, if Gabe had laid sole claim to her, Connor wouldn't have been overly put out. Sure, his male pride would have taken a beating, but it wouldn't have been too bad in the long run. Tina and Gabe would have made a good couple.

"Tossing the question back at you, mate," Gabe said. "Ever fallen for one of our women?"

Connor stared into his mug, contemplating his drink.

"Regan?"

He walked over to the sink and tossed out the dregs of his coffee. What could he say?

"Fuck me! You have, haven't you?" Gabe asked. "You knew about Tina. How come I don't know about...?" His voice drifted off. "Who don't I know about?"

No way out now. He should never have started this conversation. What was he thinking anyway opening his big mouth like that?

"Sally? Megan? Pammy?" Gabe thought loud. "No, no, no." He ticked each one off. "Tina? We know that one. Justine? Nah. Too quiet for you. Desi? Uh uh. Too thin. You kept trying to force feed her and she kept refusing."

Then there was silence.

Long, taut silence.

A kitchen chair scraped against the floor. Footsteps. The fridge opened then closed.

The silence stretched out.

Connor stared out the window, thought about Maddie. Thought about Gabe.

"Fuck you, Regan." Gabe's voice was frozen.

How could he answer? Gabe had a right to be pissed.

"What did you say to her? What did you do while I slept?"

Connor turned to face his friend, accept his anger. "Nothing you wouldn't have said or done." It was true. Sharing a woman did not mean they shared her every time. There were occasions when only one of them was involved. It was okay, a part of their understanding. "She asked questions about us, I answered. Things got a little hot, I cooled her down. Nothing you wouldn't have done."

"I didn't fall in love with her," Gabe pointed out, his voice still bitter.

"I did," Connor said with a calm he did not feel, but it was useless denying the truth now that it was out in the open. "I didn't mean for it to happen. Soon as I realized, I walked away." He lifted his hands in surrender, like Gabe had done. "Rules are rules, mate. She was yours first so I walked away."

"So did she. Is that supposed to make me feel better?"

Guilt stabbed at Connor's gut. "I fucked up, mate. I fell for your woman." He shook his head in defeat. "I'm sorry. You know I never intended for it to happen."

Gabe didn't answer, just regarded him with cold eyes.

"There's a plane at twelve-thirty." Connor said. "I'll be on it."

"You running away from this, you dipshit?"

He nodded and walked to the door. The option was to stay and fight—but that would fuck up their friendship altogether. The way things stood, if Connor got out of Gabe's way now, they might be able to salvage something. Hell, they'd survived Tina, they could get through Maddie. "Yeah, mate. I'm running away. But you're not. Go after her. Make it right. You like her, she likes you. Go and set things straight." Connor walked slowly to his bedroom to pack.

"You know what?" Gabe called after him. "You're right. It's about time matters were set straight. I'm going after her, Regan. Deal with it."

♋

The insistent banging on her door did not cease. Hard as Maddie tried to ignore it, whoever was out there did not plan on leaving anytime soon.

She couldn't face anyone. She looked like hell and she felt worse. Her eyes were all red and swollen and her nose still ran even though the tears had stopped about an hour ago. Besides, she wasn't exactly in the mood for company. Couldn't a girl just be by herself? Wallow alone in self pity while she lamented the love that would never be?

Maddie pulled a pillow over her ears, determined to outlast her persistent visitor.

That's when the doorbell buzzed. And buzzed and buzzed and buzzed.

Damn it. Old Mr. Finton from next door would never let her live it down. He'd already lectured her endlessly about the earsplitting ring. If he was home now he'd probably organize to have her kicked out the building.

She threw off the pillow and climbed reluctantly off her bed. Fine. She'd let whoever it was in, but she wouldn't be happy about it.

"Okay, already," she griped at the door. It had to be Julia. No one else had the audacity to ring her bell more than once. "I'm coming. Don't get your—! *Gabe?*" The last person on earth she'd expected to see. "Wh...what are you doing here?" Okay, it was rude to ask, but his arrival had knocked her for a six.

"I need to speak to you." He pushed past her and walked into her flat.

"About what?"

"About us. And Connor."

Maddie's heart sank. She was too exhausted and too emotionally fragile to deny him the truth. If Gabe pressed her on their relationship she'd surely blurt out her real reason for calling things off. She'd tell him how, without expecting to, she'd tumbled and fallen for his friend.

"Don't do this, Gabe. Please. Don't do this." Perhaps if she prevented any kind of conversation from taking place she could avoid hurting him with the truth. "It's over. It has to be."

Gabe turned to her. "Connor and I have rules," he blurted out. "A policy we established years ago, when we realized how tricky threesomes could get."

Okay. So much for stopping the conversation. Maddie gathered her composure together. She'd handle this like a lady, and not like a complete moron. "I...I know about the rules." Connor had told her—right after she'd realized she was in love with him.

Gabe gave a sharp nod. "Good. Then you know the rules are simple. Only the man who meets the woman first gets to fall in love with her. She is off limits to the other guy. He is simply there for the ride, for the pleasure. Nothing else."

Maddie stared at him, confounded. Did he know? Had he guessed how she felt? "Yes. C...Connor told me that bit also."

"Did he tell you the rules had been broken?"

Oh, Lord. He must know. Why else would he be here? Her head grappled for logic, for reason. Had she broken the rules? Technically, she wasn't sure. She had fallen for Connor, not the other way around. Weren't the rules there for the men—and not for the women they slept with?

Did it matter?

Her heart began to pound. "Gabe, please, I didn't know—"

"It was me. I broke the rules."

"What?" She was lost, had no idea what Gabe was talking about.

"Four years ago. Connor introduced me to his lady friend. Tina." He grimaced. "I broke the rules, Maddie. I fell in love with her. I fell hard, harder than I'd ever fallen for anyone."

Maddie stared at him, stunned. Of all the things she'd expected Gabe to say, this was not one of them. Her instincts about threesomes, on the other hand, had been spot on. There *was* no way two men could share a woman and not struggle for possession.

"I tried to pretend nothing had changed. God help me, I tried. Even carried on sleeping with her while she slept with

Connor. But you know what?" His eyes were dark with memory.

She shook her head, agog.

"I couldn't do it. Every time Connor touched her I wanted to kill him." His hand curled into a fist at his side. "I stopped seeing her, stopped joining them. It was either that, or beat the crap out of Connor while he fucked the woman I loved."

"Gabe," she breathed. "I had no idea." But she did have an inkling of his pain. Simply hearing about Connor with another woman had a crushing effect on her ribs.

"Connor figured it out. A couple of days later he stopped seeing her too. Never said a word about it, mind you, just quietly called things off. We never discussed it, never argued about it, we just moved on—without Tina."

The pain on his face was raw, as if all of this had taken place yesterday. "You still love her, don't you?" she asked.

"Never stopped," he answered in a strained voice. "Not a day goes by when I don't think about her."

Aw, heck. Would a day go by when she did not think about Connor? About what could have been? "Gabe—"

He cut her off before she could tell him how sorry she was. "He loves you."

"Pardon?" Someone must just have smacked her over the head with a concrete slab. Either that or she was having auditory hallucinations.

"Connor. He loves you. Don't know when it happened or how, but there you have it."

"Why..." She swallowed, finding it suddenly impossible to talk. Her heart took up too much space in her mouth. "Why are you here? Why are you telling me this?" Had he honestly just said Connor loved her? Did Connor love her? Did he?

"I lost the woman I love. Doesn't mean Connor has to endure the same fate." He sighed. "His flight leaves in just over two hours, Maddie. If you feel the same way he does about you, you'd better get to him, quickly. Coogee is a much shorter drive from your place than Melbourne is."

Maddie collapsed into the chair behind her, overwhelmed. For now she had to put her thoughts about Connor aside and focus on Gabe. "You know how I feel about him?" She'd tried her best to avoid him finding out, to avoid hurting him.

Obviously her best had not been good enough.

"I figured it out. You ended things with us after making love to Connor. It doesn't take a genius to work out that you fell just as hard as he did."

She nodded. It was impossible to lie to him. With Gabe she always ended up telling the truth. "I did." She felt awful. "I'm sorry, Gabe. I wish it could have been you. Especially under the circumstances."

"I'm not. I don't love you either, Maddie."

"You still love Tina."

He nodded.

"What are you going to do?" she asked.

"The same thing you are. I'm going to find the person I love and tell her how I feel."

♋

Connor heard the key in the door, and his spine stiffened. He eyed his bags warily. Maybe he shouldn't have waited. Maybe he should just have gotten his ass to the airport before Gabe arrived home.

No, damn it. He was bigger than that. He'd screwed up, but he wouldn't flee with his tail between his legs. He'd face his friend like a man, shake his hand and wish him luck for his future with Maddie.

Lucky bastard.

"So," he called out as the door opened and then closed. "Did you do it? Did you set her straight?" He didn't get up from his position on the couch immediately. First he had to steel himself, prepare himself mentally for Gabe's imminent news that he'd won Maddie back over.

Keys clunked on the table behind him. "Yeah, Connor. Gabe set me straight."

Jesus, fuck. Connor leapt off the sofa and spun around.

"Maddie?" Christ, she was beautiful. Her very presence sucked the air from his lungs.

"Hello, Connor." Her face was a blank mask, controlled. It gave away nothing of her thoughts.

Gabe's girl, he told himself and nodded a greeting. Daggers of pain knifed through his gut. Gabe's girl.

Damn it. He hadn't counted on this, hadn't expected to see her before he left. Why was she here anyway? Had Gabe brought her back to brag, to add insult to injury?

No way. He couldn't believe that of his friend.

He glanced over her shoulder—a difficult task since all he wanted to do was feast his eyes on her face. "Where's Gabe?"

"He's not here." Her voice trembled, telling him perhaps she wasn't as controlled as she pretended to be. "But he asked me to give you a message."

Connor rubbed a hand over his eyes. Maddie was here, in Gabe's apartment—without Gabe. Shite. Was this a test? Had Gabe sent her here to test his will power? His loyalty? Uh uh. Not Gabe. "What message?"

"He said, and I quote..." she raised two shaky hands and used her fingers to punctuate the quote, "...*fuck the rules.*"

Connor's jaw went slack. "He did?" Gabe was setting the rules aside? Rules that they'd both adhered to for twelve years?

Maddie took a hesitant step towards him and his heart thumped beneath his ribs. "He did. Right before he went to see an old friend of yours."

Connor raised an eyebrow. Oxygen couldn't reach his chest. Gabe had just rendered their rules defunct and Maddie had stepped closer.

"Tina," Maddie answered his unspoken question.

"Tina?"

Another tentative step forward. "Apparently there's some unfinished business between the two of them."

And just like that the shackles of guilt were broken. *Gabe was going after Connor's ex-girlfriend.* Relief almost brought him to his knees. "There is," he agreed and prayed for his friend's sake that Tina was not involved with anyone at the moment.

"There's..." Her voice caught, and she cleared it and tried again. "There's unfinished business between you and me too."

He gave up trying to breathe. It was too frigging difficult. Maddie stood a couple of meters away, an unexpected visitor wreaking havoc on his equilibrium, his thought processes. "There is," he said again. Christ, he wanted to touch her, wanted to take her in his arms, tilt her chin and kiss away the distance between them. "Although I'm not sure business is the term I'd use to describe what is unfinished between us." Visions of a wife and babies danced before his eyes. Vision of Maddie and babies.

"You're right." She smiled tentatively. "It's not business. But it is unfinished. Unresolved, you might say. Like...a lateral thinking puzzle."

Maddie was doing this his way, the lateral thinking way. His chest burned. He had to answer, but he needed oxygen to talk and at this precise moment in time, with Maddie smiling at him, he did not have a drop to spare. Her presence had scrambled his brain.

Connor forced air into his tortured lungs. He didn't have a choice. It was either breathe or pass out. "Just so happens I'm an expert at lateral thinking," he managed at last. "Hit me. Maybe we can work out the puzzle together."

Indecision flashed across her face. Her gaze dropped to his chest. A minute passed. Or maybe it was two. Or ten. Then she looked him in the eye. "A woman meets a man, her boyfriend's best friend. And the unthinkable happens. Without meaning to—" Maddie hesitated, bit her lip. "Without meaning to sh...she slips and falls in love with him."

Her words hit him with the force of a canon ball, tearing his defenses apart. *She loved him.*

She dipped her head again, trying to hide something.

Too late. Connor had already seen it—the vulnerability in her gaze. His stomach clenched, and he fell a little harder for her. "You want to know what happens next?"

She nodded but did not look up.

"That's an easy one." It was? Well if so, why was the simple task of speaking so damn impossible? Why could he hardly string a sentence together? Why did he suddenly feel as though the rest of his life hinged on this answer? "The best friend tells her he's slipped and fallen too. He's in love with the woman."

Maddie dropped her head in her hands. Tremors shook her shoulders. "Is it that easy? There are other issues at play. Issues as yet unresolved."

Gabe.

"The boyfriend's moving on, Maddie," Connor said, silently

205

giving thanks to Gabe. "He's no longer an issue."

She looked up at him. Apprehension clouded her eyes. "The best friend's moving on too. He's going back to Melbourne."

Connor let out a growl borne of relief and frustration. In two steps he crossed the room, closing the space between them, and hauled Madeline into his arms. "He was only going back to Melbourne so he wouldn't have to see the woman he loved with her boyfriend."

Maddie melted into him, molded her frame to his. He held her tighter, wouldn't let her go.

"Turns out the best friend is a jealous man," Connor said. "He can't tolerate the idea of anyone, even his closest mate touching the woman. He wants to be the only man who ever gets to touch her again. Ever gets to make love to her." She felt so good there, as though his body had been designed to fit against hers. Inside hers.

"So...so the best friend doesn't have to go back to Melbourne?"

"All he needs is for the woman to ask him to stay."

Maddie pulled her head back, looked up into his eyes. Hope and fear shone in her face. "Will you stay in Sydney, Connor? Will you give us a chance?"

"Nothing on earth would make me happier," Connor said. Then he groaned. "Christ, Maddie, I thought you'd never ask."

"I love you," she told him. "I swear I never meant for it to happen, never meant to hurt Gabe, but you...you just bewitched me. I couldn't help it."

"I love you too. The minute I saw you I knew you weren't just another woman I could share with Gabe. I knew I would ultimately have to have you for myself."

"Keep me to yourself. Promise you'll never share me again."

"Never, Maddie. From now on you are all mine. Period."

"Then kiss me, Connor. Kiss me now and never let me go again."

He did. He caught her mouth in a kiss so sweet and so hot the very air around them seemed to shimmer. As her lips parted, allowing his seeking tongue access to the velvety depths of her mouth, Connor felt his restlessness and his agitation flicker, fade and finally evaporate.

Right there, in Maddie's arms, he had finally found home.

About the Author

To learn more about Jess Dee please visit www.jessdee.com. Send an email to jess@jessdee.com or hop on over to her blog at http://jessdee.wordpress.com/.

Look for these titles by
Jess Dee

Now Available:

Ask Adam
Photo Opportunity
A Question of Trust

Circle of Friends Series
Only Tyler (Book 1)
Steven's Story (Book 2)

Nice and Naughty

Jayne Rylon

Dedication

To AMA.

Thank you for your suggestions, both for this story and that I should write at all.

"Keep true to the dreams of thy youth." ~ Friedrich von Schiller

P.S. The answer to my previous dedication: 7 days. I stand corrected even though it did take you a year to mention it.

Chapter One

Alexa shifted her convertible into fourth gear with the steady confidence of a seasoned racer. Wind gusts turned shocks of her hair into stinging whips. Her eyes squinted against the sunrays streaming down, guaranteeing sunburn that would peel half her face off. The noise was deafening.

She loved it.

Flying around serpentine curves in the rural landscape, she drank in the fresh mountain air and the beat of the heavy-metal rock screaming from her stereo. Warm, supple leather seats cradled her skin beneath the denim cutoff shorts and halter top she wore.

A refreshing ride provided the escape she needed to blow off some steam after a crazy week wrapping up a consulting project that had consumed her personal time for months. Before shifting lanes to hug the inside edge of the next turn in the deserted road, she glanced in her rearview mirror. A reflected point of light dazzled behind her.

Another vehicle.

Please, don't be a cop.

Alexa slowed to a modest ten miles an hour over the speed limit while debating the likelihood of talking her way out of yet another ticket. This time properly using her turn signal, she merged into the right lane.

When she checked again, the flicker had turned into a full-on blaze. But the machine rapidly gaining on her was no police car. Instead, the silhouette of a man on a motorcycle came into focus. The distance between them shrank steadily as the man partook of a little joy riding of his own.

Mmm mmm.

This was no plastic crotch rocket. A beefy, chrome-and-leather Harley with matching rider closed the gap between them when he accelerated. His black helmet with mirrored visor blocked her view of his face, which beat seeing him clearly. It left her imagination free rein to fill in the blanks, painting him rugged and handsome.

I bet he'll play with me.

She waited until he pulled alongside her sleek, silver graphite car with momentum to pass before she revved the engine. The visor swiveled in her direction, catching her in its reflective surface. Her windblown hair, the glow on her face from the thrill of the ride and her broad smile shone through despite the distortion.

Alexa might have imagined the searing heat of his perusing gaze, but she didn't think so. Raising her eyebrows she mouthed, "Race?"

His leather-gloved hand came off the handlebar and formed a thumbs up. Damp heat that had nothing to do with the scorching summer day spread between her thighs in anticipation.

Verifying no one else approached behind them, she slowed her car to a stop in the middle of the road. The mystery rider followed suit. He dragged his arm through the air, depicting the likeness of a bridge about a mile down the road.

She nodded in understanding.

A thrill borne from their impending competition raced through her as they both prepared for the launch while the heavy beat of music pumped her up, a perfect background for driving.

This is crazy. What am I doing? Her practical side struggled to surface. Another car could happen along any second, though honestly, the road didn't get much traffic being out in the middle of the national forest. And, hell, hadn't she gone out today looking for some excitement?

She might have backed out if given more time to debate and waffle. The rational facet of her personality dominated most often but at that moment the opportunity for thinking ended. One black-booted foot on the ground, Harley held up three fingers above his palm braced on the broad handlebar. Her calves tensed, poised to let out the clutch and step on the gas as his ring finger folded down leaving two, one...

They both took off, burning rubber that stained the highway behind them.

Alexa timed her start perfectly. Unconcerned, she paced herself as her opponent edged out in front. He easily had her off the line. Nothing she could do about that. The dark rider probably thought the raw power of his bike guaranteed an easy win. But he wouldn't suspect the modifications she'd made to her car. When she pushed the gas pedal to the floor, the high-pitched whine of a turbocharger spooling up overpowered the roar of the engine. When the extra horsepower kicked in, she shot forward, making progress toward catching the man on the bike.

Some part of her mind registered the broad expanse of his back and the way his leather chaps highlighted his jean-clad ass like a gilded frame around a priceless work of art. The ease with which he balanced astride his iron pony seamlessly merged machine and man.

It was like dangling a steak in front of the hounds at the dog track.

She tightened her grip on the gear stick. They weaved down the side of the mountain. Precise maneuvering as she attacked each bend in the road made up for the extra power of his motorcycle. Back and forth. They traded places as the light filtered between the trees in blinding flashes that marked the passing distance.

Off to the left, glimpses of the bridge came into view between the pines. It was going to be close.

One final switchback turn separated them from the finish. She assured herself she'd done this many times before. In fact, she generally drove this way just to see how fast she could make it, each time pushing the limits a little further. Exhilaration blossomed in the pit of her stomach. She'd never dared to try this speed. She had the advantage, though. The optimal line for making the turn originated from her inside lane.

Side by side, they entered the winding section of asphalt. When the biker hesitated, for a fraction of an instant, she gunned it. Tires squealed but held as she zoomed over the wooden structure, overtaking the sexy rider at the finish.

Pumping one fist in the air, Alexa coasted to the shoulder of the road.

A section of the grassy area past the bridge had worn down over time to create a patch of hard-packed dirt people utilized as a parking area when they stopped to admire the view. The rustic arch spanned a sparkling river that cut a swath through the verdant forest surrounding it. Not steep enough to prevent people from walking down safely from above, the hillside tumbled down to form a gorge, which trapped the cooler air coming off the water. It made an ideal spot for swimming, fishing or savoring the peace and solitude of the secluded area.

She burst from her car, still cheering. Mindful not to slam the door, she made her way toward the man on the motorcycle even as he swung his leg over his bike. The elation over victory was heady, making her bolder than usual. She appraised his long limbed frame with blatant curiosity.

Holy hot guy, Batman.

A wave of desire struck her. The aftereffects of her adrenaline rush spiked, demanding an outlet. She absorbed every detail of the fine male specimen standing legs apart in front of her. His impressive build dwarfed her average height, making him well over six feet tall. In addition to his black leather boots, chaps and gloves, his trim hips and athletic form sent a clear message. This was not a man to be messed with. His broad shoulders and bulging arms filled out a scuffed leather jacket creased from molding to his muscles as he rode.

No man had ever looked so good. She wished he would leave his helmet on, allowing her to preserve her mental picture of his matching good looks. That wasn't going to happen, though. He'd already reached up to tug it off.

Breath stuck in her throat as the lower edge of the helmet revealed his gorgeous face inch by inch, like a curtain going up on an ornate stage. Time slowed. In detail unmatched by her wildest fantasies, he showed first the tan skin on his corded neck followed by a strong jaw covered in scruffy stubble the color of expensive cognac. His full, sensual lips showcased his amazing smile. By the time she saw his defined cheekbones and classic nose, she had a serious case of lust. His deep emerald eyes and sandy hair polished off the package.

Her fate was sealed.

Air whooshed from her lungs as the Earth began to rotate again. The intense reaction of her body caused her confident stride to falter. Luckily, he didn't seem to notice. As he hung his helmet on the handlebars with false nonchalance, Mr. Motorcycle kept himself too busy conducting a similar inspection of her physical features to detect the disruption he caused to her system. Alexa felt a little smug, instead of insulted, when his gaze lingered on her curves. She was in deep shit.

"Nice race." He broke the silence before it became awkward. The smoky timbre of his voice curled around her insides, making her shiver despite the heat.

"Not so bad yourself." If genuine arousal didn't course through her, the obvious implication might have embarrassed her. But, somehow, this man triggered a primal reaction. This kind of instant attraction had never happened to her before. It was potent.

You need to get out more.

For such a tall and muscular man, he moved with fluid agility. He peeled off his gloves and tucked them in his back pocket. The gesture caused his black T-shirt, visible between the folds of his now unzipped jacket, to stretch tight over defined pecs. His boots settled directly in front of her thin-soled racing sneakers as he extended his hand.

"Congratulations."

Warmth spread from the intersection of their flesh when she wrapped her fingers around his substantial hand. The brief contact ratcheted up the hormones already raging inside her. After a firm but reasonable squeeze, his fingertips caressed the back of her hand for a moment before they slipped away. Face to face with him, his size, strength and stranger status might have intimidated her on an average day, when she lived in a world of rational thought and practicality. Instead, in this moment, her thoughts centered on what it would be like to be surrounded by all that strapping muscle.

"Thank you." The response meant more than a courtesy. She only indulged her wild streak on rare occasions and he had provided the perfect opportunity with their impromptu race. Although her voice sounded breathy to her own ears, relief flowed over her when he remained unaware of her body's haywire reaction.

His firm bicep brushed the side of Alexa's breast as he continued past her to inspect her car.

Was that an accident? Her nipple didn't care either way. It responded instantly by hardening against the silky fabric of her halter top. Wild and crazy this morning, she'd decided against wearing a bra though she'd never left the house without one before. It was turning into a day of firsts.

She stole the opportunity to verify the view from behind lived up to her memory based on the brief glimpse she'd caught during the race. It did. The man had a killer ass. When he threw a glance, and a devilish smirk, over his shoulder, she guessed he wasn't as oblivious as he seemed.

Their eyes met and she saw an answering spark in his.

"She's beautiful," he murmured reverently.

The car. He's talking about your car. She tried to convince herself, but the rationalization rang false. While he admired the convertible, something more arced between them. Attempting to shake off the unusual reaction inflaming her senses by focusing on her vehicle, Alexa stepped a little closer.

"I've done a lot of work on it."

"Can I touch her?" His implicit understanding of her dislike for people handling her vehicle made her confident he would treat it with the respect it deserved.

"Sure, go ahead." Plus, she got to watch the way his broad finger stroked the defined contour in the flawlessly waxed side panel, which inflamed her senses nearly as much as if he'd placed the caress on her skin instead.

Before she could stop to analyze what her subconscious offered, she asked, "Would you like to take a look under the hood?"

"Hell, yeah."

She had to laugh at the look on his face. "You look like a kid on Christmas."

"It's not every day I come across an opportunity like this." The dark undercurrent of the statement and his piercing green stare made it clear he referred to more than a fancy sports car.

Oh God. He feels it, too.

Alexa should have been freaked out. Alone with a stranger, on a deserted stretch of highway, in the mountains far from the city, sounded like an unwise situation to put herself in. She should be nervous but a remarkable calm surrounded her instead. In fact, she just now realized she'd stopped on the side of the road without a second thought to safety. Today, she threw caution to the wind. The chemical reaction between them affected her like a drug.

As though he sensed her train of thought, the man backed away a few steps, displaying his non-threatening intent. He left the path clear for her to get in her car and drive away but her instincts shouted that she could trust him. She wanted to explore this attraction just a little bit further.

She leaned over the door and rested her fingertips on the hood release. The man's gaze tracked her movement yet he didn't encroach on her space. For a moment, the only sounds breaking the silence were the babble of the stream below, the gentle rustle of leaves from the tree branches overhead and a soft birdsong.

The air between them crackled with tension.

Then, the metallic click of the hood's latching mechanism disengaging relayed her decision to stay. A broad smile spread across his face, raising faint dimples that heightened his attractiveness. Alexa inclined her head in a "come here" gesture as she circled around to the front of the car.

He ambled to her side with a steady gait that made her cognizant of his confidence she wouldn't run. Reaching for the edge of the hood simultaneously, their hands met. Sparks shot up her spine and she jerked. His arm wrapped around her waist in a protective hold. The solid strength kept her from losing her physical footing, but not her emotional balance. This close she could smell the unique combination of his leather gear and subtle, earthy cologne.

"Easy." His hand smoothed down her side and across the top of her ass as he went back to lifting the hood. The blatant touch imbued her with respect for his natural ability to handle a woman. However, she retained enough rationality to admire the gleaming chrome of the engine that she cleaned with painstaking diligence each weekend she could manage the time. Together they leaned forward, caught by the lure of a ridiculously overpowered motor.

"This is an aftermarket addition. Did you do this yourself?" His raised eyebrow conveyed his surprise.

"Yeah."

"I'm impressed. Are you a mechanic?"

"Nope, this is just a hobby." She smirked.

"Some hobby. I *am* a mechanic. This is a damn fine job."

Alexa basked in his appreciation for details. None of her friends understood her devotion to this machine. They couldn't comprehend why she spent the majority of her precious free time refining each tiny part until it was flawless. This man obviously did.

He ran his hand along the connections, searching with deft flicks of his fingertips for imperfections where none existed. His satisfied nod had her beaming.

"Jesus, woman. If someone told me I'd have the chance to play with a car like this today, I'd have said that nothing could distract me. But the way you're looking at me..."

His voice trailed off as she reached up to do a little exploring of her own. Her hand moved on autopilot, following her desire, cupping the side of his stubbled face.

Is this guy for real?

The wet heat of his lips on her palm rasped against her nerves, stronger than any dream. She whimpered as he turned his head to lick the center of her palm before catching the sensitive skin between her thumb and index finger in his teeth in a gentle nip. The move set her ablaze, destroying common sense.

"Kiss me," she demanded.

He didn't need to be told twice. With a low groan, he closed the narrow gap between them, sealing his mouth over hers. He dropped the hood in place and put his hand to better use, wrapping it around her hip, yanking her tight against the hard plane of his chest. His height made Alexa strain on tiptoes to return his kiss. Eager to help, he tucked his other hand around her thigh, just beneath the curve of her ass, and hoisted her up higher on his body.

Even as he bit at her lips, the growing evidence of his desire prodded the fly of her shorts. The denim she wore couldn't prevent the thick ridge of his dick from imprinting the soft curve of her belly as it filled with each rapid beat of his heart, pressing into her. She squirmed against him, instinctively aligning them so her pussy rubbed against the bulge in his jeans.

They fit perfectly together.

Her hands tangled in his hair, loving the way the silky strands teased the sensitive crevices between her fingers. She kneaded his scalp, urging him to take her mouth deeper. His head angled over hers, intensifying the kiss as his tongue lashed playfully against the seam of her lips. She drew it inside her mouth and sucked. He tasted like peppermint.

She moaned with regret when he pulled away.

"I'm going to set you on the hood." He rumbled in her ear in between nibbles of her neck.

"No! Wait."

Though he looked disappointed, he stopped without hesitation.

The heat suffusing her face highlighted her discomfort with being so brazen. "I...I don't want to scratch the paint. Take my shorts off first."

Strained laughter burst from his chest. It transformed his features from rugged to unbearably handsome.

"Honey, you're my every fantasy."

Kneeling in front of her, he flipped up the hem of her shirt to place hungry kisses on her stomach as he unbuttoned her cutoffs. He lowered them down her legs, following the fabric with his mouth, kissing a trail of fire down her inner thighs.

Alexa shuddered when work-roughened hands grabbed her ass and placed her on the car like some erotic hood ornament. Guiding her feet, he rested them on the front fender, straddling his torso. Her arms fell back, braced behind her. Although the metal warmed her skin, bare now except for the sexy thong she wore, the shade kept it from burning her.

His hands ran up her abdomen, pushing the halter top higher to expose her breasts. She would have begged him to touch her but he seemed to know exactly where and how she wanted to be stroked. One of his hands cupped a breast while his tongue laved the aching center of the other. With the side of his face tucked against her skin, which glistened with a fine sheen of perspiration, he looked up.

The desire burning in his eyes matched the lust roaring inside her. Their gazes locked. He waited for her to take the next step.

"More," was all she could say.

"Yes." His hands raked down her torso, fingers grazing each rib with tantalizing precision. When they feathered over her abdomen, her muscles reflexively tightened. Alexa wasn't sure who moaned when the contraction caused the arousal building inside her to flow out onto her pussy lips, soaking the tiny cotton band tucked between her legs.

She thought she heard a gruff, muffled curse just before he tugged the strip of her underwear to the side and buried his face between her legs. Then she didn't care. The combination of her copious fluids and the heat of his mouth against her shaved mound wiped away everything else. When his tongue dipped between her labia to circle her clit she almost came on the spot. His enthusiastic lapping drew out her arousal, which he devoured as though he couldn't get enough of her taste.

Pleasure flowed from his skilled mouth directly into her veins. With her head tilted back, her half-closed eyes facing the fluffy clouds in the perfect blue sky, she concentrated on the intoxicating way he manipulated her flesh and didn't notice his hand moving until the blunt tip of his finger tested her dripping pussy.

She moaned and thrust her hips at his seeking hand. He worked her open, dipping in further each time he drove the digit inside. When his finger tunneled within her, palm facing upwards, he curled the long length until it pressed against her G-spot. The sensation overwhelmed her with pleasure. This man had moves she had only read about.

Hovering on the edge of an orgasm, she shrieked. Mistaking the cry of pleasure for surprise or pain, he paused, keeping her climax just out of reach. In that moment of clarity, she craved more. Having the most amazing orgasm of her life no longer seemed like enough.

"I want you inside me. Now."

It may not have been the most graceful move she ever saw, but he somehow managed to balance her thighs on his shoulders while he ripped his wallet from his back pocket. He retrieved a condom before dropping the billfold on the ground, unconcerned about the rest of the contents. With one hand, he got the button of his jeans undone and the fly spread open. The other hand shoved his pants and dark gray briefs out of the way, allowing him to thread the most magnificent cock she'd ever seen through the opening of his leather chaps.

As he rolled the condom over his raging hard-on, he stepped between her legs and claimed her mouth. This kiss was a thousand times more potent than the first, so stimulating it shocked her. Unrestrained now, he possessed her with a natural dominance that coerced her body to bow even closer to his. While he claimed her mouth, he massaged her clit. The contrast of his harsh kiss and tender teasing had her writhing beneath him.

"Now. Please, now."

His knees bent forward, resting on the edge of the hood, and the head of his cock notched against her a moment before he thrust, driving his broad shaft a few inches inside her tight, clinging sheath. Her arms came up, banding around his solid back.

"You feel so fucking good." He groaned. "I'm not going to last."

The pure passion inflecting his words, combined with the forbidden intensity of the moment, poised her on the edge of climax. He withdrew until only the bulbous head of his cock remained before thrusting. His long, thick cock exhilarated each sensitive nerve ending along the way until her pussy completely encased him. When he tucked his pubic bone against her clit and ground his hips in a provocative circle, she shattered.

His hands clamped around her shoulders, anchoring himself deep inside her. His teeth raked the side of her neck as the waves of orgasm crashed over her again and again. The guttural cry that echoed in the empty ravine as he joined her mirrored her own sense of relief and utter completion.

A startled bird left the tree overhead with a flutter. Then the only sounds filling the void were their harsh breathing, the rustle of leaves in the gentle breeze and the tick of the engine cooling beneath her ass.

Limp, Alexa lay draped across the hood of the car, her legs splayed on either side of his tapered waist as she struggled to catch the breath he'd stolen from her. Slowly, very slowly, the world sharpened into focus. He shifted above her, slipping out of the swollen channel of her sex. She sighed at the loss.

He braced himself on his elbows and looked down into her eyes with a soulful gaze before speaking.

"My name is Justin."

And just like that, the spell broke.

She flinched and rolled from the hood, forcing him to step back to keep his balance.

He must have read the horror on her face because he started scrambling to adjust his clothes.

"Shit, don't do that. Don't go." Instead of halting her, the frustrated order spurred her on.

She grabbed her shorts from the ground and stepped into them with the practice of someone who often gets called out of the house on emergencies during the night. She was already in the driver's seat, starting the car, by the time he had gathered his wallet, its scattered contents, and regrouped enough to start after her.

"Damn it, tell me your name!"

Alexa shook her head in denial before throwing the car in gear and peeling out of the parking area without a thought for the damage rocks or sticks kicked up against the paint could do. She fought tears when she looked in her rearview mirror and saw him kick the trunk of the tree they'd made love under.

No, fucked under. She'd gone temporarily insane and had sex with a perfect stranger whose name she hadn't even known.

What the hell came over me?

Chapter Two

"It was bound to happen sooner or later." Jamie sat across the high top table from Alexa and tried to alleviate some of the misery bubbling inside her best friend. "Sweetie, you were like a sexual pressure cooker. Something had to give."

"Jamie, were you listening? I had sex with a total stranger. In broad daylight. Where anyone might have seen us. I must be insane!" Alexa dropped her head between her hands. Her professional façade never cracked like this at work. Even now, most people wouldn't see the distress harbored within the polished businesswoman perched on the stool next to Jamie in their office building's coffee shop. But she had taken one look at Alexa's normally meticulous appearance this morning and noticed her mismatched earrings. Then, when the other woman almost forgot her eight o'clock meeting, it confirmed Jamie's suspicions. Something serious had upset her friend, she never missed an appointment. Maybe...

"Were you careful?"

Alexa grimaced. "No, I just told you..."

"I mean, did you use protection?" If she didn't look so wretched, Jamie might have laughed.

"Oh. Uh, yeah, he did." Her friend turned a delicate shade of red, her fingernails tapping on the paper wrapper around her drink. "But, honestly, if he hadn't thought of it, I probably wouldn't even have noticed."

"Then it was good?" Jamie grinned, delighted someone had blasted through the calm reserve Alexa wrapped around her like a shield.

"God, I've never felt anything like it before," she admitted.

Her eyes glazed in reverie for a moment before she stammered. "But that's not the point. Jamie, I can't believe I did something so stupid, so fucking irresponsible."

"Well I, for one, am glad you did. I keep telling you these men you date can't give you what you need. You're never satisfied with them." Jamie sighed. Sometimes a friend just had to tell it like it was. "Girl, I wouldn't even call most of them dates. The suits attend professional functions with you. They have different names, sure, but they're all stamped from the same mold. Boring, boring, boring."

Jamie knew she might be getting somewhere when Alexa didn't even try to refute it. "They may be boring, but they're dependable, conservative and respectable. Wild guys aren't good relationship material."

"How would you know, Alexa? Just 'cause one jerk burned you doesn't mean men who are adventurous and trustworthy don't exist."

"I don't believe it. Those traits are mutually exclusive. And that's the problem. I want both. No, I *need* both but it's not worth wishing for the impossible." Jamie could practically see her friend rebuilding herself, reassembling the fractured pieces of her emotions as she fortified her resolve by chugging the last of her hazelnut coffee. "And right now, I have to get upstairs and start researching the Winston project proposal."

The discussion effectively closed, Alexa hopped off the stool onto her sleek, four-inch heels.

Jamie smiled. Alexa would recover. Too bad. She could have used an insatiable, daring man to help her relieve the tension from her stressful job. "Well, you know I'm always here if you need to talk. Or decide to give me the juicy details."

Alexa closed the distance between them and embraced her in a brief but tight hug. "Thanks, Jamie."

Alexa tucked the tall leather chair under the polished surface of the substantial boardroom table and began unpacking her briefcase. She represented Therber Management Services at today's proposal. If she won this contract, as a merger and acquisition consultant for Winston Industries, her burgeoning career would be assured.

Instead of rehearsing her strategy, as she normally would while organizing her documents in precise rows before her, she surveyed the scenery out the twenty-third-story window. In addition to the traffic rushing below her in a blur of lights, and the faint sounds of the city drifting up in a cacophony of horns and squeaky breaks, she glimpsed the rolling hills on the horizon. Larger steel and glass buildings, like this one housing Winston's corporate headquarters, surrounded her own office and blocked the distracting view. Otherwise, she might never get any work done.

Her gaze landed on the distant landscape, causing memories of the race to flare in her mind. No matter how stupid it had been, that stolen afternoon's passion still had the power to set her body on fire weeks later. The grueling hours spent on this proposal had kept her from dwelling on the incident overmuch. Add mental distraction to the list of reasons this contract was essential. If she won it today, her work would have just begun. Otherwise, she'd have lots of time on her hands to brood when she got fired for losing such an important opportunity.

She tore her focus from the lulling purple hue of the distant mountains and wondered if she should switch places to face away from the distraction. J. Winston, CEO of Winston Industries, possessed a reputation as a fierce negotiator and competitor. She required complete concentration to deal with the eccentric entrepreneur. He hired only the best on a regular basis and this deal was anything but ordinary. The top secret project required intense business acumen, speed to market and a reliable partner.

The venture had the business community talking. J. Winston always inspired gossip due to his reclusive nature. Some called him The Wizard because no one but his innermost circle ever saw him, and no picture of him existed that she could find in her extensive research. He stayed in his tower, pulling levers, deciding the fates of companies from a distance.

If you believed the buzz, he'd reached out for a consultant because he didn't trust even his top staff with the sensitivity of this latest project. He needed someone new, fresh and unbiased. Someone a competitor couldn't have persuaded to go mole. The full extent of the assignment remained hidden from the management firms bidding for the contract but that didn't squash Alexa's confidence that she could facilitate whatever scheme Winston Industries, and their mysterious leader, cooked up.

The heavy solid wood door swung open admitting an intimate group of executives she recognized on sight, either through the numerous networking events she attended as part of her routine duties or due to her background investigation on Winston Industries.

Game time. She stood, greeting each one by name, utterly calm and collected. The rush brought on by intense situations filled her now, just as it did when she went out driving. When everyone claimed a seat, only one chair—opposite the broad table from her—remained unoccupied. She flicked a subtle glance at her watch with thirty seconds to the scheduled meeting time.

Alexa flipped through her mental notes on the interests of those present, constructing calculated filler to entertain the staff and start selling herself to them in the ten minutes or so that it would take for J. Winston to arrive fashionably delayed. Many executive officers channeled a more powerful image by making their appointments wait. Therefore, he surprised and impressed her with his punctuality when he appeared through a private entrance just a few moments later, precisely on time.

She recovered from that slight miscalculation with tact, but nothing could have prepared her for the man that strode past the wall of windows, stopping right in front of her, hand outstretched. Automatically, she took it, wondering at the difference in his firm grip now that he tendered it in a professional gesture rather than the fiery grasp of their tryst. She squeezed his fingers, trying desperately not to think of the time they'd spent exploring deep inside her.

Holy shit.

At least she knew what the J. in J. Winston stood for now.

Justin.

Their grip extended longer than etiquette required, or found polite, but she couldn't seem to disengage from the desire that bloomed inside her at even this miniscule touch. She studied his face, instantly recognizable and somehow different from the day they'd met out on the road. His smooth jaw, shaved clean of the scruffy stubble, complimented the impeccable hairstyle that probably cost more than she made in a month. The charcoal suit he wore packaged the sexy body underneath like an exquisitely wrapped gift, making her want to rip off the covering to find the goodies hidden beneath it. His gleaming smile seemed genuine, and innocent.

Justin's professional reaction doused her initial fear that he would recoil upon finding her in his boardroom. She could act cool, too.

In the next moment, she expected him to say something like, "So good to see you again." Or "I'm glad to officially be introduced." But, instead, he said, "It's very nice to meet you. I've heard many good things about your work and look forward to hearing your presentation today." Then he crossed to his side of the table and sat down with an expectant nod, cueing her to begin, as though he hadn't just dropped a bomb on her.

To steady her churning thoughts, Alexa turned away under the pretense of tweaking settings on her laptop and the attached projector, although she had taken care of those details long before the meeting started. Several emotions crashed through her system at once. A dose of relief he hadn't called her out mixed with embarrassment.

Does he think I'm a slut? Her uncertainty washed away beneath the force of lust, which spiked off the charts as that amazing chemical reaction spread through her again. Finally, anger joined the swirling mass inside her and stuck. *He doesn't want anyone to know we've met.*

A ball of emotion lodged in her throat but she wouldn't let Justin ruin this chance. Even if he played some cruel game, she wanted the other powerful attendees to maintain their good opinions of her work. Afterward, she would deal with him in private.

Professionalism rose to the surface, driving her onward, and she buried her doubts.

She collected herself, drew a deep breath and focused on the strategy she had devised as she began to work the room. "Today, I will prove to you that I am the only consultant that measures up to Winston Industries' standards for your upcoming project."

J. Winston observed the polished performance of Ms. Alexa Daniels in utter fascination. An underlying aloof chill, which mesmerized and intrigued him, marred her perfect façade. The unexpected, illogical reaction roused his mistrust as well. He couldn't afford surprises on this deal and he had considered her a sure thing.

What is she trying to hide?

He reclined in his chair, linking his fingers together over his abdomen. Though she continued the well-executed presentation, he noticed the dilation of her pupils and the tiniest shake of the red laser pointer's dot on her screen each time she glanced at him. Did desire cause this anomaly in her behavior? He didn't consider it conceited to appraise her attraction to him. If he hired her, they would work closely together. This deal had the potential to boost his company out of reach of their competitors for a hundred years. The revolutionary technology he had discovered would be profitable only if they could harness the competitive advantage first. He wouldn't risk an opportunity like that on something as fleeting as lust, no matter how sizzling.

He had studied Alexa for a long time, tracked her career for years as she rose through the ranks at Therber, gaining the experience she needed to become a valuable asset to his organization. He'd joined today's meeting convinced it would conclude with an offer. Maybe a permanent one.

Now, he considered her behavior and knew that he didn't have all the pieces. He hadn't factored in the obvious magnetism that drew them to each other. Her file photos had always struck him as oddly attractive, though her beauty wasn't conventional. Still, that didn't explain her unusual reaction to him. She impressed him with her ability to mask the turmoil the others didn't notice, only allowing subtle hints through for him to perceive.

She's angry. In addition to the attraction rolling off her, he distinguished the other variety of heat. He prided himself on being able to read people, that skill alone contributed greatly to his success. She wrapped up the briefing having convinced the others on the panel of her worth. He interpreted their sanction in the way they nodded with her every assertion, hungry for more, leaning forward in attention. Everyone turned to him, waiting for his response.

"I'd like to speak with Ms. Daniels privately." Collectively, they rose, filing out of the boardroom, offering their support to her via handshakes and nods of approval when they passed.

Her disposition changed the moment he heard the door thunk closed.

"What the hell is going on?" She leaned forward, her arms locked straight, palms flat on the table as she unleashed the blistering sentiment he'd glimpsed earlier. Her auburn hair bounced in soft curls, framing the deceptive softness of her face, tumbling into the V-neck of that delicate lace camisole beneath her tailored suit jacket. He pried his eyes from the hint of soft, round flesh.

Whoa. Years had passed since a prospective client dared talk to him like that. Her attitude shouldn't have thrilled him and, yet, it did. Something dark awoke inside him as the hunt began in earnest. Usually, he could tamp down the primal segment of his nature but this woman drew it out of him in spades. Now that she showed her hand, instead of trying to deceive him by shuttering her buried emotions, he knew he wanted her. For his project.

Yeah, and that's not all.

"I believe we just completed your proposal process. This is the part where I offer you the job." He selected his words with care. Her reaction perplexed him but determination ensured he would discover the source of her hostility and eradicate her objections. He would have her.

"Process? So this has been an ongoing interview?" Her voice chilled further.

"Of course. You're too savvy to assume I'd hire you without considerable investigation." He thought of the hours he'd reviewed reports on her over the years. She controlled her flinch but he caught the ghost of the motion anyway.

"I didn't expect you to come off your throne to inspect me so personally. If you think for one minute that I would take a position with you after this, you're crazy. I don't care how powerful you are or how important this deal is. Count me out." Alexa gathered her briefcase, abandoning the presentation materials where they lay, broadcasting her intention to walk out if he didn't stop her.

"Wait." He rose, blocking her path. The warm scent of

spring wafted up to him.

One of the reasons he kept out of the limelight was to avoid the women who came on to him for his money or for advancement. Under usual circumstances, attraction sent up a red flag, a warning to avoid a female business partner but, for once, he felt compelled to investigate. Electric sparks of desire lured him closer to this woman when he should have dusted his hands.

She stopped practically on top of him as she tried to squeeze past. Her chest pressed close to his upper abdomen, more petite than the shadow her iron demeanor cast. When their eyes met they both hesitated, stunning him with the force of his reaction to her.

"Don't go." He couldn't prevent the command from sounding so harsh.

"I didn't listen the last time you ordered me to stay, why do you think it'll work now?" Her bitterness sliced through the haze infiltrating his mind.

"We've met before?"

"Yeah, when I was crazy enough to let you fuck me. Or do you nail women on the hoods of their cars so often that you actually forgot?" Disgust permeated her voice and her features. It cut him to know that she aimed some of the hostility at herself.

Oh, God, it can't be her. Some glimmer of realization must have crossed his face because she snapped off their eye contact and bustled past him to the door. Just before it closed completely she spun around. Hurt mixed with the heat that, even now, lingered in her gorgeous brown eyes.

"Go to hell, Justin."

He stared at the spot she had stood only a moment ago as reality sank in. His mind formulated a plan while he made his way into his personal office. From there he followed her descent down the elevator and exit from the building on the security cameras even as he hit the first speed dial number programmed in his cell.

Ringing came over the line as she stormed out to the parking garage.

Come on, answer!

"Yo." His brother's characteristic, informal greeting came at the same moment Alexa reached her car.

"Son of a bitch!" On the screen, she tucked her slender frame into a hot little convertible.

"What's up, Jay?" The voice picked up some uneasiness.

"Justin, I found your woman."

Chapter Three

"What? Who is she?" Justin's inflection became alert, the lazy cadence exchanged for rapt attention. "Where is she?"

"We have a problem." His seriousness dissolved the initial thrill in his brother's intonation. Even over the phone their communication extended beyond words. They understood each other in ways other people could never fathom.

"Fuck. Why does everything have to be complicated?"

Jason laughed despite the situation. For twins, identical in so many ways, they possessed polar opposite personalities. Where he required structure, Justin enjoyed being carefree and uninhibited. It was one of the reasons they made a perfect team. Together, they would sort this out.

"Can you meet me at 534 Lennox Road in thirty minutes?" Jason read off the address from Alexa's file lying open on his desk. He multitasked, clicking through his calendar, clearing all his other appointments for the afternoon. This woman held the key for them both.

"I'll make it in twenty." Justin loved speed and, on top of that, he'd spent weeks obsessed with finding this woman.

Jason looked at the phone. The severed connection didn't stop him from admonishing his brother. "Be careful."

Alexa fumed as she maneuvered her car through heavy rush hour traffic.

Shit, why do I care if he wants to pretend it never happened?

Mr. Winston, she thought snidely, presented her with a golden opportunity to banish her indiscretion into oblivion and take on a professional challenge of a career-making magnitude. But how could she stand to work for a man capable of such complete deception? Her morals wouldn't allow it. After all, that asshole had pursued her for business purposes and didn't even have the decency to feign guilt for enjoying fucking her on the side of the road under false pretenses. She didn't doubt that he'd enjoyed it, some things a man couldn't fake, but apparently their interlude had been a necessary evil. She wondered if he'd given himself hazard pay for that duty.

You're just pissed he wasn't as affected as you.

Every day of the past two weeks she'd buried herself in work only to find that nothing could douse the yearning he'd ignited. His calculated seduction stung and confused her. What purpose could it serve? Logic suggested insurance, an imprudence to hold over her as blackmail in case she attempted to reveal his trade secret. *Damn, this must be one important deal.*

Not even for that would she risk her heart. As much as it frustrated her, she admitted the truth—that Justin had turned out to be a slimy dirtbag—hadn't obliterated her physical attraction to him. She wouldn't lose her head over another undeserving creep. She made a point of learning from her mistakes so she understood this insane attraction would have her tangled up in emotions before long if she didn't escape while she still had the chance.

God, he looked good in that suit.

"Shit! I am so screwed." Not only did she face getting fired for blowing the proposal, but also she hungered for something she could never have. The rough and wild man she met on that sunlit road never truly existed.

Alexa turned into the underground parking facility attached to her well-maintained condo, surprised to find herself home so soon. Her wandering thoughts had kept her driving on autopilot. A creature of habit, she pulled into her usual spot and dropped her forehead on the leather steering wheel while gathering energy to make the hike through the desolate cement garage in her power heels.

Fat lot of good those did you. She climbed from the low seat, bitching to herself as she discovered her day hadn't hit rock bottom yet. When she reached for her briefcase on the passenger seat, something hard and cold jabbed the ridge of her spine. One clammy hand covered her mouth as a steely arm encircled her chest, jerking out of the car.

"Keep still, be quiet and I won't hurt you."

Like she believed anything a man holding a gun on her promised. She kicked backward and her stiletto gouged his shin. The rasping voice turned shrill and mean as he cursed her.

"Nice try, bitch." This time when he grabbed her, he didn't pretend to be rational. His fingers latched onto her upper arm with bruising force. He slammed her face down on the trunk of her car causing agony to radiate from her ribs, driving the wind from her momentarily.

"I don't have any cash on me." She masked her fear by giving rage free rein.

"It's not your fucking money I want." The coarse sound he made couldn't be called a laugh. "I need to know what he's planning."

"Who?" Genuine confusion colored her reflexive question.

"Don't play dumb, whore. I can make you talk." She fought the urge to retch when the man pinned her with his body, trapping her tight enough to show her how much hurting her excited him. "What is Winston up to?"

"I don't know." She answered honestly, understanding he'd never believe her.

Her assailant shook her with rough jerks, twisting her arm up behind her back. She thrashed in his hold and heard her skirt rip as it caught on a metal edge that sliced her skin beneath it. Alexa couldn't stifle the cry he wrung from her as he applied more pressure.

"Hello?" A deep voice rang out from several rows away, echoing in the cavernous space. "Is someone down here?"

Her captor tried to cover her mouth but, with the gun in one hand and the other holding her arm, he couldn't move fast enough.

"Help!" She screamed so loud the raw sound that tore from her throat hurt her own ears. With her head forced to the side, mashed against the trunk, she glimpsed a mop of sandy hair bobbing as the newcomer ran closer. His sharp footfalls grew louder as the man behind her dragged her toward a beat up old van parked nearby.

"Hey, you!" Her would-be savior bore down on them as he sprinted between the cars. "Get your fucking hands off her."

She struggled, kicking and fighting every inch of the way, but when the sharp corner of the vehicle's sliding door banged against her elbow, she knew time had run out. By mere chance, her thrashing knee connected with something soft as the lunatic attempted to shove her through the opening. She half-fell, half-scurried away as his hold loosened for an instant. His moan of pain and frustration cut off abruptly, silenced by the peel of tires, as his driver carried them away a moment before the helpful stranger reached her.

He skidded across the last few feet, rushing to her side.

"Jesus Christ! Are you okay?" He knelt next to her, his hands searching for injuries. "Where are you hurt?"

"I'm fine." The thready croak didn't inspire much confidence.

"We have to get out of here. If they didn't know where you lived before, they do now."

His familiar voice arrowed through her shock and thawed her stunned mind. "Justin?"

"Yeah, honey, it's me." She hadn't recognized him at first. The polished businessman had morphed into the rugged rebel of her dreams. Alexa flinched when her hand touched the short whiskers she remembered so well. "You're safe. It's okay now."

He seemed to be trying to convince himself. While he cradled her in the crook of one arm, sheltering her, he extracted a sleek cell phone from the inside pocket of his leather jacket. Scrambled thoughts untangled themselves as she wrestled to contain the tremors beginning to shake her.

"You have a beard." Unsteady fingers pressed against scruffy hairs and the tense jaw beneath them.

"Hate to shave." He might have continued their surreal conversation but someone answered his call. "Jay, where the hell are you?"

J. Not Justin.

Oh, shit. J. must think she was insane. She feared she

might be sick as her thoughts zigzagged between the attack and her colossal screw up in the boardroom. She barely registered Justin arguing in the background.

"I don't give a fuck if it's reserved for residents. Just get in the damn garage. Someone attacked her." He snapped the phone closed.

"Can you stand up?" He searched the lot, his eyes never resting on one spot for long. His vigilance bolstered her survival instincts, giving her the strength to start moving again. As he helped her gain her feet, a luxurious sedan rolled up beside them. "Just a few more seconds, honey."

He ushered her inside the door he yanked open. Her scraped knees burned as she crawled across the backseat. She met the driver's gaze in the rearview mirror.

"Someone better tell me what's going on here." The shaking of her body affected her voice, making the words jitter. Both men exchanged looks, drawing her attention. They were so alike and, yet, so different. "You're twins."

"Yes." Clean-shaven answered the rhetorical question. "Justin, make sure we're not followed."

"Where are you taking me?" Neither brother answered, their attention on the traffic streaming by.

She declined to object further since throbbing pain began to seep through her adrenaline rush. The first few minutes passed in a tense silence. Both J. and Justin concentrated on the cars surrounding them but Justin never let go of her hand. The warm reassurance his touch instilled bolstered her courage as she recovered from the surprise of the attack. She began to relax into the plush upholstery.

"Jay, we're clear, pick up the pace." Justin sat tense beside her, his foot in constant motion, tapping against the floorboard.

"I know it kills you to let me drive," J. said. Truth be told, J. irked her, too. He drove like a ninety-year-old woman, exactly at the speed limit, a precise four-second gap between his suave-but-safe vehicle and the car in front of them, never violating a single rule. The steady calm J. harnessed clearly escaped his brother. "But anyone watching has to believe there's nothing out of the ordinary if they're looking for Alexa."

"Alexa, nice." Justin tested out her name, causing a shiver to run down her spine at the way he savored the word. Still, she couldn't afford to be distracted.

"We're not going to the police?" They headed in the opposite direction of the station on the freeway.

"No. It's too dangerous. They'll expect us to, and I'm afraid the stakes are too high now." J. met her eyes with a brief stare in the rearview mirror. "I'm sorry for getting you mixed up in this."

The dark-tinted windows sheltered them from unwanted attention, cocooning them in privacy. Convinced they'd reached safety, Justin turned his attention to her. His eyes darkened as he took her in.

She opened her mouth to continue questioning them when he interrupted.

"You're bleeding."

"Shit, I'm sorry. Did I get any on the seat?" Alexa glanced down at the gash in her leg she hadn't noticed while checking for suspicious vehicles. She tugged on the ripped material of her suit skirt, tearing off a dangling section to compress against the cut. A red stain grew across the patch in a few seconds.

"Like I care about that." J. muttered from the front. "Does she need a doctor?"

Justin reached over to add light pressure with one hand while he probed her side. "I saw that bastard slam you against your car. You're going to be bruised, but I don't think anything's broken. Nothing we can't handle ourselves, Jay." Fury turned his words to acid. He lifted his head, meeting her gaze full on for the first time since he rescued her.

The combination of his fingers on her thigh and his palm so near her breast had her gasping for air.

"Does that hurt?" Worry crossed his face, drawing his mouth into a thin line.

She shook her head and scooted away from him. It was impossible to think when he touched her. "I want to know what's going on. Right now."

"You got me." He shrugged. "But I'd sure as hell like to know, too."

Chapter Four

J.'s audible exhalation reached Alexa. "I knew this was going to turn into a cluster fuck."

"What are you into, Jay?" Justin asked the question she burned to know the answer to.

"First things first." J. couldn't ignore the social niceties. "I'm Jason Winston. Justin, I believe you've met Alexa Daniels before."

She caught the knowing look the twins exchanged but her attention shifted when Justin made a sound somewhere between a moan and a sigh. "Yeah." He turned to her with an honesty she couldn't deny. "I've been looking all over for you. I had no idea you knew my brother."

"I don't." Some of her indignation returned. "Are you saying all of this is coincidence?"

"Considering I don't even know what 'all of this' is? Yeah, that's what I'm saying." Frustration escalated in his words. Every one of his reactions seemed frank and uncensored.

"He didn't know who you were. I swear it." A promise from a man like Jason could be trusted implicitly.

"And you?" Her eyebrow arched.

"I've followed your career for several years," he admitted.

"What!" Betrayal colored Justin's outburst. "You knew I wanted her, I've been going crazy trying to track her down."

"Relax." Though he addressed Justin, Alexa understood he intended his words for both of them. "I didn't realize she was your woman. I never would have matched her profile with your description."

"I'm my own woman." Her face flamed with a mixture of

irritation and arousal. She averted her eyes in an attempt to hide the reaction. The four-lane road had given way to a rural street. No pursuers could hide from them here, she could see for miles on the secluded road in either direction. By the looks of the pristine lawns, manicured formal landscaping and winding drives, the neighborhood catered to wealthy residents seeking privacy.

"Amen." Justin's rough reply accompanied a soft laugh from the front seat. The temperature climbed a few degrees inside the cabin of the car.

"We made it." Jason's announcement couldn't have come at a better time. It cut off their discussion. Both men focused on scanning the yard in front of the massive stone wall and iron gate as Jason buzzed it open.

He guided the car into the bay in front of them. They stayed in place until the garage door shut, concealing them from outside, then Justin slid his arms beneath her and plucked her from the car. He carried her into the house through the door Jason held for them, their actions so synchronized they appeared choreographed. The brothers moved, working as one, without talking. Justin acted while Jason took care of the details, flicking on lights, turning off the security alarm and heading upstairs to gather supplies.

The thick muscles of Justin's arms secured her to his chest. She gave in to temptation and snuggled close to him, drinking in his body heat and laying her palm over his collarbone.

"You smell like motor oil," Alexa mumbled against his neck, insanely enticed to lick it.

"Came straight from work."

"I love that smell." She felt, rather than heard, the rumble he made low in his throat.

His fingers tightened on her knee and he brushed her forehead with his lips a moment before he deposited her on the marble top of the kitchen island. The stone shocked her, so cold compared to the toasty security of his body. It snapped her from the sensual trance being too near him lulled her into.

She took in the well-appointed cooking area with its stainless steel appliances and large eat-in dining area. For a space so richly designed, it managed to maintain a cozy, welcoming atmosphere.

"You both live here?"

Justin nodded as he turned on the faucet in the sink beside her. He grabbed a large ceramic bowl from a cabinet behind them. His shoulders rippled and flexed beneath his form fitting T-shirt as he reached up to the top shelf.

An answering clench echoed through her abdomen, her body responding to his nearness. The need to touch him, to have him close to her again, grew inside. One thing was certain, the wild attraction they'd shared that day on the side of the road hadn't been a one time, freak occurrence. No matter how she'd tried to reason it away while falling asleep over the past two weeks, their affair hadn't been the result of her too long stretch of abstinence, high stress levels or a bout of temporary insanity. He turned her on like no other man.

Except his brother.

She squashed the stray thought before she could examine it further.

Jason strode into the room, first aid kit in one hand and a large fluffy bathrobe draped over a sinewy forearm. Somewhere along the way, he'd gotten rid of the suit jacket, rolled up his shirtsleeves and unbuttoned his collar. He'd maintained his crisp appearance, looking totally unruffled, even after the hectic afternoon. His steady reliability appealed to her as much as Justin's untamed streak.

Justin soaked a clean dishrag in the lukewarm water and placed it on top of the cloth sticking to her oozing cut. "You got it in there?" He didn't even have to look up and make eye contact for his twin to understand his meaning.

"Yeah." The soft light of regret in Jason's eyes made it clear she wasn't going to like whatever they implied.

"Have what?" She asked, lost amid their unspoken conversation.

"Suture supply kit." Justin's blunt answer made her cringe. She turned squeamish at the thought of metal piercing the raw wound on her leg.

"I don't think that's necessary," she tried objecting. Alexa started to shove off the counter but each brother put out a hand in unison to prevent her from hopping down. Jason held one hip while Justin stroked the other.

"You don't want a scar to mess up that sexy thigh." Justin slipped between her legs, his abdomen pressing against her core. One broad finger reached up to tuck her hair behind her ear. The sight of his blackened fingernail, where he'd obviously smashed it, and calloused hand only increased his attractiveness. Her body betrayed her, turning pliant and greedy. Instead of pushing him away, she wrapped her fist in his shirt and tugged him closer.

His smile hovered a millimeter away from touching her. "I missed you," he whispered and licked her with the tip of his tongue, soothing the swollen spot where she'd bitten her lip earlier. She moaned, all thoughts but sinking into his touch vaporized when he kissed her. He cupped her breast as his tongue probed her mouth, stroking her with a sweet, candid fervor. Alexa arched closer, her skirt riding high up on her thighs.

Then something cool and slippery spread across her skin before the initial sting of the needle pricked her leg. *What the hell?*

The passion Justin sparked in her narrowed her world to his touch and the intense pleasure he gave her. She'd forgotten his brother stood less than a foot away on the other side of her leg. She struggled against Justin's hold but he clasped her tighter and continued to seduce her.

"Let him distract you, sweetheart." Jason's metered voice came soft and rational in her ear. His unwavering hand guided the thread. "I'm trained in first aid. I used a topical anesthetic but it's still going to be uncomfortable. I don't want you to hurt any more than you have to."

She whimpered. She had no desire to experience more than the first few passes he'd already made. She surrendered to Justin's touch. His mouth persuaded her to forget everything but him. She sipped at his lips and leaned into his embrace.

"That's it, Alexa." Jason crooned his encouragement. "Good girl."

She spread her thighs wider, allowing Justin room to fit tight to her. The cool air of the kitchen washed over the saturated crotch of her racy panties a moment before the ridge of his hardening cock stirred against her aching pussy. Breaking the taboo of privacy by inviting Jason to watch their carnal interaction unlocked a secret chamber of arousal she hadn't known existed within her. Nervousness fought with the desire attempting to overwhelm her.

"Just relax, baby." Jason soothed both her worry over the physical discomfort and the greater panic threatening her when she realized how much she enjoyed their forbidden display. She hardly felt the deft touch of Jason's hand on her thigh. "Justin will give you an orgasm if you let him."

The combination of Jason's reserved narration and Justin's scalding touch fueled her needs. It was like being trapped between fire and ice. She moaned as Justin rocked against her. One hand supported her back while the other teased her steel hard nipple. Lust built inside her quickly, just as it had two weeks before. She strained against him, helping him stroke her clit just the way she needed it.

"You like that?" She couldn't have answered Jason's question even if she tried. The domineering control in his voice set her nerves on end, coercing her to submit.

Justin took the opportunity to explore her neck, licking and biting, as he became engrossed in the moment, trusting his brother to guide the encounter.

"Yes. Please," she begged. Her head dropped against her shoulder blades as every muscle in her body devoted itself to enhancing the sensations driving her closer to rapture.

"Please what?" It seemed natural to meet Jason's commanding gaze. The banked yearning in his eyes urged her higher. His discipline coupled with the wild abandon of his twin plunged her deeper into the exhilaration of the moment. She had never considered exhibitionism before, but having both men focused on her created a whole new level of pleasure. Her insides fluttered as she spiraled closer to climax. Just a few more seconds of Justin's intimate grind and she would go over the edge.

She kept her eyes on Jason's smoldering look when she said, "I need him to make me come."

Jason's broad smile dripped with hunger, "And I need to see it."

As soon as the words left his brother's mouth, Justin rotated his hips in an irresistible rhythm. Contractions started forming deep in her pussy and her channel clenched desperately.

"Now, Alexa," Jason ordered, his voice clear and in control. "Come for us."

In front of her, Justin roared as she grasped him around the waist with her legs and clung. He tried to wrench away but she rode his erection through their clothes. The orgasm shattered her. Even as her body shook and spasmed, she stared into the deep, still pools of Jason's eyes until Justin's groan of completion took her by surprise.

He recaptured her mouth and thrust against her in short, rapid jerks of his hips that enhanced her never-ending orgasm as he spilled his come. For a moment, all three of them maintained a stunned silence filled only with their harsh breathing in the aftermath of their outburst of passion but Jason broke the tension with a derisive laugh and a slap on his brother's back.

"I swear I haven't come in my jeans in twenty years." Justin's humor tempered his dismay. He rested his forehead against Alexa's and framed her face with his hands. His thumbs rubbed her cheekbones in a tender gesture. "You're amazing."

She avoided the emotion bared in his expression—too much, too soon.

"Will you finish the stitches now, so I can go take a shower?" She regretted the puzzled look her withdrawal caused Justin but Jason nodded in simple understanding.

"It was done a long time ago." He helped her slide out from Justin's loose hold and set her gently on the ground before handing her the fluffy robe he'd set aside earlier. "Go ahead, everything else you need is in the room at the top of the stairs. Make yourself at home."

She turned and walked away, desperate not to limp or glance over her shoulder. One moment of weakness and she'd end up right back in their arms, but she needed time to sort out all that had happened.

The light blue walls and deep, plush carpeting of the guest room soothed her frazzled nerves. She undressed gingerly, careful of the aches and pains becoming more evident with every minute that passed. Her ruined suit went straight into the garbage. Alexa avoided a peek in the mirror. If she looked anything like she felt, her ego couldn't survive that feedback.

Unlike being desired by two incredibly sexy men.

Her head thunked against the travertine tile of the luxurious shower's wall as the water heated up. She debated whether the show she'd given downstairs should be classified as the most amazing, or stupidest, thing she'd ever done in her life. The afterglow of her orgasm still diminished the part of her that had been scared to death by the attack earlier but, damn, it complicated things.

Denying her scalding attraction to both brothers would be pointless. Justin's wild, open, adventurous spirit made the ideal counterpoint to Jason's practical, organized, responsible character. All her life, she'd struggled to reconcile her prerequisite for stability with her craving for spontaneity. Together, the brothers could meet her every need. She didn't try to delude herself, Jason's eyes had promised her their experiment downstairs meant more than simple act of kindness or distraction.

No, it was a test. He's smart enough to know I'd freak out, and restrained enough to wait for me to cave.

She shut off the water with a snap of her wrist that sent sparks shooting down her arm. Damn, she'd banged her elbow pretty hard. The bruises sprinkled across her side and around the top of her arm had already begun to darken. She said a silent prayer for Justin's timing as she toweled dry. She would be lying dead in an alley somewhere by now if he hadn't stopped her attacker.

Poor Justin, does he realize that his brother intends to have me too?

She added guilt to the pile of emotions bearing down on her, belted the thick robe around her waist and prepared to find out what the hell was going on.

Justin rejoined his brother after changing his clothes. He grimaced when he imagined Alexa's opinion of his juvenile reaction.

"Don't worry." Jason took one look at him and understood his thoughts. Nothing unusual there, it happened all the time.

"I must have missed the day in health class where they

taught that coming in your pants was a recommended method of impressing a woman." He snagged a beer out of the fridge and plopped down on the deep leather couch in the living room just off the kitchen.

"Trust me, she enjoyed it." His brother's voice thickened. "The look on her face..."

"Maybe you should have let it rip in that fancy suit of yours, too. At least you wouldn't be so damn horny now." He laughed at Jason's horrified expression. He would never think of messing up his fine, tailored wardrobe.

"Listen." His twin turned serious. "I want you to know that I didn't do that on purpose. I thought you could kiss her, take her mind off the pain, but things sort of got out of hand."

Hmm, interesting. "Since when am I opposed to sharing my women with you, Jay? Last I checked, I enjoyed it. We both do."

"Alexa isn't some party girl looking for a wild time." Jason got defensive. He leaned forward, setting his soft drink on the coaster protecting the coffee table. He reached one hand back and rubbed his neck.

"No, you're right about that." Jason never acted this uncertain. Justin found it awkward to reassure him. "I wasn't giving her some line before. I think she's amazing."

"Exactly my point. I don't want to ruin what you have going with her. I know you just met her, but this could be the real thing for you. She's different."

"Jay, I may not have several flashy degrees or rule a corporate empire but I'm not a fucking idiot." Before his brother could object, he barreled on. "I *know* this is the real thing. But not just for me, for us both. She's the hottest woman I've ever laid eyes on. That day in the woods... Shit, Jay, I already told you how it was, like I'd die if I couldn't have her. But just now, with you there, it ratcheted things up until I thought she'd start glowing like white-hot metal. Seeing her in that suit made me realize she's not only wild at heart. She lives in both our worlds. She needs us both."

In another rare moment, Justin's discourse rendered Jason speechless. Clearly, he wanted to pursue the matter further but they'd both heard the shower shut off a minute ago. Neither wanted to risk being overheard. Sure enough, light footsteps sounded on the stairway behind them.

He covered for them. "Now, quit stalling and tell me why someone wants to know about your business enough to face felony charges over it."

Chapter Five

"That's a really good question." Alexa entered the room and faced the brothers. Justin sprawled on the beefy leather couch while Jason sat, with perfect posture, on the elegant wingback chair beside it. The eclectic mix of furniture suited the room.

Justin patted the cushion by his side. "Sit down, you're still pale."

He looked delicious in his faded rock band T-shirt and jogging pants. She couldn't explain why the sight of his masculine bare feet turned her on but the flip of her stomach that resulted grew into a full out lurch when her stare darted away and landed on the hint of smooth, ripped chest that peeked through Jason's button-down shirt. Not to mention the sinewy forearms that rested next to each other as he crossed his arms over his lean stomach.

Everything about them turns you on.

She grabbed a sage microfiber blanket off the opposite arm of the couch and tucked it around her like a shield before settling a safe distance away from Justin. The combination of the central air conditioning and her wet hair made the velvety cover seem rational, though they scalded her with the appetite in their eyes. It also ensured she didn't flash them by accident and cause the whole house to explode from the sexual tension her bare flesh might incite. She needed to gather information without distractions.

"Don't bother trying to shut us down." She could tell Jason was preparing to dodge their questions about the business again. "We're in this together now."

"I've decided this venture is too risky." His face became

stony, determined. "I'll spread the word I'm withdrawing my bid."

Justin ignored him and turned to Alexa instead. In a stage whisper he said, "He's lying. Sometimes he goes all big brother on me, since he's a whole two minutes older, like I can't take care of myself."

The thought that Jason considered his six-foot-something, muscled, badass brother in need of his defense inspired a grin but she played along, nodding in sympathy. "He does seem to have that protective streak down."

"But, really, he'll keep working this deal on his own. It's too intriguing for him to pass up." He winked and her insides compressed with longing. "So we'll just wait until he thinks we're not looking and then jump in on our own which will be much riskier than if he'd let us work together in the first place."

Jason rolled his eyes in exasperation. She burst out laughing at the sight of one of the country's most influential businessmen acting like a teenage girl. "Oh, for the love of God. You're not going to quit are you?"

"No." Though Justin acted playful, his emotions ran deep. She read the tension in his whitened knuckles grasping the beer bottle so tight she feared it might crack.

"And neither will I." She committed to helping now, if only to screw the people who had tried to kidnap her. "You offered me a job, and I accept."

Jason's eyes darted between them, weighing his options for a moment, before he stalked into the kitchen and retrieved a steel case. In the confusion earlier, Alexa had assumed it was a briefcase but now she saw it was far too bulky and heavy for that.

He set it on the sturdy coffee table in front of them and snapped open the lid.

She slid closer, enticed by the electronic gizmo inside. Her elbow bumped Justin's when he leaned toward the puzzling object. Circuits made of precious metals glinted, reflecting the halogen can light from overhead.

Justin reached into the case, hesitating a second to peer up at his brother.

"Jay, this isn't what I think it is, is it?" He'd obviously made the leap ahead of her. She recognized a fuel cell and a miniature engine but...that would make the cylinder on the end...

"Wow." She had to concentrate on keeping her mouth closed.

The tiny motor fit comfortably in Justin's hands as he lifted it to examine the modified attachment.

"Exactly." Jason sounded weary. "About three weeks ago, a small research and development start up approached me, claiming to have invented a highly efficient technology powered by a revolutionary biofuel source. They promised their engine ran on renewable, cheap and environmentally friendly fuel. One that could eliminate our reliance on oil and other petroleum products forever. "

"And this is what? A prototype?" Justin tested wires and fittings, he twisted and removed a component.

"Should you be doing that?" The magnitude of change such a technology could bring staggered her. Watching Justin dismantle it without a thought to the consequences set her on edge.

"Yeah, I get engines." He barely paid attention to his response, his focus absorbed in the mechanical parts.

"So do I, but this is unique. Stop. Let's take some pictures first, draw up a diagram..."

He paused to grin up at her. "You're going all Jay on me there, babe."

"Don't worry, Alexa. I documented every detail as soon as they delivered the prototype." Jason smiled down at her in commiseration. "Then I put out word that I was looking to hire a technology consultant. The best of the best."

"So you've had this for weeks and didn't show it to me?" Justin acted pissed but she knew the emotion stemmed from hurt. "I fucking knew something was up with you. Why did you keep denying it?"

"Because you would've wanted to dive right in and I had to do more research first. Then you were...preoccupied." He sighed.

"You did what you thought was best, Jason. You couldn't have known how dangerous the situation would get." Their eyes met and held. She detected regret, longing and, not least of all, desire. The longer they watched each other, the more his gaze heated until Justin interrupted.

"Something's not quite right." He pointed to a gear and hose component. "Here."

"That's the problem." Jason sighed. "It doesn't work. There's an integral component missing."

"How much do they want for it?" Justin pushed back on the couch, the engine abandoned where he laid it on the table.

"Fifty billion." Jason's calm declaration nearly sent her through the roof. Fifty billion dollars. For just one part. Not to mention the cost of R&D, production and marketing. A deal of this magnitude was out of her league, light years beyond even her last project. Jason's faith in selecting her for this position staggered her.

"And I would gladly have raised it. I only wanted to gather a team of experts before word got out. People I could trust. I needed Alexa to head up the program while I was out campaigning for funds and building a consortium to protect our investment. Even Winston Industries can't secure the kind of a bond that will be necessary to develop this on its own."

He beamed at her before continuing. "She's the best in her field. Her reputation, and my research, guaranteed she could handle the political posturing, maintain the level of detail necessary, coordinate all the departments involved and her mechanical capability would allow her to interface with the technical teams, which I hoped to recruit you for. I've been eying her for Winston Industries for some time and this was the golden opportunity. It seemed rational at the time, but you're right to criticize my over planning."

"We're in this together now, Jay. We'll work it out." Justin reassured his brother.

There were no hard feelings but Alexa could tell from Jason's stiff posture that they hadn't heard the whole story yet.

Again, the brothers had an entire subliminal conversation she couldn't quite follow. First, Justin raised his eyebrows. Then Jason shook his head. In response, Justin muttered a curse under his breath.

"What am I missing?" She glanced from one to the other, trying to gauge their expressions.

"The start up's head scientist had a heart attack and died this morning." Jason's cynicism made it clear he didn't believe the fatality a natural death.

"Fuck." Justin scrubbed his fingers through his hair.

"I'm assuming that's when the thieves realized the design had already been shared with Winston Industries and decided to hunt down the details. I'm sorry, Alexa, I didn't know. The message was highly classified and I missed my assistant in the hallway en route to our meeting. I never would have let you leave alone if I'd realized. Once the information leaked, I put us all in jeopardy. I almost got you killed."

Reminded of her narrow escape earlier, she shivered. Her attackers hadn't been playing around. People had been killed for far less than billions of dollars.

"Come here." Before she could protest, Justin tugged her into his lap and surrounded her with his body, which radiated warmth. She could tell he needed to hold her as much as she wanted him to by the desperation in his clutching hands. They were in deeper than she'd ever imagined. "Son of a bitch! We might have lost you before we really knew you."

Her pulse raced. "We?"

"You want us both. Don't you, honey?" Justin trailed his hand down her shoulder, swiping the blanket away from her.

"I..." Her mind still reeled from the revelation of the invention. Switching focus, she thought about what he implied. Could she really be with two men? Sex on the hood of her car had been a serious departure from her comfort zone. This...

"Don't pressure her, Justin." Jason's warning unfroze her. She shook off his concern and decided to be blunt.

"You're okay with sharing?" She couldn't keep the incredulousness from her voice.

"Hell, yes." Justin played with the knot in the terrycloth belt. "Let us show you how good we can make it for you."

His daring didn't surprise her but Jason's slight nod of agreement shocked her. For someone so careful and proper, their proposition shattered logic and promised chaos for ignoring the consequences.

"We're two halves of a whole, Alexa," Jason explained without trying to persuade her. "It's always been this way."

"You've done this before?" she asked, though she suspected the answer.

"Yes," they answered in unison.

Time suspended as Justin's energy crackled, practically stinging her with its restlessness, while Jason's level stare permitted her room to decide. His reserve challenged her more than his twin's exuberance. Experience had taught her that passionate emotions could burn out in a flash but Jason's patient desire coaxed her into a situation that could only result in disaster.

She knew her weaknesses. Falling for the wrong man ranked high on the list. She barely knew these men and already she craved them. What would happen if she let herself care for them?

Jason turned away and said, "She's not ready, Justin."

The stab of disappointment that tore through Alexa convinced her to act before she regretted this moment for the rest of her life.

"Wait." Both sets of green eyes turned on her like lasers. She wiggled off Justin's lap and stood between them. Throwing caution to the wind, she shrugged the bathrobe off her shoulders and let it drop to the floor. She'd never felt as sexy as when they both drew nearer, as though they couldn't resist.

Justin rotated forward and dropped to his knees at her feet in front of the couch. Jason closed the gap between them with one long stride. She shivered when Justin's hands bracketed her hips and his warm lips kissed her reverently just below her belly button. Jason stood close, his chest brushing hers every time she drew another rapid breath. He refrained from touching her when he asked, "You're sure?"

In response, she locked her arms around his solid back and pulled him close, angled to the side so both brothers fit against her. "Yes." She couldn't stop the moan that escaped a moment before she rose up on her tiptoes to place her lips on his in a light kiss. Eyes wide open, she watched desire dilate his pupils when he reciprocated. Kissing Jason was a sweet, intoxicating experience. His fingers supported her neck as he deepened the contact, his tongue nudging her lips, teasing her. Her legs trembled and she might have fallen if not for the two men holding her steady.

Without a word, Jason stepped away, breaking their embrace. She groaned at the loss but, before she could protest further, Justin scooped her into his arms and followed Jason up the stairs, taking them two at a time. They turned into the blue room. Jason peeled the thick comforter out of the way even as Justin leaned forward and placed her in the center of the huge, king-sized bed. The smooth, high thread count sheets cradled her, caressing her skin. Justin followed her down, his mouth surrounding one of her nipples. He licked, laved and nipped her playfully as she watched Jason strip off his clothes.

He didn't hurry. Instead, he unbuttoned the crisp blue shirt with deliberate movements as he observed his brother feasting on her. He studied her reactions while untucking the Oxford and setting it neatly aside, draped over the arm of a nearby chair.

"You like it when he sucks just that way." Jason's words thrilled her. Justin adjusted his technique based on the observation, increasing the waves of pleasure his wet mouth produced. Jason slowly unbuckled his belt. She couldn't take her eyes away from his fingers hovering over the button of his slacks. The material formed an impressive tent where his cock lay hard and aching beneath. Instead of freeing it, he continued to tease her by drawing the leather from around his waist inch by inch.

He coiled it around his fist and the image he made, bare chest gleaming with a light sheen of perspiration, looming over the bed, in complete control caused a spasm to run through her pussy. "Have you ever had a man use a belt on your lush ass before, sweetheart?"

She shook her head before gasping, "No."

The thick, erect length of Justin's cock thumped against her thigh through the soft cotton of his pants as it twitched in response.

"Hmmm," Jason nearly purred. "Maybe next time."

Her nipple hardened further as Justin blew cool air across the damp skin before switching to sweep his tongue across the other breast. The unhurried strip tease continued to torture her. Jason flicked open the button on his slacks and unzipped them before nudging them down his long, muscled legs, leaving him standing in his black boxer briefs, the prominent bulge stretching over nearly to his hip bone. He looked like a picture clipped out of a Playgirl magazine.

Justin trailed his hand down the center of her body, heading straight toward her soaking mound. Her back arched as she tried to direct herself closer to his wandering palm. She needed him to touch her, to still the lust his expert manipulation of her flesh and the sight of his brother's hard, six pack abs generated.

"You want him to pet that pretty pussy, don't you?" She writhed beneath Justin's strokes and Jason's infatuated stare.

"Yes. Oh, yes." She couldn't believe the frenzied plea in her voice but, damn, she'd never wanted a man's touch as desperately as she did right now.

Jason pushed his underwear down his thighs, liberating his full hard-on, which bounced heavy against his ripped thigh. A single drop of pearly liquid beaded at the tip and she licked her lips.

Her eyes closed when Justin's fingertip invaded the top of her drenched slit and followed it downward. Her hips bucked at the intensity of that glancing touch, driving the digit further between her swollen lips. Justin licked her stomach as he moved lower, his fingers flitting over the folds of her pussy. When the mattress dipped, her eyes flew open to discover Jason sitting near the top of the bed, his hips angled toward her, his legs extending down her side as he lounged against the headboard. He pillowed her head on his abdomen, stroking her hair, tracing the shell of her ear, smoothing along her eyebrows with one fingertip before brushing it over her mouth.

She opened her lips, sucking it into her mouth on a moan even as Justin's finger snuck just inside the entrance of her tightening channel. Alexa glanced down to see Justin, now naked—his clothes thrown in a hasty pile at the foot of the bed—nestled between her thighs. His broad shoulders spread her legs further apart to accommodate him.

"You smell so good, baby." He buried his face against her skin, inhaling deeply. His desire was organic. Jason's cock jumped at the sight, branding her collarbone with its heat as it bobbed against her. She turned her head from the erotic sight Justin made and reached forward. Jason helped by shifting his body, cradling her head.

"That's right, sweetheart. Go ahead, suck me." He guided her mouth over the engorged tip of his cock. The moment her tongue swiped the tangy fluid from the slit in the head, Justin sank his finger inside her clenching pussy, spreading the rings of muscle to accommodate its broad length.

She moaned when he followed the thrust with his tongue on her clit, causing Jason's cock to slide further into her mouth. Alexa devoured him with eager swallows. Her enthusiasm was rewarded with Jason's groan of approval and the beginning strokes of Justin's finger deep inside her. She palmed Jason's balls in one hand, loving the way they flexed and tightened in her light grasp.

He leaned forward, testing her nipples with firm squeezes that sent shockwaves to her pussy. Justin added another finger, preparing her for his oversized cock. His lips encased her clit with liquid warmth, sliding over the sensitive nub as he gently licked it. Her muscles gathered tension and she drove Jason's cock deeper into her mouth, causing the head to bump against the back of her throat.

"Right there, Justin." Jason's gravelly instruction directed his brother to the perfect spot. "Make her come. Now."

Justin's fingers curved inside her, the pads of his fingers stroking the front wall of her vagina, locating the ultimate pleasure point, trapping it between his skilled fingers and her pubic bone. Sensation overwhelmed her in a tsunami of passion. She came hard around his hand. Her slick juices coated Justin's face as she swallowed Jason's cock in time to the spasms wracking her body. The waves of orgasm lessened but didn't die out within her as Justin continued to wring pleasure from her body.

Jason's harsh breathing penetrated the roaring in her mind but Justin's voice captured her attention.

"I need to fuck you." He dislodged his fingers from the still clutching grasp of her pussy and crawled up her body until he knelt between her thighs and the plump head of his cock lined up with her dripping opening.

Alexa tilted her head just enough to beg around the proud shaft filling her mouth. "Please. Yes."

Justin groaned as his hips thrust forward, burying himself several inches deep inside her. "I can't hold back, honey." He jerked his cock out then rammed into her again, scooting her up to press tight against the muscled wall of his twin's abdomen. He stretched her impossibly, only causing her desire to spike with the edge of pain.

She tasted the salty musk of Jason's precome and knew he was close to surrendering.

"So small, you're stretched tight around him." Jason's rough, broken words spurred her higher and the ripples of her extinguishing orgasm flared to life.

He gave a harsh moan and tried to pull away but she increased her hold on his balls, keeping him in place, right where she wanted him. "No. Justin." The urgency in Jason's voice broke through to his brother, keeping all three of them poised on the razor edge of pleasure when Justin paused his pounding rhythm. "Condom."

Alexa didn't stop worshiping Jason's steel-hard flesh long enough to tell him she took the pill. She just shook her head no as emphatically as she could with his thick cock buried in her throat and flexed her pussy around Justin, encouraging him to deliver what he promised.

"Oh, God. Can't stop." Justin grabbed her ass, tugging her down onto him even as he buried himself as deep as he could get inside her, grinding his pubic bone against her clit. She felt full to bursting as the head of his cock pressed against her cervix. He thrust inside her fully, extracting all the way out before shoving completely inside her again. Once, twice, and then her world erupted in a flood of lights and ecstasy.

Jason's sac tightened in her palm, and the contractions of his body prepared her, moments before jets of hot come scalded her throat and soothed the flaming need in her pussy. Simultaneously, Justin pumped his seed deep inside her, calling out her name over and over as Jason fed her his own ardor.

She greedily swallowed one last time and whimpered at the hollow sensation left behind when Jason's cock slipped from her lips. He glided down her body, grabbing the comforter from the foot of the bed. He turned her onto her side and gathered her close, her back to him even as Justin pivoted to lie in front of her, still locked deep.

The blanket settled over them and she drifted off to sleep, exhausted from adrenaline and spent passion. Their hands stroked her mindlessly, her aches and pains long forgotten, thoughts of lurking danger banished by the two men bracketing her.

They would keep her safe and satisfied.

Chapter Six

Alexa surfaced in stages from a sound sleep. Bobbing into consciousness, she became aware of shreds of reality each time she struggled to open her eyes but lost out to the utter relaxation sedating her. First, she noted her bed felt luxurious and more comfortable than she remembered. Next, she sighed and nuzzled closer to the warm, firm body nearby. Finally, enough awareness returned to allow her to chastise herself for the wild abandon of the night before.

She bolstered her nerve and peeked out from under heavy lids at the tousled, sexy man lounging on his side, elbow propped in hand, monitoring her rest.

"Morning sunshine." His lazy, smug voice spoke of his absolute contentment.

"Mmm. Justin." She hadn't intended for her reply to sound so welcoming but truth outpaced her instinctive denial of enjoying such a taboo affair. She had loved every minute of the night before and couldn't wait to do it again.

He reached out, stroking the side of her face as she lay next to him on her back, her head propped up on his sculpted biceps. The tenderness in his eyes swamped her and she started to retreat. Smoking hot sex was one thing, but affection from a man like this could be fatal to her heart.

"Shhh. Lay here a minute more with me." His free arm snaked around her waist, pinning her to the ultra-plush mattress. "Jay is downstairs making some food to bring you in bed. You wouldn't want to spoil his surprise, would you?"

Her stomach growled and she relaxed beneath him, defeated. It would be impossible to argue since she wanted to soak in the moment. Jason's thoughtfulness touched her. Of course he realized she'd be starving. They hadn't eaten dinner last night. He probably even deduced that her nerves had prevented her from eating lunch before the big meeting yesterday. Breakfast sounded heavenly.

"How are you feeling this morning?" Concern replaced the affection in his expression. That she could handle. Alexa stretched, testing her muscles with tentative movements. She winced when the stiffness in her ribs and leg penetrated the lingering haze of waking.

"Not too bad," she lied.

Justin lifted the thick down comforter away from her in stages. He paused to inspect the bruises ringing her upper arm first. He bent over her, pressing a soft kiss just beneath the obvious finger marks.

"Poor baby." He grunted as he tugged the quilted blanket to her waist and saw the discolored flesh stretching over her ribcage. It must have looked pretty nasty because his attention didn't waver from the injury to her fully bared breasts. He trailed his fingertips over the area, light enough to tickle a bit, before taking his hand away and touching his lips to his palm. Justin laid it over her side in a gesture that melted her further.

He made his way down to the top of her thigh where a trimmed bandage smacking of Jason's attention to detail covered the neat row of stitches. His hand trembled when he traced the outline of the gauze.

His attention snapped up to her face. "I'm sorry I wasn't more careful with you last night. Did I hurt you?"

"No." She shook her head, she hadn't felt pain, only pleasure. But if he hadn't shown up when he did...

"I just wish I'd gotten there sooner." Regret marked his features before simmering anger covered it over. "If I find the bastard that did this to you, he's dead."

"I never said thank you," she whispered.

Justin leaned forward until his forehead rested against hers and avoiding his gaze became impossible. "You could thank me now."

The steamy look accompanying his words dared her to ask, "What did you have in mind?"

His broad smile betrayed his trickery and she anticipated a

naughty request. "I want to know why you ran from me that day in the mountains. Why you're still running now."

"Are you sure you wouldn't rather have a blow job?" she bargained.

"Very tempting." He chuckled at her audacity. "But I need to understand what's holding you back."

"The fact that I slept with two men at once last night isn't enough?" She hoped her attitude masked her vulnerability. She teetered off balance, torn between the strength of her emotions for two men, practically strangers, and her logical conclusion that nothing lasting could come of the situation.

"Honey, you can lie to yourself, but you can't fool me. I tasted your desire when it flooded my mouth." She couldn't deny it. "You loved every moment of it."

"That doesn't mean that I think it was prudent." She fought to keep herself cold and rational. Pushing up from the bed, she tried to escape but Justin wouldn't allow it. He snagged her wrist and returned her to her place beside him.

"It wasn't prudent to let me come inside your hot pussy without protection?" He thought the lack of a condom bothered her. "I swear I've never done that before. I'm sorry, we should have talked about it first but, for the record, I'm healthy."

"I'm on the pill. My *body* is safe." She worried about her heart.

"Someone hurt you." His scrutiny cut too deep for her comfort. "Worse than these bruises."

Tears stung her eyes as she frantically tried to blink them away. She wanted to slap him with her words, gain some space to think. "Just like you will, too."

He didn't even flinch. "It's not going to happen, babe. You can trust us."

"I know your type, Justin." She couldn't keep the bitterness from her voice. "You're reckless, fickle, unfaithful and commitment phobic."

"No, darlin'." The volume of his retort escalated. "You're the one who's afraid, not me. I'm willing to admit that I've fallen head over heels for you. You want to hear me say it? Fine. I. Love. You. And that's not going to change."

"What? That's crazy! I just met you!" She lurched in an

attempt to jump up but collapsed gasping and pushing a hand against her ribs. The gesture granted him a reprieve from the tirade she prepared to launch.

"It's fucking true! The world feels right when I'm with you. I don't need a year or ten to know that I'll never find a woman like you again. I won't throw that away because you're scared."

"Yelling in her face probably isn't the best approach to convince her of what little self-control you possess." Jason's deadpan delivery came from the doorway in an attempt to diffuse the situation but Alexa lay stunned by the impact of Justin's words and emotions.

He scrubbed his hands over his face. "Shit. You're right, that was...stupid."

The shrill ringing of the house phone drowned out his last syllable. Both brothers stiffened, becoming instantly alert. Jason set the tray he carried on the bed and grabbed for the receiver on the nightstand.

Angling closer, Justin whispered in her ear as Jason punched the talk button. "Only a few emergency contacts have access to that number."

"Hello?" Tension emanated from each stiff muscle in Jason's body. "I see. Yes. We'll be there." He replaced the handset in the cradle with a precise snap of his wrist.

"When and where, Jay?" Justin asked as though he'd heard the conversation himself.

"You have to stop doing that!" She squirmed from beneath him and faced them with hands on hips, unconcerned by her nakedness. "What the hell was that about?"

"Seems someone from the R&D lab kept process notes and they're willing to make a deal." Jason looked between her and Justin in silent communication but this time she understood exactly what they intended.

"Oh, no you don't." She stepped between them, cutting off their line of sight. "I'm going too."

Justin watched his brother cross the gloomy street in front of their parked car. The tinted glass made surveillance possible, hiding them from any onlookers. The caller had demanded Jason come alone but neither he nor Alexa would have permitted a solo excursion. He hoped the fact they refrained from calling the cops would satisfy the informant.

"Son of a bitch," he muttered under his breath as Alexa unfolded her lithe body from the backseat and climbed upfront. The awkward position must have hurt like hell considering her injuries but it gave him a world-class view of her luscious behind.

"Are you looking at my ass?" Her scathing tone implied he better not be.

"Yup."

"How about you watch out for Jason instead?" She had a point there. He swiveled his head to face out the windshield. Although his brother trained in self defense to protect against money seeking schemers, it never hurt to have help.

"How did you talk us into letting you get involved in this again?" Justin fired the words from where he fumed in the passenger seat.

"I was already involved, remember?" Like he could forget the horror of witnessing her half-jammed into the hatch of that van. "Besides, no matter what he thinks, Jason needs someone to cover his ass while he's exposed out there. From the way you're holding that gun I assume you actually know how to use it, but it probably requires some concentration. In addition, you couldn't refute that it would be easier to protect him if someone else were in charge of the exit plan. I happen to be an excellent driver. Plus, I'm an even better negotiator. It's one of the reasons Jason hired me in the first place."

"I'll keep that in mind." The sly smile she sent him caused his cock to harden, a distraction he couldn't afford right now. He had to clarify one thing, though, in case this situation went to shit like his instincts screamed it would.

"About what I said...you know, before." Justin cleared his throat while keeping his attention glued to the surroundings, monitoring every nook and cranny of the shadowed alley for signs of trouble.

"Don't worry about it." Alexa attempted to brush him off. "Lots of people say things in the heat of the moment they don't mean."

Huh?

He heard her fidgeting, fingers toying with the zipper on her purse as she removed something metallic from inside and fiddled around with it. He risked a glance in her direction and caught the uncertain expression she wore as she chewed on her moist bottom lip. He nearly groaned.

Eyes forward, chief.

Jason stood with his back to a brick wall, vigilant, awaiting his contact's arrival.

"You have it all wrong." How could he do anything but love her? She was sweet, sexy, brave, smart, daring and a perfect fit for both him and his twin. "I want to apologize for the way I told you. I know you're not ready to deal with it yet. I'm not going to rush you. I just wanted you to know I'm not fucking around here."

He paused for a moment, double checking their surroundings. Her unusual silence urged him to continue. Maybe she would actually listen.

"Look, I don't know what that jackass did to you..."

She interrupted. "He promised to love me forever but he really meant until he got bored. I walked in on him with the next gullible woman he met."

Justin snuck a glimpse at their woman. Her curt explanation didn't obscure the agony in her beautiful eyes but it did demonstrate how she had evolved to protect herself, by controlling her emotions and playing things safe. When a woman like Alexa loved, her whole soul would be exposed with nothing held in reserve. Giving that trust, and having it betrayed, had scarred her heart.

He was determined to heal it.

"Damn, honey. I can't say I'm sorry 'cause if he wasn't a supreme fool, you wouldn't be here now. I'll never let go of what we have but I'll try to give you room to accept it. I'll be right here waiting for you to tell me you're ready. That's a promise."

He cursed his timing when a lone figure in a black trench coat approached, preventing her from responding. The man's innocuous appearance contradicted Justin's expectations for the bearer of information that had already cost the life of one person. His average height, plain brown hair and nondescript form helped him avoid attracting attention as he made his way in front of the car.

Justin's fingers tightened on the grip of the S&W he held at the ready when the stranger's hand dipped into the front pocket of his long coat. He relaxed marginally when the man retrieved a manila envelope instead of the weapon Justin feared. Maybe they'd get the info and get out of here quick and painlessly after all.

Jason prepared himself to knock the newcomer over and bolt for the car if he so much as looked at Jason funny, confident that Justin would have him covered. He wanted to stay and force some answers from the man but he wouldn't risk Alexa's safety by keeping her out in the open any longer than necessary. The thought of losing her had already become unbearable. As crazy as it seemed, Justin's bold declaration this morning had been the truth. A better partner for them didn't exist.

The man barely made it up to him before he dug inside his coat and flipped out a packet of papers. "Take them. Hurry, I'm being followed." The strained words accompanied a paranoid glance behind him as though someone might be standing right over his shoulder.

Jason held out a wad of money, the amount specified for the trade.

"Keep it. I just want to get out of the game." He spun on his heels and headed off.

For one split second, Jason considered inviting the man to the sanctuary of their house but he couldn't risk a trap. Not with Alexa involved.

"Thank you," Jason called to the retreating form.

The brisk footsteps paused as he turned back, nodding stiffly, a moment before his face froze in a grimace of shocked pain and a red stain blossomed across his forehead.

"Oh fuck!" Jason rushed to the spot where the man had collapsed but his eyes already glazed, his limbs folded, completely lax, in a unique state reserved for death.

A distant corner of his mind registered the car screeching up to the curb and the telltale ping of a bullet ricocheting off the pavement near his feet before Justin's shout rang out.

"Let's go, it's too late for him." Then, a second later, "Jason!

Move it, now!"

Jason stumbled to the car waiting open for him and slid inside. Justin reached through the open window to slam the door shut with one hand while firing a few shots at a target Jason couldn't see.

The memory of the stricken informant obscured everything else.

Chapter Seven

Alexa set her iPod on the center console, thankful that Jason had arranged to have someone grab a few essentials from her apartment last night. She attached the cables to the car stereo a moment before all hell broke loose. Justin shouted at her to pull forward, Jason stumbled back into the car and shots echoed with an eerie whine when Justin returned fire on an unseen assailant. She slammed the stick in gear and peeled away. Filtering all distractions from her mind, she focused on the job at hand.

Rounding the corner, she forced her muscles to relax and let years of training take over. "Turn on the music," she instructed Justin without removing her eyes from the road flying by faster with every gear change.

"Holy shit, now is not the time!" He spun around, scouting out the road behind them. "There are two black sedans and a motorcycle in pursuit."

She waited for him to finish reloading the gun before reiterating. "Press the dial at 6 o'clock and hang on."

Avoiding a semi, she tucked them into a space barely larger than the car itself. Justin's shoulder slammed against the door, resulting in additional cursing.

"Sit down, put your belt on and play my damn music!" Her command left no room for argument. He settled himself as she wove into the current of traffic on the highway, avoiding another injury.

"Not like I can keep a steady line now anyway." He grumbled before flipping down the mirrored visor to check on Jason. "You are okay, aren't you?"

"Yeah." Jason's monotone response reached them.

"Alexa, step on it, they're still right behind us."

She observed the vehicles in her rear and side view mirrors, aware of their exact positions. "Turn it on."

"Jesus Christ, you're stubborn. Fine. Here." He stabbed the button harder than necessary, the result of too much adrenaline, and the heavy beat of her selected score enveloped them.

She always accompanied her drives with music. It helped her get lost in the rhythm of the lines blazing by and focus on the opportunities between the drivers she streaked past. She edged ahead within moments, taking carefully weighed chances. She calculated each turn, pass and merge before accepting the risk.

Beside her, Justin whooped with her successful movements, each increasing the distance between them and their tails. His enthusiasm faded to the background as the song transformed into a precise staccato refrain. She evaluated her options and studied the pattern of traffic before ditching from the highway at the last safe moment to exit onto an industrial strip of road. Warehouses lined the narrow street and huge trucks transporting goods abounded.

Only the biker remained behind them.

The skilled rider had the advantage, his motorcycle faster and more agile than Jason's sedan, though Justin had obviously worked his magic on the car at some point. It responded with a roar when she needed power and accelerated quicker than she expected. Still, her chance to get away lay in being a smarter driver.

"What time is it?" She spoke in a calm, even tone.

"Time to go home," Jason protested from behind her and she risked a quick glance at him. His pale face glowed against the dark leather interior and he gripped the oh-shit handle in the door hard enough that it would bear permanent dents.

Thank God he's okay. Her heart shuddered when she reflected on what might have happened, causing her to lose focus for a moment.

"Watch out!" Justin's warning swung her attention back to the road in front of her where she avoided a parked car with inches to spare.

She accelerated, bringing them up to speed, regaining her composure with fluid grace.

"Who set the clock in this car?" She asked. When Jason grunted a response, she counted on it being exact. "The time?"

"Five thirty-three." Justin didn't bother asking why anymore.

While they'd waited for the doomed man to deliver his notes to Jason, she'd spent her time plotting. She traveled a route parallel to this road on her way home from the office on good weather nights, when she used an evening tour to unwind. Nothing ruined a drive in her convertible faster than being stuck in miles of traffic, choking on exhaust fumes. Therefore, she tracked most of the possible pitfalls in the city.

She nodded. "We'll make it."

"What are you doing?" Jason's censure shone through.

"Taking you home, safe and sound." She navigated on autopilot, maneuvering the vehicle with efficient tactics. She managed to sneak away from the motorcycle at times but he always caught up again. She didn't have a choice.

"Time?" Alexa checked her speed, too.

"Five thirty-six." Justin read off the glowing numbers. "You have a plan?"

"Yeah but we're too early." She swung out wide and doubled back on their path, heading straight toward the man on the bike. He dodged out of their trajectory, expecting her to attempt to ram him but she couldn't do that.

"Tell me when the clock turns to five thirty-eight." She continued to backtrack until Justin gave her the signal.

"Now."

As soon as the road cleared, she swung the car around one hundred and eighty degrees with a screech of tires to finish the loop.

"Five thirty-nine," Justin announced. "But he's still there, about five hundred feet behind us."

Perfect.

She came over the ridge on West Hamilton and Jason shouted from the backseat. "You're not going to..."

Alexa judged the gap sufficient and committed to the stunt, slamming the gas pedal to the floor.

"Wahoo!" Justin howled as they dove into the center ghost island, around the stopped cars, and flew across the tracks in front of the five forty train from downtown. The bike had no choice but to stop or be flattened.

Either way, he couldn't follow.

Justin laughed as he whirled her around in circles across the middle of the living room floor. "Fucking brilliant."

Then he ensnared her with a fierce kiss, letting his relief infuse the gesture. Dizziness swamped her senses, but not as a result of being spun. He left her craving his touch when he separated their mouths. He brought his lips close to her ear and whispered, "I need you to take care of Jay for a while."

She nodded.

He lowered her feet to the floor, rubbing her body down every inch of his muscled front along the way, before facing Jason. He sat, still as a statue, in his usual chair with his head buried in his hands, his fingers locked over his fine hair, rumpled for the first time since she'd met him.

"Jay, I'm going to the shop to get some tools. We'll need them if we're going to crack those notes and file a patent on the engine."

Alexa read between the lines. They would only be out of danger once others couldn't profit from the secret.

"It's not safe." Jason's answer sounded hollow.

"No one knows about the second entrance to the house, it's secure."

Even Jason couldn't argue that point. "Don't do anything crazy."

Justin clapped a hand over Jason's shoulder. She witnessed the compassion in Justin's eyes before he turned to go.

When the door shut with a quiet snick, she crossed to Jason. She couldn't bear the sight of his suffering a moment longer. She understood him well enough to grasp the problem he faced. That insight highlighted the seriousness of the affection growing inside her. She'd never experienced such a deep, instinctive bond with anyone before these two incredible men.

She sank to her knees between his feet and laid her head in his lap. "It's not your fault, there's nothing you could have done."

Alexa stroked his leg, surprised to feel him shaking beneath her touch. "I almost invited him to come here, with us. He would have been safe." Jason drew a deep breath. "He didn't even take the money."

"You couldn't have known he was legitimate." She needed to ease his suffering.

His hands slid down from behind his head to settle in her hair. He rubbed it between his fingers, soothing himself by touching her.

"I should have thought to provide him protection." His disappointment and fury radiated through the rigidity of his body.

"You're not superman." She peered up at him, meeting his liquid green gaze. His pain nearly broke her heart.

Oh no, it can't be. I can't care that much. The sudden realization burst free from her soul and she evaluated it with brutal honesty. She did care, and she would give him whatever he needed even if this primal side of him frightened her a little. "Sometimes, we have to take calculated risks."

The fire in his expression singed her, but he still wouldn't accept the solace she offered.

"Take me, Jason." He wavered on the edge of his control, his hand fisting in her hair. "I'm yours, too. We're not only connected because of Justin."

"You don't understand what you're doing." His breath came harsh and uneven. "Don't tempt me. Not now."

A darkness he kept under wraps with sheer force of will seeped through the cracks in his resolve, weakened by the strain of the day. Alexa yearned to discover what the intensity of his emotions would feel like swirling around her. She anticipated his need to regain control and accepted the burden, even at the risk of sacrificing her own.

"Use me." She trusted implicitly that he would not harm her. That bone-deep knowledge provided the freedom to explore the source of the struggle within him. "I want to help. You can't keep this bottled inside."

He drew a harsh breath and scrunched his eyes as though offering up a silent prayer. "Our first time alone should be gentle and romantic. I can't give you that right now."

"That's not what I want." She stood and tugged on his hand. "Please."

His control fractured. Jason lunged from the chair, shoving her in front of him until her back bumped up against the side of the stairwell. He groaned and buried his fingers in her hair. "Last chance, sweetheart." His lips hovered a hairsbreadth from hers.

"Do it." Alexa surged forward, closing the gap between them.

His touch enveloped her. His hands flew over her, unsnapping her jeans as his mouth plundered, stealing her breath through his kiss. They turned, banging their way up the stairs, one or the other pinned against the wall as they stripped clothes away, never breaking contact for more than a moment.

By the time they made it to the top of the stairs, she had wrapped her legs around his waist. Her bare pussy, slick with arousal, slid against the smooth skin of his lower abdomen. His hard-on nestled against her ass while he walked them down the hall to his room. He kicked open the door and deposited her on the cool black satin sheets of the large, artistic, wrought-iron bed. She didn't waste time examining his space but the overall ambiance impressed luxury on her senses.

He came over her on the bed, his hard cock nudging between her legs, and reclaimed her mouth with an animal grace. She wrapped her arms around his powerful back, delighting in the flex and ripple of the muscles there.

Where sex with Justin was playful, Jason's intensity made her feel delicate and oh-so-willing to submit to his inherent domination. Her legs locked around his waist and she attempted to use her heels on his tight ass to urge him inside her, testing him, goading him.

He didn't disappoint.

Jason shook off her efforts, breaking free of her grasp. He deprived her of his touch and the loss caused a physical ache.

"You gave me control." The fire in his eyes set off another wave of desire inside her and she writhed on the mattress beneath his measuring stare.

"Yes, whatever you want," she practically begged.

He climbed from the bed and her attention caught on the sight of his magnificent cock waving in stiff bobs as he crossed the room to his closet in two steps. He retrieved a handful of silk ties and a small leather chest that he placed at the foot of the bed.

With careful deliberation, he knelt at her feet and yanked her ankles apart. The movement shocked her, making her exposure complete. The thrill that rushed through her left no doubt as to how much she loved it and wanted to continue this game.

"You like this?" His gravelly question required no answer but the moan slipped out of her throat anyway.

His strong grip collared each ankle, making them appear dainty in comparison. Jason bent low to brush a kiss over each one before selecting an expensive-looking tie from the pile. He lifted her right ankle, winding the material comfortably, but inescapably, around it before securing the ends to a loop of metal camouflaged by the ironwork in a convenient spot at the corner of the bedframe.

He caught her glance and resolved her curiosity while binding her other leg. "Yeah, it's custom made."

Alexa tested the strength of the knot work and found it secure. She couldn't break free. Unbidden, she whimpered and squirmed on the silky sheets. Every tactile stimulation inflamed nerve endings sensitive to the touch. With her feet immobilized, he slithered up her body, the two remaining ties in hand.

"So beautiful." He trailed the strips over her legs and abdomen.

She arched her hips, trying to reach the dangling fabric with her clit, which throbbed, desperate for attention.

"Not yet." His stern command stilled her attempts and she watched, fascinated as he dropped his head between her legs. His mouth teased her, staying out of reach. "You're so wet, you're spilling your desire on my sheets."

"I'm sorry." She tried to lift her ass off the bed but he delivered a light slap to the inside of her thigh.

"Never apologize for your passion. It's one of the things I love most about you." The declaration startled Alexa but his direct eye contact left no room for deception. His honesty caused her channel to clench and squeeze out more of her fluids. He stooped lower and licked the dampness from the material between her legs. After cleaning the spot, he turned his head and nipped her.

"Please, Jason, hurry." She reached down and attempted to position his head closer, but he refused to budge. "I need you to touch me. Fuck me. Anything. Please."

With a growl, he lurched up and pinned her wrists to the pillow beside her head. Every inch of his body molded tight to her as she panted beneath him. He licked and kissed his way up her throat before slanting his lips over her mouth. His finesse transformed into pure desire as he sucked on her tongue.

She lost herself in the journey he led her on, stealing her sanity as his wet warmth took her mouth. When he pulled away, she resurfaced only to find her wrists bound to each other and the headboard. She struggled a moment, a brief flash of panic setting in before he soothed her with a kiss and a promise.

"You're going to like this. I'll take care of you."

He yanked two pillows from the side of the bed and tucked them beneath her hips, angling them upward. He towered over her. A web of veins, which pulsed in time to his pounding heart, decorated the bulging muscles of his arms and neck, announcing his command over the passion and strength flowing through them. A bead of precome rolled down the head of his cock and dripped a few inches above her pussy. She felt so hot she expected to see it sizzle on her skin.

"Oh God. Please." She couldn't still her body as it undulated beneath him.

"Patience, love." His wide hand smeared the glistening drop across her belly, massaging it into her skin. Nothing in her life had ever been so erotic as this moment.

He turned to the chest she'd all but forgotten and raised the lid. She strained her neck, trying for a glimpse of the contents, but no matter how she struggled, she couldn't see what mysteries the box held. She heard the crumple of packaging opened for the first time a moment before he swung around with a feral gleam in his emerald eyes.

"You've never taken a man in your ass, have you, Alexa?" Her attention flitted between his straining cock, the perspiration dampened muscles of his smooth chest and six pack abs. So focused on his form, she almost missed the question entirely.

"No, never." But she wasn't clueless. If she stayed with the brothers, it would happen sooner or later.

Jason tipped forward, supporting himself on one forearm while the other rested at her hip. He whispered in her ear. "I'm going to prepare you for us. It will hurt less if you cooperate."

She couldn't still her reflexive jerk when the cool, blunt tip of a toy pressed against the opening of her pussy. She bucked beneath him, increasing the contact of their bodies, trying to force it in deeper. He let her have her way this time.

"That's it, sweetheart." His voice rasped in her ear as he teased it with his tongue. "Get it good and wet."

His head lowered to suckle the tip of her breast, alternating broad licks with the sharp edges of his teeth on her nipple. Her pussy contracted so tight the bulbous rubber object squeezed from her grip. She moaned at the loss.

"You want it back?" He dared her to ask for it.

A tremor ran through her entire body at the raw sensuality bursting from him.

"Yes."

He pressed the lubricated tip against her asshole, drenched from the arousal that ran down her crack from her weeping pussy. The bite of discomfort only spurred her higher but instinct caused her to fight the intrusion and the bonds holding her in place. Her head thrashed on the pillow as Jason forced the toy to invade her with steady pressure. He crooned reassurance and pet her hair until the base nestled against her ass, the toy fully seated inside her.

His cock rode her thigh when he buried his face in the crook of her neck, holding her until the sting faded and arousal took its place. "You have no idea how badly I need you."

"And I, you," she promised. Both spoke of more than the psychical.

Some of the desperation seemed to drain from him as he nuzzled her. He lifted his head just enough to fit his mouth over hers. His kiss suffused her with gentle heat that, when combined with the pressure of the object spreading her anus, threatened to make her come apart.

The forbidden act increased her excitement, multiplying the desire inside her.

Finally, his hands framed her face as the heavy head of his cock fit against the entrance to her pussy. Her labia hugged around him, inviting him in. He rocked against her with miniscule movements that began to nudge apart the tight rings of muscle.

"I need all of you, Jason." Instead, the ties restricted her movement, leaving her at his mercy, unable to force him deeper.

"Not yet, sweetheart," he whispered in her ear. "You're going to come so hard around me. I can't wait to feel your wet pussy sucking at my cock. You're so petite , it's going to take a while for me to open you to all of me with that toy in your ass."

His fingers flexed restlessly as his hips continued their relentless torture, driving his shaft a tiny bit deeper with each pass. His cock rubbed and teased the thin wall of flesh separating it from the plug. The sensation triggered a response in nerve endings she never knew existed before. She wondered what it would feel like to have Justin buried deep inside her.

"That's right, Alexa." His hips thrust harder as the same thought occurred to him and spurred him on. "Imagine what it will be like with both of us fucking you."

"Oh God." Her orgasm spiraled closer as his pelvis began to stroke her clit. "I'm going to come."

He froze, leaving her dangling on the edge of oblivion.

"Not until I tell you to." His piercing stare promised her it would be worth the wait.

He began to move again, almost halfway inside her now, and she already felt full to capacity. Her tissue stretched and accommodated him gradually. The waves of pleasure built again.

"Jason." Her moan was ragged. "Can't wait. Need to come."

He pulled back once more before ramming inside her. His cock reached impossibly deep, drawing a gasp as her back arched in astonishment. His balls slapped against the base of the toy in her ass, sending shockwaves up her spine. She tried to suppress the sensations pushing her toward a gigantic release but he noticed and let her off the hook.

"Come for me, Alexa." His command sent her flying. Jason rode through the spasms of her climax, extending the explosion of passion that threatened to overwhelm her.

He fucked her hard, deep and fast until the pulsing pleasure rose again. Her head swished from side to side, trying to escape the intensity radiating from their joining. The wild grunts and moans of Jason's impending orgasm, coupled with the sliding action of his body pressed tight against her clit, threw her into another round of contractions.

"Yes," he moaned. "Milk my cock."

She did just that, clamping around him in rhythmic pulses until she heard him shout her name. The searing heat of his come filled her as he gave her all the pent up need and emotion raging inside him.

Chapter Eight

Alexa slunk down the stairs in search of Justin. She grabbed the handrail to steady her liquefied muscles. Following her earth shattering release, Jason had tended to her, untying her and carrying her to the shower. The calm after the storm of passion they'd shared allowed her time to consider the ramifications of their actions.

The etiquette of a relationship like this escaped her. Would Justin be angry? Had she cheated on him? Uncertainty and fear festered inside her with each passing moment. Although Jason acted like nothing depraved had happened and certainly he wouldn't intentionally hurt his brother, she needed Justin to confirm it. Her confidence in her actions dissipated with each passing moment. Had desire colored her judgment?

She'd excused herself from Jason's sophisticated, dark-wood paneled office where he researched the startup that had originally contacted him, kicking off this chain reaction of disaster. She intended to wait in Justin's workshop for his return. Then, she could confess what they'd done and beg for his forgiveness if he didn't approve.

If only it hadn't felt so right.

She made her way through the kitchen toward the space Jason had indicated adjoined the garage. Light spilled from beneath the door and, as she drew nearer, she heard the pounding rhythm of hard rock music accompanied by the whir of a power tool.

Her pulse skittered when she considered Justin's reaction. He might see her betrayal as grounds to call off their developing relationship. Her sweaty palms and the sinking dread in the pit of her stomach convinced her that the attachment she had to both men transcended simple desire. True, she craved their touch, had become addicted to the potent sexuality they embodied but, more than that, they captured her soul. Being with them was like finding a piece of herself she hadn't realized was missing.

She laid a hand on the door, frozen for a moment, before gathering her courage and shoving it open.

As though he sensed her presence, Justin pivoted when she entered. He clicked off the buffer he used to smooth a chunk of metal while she took stock of the workshop. Clamps, rulers, bits, blades and various accessories lined the walls. Tool chests bursting with supplies sat in each corner and machines ringed a huge raised bench table.

"Exactly what did you need that you didn't already have two of in here?" Her foot tapped the smooth concrete and her arms crossed over her chest as she declared shenanigans.

"Uh...alright, busted." He shook his head ruefully. "I just checked the perimeter with a walk around the house to give you and Jay some time to come to your senses and realize that a good, hard fuck was the best way to work out all your leftover stress. It was driving me crazy. I need to concentrate on this without a major distraction hanging over my head."

"Wait. You *wanted* us to do it?" Some of her uneasiness seeped out. "Without you?"

His smile lit up the room. "You needed it almost as bad as Jay." Then he turned serious. "Look, he's never taken a woman he understood or connected with before. Sure, we slept with women, probably more than was wise. But they were never a serious thing. They were party girls, looking for a fun time. You're the only woman who's ever tempted him to love or challenged his self-control. And by the looks of you, it suits you both."

Justin stalked closer, taking her hand in his own tender grasp. He brought it to his lips and kissed the red lines decorating her wrists like bracelets.

"You enjoyed this?" he asked with genuine curiosity.

Alexa shivered and nodded.

"And this?" He brushed his mouth over the dark spot on her neck she'd glimpsed in the bathroom mirror when Jason toweled her dry earlier.

"God, yes." Admitting it caused a blush to crawl over her face. She attempted to regain influence by focusing on her anger. "But how was I to know you approved?"

He tugged her into his arms, cradling her against his chest. She listened to his steady heartbeat and relaxed.

"I'm sorry, honey. I didn't mean to upset you." He settled his chin on top of her head. "You didn't do anything wrong."

He cupped her shoulders in his hands and braced her. "Hey, look at me, baby." The tenderness in his eyes warmed her heart instead of frightening her this time. "I'm even more thrilled for you and Jay than I am for myself. You're the two people I love most in the world. Whether I'm there or not, you should do what feels right with him. I know he would say the same. You belong with us."

They embraced for a long minute, neither having to speak. He ended the silence when awkwardness infiltrated her for not reciprocating his declarations. Justin didn't pressure her for more than she could give.

"Come on." He led her over to the component he'd been working on when she came in. "I need some help."

Jason clicked the print button, sending the last of the supplier documents to the queue. He supplemented business acumen with expert research skills, enabling him to make strategic decisions. Over the years, he'd learned to double check information provided by prospective partners who targeted his successful firm for scams.

Before things went to hell in a hand basket, he'd intended to hire Alexa as the program manager of the new operation. A large part of her position would be to act as a liaison who could decipher the technical specifications and translate them into terms he could understand. She often performed a similar function in her role as a top consultant in the field.

His file on her proved her commitment to her career. She spent months working high intensity projects with ridiculous, long hours. On call, she had to be available 24/7 to extinguish any fires that popped up related to an initiative. Analyzing the information he now possessed would be second nature to her.

Jason straightened the papers, whistling a cheesy song as he made his way out to Justin's workshop. The racket of metal and gears floating up to his bedroom earlier had clued him in to his brother's ruse even if Alexa had been too preoccupied to notice. He nudged open the door so he could steal a look inside undetected. He scoffed at his own silliness. He'd never craved a simple glimpse of a woman before, but a man in love for the first time wanted to savor every moment.

Alexa perched on a high stool, tinkering with random parts that made little sense to him. Close behind her, Justin stood relaxed, watching over her shoulder, one arm wrapped casually around her waist as they collaborated on a solution.

Jason wondered how he could have known of her all these years and never realized she would be the perfect woman for them. Her profile hadn't captured the adventurous part of her spirit and the chemistry between them had remained untested since he avoided public appearances.

So much time wasted.

He entered the room, making his way toward them. Their ability to concentrate with the radio blasting baffled him. Together, they turned and Alexa's face reflected the same joy he experienced on reuniting with her after their brief separation. Her eyes smoldered with remnants of heat from their earlier interlude. Her submission thrilled him with its beauty and intrinsic trust.

Her protection was a responsibility he took seriously. If they could crack the secret and apply for a patent, their safety would be assured. Only once they eliminated the possibility of someone else profiting from the invention would they be free to continue their lives in peace. Even if they gave up pursuing the engine design, they'd be at risk. Some crazy person might not believe the final piece of the puzzle eluded them.

Suddenly, he wanted to finish this deal and get to the truly important part of his future. Just a few days ago, he'd have sworn the biofuel engine was the most significant development in his life but one sassy woman had changed his mind.

"What do you have, Jay?" Justin's concerned grimace and insightful stare made it clear he shared the same train of thought.

"A present." Jason pressed a quick peck to Alexa's cheek as

he set the documents down in front of her. More than a glancing touch and they wouldn't get any work done.

She rifled through the stack to get a sense of the information. On the third or fourth page she paused.

"Why didn't I think of this?" She spoke to herself, engrossed in the data. Ignoring Justin's bewildered look as he tried to interpret the rows of numbers, she began to organize the sheets into piles. She continued to talk to herself.

"We already know what that was for." She crumpled one of the papers and tossed it into a heap of scrap metal that appeared to be bungled attempts at replicating the component.

"No." She added another wad to the trash. "Nope. Got that one. Not it." Garbage. Garbage. Garbage.

"I take it things haven't been going well down here?" Jason raised an eyebrow at his brother.

"Using the notes, we were able to recreate all but one critical piece of the component." He sighed. "We thought we had it but it looks like our friend trusted no one. For the vital connection he removed the full details of the materials used and replaced them with some kind of code. CP. We tried copper pipe, chrome plates, chipped platinum and any other conductors we could think of but, so far..." He shrugged wearily.

Alexa swiveled around, displaying an invoice so they could read it. The letterhead stated *Chastal Partners—your source for fine specialty metals.* Below that, a quantity of one sat beside a single line item—*half-inch gold conduit.*

"Tell me you have some," she pleaded.

Justin yanked open a drawer. Things rattled and banged as he rummaged through it. "One eighth, three quarters, one sixteenth..." He grinned, selecting a piece and screwing it onto the fitting. He dropped the component into the chamber and attached the necessary wires.

The three of them stood silent, staring at the completed engine.

"Go ahead, honey." Justin rested his hand on Alexa's lower back and Jason reached out to squeeze her left hand. "Start it up."

She inhaled and looked at them in turn, then nodded. They held a collective breath as she pushed the ignition button.

The engine roared to life.

For a moment, they stood stunned. Then Alexa squealed and dragged them both to her, kissing Justin as her arm crushed Jason's waist.

She faced Jason. "You gave us the key." She followed her words with a sweet, tender kiss that sucked the breath from his lungs.

He smirked as she turned to Justin. The pride and desire in her eyes melted his brother. Justin swooped back in for another quick kiss before she whispered, "And you made it work."

They both said, "But we couldn't have done it without you."

"Jinx." Her laughter was infectious.

She reached out and shut off the engine. "What do we do now?"

"I set up an appointment with a patent officer for first thing tomorrow morning. I knew you two would figure this out." Jason had used his connections to score a time slot that usually took months to schedule. "There's nothing else we can do until then."

"I can think of a thing or two to pass the time." Justin's wicked smile left no room for misunderstanding. "Let's celebrate."

Chapter Nine

"I've died and gone to heaven," Alexa purred.

She reclined on the huge, downy bed in what she had come to think of as her room. The twins alternated feeding her from a decadent selection of berries, cheese and champagne as they lay propped up on either side of her. Naked, their statuesque bodies made a feast for her eyes that rivaled the gourmet food they proffered.

"That would make Justin an angel, which is clearly not accurate." Jason's dry wit made her laugh and some of the sparkling wine Justin held out to her dribbled down her chin, onto her chest, landing above the lacy edge of her turquoise negligee. Both brothers had insisted she keep her underwear on until she ate, but the deepest hunger she had was for them.

She peeked up at Justin to find his stare glued to the curve of her breasts and the droplets of amber liquid pooling on them. Alexa turned to Jason, manipulating his sense of propriety by arching an eyebrow in false indignation. "You're not going to let it stain my bra, are you?"

Justin growled from her other side as Jason's head dipped down and his tongue flashed out, lapping up the spilled champagne. The flowing touch on her skin coaxed a moan from her.

Each brother took one of her shoulders and raised her up. Justin's hand snaked behind her back and untied the top with one smooth flick of his fingers. They each peeled away a side of the garment. Justin removed it, flinging it over the side of the bed, while Jason continued to lick and suck her flesh. He lifted his head and reached for the bottle of expensive bubbly resting in a bucket of ice.

"It's exquisite mixed with the taste of her." The smoky tone of his voice bolstered her arousal as they settled her against the mountain of pillows until she lay nearly horizontal. He tipped the bottle in miniscule increments. She watched the liquid hang over the spout of the bottle as the meniscus stretched, surface tension and his control keeping her in suspense. Then a rivulet poured out onto her chest and meandered down the center of her body inch by inch.

The cool liquid fizzled on her skin for a moment before Justin murmured a low curse and dove for the trail sliding down her. His sultry breath bathed her as his tongue swept the intoxicating drink from her torso. When nothing remained, Jason renewed the flow from the green glass bottle and Justin continued his deliberate cleansing. The contrasting temperatures drew her nipples tight. Jason tugged on the hardened peaks, sending a ray of sparks straight into her core.

Distracted by Justin's mouth, now sipping a larger splash of champagne from her belly button, Alexa didn't see Jason take a raspberry from the silver dish at her side. She jumped when he pressed the fruit against her stomach then drew a heart on her with the sticky red juice. Justin followed the path of the crude drawing and his mouth curved up in a smile against the sensitive surface of her belly.

"It's true, you know," he murmured against her in between licks and nips. "We love you."

Her eyes met Jason's piercing gaze and, in the profound green pools, she recognized his tacit agreement with Justin's declaration. They echoed the overwhelming sense of belonging and homecoming that permeated every fiber of her being in their company. She knew, without a doubt, these two virile men were destined to be her soulmates and she thanked every power she could imagine that she had been given this opportunity for happiness with them.

This is a chance worth taking.

"I'm ready. It's irrational. I've only just met you, but I know it's true." She buried one hand in Justin's hair, tugging the strands with delicate pressure until he looked at her, and palmed the side of Jason's jaw. "I love you, too. Both of you."

Justin's fingers tightened on her hip as he buried his face against her breasts and held her close. Jason leaned down and took her lips in the most romantic kiss of her life. He caressed her with his mouth, stroked her with his tongue and never once looked away from the moisture filling her eyes with happiness. He rested his forehead on hers and rubbed their noses together before pulling back to let his twin have a turn.

Justin's kiss scalded her with the fury of his passion. His big body overwhelmed her when he pressed close, his cock resting against her hip, throbbing in time to the pounding heartbeat vibrating her breast where their chests melded together. Jason traveled down from her neck, stimulating every part of her that he passed. He bit her shoulder hard enough to sting before drawing away the sensation with a soothing sweep of his lips. When he reached her breast, he moaned—a husky sound of need—and drew the aching peak into his mouth. He swirled his tongue around the nipple, causing her to arch against Justin's body, pinning her in place.

Justin fractured the contact between them, descending to mimic the treatment on her other breast. Her feet propped flat on the comforter as she tried to force herself closer to the source of her pleasure. Hands roamed over her abdomen and thighs, and a single fingertip traced the scalloped edge of her panties.

"Yes, please, touch me." She squeezed her thighs together, trying desperately to cause some friction on her clit through the restless movement of her legs.

Jason lifted his head from worshipping her chest and smiled up at her. He covered her mound with his palm. She rubbed against him, too turned on to be embarrassed by her wanton behavior. His long fingers cupped her, the ends tapping against her ass. She shrieked, the sensations too intense at first, then sank by degrees into the resulting delight.

"Do you want to show Justin our surprise?" His innate control returned, guiding their encounter.

She glanced down to the other man eagerly devouring her breast, driving her insane. It would be nice to turn the tables and see him awed by the power of their connection. Alexa nodded, words beyond her capability at present.

The pads of Jason's fingers worked up her slit, stroking her over her underwear. Slick arousal coated them through the fabric, making them glide across the ridges of her silk encased labia. She groaned, a sound she didn't recognize coming from herself, when his finger slipped around the edge and entered the tiniest bit inside her swollen opening.

"Alright, sweetheart. If you're sure." His reassuring nod bolstered her confidence. "Justin, get rid of her underwear."

He grabbed the side seam and ripped, tearing them from her body. The pressure of the band on her skin just before it snapped made her aware of his strength and determination to have her. Still tormenting her chest with his skilled foreplay, he couldn't see what Jason referred to and didn't seem to be able to tear himself away long enough to find out.

She attempted to hurry them, but they conspired to hold her in place, each pressing against her until, eventually, she gave in and accepted their sweet torture. Jason's finger lodged inside her pussy at the first knuckle. Despite her wetness, even that single digit needed to be cajoled through the muscles clenching furiously around it. He worked her open before adding a second finger.

When the tide of desire overcame her without warning, she naturally looked to Jason for permission. He studied her reactions, observing her with close scrutiny as he manipulated her sensitive pussy. "Wait for it. It'll be better that way."

She grit her teeth, trying to still the rhythmic tightening inside her, but she wouldn't be able to refrain for long.

"Justin, turn her over. Alexa has something she wants to show you." By the way his cock bobbed in excitement, she knew Jason enjoyed it just as much as she did.

The room rotated around her as Justin's strong arms flipped her like she weighed no more than a feather. Her knees curled up instinctively and she rested on all fours, her head and shoulders lying against the pillows, her ass thrust up into the air.

"Oh fuck!" Lust distorted Justin's voice into a rapsy expression of desire. She nearly collapsed when he caressed the base of the anal plug tucked inside her ass. "Were you wearing that the whole time we were downstairs?"

"Yes!" she shouted. Whether in answer to his question, or because the vibration of his exploratory touch felt so damn amazing, she didn't know. Justin swept light kisses across her displayed ass cheeks while Jason thrust his fingers deeper inside her channel.

"Shit, I almost came just thinking about that." Justin's rough laugh accompanied a crisp spank. She jumped in surprise, increasing the contact. His cock rubbed against her leg as his hips rocked and his touch rimmed her rear entrance near the intrusion. "You have no idea how sexy this is. I can see your hole spasm around it when I touch you."

Jason's fingers rotated, stroking the wall of her pussy, trapping it against the pliable object on the other side. "Please, let me come. Someone fuck me, please." She could hear irregular breathing behind her and knew they couldn't tease her much longer.

"Will you let me take your ass, honey?" Justin displayed uncharacteristic self-control as he waited for her answer. His fingertip trembled on her ultra-sensitive ring of muscle.

A grain of trepidation snuck past her guard. Before she could filter it out, she asked, "Will it hurt?"

"Probably," he admitted though it didn't sound as though that would deter him. "At first, almost definitely, but I bet Jason can distract you." He pressed harder now. His finger prodded the opening a bit wider, causing a moan to break free from her chest. The new sensation excited her far more than it scared her.

"Yes." She moaned as his hand disappeared suddenly. "Do it."

The bed dipped as he left and she would have felt abandoned if not for Jason holding her steady. While Justin was gone, Jason raised her leg and slid beneath it so he lay on his back under her and she straddled his face. His breath whispered over her clit and Alexa dropped down, pressing her soaked pussy against his mouth. She rode his lips while he firmed his tongue and began poking it inside her. Every time she thought she would fall over the edge into climax, he nipped the outer edges of her pussy enough to return her control.

She got lost in the seduction of Jason's mouth and was startled when something cool and slippery ran down the crack of her ass. Justin had returned and began preparing her. She shuddered in anticipation, causing her clit to rub across the tip of Jason's tongue. "Hurry. Please."

"That's not the way you want to do this." Justin's voice

came close to her ear as he bent over her back. He greased the base of the plug, swiping his fingers in a circle around it, spreading the lubricant over her asshole. "You're going to have to push out now, baby. On three. Ready?"

Jason kept licking her pussy, driving her wild, and Justin stroked her flank with one hand.

"Yes." Alexa prepared herself.

"One." He counted as he took the base in a firm grip with one hand. "Two. Three." She almost forgot to follow his directions because the bulbous middle of the toy stretched her to impossible proportions. It felt so much larger than it had when Jason penetrated her with it earlier. She stiffened, causing the pain to worsen. Justin inserted two fingers inside her pussy and caressed the rough patch of her G-spot, unfreezing her with waves of heat that melted her defiance.

The widest segment of the toy passed her anus and the rest slipped from her with a pop. She moaned and her hole flexed against the cool air. Justin growled behind her and she heard the toy thunk to the ground, forgotten.

"Oh God. You should see this, Jay." But Justin had already positioned himself behind her. He rubbed the full head of his cock against the susceptible opening. "It's nice and stretched open for me."

Alexa noted the snick of a flip cap before he squeezed a generous dollop of lube onto his cock, heard the wet, fleshy sounds it made when he took the engorged length in his fist and slathered the slick substance over it. Then he scooped the excess warmed gel into her waiting orifice. Her body convulsed in response, tightening all her muscles, clenching around Jason's hand. He moaned against her pussy.

"Jay, I want her to come. I want her to enjoy it when I slide my cock inside her sexy ass for the first time." Justin's hands clamped on either side of her waist drawing her to him until the tip of his cock fit against her.

The suspense drove her wild. She lurched back, trying to fill the emptiness with his hard-on but Justin dodged her movement. The crack of his palm on her ass resounded in the room but the resulting burn only heightened her arousal.

Jason sucked her clit into his mouth on a groan when she said, "Again. Please, spank me harder."

A harsh laugh came from behind her. "That's Jason's specialty, honey, but don't try to force this. You're too tight to take all of my cock at once."

Peeking over her shoulder, she saw him wrap his hand around his fully erect cock and guide it to her ass. Jason stopped eating her long enough to watch the action close up as Justin crouched over them both. A constant pressure built against her rear entrance and his mouth flattened in a grimace as he restrained himself from thrusting inside her.

"You have to let me in, baby." With the tip of his cock nudging inside, he leaned forward, blanketing her back so he whispered encouragement directly in her ear. "Relax, trust me."

"I do." She promised, concentrating on loosening the muscles. "I trust you."

His cock penetrated another fraction of an inch, setting off an avalanche of sensation. Pleasure, pain, shock and longing mixed in a whimper that sounded more animal than human.

"That's it, honey." He kissed her cheek, his gentleness at odds with the tension broadcast by his tight abdomen. Jason renewed his efforts, the double stimulation causing her eyes to close as she fought to hold herself together.

"You're doing great, push back against me. The head of my cock is almost inside you now. The rest will be easier."

His constant stream of commentary made it all too easy to visualize what he did to her. It added another layer of ecstasy to the moment. Jason increased the suction on her clit and drove a third finger inside her. The combination of his mouth and hands with Justin's cock and dirty talk were unstoppable. She surrendered to the rush of sensation.

Justin sank several inches deep when the clasp of her ass relaxed in the instant before she shattered. Jason's fingers scissored inside her, spreading her pussy even as it clamped around him. Full to bursting, Justin bore inside her more completely with every surge of his hips. It hurt, more than a little, but pleasure consumed her and drowned out the pain.

"Fuck!" He buried himself further, rasping against pleasure centers she didn't know existed, prolonging her climax. "That's it. Come on my cock, squeeze it so tight."

Jason sucked her clit with steady draws of his hot mouth, swiping the arousal running from her into his mouth periodically, until she couldn't take anymore and tried to squirm away.

"Oh, no you don't. You're not finished." Justin clutched his arm around her middle, pinning her back tight against his front, then turned them both so he reclined on the bed, with his shoulders leaning against the headboard, and she sat on his ripped abdomen. She collapsed against the muscled expanse of his chest, trying to catch her breath as gravity impaled her on the entire length of his shaft.

"You're too big." Her disgruntled complaint met with his strained laughter.

"Seems just right to me." He kissed her neck, fanning the embers of desire until they rekindled to her amazement. She turned her head and greeted his seeking lips in an unspoken, passionate communication. She lay, cushioned by his strength, his stature emphasizing her petite build. Alexa felt loved, secure, treasured, and knew he understood her reciprocal emotions in the same intuitive way.

Jason rolled to his knees and crawled between their legs. His hands encircled her waist as he positioned her to fit better against his twin. He lifted her a few inches, then guided her down until her ass rested snug to Justin's pelvis.

"Son of a bitch, Jay," He snarled, his teeth clenched. "I'm going to come right now if you don't leave her alone. She's so hot, her orgasm's lingering, squeezing her ass around my cock."

He groaned and his head banged against the headboard as he fought for control.

Jason grinned down at her, petting her chest, stroking down to the sensitive spot just above her pussy. Her muscles clamped in response and Justin thrust his hips, grinding into her.

"Can you handle both of us, sweetheart?" Jason's hand sheathed his cock, as he idly stroked up and down the long shank glistening with precome.

"I'm going to try." She reached out, bringing him close for a kiss. She tasted her own sweetness on his mouth and suddenly she needed him as though she hadn't just had the most intense orgasm of her life.

Justin cupped her breasts, weighing them in his palms before tweaking her nipples. She arched into his touch, increasing the pressure. Jason's cock lay at the apex of her thighs, gliding through her slit as he sucked her tongue into his mouth. She tilted her hips and the dark purple head nudged against her wet hole.

"Shit, yes." Justin moaned beneath them, his hands shifting to guide her hips, lifting and dropping her on his engorged flesh. The motion wedged Jason's cock inside her further and stretched her with both of their girths. "I can feel him opening your pussy. Take us. Take us both."

Jason retreated enough to allow them to watch his cock disappearing inside her with rapt attention. As he began to thrust, delving deeper and deeper, she could no longer hold herself up and her head fell back against Justin's collarbone. Just when she thought she couldn't take it anymore, Jason changed the angle of his penetration and slid home.

All three of them lay still for an instant, caught by the raw power flowing between them before Jason and Justin began to fuck her simultaneously. They moved inside her, deep and hard, gaining speed and groaning louder in her ears. Overflowing with their heat and power, she relinquished all control and gave herself over to their demands.

One of Justin's hands moved to her mound, his fingers split in a V around Jason's cock plunging inside her with full, furious strokes. He traced the seam of her pussy up to her clit and began to rub it in small circles she couldn't resist.

"Yes," Jason shouted above her as his pubic bone forced Justin's fingers to tap against her clit. "I can feel you gathering. Let go. Come for us."

Jason slammed inside her, shoving her back against Justin's sheltering embrace even as he drove into her from behind, sandwiching her between them. Their cocks pinched the thin layer of skin separating them, stroking it with provocative glides of their steel-hard flesh.

Alexa came, shuddering in their arms, cresting one peak only to be propelled to another by their shuttling cocks. Behind her, Justin bellowed his release a fraction of a second before Jason ground and bucked against her. Their cocks pulsed together, wringing another climax from her as they spilled their semen inside her. Come filled her pussy and ass as jet after jet spurted onto swollen, sensitive tissue.

Pleasure overwhelmed her and she collapsed, pliant onto Justin's chest. She only became aware of the room around her and the men embedded in her heart when they rolled to one side, still locked together, sheltering her between them.

Jason brushed her hair away from her eyes and tucked it behind her ear.

"I love you." All three of them whispered the declaration at the same time.

"Jinx. Again." She grinned as her eyes fluttered shut, lulled into a deep sleep by the bone-deep satisfaction coursing through her.

Chapter Ten

Justin couldn't stop touching her. Long minutes after Alexa had drifted off to sleep, he continued to stroke her hair in complete awe of the emotions she instilled in his heart. He could no longer imagine his life without her. Jason propped himself on his elbow, tracing a path from her shoulder to her hip with a feather light touch.

Justin broke the reverent silence with a whisper. "Jay."

"Yeah." His brother's lazy, satisfied voice drifted to him.

"She was made for us." He pressed a tender kiss to her forehead. Even in sleep, she angled closer, welcoming his caress.

Jason's eyes turned misty and Justin panicked, afraid his brother might lose his unflappable restraint. "Hey, none of that shit, Jay."

Jason buried his face against the curve of Alexa's neck and nuzzled her, breathing deep of her sweet scent to ground himself. "I just never imagined we'd find her. I couldn't let myself hope. Now, she's here. Our perfect woman. Real. I can't bear the thought that we might fuck it up and lose her."

"I know." Justin recalled countless women they'd shared, none lasting more than a night or two. Though they sated the twins' carnal hungers, he'd watched Jason battle despair each time it became clear they couldn't compliment the brothers out of bed. "That's why I think we should ask her to move in with us after the meeting tomorrow. I can't let her go even when there's no more threat."

Jason agreed. "I can't either. I just hope it's not too soon for her. Justin, we have to be patient. Do whatever it takes to prove to her what we know. She's ours."

"And we're hers." The brothers sealed the pact with a knowing gaze before they wrapped around their woman and joined her in sleep.

Justin shifted in the uncomfortable office chair and wondered how Jason and Alexa thrived in such stifling environments. Granted, the musty, dim corridors they'd navigated, past dingy, government-issue cubical walls differed vastly from the elegant fixtures of his brother's high-end building, but any office seemed like a cattle pen to him. Trapped here day after day without even a glimpse of the sun he would go insane.

Alexa, on the other hand, had tugged her suit jacket around her slender shoulders like armor earlier this morning and turned with a grin to leave as though she anticipated the task. In fact, when they arrived, she dove into the duty of convincing the squat man with thick glasses of their eligibility to claim the patent for the biofuel engine with a fervor that couldn't be entirely false. *She really enjoys this.*

A combination of irrefutable logic, precise language, precedents set by similar cases and her undeniable charm convinced the patent officer. Within fifteen minutes, he ate out of the palm of her hand. While the official hunched over the documents, signing and sealing where appropriate, Justin wondered if a man existed she couldn't wrap around her little finger.

He caught sight of Jason shaking his head in wonder and winked at him. Justin's palms dampened with nervous sweat. Now that this business concluded, they could move on to the future. What if Alexa rejected their proposal? She was a priceless gift, irreplaceable. The thought of losing her caused a bead of perspiration to form on his brow.

Her enthusiasm rescued him from further worry when she rose and pumped the little man's pudgy hand. Justin mimicked Jason, reaching forward in turn to complete the transaction with a handshake of his own. Victory sparkled in her eyes. Her excitement and pride captivated him. She laid her fine-boned fingers on his forearm and subtly guided him from the room while Jason followed close behind.

She waited until the metal doors of the elevator trundled closed, locking the three of them inside, before doing an adorable happy dance that jiggled all the right parts of her anatomy. She smacked a quick kiss on his cheek and squeezed Jason before composing herself in time to maintain her respectable appearance when the lobby opened up in front of them moments later.

"We did it." She passed the briefcase containing copies of the patent documentation to Jason then reached out to hold one of their hands in each of her own as they crossed the polished granite floor. They headed toward the secure garage where they'd arranged to park this morning to avoid the main lot and entryway.

"Wait." Justin stopped short, causing a chain reaction, tugging them all to a halt in the middle of the bustling crowd.

"What's wrong?" Alarm tinged Alexa's reply.

"Nothing." Justin attributed his uneasiness to the life change he and Jason planned to discuss with her when they returned home. Though certain of his desires, he feared scaring her off. Spontaneously, he decided she deserved the proper atmosphere when they asked her to become a permanent part of their lives, something fancier than the living room couch. Jason's connections ensured a table at an exclusive restaurant for lunch. "Let's go out. Le Chic is just around the corner. We should go someplace special." His brother understood what he intended but he shook his head in opposition.

"I don't think that's wise." Jason waggled the handle of the briefcase. "Until this is announced, some risk exists."

Still riding the high of accomplishing their objective, Alexa beamed up at Jason and broke the tie. "It'd be nice to get away for a little bit before all the real work preparing and marketing the product begins. Plus, I've always wanted to eat at Le Chic."

Justin knew his brother couldn't deny her. Jason's trepidation gave way to a shrug and a grin. She had a way of relaxing him. "What the hell? It's just an hour. Sure, let's go."

Together, they pivoted toward the main entrance. Always the gentleman, Jason held the heavy glass and metal door for Alexa who started down the wide limestone staircase with

Justin trailing a few feet after her.

Too late, Justin spotted the brawny mercenary who stepped from behind one of the massive fluted pillars, gun drawn, aimed pointblank at Alexa's chest. His leathery face hosted evil eyes, on fire and out of control. Justin could see the man riding the edge of sanity. He'd always pictured assassins as calculating and cold, but this man's emotions flew all over the charts. Now his life, and the lives of the two people who made up his world, were at the mercy of a deranged killer for hire.

"I knew you'd show up here eventually." The grin he flashed revealed crooked, yellow teeth. "Now, toss me the case." The steel conviction brooked no argument but Alexa defied the bastard, sending shards of razor sharp terror through Justin's heart.

"You're too late." She stood firm, blocking the path to Jason. Justin had no opportunity to quiet her or get between her and the deadly threat. "We already patented the design on behalf of Winston Industries and the surviving members of the original research team."

"Liar!" the man snarled. His gun wavered when frustration and rage deteriorated his shaky control. "If I fail to recover the design they'll kill me too."

Justin coiled, preparing to spring at the slightest chance to intercede but no opening presented itself. Jason dismayed him further by edging to the side, drawing the insane light burning in the gunman's eyes onto himself.

"Here. Take it." He thrust the leather satchel outward. "Just let her go."

"The bitch is right, it's worthless! Unless the patent holders are dead." The man's trigger finger tightened, his knuckles white on the grip of the pistol.

Jason flung the case at the man's arm at the same instant Justin launched for Alexa. He tackled her, tucking around her in mid-air, attempting to shield her. The rapid double bang of the gun firing twice, before the case knocked it from the man's hold, corresponded to the sick lurch of her body now falling beneath him, making it obvious he had failed.

Jason's primordial scream of fury and pain echoed the despair flashing into Justin's soul. Some far corner of his brain registered the dull thud of fist on face accompanying Jason's dispatch of the monster who had tried to destroy their future. Justin left their defense to Jason and concentrated on their woman.

"Alexa!" he cried as the first hot gush of her blood streamed through his fingers clenching her back. Terrified to see the extent of the damage, he pulled himself away from her limp body. A giant crimson stain spread across the right side of her upper chest. Simultaneously horrified and relieved, he watched the blood throb from the gaping hole in her tattered shirt in time to her racing heartbeat. At least she still had a heartbeat.

Jason fell down beside them and applied pressure to staunch the wound with the jacket he yanked from his shoulders. A painful, unnatural sound emanated from the mask of shock her face had become as she gasped for air. She attempted to get up but her blood-slicked hand slipped feebly on the stone beneath her.

"Oh God, no." Justin stared at her in abject horror.

Jason worked over her with deliberate efficiency but Justin could only gape.

"Lie still, sweetheart." His brother's calm reassurance worked on Justin as well. He gripped Alexa's hand, trying to conjure a million words at once. He needed to tell her so many things. He couldn't bear for her to die never knowing she was their life.

"Jason. Justin." Their names rasped wetly between her shallow wheezing. Blood flecked her luscious lips when she whispered. "Love you."

Justin's chance to pledge it in return disappeared when her eyelids closed, every muscle in her body lax, and his sanity evaporated.

Chapter Eleven

Jason tamped down the cocktail of frustration, pain and concern brewing within him as he stared at his brother, feeling more helpless than ever before in his life. Justin drooped, half reclined in the hospital bed. IVs hydrated him to assist his recovery from the loss of blood he'd suffered but Jason figured his blanched complexion had more to do with their argument than the bullet wound piercing the thick muscle of his twin's upper arm.

His dumbass brother hadn't even realized he'd been shot. Overcome by dread and misery he'd plowed on to the hospital, only receiving treatment when he collapsed in the waiting room. Thankfully, the doctor assured them the damage would heal with minimal inconvenience.

The same did not hold true for Alexa.

Bile rose in his throat for the millionth time since he'd watched the sinister handgun come up in front of her. No matter how often he replayed the scene in his mind, analyzing the options, no other possible outcome presented itself. They'd done all they could.

"I'll never forgive myself for what happened today." Justin's misery permeated every word, every movement, every breath he took.

"Damn it." Jason couldn't bear to lose his brother on top of everything else that'd transpired today. He continued attempting to convince him. With a firm hand on his shoulder, he subdued his weakened twin. "You're being ridiculous. Don't go. This is not your fault."

"You warned me of the danger. I ignored you. I risked her

life but she suffered the consequences." Justin didn't seem aware of the tears making silent tracks down his face. Panic flared in Jason's chest, he hadn't seen his brother cry since childhood. "Fuck! Why can't I ever fucking think about these things before I do something so fucking stupid?"

"We made a mistake, Justin. I agreed, too. Slow down. Consider the consequences this time."

Despair clouded Justin's rationality. "No, I don't deserve to be around you. I'll only fuck up your life more than I already have."

"We're two halves of the same whole, remember?" Stark terror had chilled Jason earlier, when he feared he might lose both Alexa and Justin. It had reinforced the importance of their bond. "I need you now more than ever."

"Me. Too." The faint, scratchy words barely rose above the whir and beep of all the hospital equipment but Jason and Justin both whipped around to see Alexa fighting to stay awake.

"Sweetheart." Jason hovered over her, his chest constricting when he witnessed her labored breathing. "Thank God."

Behind them, he heard muffled curses and the rip of tape as Justin tore the tubes and needles from his arm before stumbling to her bedside. Jason grabbed a chair and pushed his brother down into it with one hand, the other never leaving her tentative grip as she tried to catch her breath after her brief speech.

The slow, fractured words scraped Alexa's throat, causing her to wince. A dull ache infused every cell of her body. Disoriented, the now familiar cadence of her lovers arguing drew her from a fog of suffering. A sense of urgency propelled her to full consciousness.

The strained lines of worry creasing Jason's handsome face frightened her as much as the liquid agony dripping from the less reserved brother's eyes.

"I nearly got you killed." Self loathing oozed from Justin.

She grappled with the situation, trying to force it to make sense, all the while resisting the insistent lull of her drug induced weariness. She blinked in an attempt to bring the room around her into sharper focus. Breathing hurt beyond belief, her throat dried from the oxygen pumping into her, and she couldn't force her vocal cords to produce the questions she needed to ask.

"Just rest. Don't struggle." Jason bent low over her to brush his lips across her forehead. "I love you more than you'll ever know. The doctor says you're going to be okay. I'll be right here with you, and so will Justin. You're safe now. Sleep, baby."

She trained her gaze on Justin but he refused to look her in the eye. *Are they lying? Am I going to die?*

"Justin, you're scaring her. Quit being a fool."

"Shit. I'm making things worse, even now. I'll go." He pried himself up to a half crouch before Alexa forced her body to respond to a fraction of her commands. Her hand rose a mere inch off the hospital bed before it dropped, listless at her side.

"No." The grotesque whisper sounded nothing like the shout she intended.

"Honey, don't." Justin laid his head gingerly on the pillow next to her, eyes squeezed shut. "I can't stand to see you hurt."

His bloodshot eyes opened, so close to her own they filled her world. "I love you with all my soul. I'm leaving you with Jay. He's good for you. He'll always take care of you. Protect you."

His abandonment broke something precious inside her. She recalled his hollered promise to love her just a few short days ago. He'd convinced her that he meant it. How could she have been fooled again?

"Liar." The rending of her spirit far surpassed the agony of her body. Comprehension dawned in the depths of his emerald eyes a moment later and she knew he remembered his vow, too.

Jason interceded. "Fine. I never imagined you were such a coward. Leave if you need to run, but quit hurting her. I won't stand for anyone causing her a moment's grief ever again. Get out."

Regret, agony, fear and resignation cycled through Justin's expression. She tried to beg him to stay, to hell with pride, but the darkness crept over her, dragging her down into the medicated void once more.

Days passed in a blur of sounds and dreams. Alexa remembered Jason's somber explanation of the surgery necessary to repair her punctured lung. Then sedation prohibited her from discovering anything further.

The next time she surfaced, she woke to darkness. A strong hand entwined with hers prevented her from panicking. She rubbed the pad of her thumb across the warm palm. The lack of calluses convinced her it belonged to Jason. The sweet visions of Justin must have been delusions.

Her light touch roused him from his fitful doze in the chair beside the bulky hospital bed. His arm distended at an awkward angle that had to be uncomfortable.

"You're awake." His sexy, sleep roughened voice allowed her to fantasize she'd stirred in the night to make love to him.

I guess I'm getting better. The sarcastic thought factored in a healthy dose of relief. Her hand clasped Jason's tighter, responding like normal as some of her strength returned. Bolstered by the small success, she tested her voice with the most important message first.

"Love you." The audible phrase sounded clearer than her previous attempt. Joy rushed through her. He had proved the strength of his character by sticking with her. Reliable, gentle, loving and kind, he fulfilled her needs. Well, at least those she allowed herself to acknowledge.

Spontaneity, laughter, adventure, unbridled emotion... What about those? She couldn't return to the half existence she lived before Justin unlocked her wild side and gave her permission to indulge it.

"I love you too, Alexa." The words carried a sacred promise they both understood. They would never be parted or give up on each other.

Tears scalded her dry eyes causing Jason to sit up in alarm. "Are you okay? Should I get the nurse?"

She shook her head, gesturing for him to sit.

"We can't live without...him." She couldn't bring herself to utter Justin's name. An abyss festered deep in her chest where his love should reside.

"Jesus Christ!" Jason's sharp response rose in volume. "How much do you remember?"

"Justin. Left. Us." Her stamina began to fade again, her

eyes shutting under the weight of despair.

"Stay awake, baby." He patted her hand, bringing her back a bit. "Just a minute more this time, please? Focus on what I'm saying."

While he talked, he stretched to the table beside her and grabbed the box of tissues. She expected him to dry her tears, not to hurl the carton at the bed on her other side.

A startled grunt filtered from the darkness.

"What the hell was that for, Jay? You hit my fucking arm."

Justin's grumpy mumble sent her pulse flying. The machine beside her clamored with the sudden rise.

"For frightening Alexa," Jason answered. "Now get your ass over here."

Justin asked, concerned, "What's that beeping? I don't recognize that one. Is something wrong?"

His head snapped toward her when he belatedly realized she was conscious. Jason stroked her arm, calming the painful trembling spreading throughout her body.

"You're here." The desperation spilling into her voice would have annoyed her at any other time but, for now, her gratitude crowded out all other thoughts. The lethargy haunting her lifted as euphoria pumped her up.

"I promised." Justin sank down next to her, careful not to jostle the mattress. "I could never leave you. God, have you spent all this time thinking I abandoned you?"

"How long?" It seemed like forever and, yet, just a moment ago that she woke up in this room.

"It's been three weeks of pure hell for us all. Did you really believe I left?" Shame colored his question when he read the truth in her expression. He took her free hand in his, completing the chain with Jason on her other side. He swallowed hard. "I love you, Alexa. The day we got shot, I went a little crazy. Maybe it was the blood loss." His self-deprecating laugh fell flat.

"You? Shot?" She examined him but everything she saw looked like healthy, strapping man.

"Yeah, you guys left me out of the fun. I guess I'm just not cool enough to take a bullet." Jason's humor didn't fully mask his concern. "When Justin dove in front of you, the second shot got him in the arm. If he hadn't knocked you over... Well, it wouldn't have been good. It doesn't seem like it now, baby, but you got so damn lucky. The doctors didn't think you had a chance at first."

"Stubborn." She smiled for the first time since Justin's emotions had made her believe there could be no happy ending for them.

"Thank God," the twins answered together.

"Jinx."

They laughed for her, since the gesture was too painful to attempt, even as contentment settled over her for the first time in weeks. But, still, she had to know if the sensation came from false security.

"Did they catch him?" She hated the fear that seeped into the question.

"Jay took him down." Justin beamed at his twin. "They've got him on multiple counts, including the murder of the informant since they matched the bullet to his gun. Jay called in some of his fancy hotshot lawyers and they swear he's going to bring in the whole operation. He's given them names, locations, descriptions and all the info they need. Besides, the patents have been verified, publically announced, and upheld by the court."

"Thank God." She surrendered to relief, sinking back into the hospital bed as the last of her tension drained out. Drowsiness returned, enhanced by the glow of safety and the comfort of her men holding her hands, stroking her hair and just being near.

"One last thing, sweetheart." Jason's tone turned serious. The nearly palpable loyalty in his eyes made her heart soar. "Recovering is going to take time and determination but we'll be here to support you every step of the way. While you're working on getting better, will you think about moving in with us for good? We want to spend our lives with you if you'll have us."

"Yes." She squeezed their hands and love poured into her from both sides. Justin's gaze burned with desire, commitment and a shred of fear that pushed her to answer. There was no need to leave them in suspense. "No thinking. Just yes."

Jason's intense sincerity balanced Justin's smoldering grin of delight.

"Well, honey." Justin winked at her. "I guess you better concentrate on healing up quicker. Looks like we have a lot more to celebrate now."

They both leaned in and kissed her cheeks before whispering promises of eternal devotion. Alexa drifted into a restful sleep with a smile on her face and love in her soul. The assurance of years of bliss to come fabricated nice and naughty dreams for her to savor.

About the Author

Jayne Rylon's stories usually begin as a daydream in an endless business meeting. Her writing acts as a creative counterpoint to her straight-laced corporate existence. She lives in Ohio with two cats and her husband who both inspires her fantasies and supports her careers. When she can escape her office, she loves to travel the world, avoid speeding tickets in her beloved Sky and, of course, read.

To learn more about Jayne Rylon, please visit www.jaynerylon.com. She enjoys hearing from readers. You can send an email to Jayne at contact@jaynerylon.com.

One lucky woman...three sexy cowboys...
she's in for the ride of her life!

Long Hard Ride
© *2008 Lorelei James*
A Rough Riders Book.

Channing Kinkaid itches for a change; a wild western adventure with an untamed man. Determined to shed her inhibitions and embrace the steamier, seamier side of life, she sets her sights on hooking up with a real chaps-and-spurs-wearing cowboy.

Enter Colby McKay—bull rider, saddle bronc buster and calf roper. From the moment he sets lust-filled eyes on the sweet and fiery Channing, he knows he's found the woman who's up to the challenge of cutting loose. What rough and rowdy cowboy could resist a no-holds-barred sexual romp with a sassy young thing starring as his personal buckle bunny?

Intrigued by Channing's bold proposition of horsing around on the road, Colby impulsively sweetens the deal; sexual escapades not only in his bed, but in the bedrolls of his rodeo traveling partners, Trevor and Edgard.

Although Channing's secretly longed to be the sole focus of more than one man's passions, Colby's demand for complete submission behind closed doors will test her willful nature.

Can Channing give up total control? Especially when not all is as it seems with the sexy trio? Or will the cowboys have to break out the bullropes and piggin' string to break in this headstrong filly?

Warning: This title contains the following: lots of explicit sex, going strong long after the cows come home, graphic language that'd make your mama blush, light bondage with bullropes, ménage a trois, and – yee-haw! – hot nekkid cowboy man-love.

Available now in ebook and print from Samhain Publishing.

Enjoy the following excerpt from Long Hard Ride...

On a drunken dare after too many kamikazes, Channing Kinkaid found herself standing on a shellacked bartop while a bartender named Moose sprayed her chest with ice-cold beer.

"Contestant number four! Strut your stuff, baby!"

Channing thrust out her enormous rack, hardened nipples leading the charge. She completely overshadowed the other contestants. She grinned saucily. It was the first time since her thirteenth birthday she hadn't been ashamed of her large breasts.

Amidst catcalls and wolf whistles she sexed it up, shimmying her hips. Stretching on tiptoe to force the tight T-shirt higher up her flat belly. Widening her stance, she spun on her boot heels, bent over, and grabbed her ankles, jiggling her ass and her boobs.

The crowd of men went absolutely wild.

The tease paid off when Moose announced she'd won the Golden Knockers trophy and one hundred bucks.

"Yee-haw!" she yelled and jumped from the bar.

Never in a million years would anyone she grew up with believe Channing would enter a wet T-shirt contest, let alone win first place.

A tiny chorus of Toby Keith's "How Do You Like Me Now?" broke out inside her head and she smirked.

After receiving congratulations from admiring cowboys on the circuit and a few frat brats, she poured a fresh kamikaze in the trophy cup. She toasted herself in the cracked mirror behind the bar and liked what she saw.

She glanced around, half-afraid she'd see Jared storming toward her, intent on spoiling her fun by dragging her off to celebrate her victory in private. The man was seriously antisocial. And dammit, she was having fun for a change.

The Western bar was jam-packed. Jared hated crowds, but he hated leaving her alone in a crowd—especially a group of horny, drunken men. Where could he have gone? Did she really care?

Sweet, warm breath tickled her ear. "Lookin' for someone,

darlin'?"

Channing tilted her head. Colby McKay—king of the rodeo circuit—stared down at her. From far away he looked a total package. Up close he was simply stunning. Icy blue eyes, dark chestnut hair and chiseled features that weren't typical rugged cowboy, but rather, brought to mind the image of a brooding poet.

His toned body spoke of his athletic prowess with horses and bulls; his thickly muscled arms and big, callused hands spoke of his skill with ropes. Mmm. Mmm. He was yummy and he knew it. He also was aware he made her skittish as a new colt.

She flipped her hair over her shoulder, a nervous gesture she hoped he'd misread as dismissive. "Hey, Colby. Have you seen Jared?"

"He's on his cell phone over by the bathroom." The eye-catching cowboy flashed his dimples. "Which leaves you unattended. Which is a damn shame. Dance with me."

Her stomach jumped, a reaction she blamed on booze, and not the intensely sexy way Colby studied her.

Okay, that was a total lie. She always acted tongue-tied whenever she got within licking distance of Colby, and his equally sexy traveling buddy, Trevor Glanzer.

Jared had kept her sequestered so she hadn't put truth to the rumors Colby and Trevor were the bad boys of the circuit. She knew they were fierce competitors; they worked hard and played hard—on and off the dirt. She'd seen the buckle bunnies of all ages and sizes constantly vying for their attention.

But she, little city-slicker nobody Channing Kinkaid, had captured Colby's interest.

So, for some unknown reason, Trevor and Colby courted her shamelessly at every opportunity. Sometimes separately. Sometimes double-teaming her with hefty doses of good ol' boy charm. It made her wonder what it'd be like to have them double-teaming her in private.

Whoo-ee. With as hard as they rode livestock? They'd probably break the damn bed frame. Or her.

"Come on, Channing," Colby cajoled. "One dance."

Jarred from her fantasy of becoming a Colby/Trevor sandwich, she stammered, "I-I'm all wet. And I smell like beer."

Colby's hot gaze zoomed to her chest. "I ain't complainin'."

"You will be once I'm plastered against you and getting you wet."

He bent to her ear and murmured, "Nuh-uh, shug. I like my women wet. Really wet. I like it when they get that wetness all over me. All over my fingers. All over my face. All over my—"

"Colby McKay!" Flustered by the image of his dark head burrowed between her legs, his mouth shiny-wet with her juices, she attempted to push him away. He didn't budge. The man redefined rock solid. No wonder bulls and broncs had a tough time tossing him off.

"You ain't as indignant as you'd like me to believe, Miz Channing. In fact—" he nipped her earlobe, sending tingles in an electric line directly to her nipples, "—I suspect a firecracker such as yourself prefers dirty talk."

The subtle pine scent of Colby's aftershave and the underlying hint of aroused male soaked into her skin more thoroughly than the beer. A purely sexual shiver worked loose from her head to the pointed toes of her cowgirl boots.

"Come on and dance with me. Let's see if we can't spread that wetness around a little." Without waiting for her compliance, Colby tugged her toward the dance floor.

"Honky Tonk Badonkadonk" blasted from the speakers.

The second they were engulfed by the mass of dancers, Colby hauled her flush against his firm body. A big, strapping man, he was hard everywhere—from his brawny chest to his powerfully built thighs. No two-stepping for them. He clasped her right hand in his left, nestling his right palm in the small of her back. That single touch seared her flesh like a red-hot brand.

Lord. And the long hard thing poking her belly sure as shooting wasn't his championship belt buckle.

"You okay?"

Channing nodded, even when her head spun with the idea the hottest cowboy on the circuit had a massive hard-on for her—right here in front of rodeo queens, stock contractors, old timers and everyone else.

"See? This ain't so bad, is it?"

Printed in the United States
220405BV00001B/2/P